These
SHALLOW
GRAVES

ALSO BY JENNIFER DONNELLY

Revolution

A Gathering Light

The Waterfire Saga

These
SHALLOW
GRAVES

JENNIFER
DONNELLY

HOT
KEY
BOOKS

First published in Great Britain in 2015 by Hot Key Books
80-81 Wimpole Street, London W1G 9RE
www.hotkeybooks.com

A CIP catalogue record for this book is
available from the British Library.

ISBN: 978-1-4714-0514-3
Also available as an ebook

1 3 5 7 9 10 8 6 4 2

Typeset in Berling 11pt

Printed and bound by Clays Ltd, St Ives Plc

Hot Key Books is an imprint of Bonnier Publishing Fiction, a
Bonnier Publishing company.

www.bonnierpublishingfiction.co.uk
www.bonnierpublishing.co.uk

TO WILFRIEDE DONNELLY,
my mother and my first storyteller,
with love and admiration

The past is never dead. It's not even past.

—WILLIAM FAULKNER

Josephine Montfort stared at the newly mounded grave in front of her and at the wooden cross marking it.

"This is the one you're after. *Kinch*," Flynn, the gravedigger, said, pointing at the name painted on the cross. "He died on Tuesday."

Tuesday, Jo thought. Four days ago. *Time enough for the rot to start. And the stink.*

"I'll be wanting my money now," Flynn said.

Jo put her lantern down. She fumbled notes out of her coat pocket and counted them into Flynn's hand.

"You get caught out here, you never saw me. You hear, girl?"

Jo nodded. Flynn pocketed his money and walked off into the darkness. Moonlight spilled over the rows of graves and the looming towers of the asylum. A wail rose on the night, high and piercing.

And suddenly Jo's courage failed her.

"Step aside, Jo. We'll do it. Oscar and me," Eddie said.

He was standing across from her, on the other side of the grave. He said nothing more as she met his gaze. He didn't need to. The challenge in his eyes spoke volumes.

How did this happen? How did I get here? Jo asked herself. She didn't want to do this. She wanted to be home. Safe inside her Gramercy Square town house. She wished she'd never met Eddie Gallagher. The Tailor. Madam Esther. Fairy Fay. Most of all, she wished she'd never laid eyes on the man buried below her.

"Wait by the vault. Go back," Eddie said. Not unkindly.

Jo laughed. *Go back? How?* There was no going back. Not to her old life of drawing rooms and dances. Not to Miss Sparkwell's School. Not to her friends, or to Bram. It had all gone too far.

"Jo . . ."

"*You* wait by the vault, Eddie," Jo said crisply.

Eddie snorted. He tossed a shovel at her. Jo flinched as she caught it, then started to dig.

⇒ CHAPTER ONE ⇐

Miss Sparkwell's School for Young Ladies
Farmington, Connecticut
September 17, 1890

"Trudy, be a dear and read these stories for me," said Jo Montfort, laying out articles for her school's newspaper on a tea table. "I can't abide errors."

Gertrude Van Eyck, all blond curls and dimples, stopped dead in the middle of the common room. "How did you know it was me? You didn't even look up!"

"Duke told me," Jo replied. Duke's Cameos were Trudy's favorite brand of cigarette.

Trudy sniffed her sleeve. "Do I smell?"

"You positively reek. What does Gilbert Grosvenor think of you smoking cigarettes?"

"Gilbert Grosvenor doesn't know. Not about the ciggies, or the bottle of gin under my bed, or that utterly swell boy who delivers apples," Trudy said, winking.

"Slang does not become a Farmington girl, Gertrude," sniffed Libba Newland, seated nearby with her friend, May Delano.

"Neither does that fringe, Lib," said Trudy, eyeing Libba's badly curled bangs.

"Well, I never!" Libba huffed.

"And I'm sure you never will," Trudy said archly.

"Stop being awful and read these, Tru," Jo scolded. "My deadline's tomorrow."

Trudy sat down at the table and helped herself to a jam tart from Jo's plate. It was three o'clock—teatime at Miss Sparkwell's—and the common room was crowded with students on break. Everyone was chatting and eating except Jo, who was busy finalizing the layout for the second edition of the *Jonquil*.

"What do we have this week?" Trudy asked. "The usual tripe?"

Jo sighed. "I'm afraid so," she said. "There's a piece on the proper way to brew tea, a poem about kittens, Miss Sparkwell's impressions of the Louvre, and advice on how to fade freckles."

"Ye gads. Anything else?"

Jo hesitated, working up her nerve. "As a matter of fact, yes. A story on the abuse of girl laborers at Fenton's Textile Mill," she said, handing one of the articles to her friend.

"Ha! So funny, my darling!" Trudy said, smiling. Her smile faded as she read the first lines. "Oh dear God. You're *serious*."

Trudy kept reading, riveted, and Jo watched her, thrilled. Jo was a senior at Miss Sparkwell's and had written for the *Jonquil* during her three previous years at the school, but this was the first important story she'd written. She'd worked hard to get it. She'd taken risks. Just like a real reporter.

"What do you think?" she asked eagerly when Trudy finished reading.

"I think you've lost your mind," Trudy replied.

"But do you think it's *good*?" Jo pressed.

"Very."

Jo, who'd been perched on the edge of her seat, shot forward and hugged Trudy, a huge grin on her face.

"But that's *entirely* beside the point," Trudy said sternly as Jo sat down again. "If you hand in the layout to Sparky with *that* story in it, you're done for. Detention for a week *and* a letter home."

"It's not *that* bad. Nellie Bly's pieces are far more provocative," said Jo.

"You're comparing yourself to *Nellie Bly?*" Trudy asked, incredulous. "Need I remind you that she's a scandalous lady reporter who meddles in other people's business and has no hope of marrying a decent man? You, in contrast, are a Montfort, and Montforts marry. Early and well. And that is all."

"Well, *this* Montfort's going to do a bit more," Jo declared. "Like write stories for newspapers."

Trudy raised a perfectly arched eyebrow. "Is that so? Have you informed your mother?"

"Actually, no. Not yet," Jo admitted.

Trudy laughed. "Not *ever,* you mean. Unless you want to find yourself locked away in a convent until you're fifty."

"Tru, this is a story that must be told," Jo said, her passion clear in her voice. "Those poor girls are being mistreated. They're worked hard and paid little. They're practically slaves."

"Jo. How on *earth* do you know this?"

"I spoke with some of them."

"You didn't," Trudy said.

"I did. On Sunday. After services."

"But you went straight to your room after services. You said you had a headache."

"And then I climbed out of my window and went down to the river. To one of the boardinghouses there," Jo said, lowering her voice. She didn't want anyone to overhear her. "A farmer gave me a ride in his wagon. I spoke with three girls. One was seventeen. Our age, Tru. The others were younger. They work ten-hour days standing at these hellish looms. Injuries are common. So is exposure to coarse language and . . . and *situations*. I was told that some of the girls fall in with bad sorts and become wayward."

Trudy's eyes widened. "Josephine Montfort. Do you really think that Mr. Abraham Aldrich wants his future wife to even *know* that wayward girls exist, much less write about them? The future Mrs. Aldrich must be pure in mind as well as body. Only men are supposed to know about"—Trudy lowered her voice, too—"about *sex*. If news of what you've done gets around, not only will you lose your place here, you'll lose the most eligible bachelor in New York. For goodness' sake, be sensible! No mill girl, wayward or otherwise, is worth the Aldrich millions!"

May Delano looked up from her book. "What's a wayward girl?" she asked.

Jo groaned.

"Never mind," Trudy said.

"Tell me," May whined.

"Very well," Trudy replied, turning to look at May. "A girl who is with child but without a husband."

May laughed. "Shows what *you* know, Trudy Van Eyck. The stork brings babies *after* you're married, not before."

"Come, May, we're leaving" said Libba Newland, shooting Trudy a dirty look. "The common room is getting a bit *too* common."

"I'll bet you a dollar Lib tattles to Sparky," Trudy said darkly, watching them go. "I just finished my detention for smoking. Now *you've* earned me some more!"

Disappointed by Trudy's lack of enthusiasm for her story, Jo snatched it back. She wished Trudy understood her. Wished *someone* did. She'd read Bly's *Ten Days in a Mad-House* and Jacob Riis's *How the Other Half Lives*, and they'd touched her deeply. She'd been appalled to learn how the poor suffered and felt compelled to follow the examples those two reporters set, if only in some small way.

She thought about the mill girls she'd spoken with. They'd looked so crushingly tired. Their faces were as pale as milk, except for the dark smudges under their eyes. They'd been taken out of school and made to work. They weren't allowed to talk or to go to the bathroom until their lunch breaks. One told her she could barely walk home at the end of the day, her legs hurt so badly from standing.

Their stories had made Jo sad—and blisteringly angry. "Trudy, why did I become editor of the *Jonquil?*" she suddenly asked.

"I have no idea," Trudy replied. "You should've joined the glee club. Even *you* can't get into trouble singing 'Come into the Garden, Maud.'"

"I shall tell you."

"I had a feeling you would," Trudy said dryly.

"I did it because I want to inform my readers. Because I wish to draw back the veil that hides the injustices that surround us," Jo said, her voice rising. "We who have means and a voice must use them to help those who have neither. Yet how can we help them if we don't even know about them? And how can we know about them if no one writes about them? Is it so wrong to want to know things?"

Heads turned as Jo finished speaking. Girls stared. She glared back at them until they turned away. "They suffer, those mill girls," she said, her voice quieter, but her heart still full of emotion. "They are so terribly unfortunate."

Trudy took her hand. "My darling Jo, there is *no one* more unfortunate than we ourselves," she said. "We are not engaged yet, you and I. We're spinsters. Pathetic nobodies. We can go nowhere on our own. We must not be too forward in speech, dress, or emotion lest we put off a potential suitor. We are allowed no funds of our own, and most of all"—she squeezed Jo's hand for emphasis—"no *opinions.*"

"Doesn't it bother you, Tru?" Jo asked, frustrated.

"Of course it does! Which is why I intend to marry as soon as I can," Trudy said.

She jumped up, snapped open an imaginary fan, and strode about the room imitating a society lady. "When I am *Mrs.* Gilbert Grosvenor and happily installed in my grand Fifth Avenue mansion, I shall do *exactly* as I please. I shall say what I like, read what I like, and go out every evening in silks and diamonds to smile at my beaux from my box at the Met."

It was Jo's turn to raise an eyebrow. "And Mr. Gilbert Grosvenor? Where will he be?" she asked.

"At home. Sulking by the fire with a copy of *The Wall Street Journal,*" Trudy said, imitating Gilbert's eternally disapproving expression.

Jo laughed despite herself. "I'll never understand how you were passed over for the lead in the school play. You belong on stage," she said.

"I wasn't *passed over,* thank you. I was offered the lead and declined it. Mr. Gilbert Grosvenor frowns upon theatricals."

For a moment, Jo forgot about her own worries. She knew Gilbert. He was smug and disapproving, an old man at twenty. He was also stinking rich.

"Will you really marry him?" she asked. She could no more see beautiful, lively Trudy married to Gilbert than she could picture a hummingbird paired with a toad.

"I mean to. Why shouldn't I?"

"Because you . . . You'll have to . . ." She couldn't say it.

"Go to bed with him?" Trudy finished.

Jo blushed. "That is *not* what I was going to say!"

"But it's what you meant."

Trudy looked out of a nearby window. Her eyes traveled over the lawns to the meadows, then farther still, to a place—a future—only she could see.

"A bit of nightly unpleasantness in exchange for days of ease. Not such a bad bargain," Trudy said, with a rueful smile. "Some of us are not as well off as others. My papa can barely manage my school fees, never mind the dressmaker's bills. And anyway, it's not *me* I'm worried about. It's *you*." Trudy turned her attention back to Jo. "You know the rules: get yourself hitched, then do what you like. But for heaven's sake, *until* you get the man, smile like a dolt and talk about tulips, *not* mill girls!"

Disappointment settled on Jo like a heavy woolen cloak. She knew Trudy was right. Sparky would be appalled if she ever found out what Jo had done. So would her parents, the Aldriches, and the rest of New York. *Her* New York, at least—old New York. Well-bred girls from old families came out, got engaged, and then went back—back to drawing rooms, dinner parties, and dances. They did not venture into the dangerous, dirty world to become reporters, or anything else.

The boys got to, though. They couldn't become reporters either—that was too grubby an occupation for a gentleman—but they could own a newspaper, run a business, practice law, breed horses, have agricultural interests, or do something in government like the Jays and the Roosevelts. Jo knew this but couldn't accept it. It chafed at her spirit, as surely as the stays of her corset chafed her body.

Why is it, she wondered now, *that boys get to do things and be things and girls only get to watch?*

"Jo?"

Jo looked up. It was Arabella Paulding, a classmate.

"Sparky wants to see you in her office," she said. "Right away."

"Why?" Jo asked.

"She didn't say. She told me to find you and fetch you. I've found you, so go."

"Libba tattled," Trudy said ominously.

Jo gathered up her papers, dreading her interview with the head-mistress.

"Don't worry, my darling," Trudy said. "You'll only get a few days' detention, I'm sure. Unless Sparky expels you."

"You're *such* a comfort," said Jo.

Trudy smiled ruefully. "What can I say? I merely wish to smoke. Sparky can forgive that. You, on the other hand, wish to know things. And no one can forgive a girl for that."

❧ CHAPTER TWO ❧

Jo hurried out of Hollister Hall, crossed the grassy quad, and entered Slocum, where the headmistress's office was. A tall gilt mirror stood in the foyer. It caught her image as she rushed by it—a slender girl wearing a long brown skirt, a pin-striped blouse, and lace-up boots. Wavy black hair formed a widow's peak over a high forehead, and a pair of lively gray eyes stared out from an uncommonly pretty face.

"You'd be a beauty," her mother often told her, "if only you'd stop scowling."

"I'm not *scowling*, Mama, I'm thinking," Jo always replied.

"Well, stop. It's unappealing," her mother would say.

Jo reached the door to Miss Sparkwell's office and paused, steeling herself for a thorough dressing down. She knocked.

"Enter!" a voice called out.

Jo turned the knob and pushed the door open, prepared to see the headmistress wearing a grave expression. She was not prepared, however, to see her standing by a window dabbing at her eyes with a handkerchief. Had the mill girls story upset her that much?

"Miss Sparkwell, I don't know what Libba said to you, but the story has merit," Jo said, launching a preemptive strike. "It's high time the *Jonquil* offered its readers something weightier than poems about kittens."

"My dear, I did not summon you here to talk about the *Jonquil*."

"You didn't?" Jo said, surprised.

Miss Sparkwell passed a hand over her brow. "Mr. Aldrich, would you? I—I find I cannot," she said, her voice catching.

Jo turned around and was astonished to see two of her oldest friends—Abraham Aldrich and his sister, Adelaide—seated on a divan. She'd been so preoccupied with defending her story, she hadn't even noticed them.

"Bram! Addie!" she exclaimed, rushing to her friends. "What a lovely surprise! But I wish you'd have let me know you were coming. I would've changed out of my uniform. I would have . . ." Her words trailed off as she realized they were both dressed entirely in black. A cold dread gripped her.

"I'm afraid we have some bad news, Jo," Bram said, rising.

"Oh, Jo. Be brave, my darling," Addie whispered, joining him.

Jo looked from one to the other, her dread growing. "You're frightening me," she said. "For goodness' sake, what is it?" And then she knew. Mr. Aldrich had been in poor health for some time. "Oh, no. It's your father, isn't it?"

"No, Jo, not ours," said Addie quietly. She took Jo's hand.

"Not yours? I—I don't understand."

"Jo, your father is dead," Bram said. "It was an accident. He was cleaning a revolver in his study last night and it went off. Addie and I have come to fetch you home. We'll get your things, and then . . ."

But Jo didn't hear the rest. The room, and everything in it, whirled together then spun apart. For a few seconds, she couldn't breathe or speak. How could her father be dead? Of the many sure and solid things in her life, he was the surest. And now Bram was telling her that he was gone . . . *gone* . . . and it felt like the world was crumbling under her feet.

"Jo? Can you hear me? Josephine, look at me." Bram was by her side now. He'd put a steadying hand on her arm.

The sound of his voice pulled her back, reminding her that their sort did not make scenes in public. And public, to an Aldrich or a Montfort, was any place other than one's own bedroom.

"Are you all right?" he asked her.

Jo managed to answer. "Yes, thank you," she said. She forced herself to continue. "I shall be ready shortly. I just need to gather a few things. Please excuse me."

"Let me come with you," Addie said. She took Jo's arm and led her out of the room. Together they headed for the dormitory. "We'll try for the 5:05. It'll get us to Grand Central before dark. We certainly don't want to arrive *after* dark. It's far too dangerous," she fretted. "The city's no longer fit for our kind. It's been overrun by foreigners, criminals, and typists."

Addie's chatter barely registered. Jo was dazed, struggling to put one foot in front of the other. The quad with its lawns and buildings passed by in a blur. She'd walked this very same path only moments ago, but barely recognized it now. In the space of a heartbeat, everything had changed.

The dormitory was deserted when they reached it. All the other students were at clubs or in the library. Addie opened the door to Jo's room and ushered her inside. "Here we are, all by ourselves. You can cry now if you need to and no one will see," she said.

Jo sat down on her bed, frozen with shock. She waited for the storm of tears, but it didn't come.

Addie started to hunt for Jo's valise, but Jo stopped her. "There's no need to pack," she said. "I've plenty of clothing at home. If you could just get my coat, gloves, and hat."

"What a brave girl you are, holding back your tears," Addie said. "It's better that way, though. No red eyes at the station. No reason for the great unwashed to gawk."

Jo nodded woodenly. Addie was wrong, but Jo didn't correct her. She wasn't holding her tears back; she had none. She desperately wanted to cry, but couldn't.

It was as if her heart, corseted as tightly as her waist, could not find its shape again.

➤ CHAPTER THREE ➤

"People pass. It happens every day," declared Mrs. Cornelius G. Aldrich III. "That's why it's so important to make more of them."

It was Charles Montfort's funeral luncheon, a somber and decorous affair—or at least it had been until Mrs. Aldrich arrived.

"Another cup of tea, Grandmama?" Addie Aldrich asked, lifting a teapot off the low table in front of her.

"No, confound it! You've asked me three times! Go ask young Beekman over there if he wants something. I don't see a ring on *your* finger yet, miss!" Grandmama barked.

Addie colored and put the teapot down. Grandmama, seated in a wing chair in the Montforts' drawing room, returned her attention to the woman sitting across from her—Madeleine Montfort, Jo's aunt. Addie and Jo sat together on an overstuffed settee between the two older women.

"I understand the family's bereaved, of course I do. But I don't see why it should delay an engagement," Grandmama said petulantly. She took a cookie from a plate and fed it to the spaniel on her lap. "Girls these days. I don't understand them. Waiting until *twenty* to marry and then having such small families!"

Jo, staring blankly ahead, vaguely understood that Grandmama was talking about her, Bram, and marriage. Apparently a proposal had been imminent, but would now be delayed because of her father's passing.

Should I be excited? she wondered. It was hard to be, given the circumstances, but it would've been hard to be excited not given them. A proposal from Bram Aldrich would hardly have been a surprise. For as long as Jo could remember, there had been an expectation that they would marry. Just last summer she'd overheard her mother and aunt talking about it in the conservatory.

"An Aldrich match would be most advantageous, Anna," Aunt Madeleine had said. "Bram is a fine young man, and the family is very well off. More so—"

"Than we ourselves?" Jo's mother interrupted, an arch tone to her voice.

"Yes," Madeleine replied. "Forgive me, but these things must be said. However, that is *not* to imply they are new money. My only point is, that if Jo were to marry Bram, she would never want for anything."

"I agree, Maddie, and I'm leaning toward the match, but keep that between us. It wouldn't be wise to let Grandmama think she's gotten her way," Jo's mother replied. "Not until I have some idea of what Bram's father plans to settle upon the couple. Grandmama married beneath her, you know. She had no choice. Her father squandered his inheritance. She's been trying to restore the blue to her blood ever since. She married her son to a Van Rensselaer, and wants a Montfort for her grandson. The Aldriches are a fine family, yes, but nowhere near as old or distinguished as our own. Jo could easily marry a Roosevelt or Livingston. Grandmama would do well to remember that."

Theakston, the butler, had chosen that very moment to walk down the hall with a tea tray, and, to her chagrin, Jo had to hurry off before he caught her eavesdropping. Had she stayed a moment more, she might've found out what she most wanted to know—did Bram love her?

Jo's mother and aunt *had* kept their thoughts about the match between themselves—at least, they hadn't shared them with her—but that hadn't stopped the rest of society from talking. Especially Grandmama.

Then again, Grandmama was *always* talking about marriage. She was the reigning matriarch of the Aldrich clan, and a Livingston herself before she married. The blood of many of New York's best families ran through her veins. She was related to everyone who mattered, and everyone who mattered called her Grandmama. Deeply attached to Herondale, the Aldriches' Hudson River estate, she only set foot in Manhattan when absolutely necessary, preferring Herondale's woods and meadows to tall buildings and traffic.

"And *another* thing I don't understand, Maddie, is the younger generation's total disregard for bloodlines," Grandmama continued now. "Margaret DeWitt's youngest is marrying a Whitney. Why, I've never even *heard* of them! I understand the boy's father is a political man. He'd do for some new-money girl, but a *DeWitt*?" She shook her head, disgusted. "Fine set of hips on that girl, too. She'll breed as easily as an Ayrshire heifer."

Madeleine blanched. She lost her grip on her teacup; it clattered into its saucer. "Tell me, Grandmama," she said, "how *is* that other spaniel of yours? Suki, I think she's called. I see that she's not with you. I hope she's not ill?"

"Not at all. Didn't I tell you? The bitch caught!" Grandmama said happily. "Mated her four times with Good King Harry, Alma Rhinelander's dog. I'd almost given up on her, but she'll whelp next month. If only it were that easy with daughters, eh, Maddie? Take a sturdy bitch in season, put her in a pen with a keen stud, and two months later, there you are with six strapping pups!"

Madeleine clutched her pearl necklace. "Addie, I do believe Mrs. Hollander is leaving," she said. "I know she'll want to say goodbye to Jo. Would you be a dear?"

"Of course," Addie said. She took Jo's hand and pulled her off the settee. "I'm so sorry, Jo. I don't even know what to say. She's *impossible*," she whispered when they were out of earshot. "Papa used to be able to control her, but now that he's so poorly, no one can."

"It's all right, Addie," Jo responded in a dull voice. She didn't care what Grandmama said. Her father had been buried that morning, and with him, a piece of her heart.

His funeral service had been held at Grace Church on Broadway and Eleventh Street and every pew had been packed. The old families still attended Grace, though few lived within walking distance anymore. Commerce, industry, and the rising tide of immigrants had forced them out of lower New York to the city's upper reaches. Grace's graveyard was as full as its pews, so Charles Montfort had been buried at the church's northern cemetery. Alive or dead, wealthy New Yorkers now sought their accommodations uptown.

Addie led Jo to the foyer, where Theakston was handing Mrs. Hollander her wrap, then bustled off to offer a cup of punch to Andrew Beekman. Jo made small talk with Mrs. Hollander, then kissed her goodbye. She started walking back to the drawing room, but on her way, she was gripped by a sense of unreality so strong, it made her dizzy. She put a hand on the banister to steady herself.

"This is my house," she whispered. "There is the ebony bench Papa brought back from Zanzibar. Above it is a portrait of Grandfather Schermerhorn. Beyond it is the drawing room, which contains a piano, a fireplace, a clock, and my mother."

But how could all these things be here, and her father not be? How could the clock still be ticking? How could there be a fire in the grate? How could her father be *dead*?

Killed by a gun. His own gun. Accidentally. That's what everyone said. But it just wasn't *possible.* Her father was a sportsman. He'd known his way around guns and had kept several in the house, for he'd always been cautious about his family's safety. To a fault, her mother said. He'd often walked the house at night, checking doors and windows.

"Dearest Jo, how are you holding up?" a voice asked. But Jo, lost in her grief, didn't hear it. The voice spoke again. "Josephine, are you quite all right?"

Jo heard it that time and turned around. It was the Reverend Willis, her family's pastor. He was peering at her with an expression of concern. She forced herself to smile.

"I'm fine, Reverend. Thank you. Would you like a cup of tea?" she asked.

"No, my dear, I've had plenty. Perhaps you should sit down. You look pale."

"I will," Jo said. But not here. She had to escape from the sad faces and hushed voices. Excusing herself, she hurried off to her father's study. As she climbed the stairs to the second floor, the skirts of her black silk mourning gown rustling around her legs, the reverend's eulogy came back to her.

Charles Montfort was a man who was genial to all. A pillar of society. A man whose professional dealings were forthright and fair, and whose generosity to those less fortunate was unparalleled. He was a devoted husband and father, kind and loving to family and friends. . . .

Yes, Papa was all those things, Jo thought. And yet, the reverend hadn't captured him. Not entirely, for he could be so *different* at times. So quiet and remote.

Jo reached the study and slipped inside. In here, she could almost believe he was still alive. She could smell him—his cologne, his cigars, the India tea he drank. She could feel him.

"Papa?" she whispered.

Emotion welled up in her. For two days, ever since Addie and

Bram had given her the news, she'd been unable to cry. Now she would. Finally. Here, all by herself. She waited, but again the tears didn't come. What was *wrong* with her? She'd loved her father. Why couldn't she cry for him?

Frustrated, she walked to the large bay window and looked out at Gramercy Square. It was a beautiful September afternoon, and the park was filled with children and their nannies. She leaned her head against the window frame, crumpling the voluminous draperies. As she did she felt a hard bump under her toe. The draperies were so long that their excess fabric puddled on the floor. Moving a panel aside, she peered down and saw something small and copper-colored tangled in the fringed ends of the carpet. It was a bullet.

Jo shuddered as she picked it up, wondering how it had gotten there. Her father kept a loaded revolver in a cabinet in his study; it was the very one that had killed him. She wondered now, as she had a thousand times in the past two days, how the accident had happened.

Perhaps he'd started to unload the chamber and had put the loose bullets on his desk, but was distracted by something. He closed the chamber to attend to the disturbance, then picked the revolver up again, forgetting that it wasn't empty, and somehow it went off. That was the only logical explanation she could come up with.

"But it doesn't explain you," she said, frowning at the bullet. She turned it over and looked at the bottom. The letters *W.R.A. Co.* arched across it. Under them was stamped *.38 LONG.*

Maybe Papa collapsed across his desk after the gun fired, sweeping the loose bullets off as he fell to the floor, she thought. *And then Theakston or a policeman kicked one across the room.*

Her eyes traced a possible trajectory from the desk to the window.

It must've been kicked with quite a bit of force, though, she mused, *to travel over a thick rug all the way to the other side of the room.*

"Oh, what does it matter how it got there?" she asked herself, sighing. "He's gone. And no amount of puzzling will bring him back."

She opened the cabinet where the revolver had been kept—her mother had made the police take the gun away—and placed the bullet on a shelf next to a box of ammunition. Her mother sometimes came in here and Jo didn't want her to see it. It would make her even more distraught than she already was.

Jo slowly walked around the room, touching the mantel, then her father's humidor. The edge of his desk. His chair. Images came to her. She remembered him handing her a kitten with a pink bow. And twirling her around at a skating party. She remembered him dancing with her mother, the two of them so handsome together: her mother a cool blond beauty, and her father with his strong Montfort features—his thick black hair and gray eyes like her own.

Often, those eyes had shone with mischief and merriment. But under the laughter, Jo had sometimes glimpsed a shadow. Her father had spent hours here in his study standing at the window, hands clasped behind his back, gazing down at the street—as if expecting someone.

Jo recalled the first time she'd found him that way. She was little, and was supposed to have been asleep, but she'd gotten out of bed, snuck up on him, and said, "Who are you waiting for, Papa?"

He'd spun around and she'd seen that his face was as white as chalk, and that his eyes were filled with emotion: fear, which she knew, for she was afraid of many things—spiders and thunder and circus clowns—and sorrow, which she did not know. Not then.

"Oh, how you startled me, Jo!" he'd said, smiling. And then he'd told her he wasn't waiting for anyone, just thinking over a business deal.

Even then she hadn't believed him, and as she'd grown older she'd wished he would confide in her about whatever troubled him. But he hadn't, and now he never would.

For a moment, Jo saw her father again standing at the window. Watching. Waiting. And suddenly it was there—the word she hadn't been able to come up with. The one word that best described him.

Haunted.

❧ CHAPTER FOUR ❧

"Park Row, please, Dolan. The offices of the *Standard*," Jo said, stepping into her carriage.

Jo's driver frowned. "Mrs. Montfort said I was to take you to tea at the Reverend Willis's, Miss Jo, then straight home," he said.

"You *were*, Dolan. But then there was a change of plan. Did Mama not inform you?" Jo asked lightly. "She must've forgotten."

Dolan, his hand on the carriage's door, gave Jo a long look. "There was no change of plan, was there now?"

Jo was nabbed. "No, Dolan, there wasn't. But *please* take me to Park Row," she begged.

"What will your mother say if she finds out you've been downtown?"

"She won't if you don't tell her. I *can't* go home. Not yet. It's miserable there with the shades drawn and Mama shut up in her room all day and Papa's portrait draped in black," Jo said, a desperate note in her voice.

Dolan shook his head. "You've been able to get round me since you were five years old. We'll go, but we need to be quick. No dilly-dallying."

Jo thanked him, greatly relieved. She'd been confined to her house for the last two weeks, ever since her father's funeral, as she was in mourning. But unlike her proper mother, who preferred darkened rooms in her grief, Jo yearned for distraction. Her lively mind withered with nothing to occupy it.

Yesterday, her uncle Phillip had given her a reprieve. He was her father's older brother, and the executor of his will, and was helping to dispose of his assets. The Montforts had made their fortune as shipbuilders in seventeenth-century New York, and all of Charles's holdings were maritime related: the *Standard*, a city newspaper that had once been a shipping-news daily; three lumber mills; and a rope factory. Jo's mother had no understanding of her late husband's business affairs, and no wish to gain one, so she'd asked Phillip to sell everything to outside parties except for Charles's largest asset—his stake in Van Houten Shipping. Charles had been a partner in the firm, along with Phillip and four other men. The firm was originally formed by seven partners—one other had died years ago. Now the surviving partners would buy his share and divide it.

Phillip had visited Anna and Jo last night to tell them that he'd already found a buyer for one of the lumber mills. He'd also mentioned that Charles had specified a few personal bequests in his will, including a rare King James bible for the Reverend Willis and a silver whiskey flask for Arnold Stoatman, the *Standard*'s editor. They would all require personal notes.

"Would you take care of this for me, Jo?" he'd asked. "You can present bequests to the household staff personally. Dolan can deliver the remainder—except for the bible. I think a member of the family should deliver that. Anna, will you allow Jo to do this?"

Jo's mother had hesitated. "It's far too soon for her to be out and about," she'd finally replied.

"I defer to you, of course," her uncle had said, "but remember that Jo is young and the young need diversions, especially during dark times. Surely a trip to the rectory wouldn't be frowned upon?"

Mourning was no longer quite the elaborate affair it had been a generation ago, but custom still dictated a period of seclusion and the donning of somber clothing. Jo would wear black for six months, her mother for two years. After that, touches of white were allowed, and then gray or mauve.

Attendance at balls and parties was not allowed for half a year, but mourners could attend church and, after three months, concerts. Visitors could not be received for several months—except for family and close friends. Nor could the bereaved pay social calls to anyone not in their immediate circle.

At Charles Montfort's funeral luncheon, Grandmama had loudly opined that the whole blasted custom was a pretentious middle-class invention and refused to have anything to do with it.

"Black dresses for months on end . . . pah! If I wanted to wear black all the time, I'd join the clergy."

Jo's mother had relented, and Jo had been grateful to her uncle for providing her with an escape. She'd been so desperate to prolong that escape that she'd grabbed the little box containing the whiskey flask for Mr. Stoatman as she'd left the house that morning, hoping she'd be able to persuade Dolan to take her to Park Row.

They were heading down Bowery now. Jo's carriage was enclosed, the better to avoid noxious smells and bad weather, but its doors had generously sized windows, and she looked out of hers excitedly. An elevated railway ran the length of the street. Shopgirls walked arm in arm underneath it, laughing and chattering. Men loitering in doorways eyed them boldly. Barkers stood on wooden boxes shouting about dime circuses and snake dancers. Newsboys shouted the day's headlines.

Jo knew she shouldn't sit at the edge of her seat, her face pressed to the glass—*Eager young ladies aren't ladies at all*, her mother would've said—but she couldn't help it. The New York before her now was so much more interesting than the one she knew, and alone in her carriage, away from the oppressiveness of her mother's rules, she could give free rein to her insatiable curiosity.

Her carriage crossed Grand Street, with the tenements of Little Italy to her right and the Jewish East Side to the left. The sidewalks were teeming with immigrants, and Jo yearned to know more about them. She'd heard stories: they lived ten to a room, spat on their fruit to clean it, ate pickles for breakfast, and were poor and wretched. But as she watched the people, she wondered if they knew they were wretched. They didn't act it. They shouted their greetings. Sang their wares. Kissed each other on the cheek. They poked and slapped and hugged their children.

One woman in particular caught Jo's attention. Her clothes were grubby and ill-fitting. Her hair had been scraped into a messy bun. She was buying potatoes from a pushcart man, and he must've said something funny because suddenly she was laughing—with her head thrown back and a meaty hand pressed to her enormous, jiggling bosom.

What's it like to laugh like that? Jo wondered. She didn't know. She never had. It wasn't done north of Washington Square.

A few minutes later, her carriage turned onto Park Row, home to many of the city's newspapers. It stopped in front of the *Standard*'s building—an old, squat brick structure nestled up against the tall new *Tribune* building.

Dolan jumped down from his seat and opened the door. "In and out, Miss Jo," he cautioned.

"I won't be a minute," Jo promised.

Her heart beat faster as she stepped inside the building. The small room in which she now stood served as the reception area. A wall separated it from the pressroom, but it did little to mute the pounding of the presses or contain the sharp, oily smell of ink. Copyboys raced down a staircase at her right, rushing finished stories to typesetters. Reporters raced up the same stairs, hurrying to the newsroom.

Jo watched them with a longing so intense, it hurt. She'd loved this place from the day she'd first seen it. Her father had owned the paper for twenty years, but he left the running of it to his editor in chief. He made regular visits, however, to make sure the *Standard*'s tone reflected his views, and had sometimes brought Jo with him—over her mother's objections. As a child, she'd thought all the noise and commotion was the most wild, wonderful game, but as she'd grown older, she understood why everyone rushed around so: they were chasing a story.

How Jo envied them. *To have a purpose in life—what does that feel like?* she wondered.

"Can I help you, miss?" the harried young woman behind the desk asked brusquely.

"Yes," Jo replied. "I'm Josephine Montfort. I'd like to see Mr. Stoatman. I have a bequest for him from my late father."

The young woman's manner immediately became more accommodating. That often happened when Jo revealed her surname.

"Of course, Miss Montfort," she said, "and please accept my condolences. Mr. Stoatman's in a meeting at the moment, but you may wait for him here or outside his office."

"I'll wait upstairs. Thank you," Jo said.

She climbed the staircase, narrowly avoiding a collision with a copyboy, and emerged in the newsroom. It was one long open space that ran from front to back of the building. Two offices, built out from a wall, stood at the left of the landing—the city editor's and Stoatman's—the editor in chief.

The sound of clacking typewriters was deafening. Reporters were yelling at copyboys and the city editor was angrily crumpling a typed story while bellowing that his grandmother could have done a better job on it. Jo made her way to Stoatman's office and stood by the closed door, spellbound.

Her father liked to say that when he inherited the *Standard*, it was nothing but a small daily devoted to maritime news and that he'd made it into a small daily devoted to marriage-time news. It was the preferred paper of the upper class: sober, genteel, and a stark contrast to Mr. Pulitzer's and Mr. Hearst's papers, with their lurid headlines. It reported on city politics, cultural events, and social happenings, and refused to print tawdry tales of murder and mayhem. More important to its readers, it also ran the birth, death, and wedding announcements of New York's best families.

Remember, Josephine, there are only three times in a woman's life when her name may appear in the papers, Jo's mother often said. *When she is born, when she is married, and when she dies.*

The merely wealthy, or worse yet—the newly wealthy, searched in vain for their names in the *Standard*'s columns. It was the doings of the old Dutch and English families—those whose ancestors had built New York from a rough-and-tumble trading post at the end of the world to a mighty port city in the center of it—that the paper documented.

"You might be a while, miss," a voice said. "Would you care to sit?"

Jo turned, startled. A reporter was standing close by, holding a chair. He looked to be eighteen or nineteen years old and had dark hair, a handsome face, and blue eyes—the bluest she'd ever seen.

"I beg your pardon?" she said, flustered. She wasn't used to speaking with strange men.

"I said you might be a while. Stoatman's got some lackey from the commissioner's office in with him." He put the chair down next to her.

"Thank you," she said. "You're very kind."

She tried to look away, but couldn't. His eyes were not only impossibly blue, but frank and amused. She felt that they could see inside her, that he could see her heart and its sudden, silly fluttering. Blushing, she sat down.

As he returned to his desk, she glanced at him from under the brim of her hat. Had she thought him handsome? He was *glorious*.

He wore a white shirt with the sleeves rolled up and a tweed vest. His shoulders were broad and his forearms muscled. Thick, wavy brown hair curled over his ears and down the back of his neck. His nose had a bump on its bridge, like a boxer's. A strong jaw and high cheekbones gave his face character. His smile was slow and easy.

Jo made herself look away. She untied the bow on the box containing Mr. Stoatman's bequest. As she was retying it, her eyes fell on the handsome reporter again. He was talking with two other young men about exciting things—a robbery, a stabbing, a three-alarm fire. Their conversation was so different from the stultifying ones that went on in her home.

Newport or Saratoga this summer? I hear Ellie Montgomery's had her drawing room repapered. Have you seen Minnie Stevens's herbaceous borders?

As Jo continued to eavesdrop, one of the reporters brought up a topic that was more than exciting; it was scandalous. She leaned forward, the better to hear him.

"Hey, Eddie, you hear about the chorus girl who fell in front of a train this morning?"

"She didn't *fall*, she jumped."

That was the same young man who'd offered Jo a seat. Now she knew his name—Eddie. He was leaning back in his chair, tossing an eraser in the air as he spoke.

"You sure about that?" the first reporter asked.

"I got it straight from the horse's mouth—Oscar Rubin over at the morgue," Eddie said.

"What happened?"

"She was carrying on with the Beekman boy. Beekman senior found out and sent junior off to an aunt in Boston. Problem was, the idiot put the girl in the family way. He told her he'd marry her, then did a bunk."

Jo gasped, horrified. Andy Beekman had unexpectedly left for

Boston just a few days ago. Now she knew why. And to think that Addie had served him tea at her father's funeral luncheon!

"Stoatman know this?"

"Yeah, but he won't run it," Eddie replied, still tossing his eraser. "He'll kill it. Just like he killed my story on Charlie Montfort."

"What story? There is no story. Montfort's gun went off. It was an accident. *End* of story."

"It *wasn't* an accident," Eddie said.

And suddenly it was no longer exciting to be in the newsroom. Suddenly Jo couldn't breathe.

"The cops said it was."

Eddie snorted. "They were *paid* to say it was. A rookie I know was there. He saw the body and he says different."

"Yeah? What's he say?" the other reporter asked, snatching Eddie's eraser out of the air.

Eddie sat up. "That Charlie Montfort put his revolver to his head and blew his brains out."

⋙ CHAPTER FIVE ⋘

It wasn't true. It *couldn't* be. Jo stood up on shaking legs and approached the reporter.

"How *dare* you. The dreadful thing you just said about Charles Montfort . . . it's a lie. Why did you say it?" she asked. Far too loudly.

Heads turned. The young man looked at her. "What's that to you, miss?" he asked.

Jo was about to tell him when the door to the editor in chief's office opened and Stoatman emerged, holding the stub of a cigar in one hand, ushering a man out with the other. Short and bald, he wore an ink-stained shirt, a vest, and ash-covered trousers. The two men said their goodbyes; then Stoatman spotted Jo.

"Miss Montfort? What an unexpected pleasure," he said. "What brings you to the newsroom?"

Jo, still glaring at Eddie, saw his eyes widen at the mention of her name. *He knows who I am now and he's worried I'll get him into trouble,* she thought. *Good. He deserves it.*

"This . . . this . . ." *Boy,* she was going to say to Stoatman. *This boy should not speak ill of my father.* But she changed her mind. ". . . bequest," she said, handing him the box. "It's for you from my father."

Stoatman's perpetually gruff expression softened. "How kind. My condolences, Miss Montfort. Please come in," he said.

He ushered Jo into his office, shutting the door behind them, and offered her a chair. He offered her tea, too, but she declined. She was still upset and didn't want to be here in Stoatman's office, choking on cigar smoke. She wanted to go back into the newsroom and make that boy answer her.

Stoatman opened the box. He smiled wistfully at the sight of the silver flask. "This was mine," he said. "Your father won it when we made a wager on the 1880 presidential election. I picked Hancock. He bet on Garfield. Charlie always backed the winners." He looked up at her. "Thank you for this."

"You're very welcome," Jo said, saddened by Stoatman's recollection. She'd accompanied her father to the newsroom during the last election. It hit her now that she would never do so again.

She rose. Stoatman did, too. They made small talk about the mild weather; then Jo took her leave. Sad as she was, she was also determined. She *had* to speak to that reporter. An opportunity to return to the newsroom wouldn't come her way anytime soon. As she walked out of Stoatman's office, she saw her chance. The reporter was standing by the staircase, talking to a copyboy. He had his jacket on and looked like he was ready to leave.

"I'll walk you out, Miss Montfort," Stoatman said.

"That won't be necessary, Mr. Stoatman," Jo quickly said. "I know my way. Good day."

She walked to the staircase. When she was a few feet away, she abruptly stopped, closed her eyes, and pressed the back of one hand to her forehead. It was a ploy she'd seen Trudy pull when she wanted to spend the day in bed instead of going to class. She hoped Eddie would see her, but it was Stoatman who did.

"Miss Montfort, are you all right?" he asked.

Jo opened her eyes. "Yes, I'm fine, thank you," she said, chagrined.

"Mr. Stoatman!" another voice said. Jo recognized it as belonging to the young woman from the front desk. She was standing at the top of the stairs, breathless. "The mayor's here. He's in a lather about your editorial on the subterranean railway."

Stoatman bit back a curse. "Gallagher!" he barked at Eddie. "See Miss Montfort home!"

Jo couldn't suppress a triumphant smile. A carriage ride uptown would give Eddie Gallagher plenty of time to explain himself.

Eddie looked alarmed. "But it's five o'clock, chief," he protested.

"Don't worry, Gallagher. The Park Row bars won't run out of beer while you're gone. Get a move on!" Stoatman ordered as he disappeared down the stairwell.

"I'm so terribly sorry to be a burden, Mr. Gallagher," Jo said, in a voice that suggested she was anything but. Eddie, looking thunderous, offered her his arm. She allowed him to lead her down the stairs. They crossed the foyer, and then he held the door for her. Out on the sidewalk, he took her arm once more and walked her to her carriage.

"Miss Jo, what's wrong?" Dolan asked worriedly when he saw her.

"I felt a bit heady," Jo lied. "Mr. Gallagher here kindly offered to see me home."

"I knew this wasn't a good idea," Dolan said unhappily, handing Jo up into the carriage. She sat in the rear-facing seat. Dolan waited for Eddie to get in and settle himself across from her; then he closed the door.

As soon as they'd pulled away from the curb, Jo dropped her wilting flower act. "Why did you say such a terrible thing about my father?" she demanded, still furious.

"You seem to have made a miraculous recovery, Miss Montfort," Eddie observed. "I'm so relieved."

Jo ignored that. "If you have information about my father's death, you must tell me, Mr. Gallagher. I have a right to know."

Eddie smiled smoothly. "Really, Miss Montfort, it was nothing. Just—"

Jo cut him off. "Do *not* patronize me. This is my father of whom we are speaking. If you refuse to explain your comments to me, I shall share them with my uncle, Phillip Montfort, and you can explain them to him."

Eddie leaned forward in his seat. His smile was gone. "I could lose my job over this," he said. "Eight dollars a week is nothing to you, Miss Montfort. You probably spend that much on fruit gums. But it's all I've got."

"I do not care for fruit gums, Mr. Gallagher. They're vulgar. Are you going to tell me . . . or my uncle?"

Eddie's gaze hardened. "You want the truth? Here it is. Your father was found dead on the floor of his study late at night. There was an entry wound on his right temple. An exit wound at the back of his skull. The slug was lodged in the wall." He paused, gauging the effect of his words. "Should I continue?"

"Yes," Jo said, shoring up her courage. The image of her father with bullet wounds in his head was extremely distressing, but she needed to hear what Eddie had to say.

"The gun was in your father's right hand. He wasn't cleaning it when it went off. Only a fool cleans a loaded gun, and Charles Montfort was no fool. It was suicide. The police know it. Stoatman knows it. Every editor in the city knows it. There was plenty of talk between cops and reporters that night. Your uncle bribed the police captain and the coroner to record the death as an accident, then threatened to sue the hell out of any paper that said otherwise. He didn't have to threaten Stoatman. Your family already owns him."

"You wish to discredit my uncle now, as well as my father? Perhaps *someone* made a bribe, but not my uncle. He would *never* do such a thing," Jo said hotly.

Her voice was rising with every word she spoke, but her brave front was crumbling. Could Eddie Gallagher actually be right? One thing he'd said was undeniably true: only fools cleaned loaded guns, and her father was no fool. From the moment she'd heard the explanation of his death, she'd found it impossible to accept.

"They teach you anything in finishing school besides embroidery, Miss Montfort?" Eddie asked. "Your uncle had a good reason for bribing the police—you. Suicide is a lot of things. It's ugly and sad, but most of all it's scandalous. If people knew the truth, they would wonder *why* your father killed himself. Maybe Charles Montfort had money troubles, they'd say. Maybe there was a woman involved. Maybe he lost his mind. The old New York families—your people—they're not too keen on scandals, are they?"

"No, they're not," Jo said, shuddering at the thought of anyone in her circle finding out that her father had killed himself.

"There'd be no doors slammed in your face. Society families are too polite for that," Eddie said. "But the invitations would stop and the proposals would never start. Your uncle wants to make sure you marry an Aldrich, a Roosevelt, or a Livingston. Otherwise you'll have to settle for new money—a fate worse than death." He sat back in his seat. "Do you see what I'm saying?"

Jo was silent. She was in shock. Not only from what Eddie had said, but from how he'd said it. No one had ever spoken to her like that. Not once in her entire life.

"What I see, Mr. Gallagher," she said when she'd collected herself, "is that you take pleasure in being cruel. Whatever you think you know about me and my *people*, know this—Charles Montfort was my father and I loved him." She turned and rapped on a small wooden door in the driver's-side wall of the carriage.

It slid open. "Yes, Miss Jo?" Dolan said. He'd turned his head, but kept his eyes straight ahead on the rush of evening traffic.

"Pull over, please, Dolan. I wish to walk the rest of the way. Kindly take Mr. Gallagher home," Jo said, struggling to keep her voice steady.

"What's the address, sir?" Dolan asked.

"You don't need to take me home. I can walk," Eddie replied.

"I wouldn't hear of it," said Jo.

"Address, please, sir," Dolan pressed.

"Twenty-Three Reade," Eddie said.

Dolan slid the door closed. A few seconds later, the carriage came to a stop by the curb.

"Miss Montfort, I . . . Please forgive me," Eddie said haltingly. His smug air had vanished. He looked ashamed of himself. "I've gone too far. It's how I react to being cornered. I come out swinging and try to knock the other fella down before he can knock me. Only this time the fella was a girl."

"Dolan will take you home now," Jo said. Her face was hidden by her hat brim. She would not let him see how badly he'd upset her.

Eddie leaned toward her. "Miss Montfort, I'm sorry. Really. For my behavior and for the loss of your father," he said. His eyes sought hers and she saw, in their depths, that he meant it.

"Everything all right, Miss Jo?" Dolan said as he opened the door.

"Perfectly," Jo said. She stepped out of the carriage and headed toward Gramercy Square without a backward glance. No one looking at her would have guessed she was struggling just to put one foot in front of the other. As she walked, she thought about what Eddie Gallagher had done. He'd upset her and insulted her, but had he also told her the truth?

His words echoed in her mind: *Charlie Montfort put his revolver to his head and blew his brains out.* Overcome by emotion, she stumbled and had to grasp the iron fence of a nearby brownstone for support.

"Miss? Are you all right? You want I should call a cop?" It was a newsboy.

"I'm fine, thank you. It was just a spell," Jo said, forcing a smile. She took a few deep breaths and continued up Irving Place.

She wished she could talk to someone about this—someone who

might be able to tell her if it was true. But who? Not her mother or uncle. She'd have to tell them how she found out, and they'd be furious with her. As she reached her house, she paused to calm herself. Her eyes traveled over the stoop, to the second floor, and the windows of her father's study. And suddenly she realized there *was* someone who could tell her if Eddie's claim was true.

"You, Papa," she said.

❧ CHAPTER SIX ❧

A cool night breeze blew through the windows of Jo's bedroom, billowing the draperies out like sails. Pale moonlight spilled across the floor. Downstairs, the grandfather clock struck the hour—two o'clock. Jo heard its deep, familiar chime.

She sat up in her bed, wide-awake, and felt for the matches she'd placed on her night table. A few minutes later, she was padding past her mother's bedroom and down the stairs, carrying a glowing candle.

As Jo slipped inside her father's study, careful to sidestep a loose floorboard right outside the door, she exhaled deeply—relieved that she hadn't encountered their butler. Theakston was a meddler and a snitch. Normally, he'd be in bed at this hour, along with the rest of the servants, but he'd been known to polish the silver or wind the clocks on nights when he couldn't sleep.

Jo placed her candleholder on top of her father's massive mahogany desk and looked around. If she was going to find any answers about his death, she'd find them here. His study had been his sanctuary. It was a masculine room, all dark wood and leather. He spent an hour or two here every night reading, writing letters, and consulting his agenda for the next day's appointments.

It was that agenda Jo was determined to locate. She wanted to see what he'd written under September 16, 1890, the day he'd died. She'd asked her mother about it at dinner.

"Do you know what happened to Father's agenda? I should like to have it as a memento," she'd fibbed.

But her mother, still fragile in her grief, hadn't wished to speak of it. She'd picked at her meal then retreated to her bedroom. She hadn't asked Jo about her day or why her trip to see Reverend Willis had taken so long. Sitting by herself at the dinner table, Jo wondered if her mother even remembered Jo had left the house.

"It has to be here somewhere," she whispered now, riffling through a desk drawer. She pulled out scissors, fountain pens, a box of matches—everything but the agenda. She searched the other drawers and looked under the blotter but found nothing.

It's not like this in mystery books. In mystery books there's always a secret compartment. Shelves that move. Something, she thought. *Help me, Papa. Please.*

She walked around the desk, searching for a false panel, but found nothing. Then she pulled all the drawers out. When she had them on the floor, she felt around inside the frame, hoping to find a latch or button. Again, she turned up nothing. Sighing heavily, she put the drawers back. She'd just slid the last one into place when she heard it—a creak.

Jo knew that sound. It was the loose floorboard outside the study's door. And she knew who'd made it.

Theakston.

⇻ CHAPTER SEVEN ⇺

Jo knew she only had seconds.

She licked her fingers and pinched the candle's wick. Its flame faded with a hiss, but no smoke. Grabbing the candleholder, she crawled under the desk, cutting her knee painfully on something as she did. She pulled the desk chair into place just as the door opened.

There were footsteps. *His.* They crossed the room slowly. She heard him plump a cushion, then wind the clock. *What's brought him up here?* she wondered. Had she heard her walking around?

Go, Theakston, she silently pleaded. *Leave.*

But he didn't. Instead he walked to the desk and straightened the blotter. "Blast that maid," he muttered. "I told her not to touch anything in here."

He was standing in front of the desk. Only a panel of wood separated them. Jo's heart was pounding so loudly, she was certain he would hear it. She could imagine him coming around the desk, pulling the chair out, and peering down at her, his smile oily and triumphant.

Miss Josephine? This is most irregular. Is everything all right? he'd ask.

By morning, her mother would be fully informed. By lunchtime, the entire household staff would be. He hated to tell tales, he'd say to Mrs. Nelson, their cook—who would tell every other servant in the house—but he was concerned for Miss Jo. She was too forward for a young lady.

After what seemed like an hour but was only a minute, Jo heard him walk to the door and then close it behind him. She let out the breath she'd been holding and crawled out from under the desk. There was blood on her nightgown from her knee. She remembered that she'd seen a box of matches in a desk drawer. She dug them out, relit her candle, and inspected the cut. It was thin but deep. *What made it?* she wondered.

Crouching down, she ran her hand over the floorboards under the desk. Something sliced the skin of her palm, and she sucked in a breath at the pain. Moving her candle closer to the boards, she examined them carefully and saw that a thin, sharp piece of metal protruded from a gap between two of them. One of the boards was shorter than the rest, and scuffed.

Jo was so excited that she sat straight up and whacked her head on the underside of the desk. "Blast!" she hissed.

She grabbed a letter opener off the desktop and wedged its tip under the short board. It came up easily. Underneath it was her father's agenda. The small hollow in which it rested was lined with tin to keep mice out. An edge of that lining was what had cut her.

"Bless your black heart, Theakston," she whispered. If he hadn't come snooping, she wouldn't have ducked under the desk.

Jo lifted the agenda out and flipped to September 16. Tucked between that page and the following one were ten one-hundred-dollar notes. Jo had never seen so much money, and seeing it now made her uneasy. She knew that her father's business transactions were conducted with checks, not cash.

She put the money on the floor, then scrutinized the page, hoping to find something that would tell her why he'd killed himself.

She saw the words *Meeting, VH partners, noon* written in her father's neat hand. That signified nothing unusual. *VH* stood for Van Houten, the shipping firm in which he was a partner. Her father routinely attended business meetings with the rest of the partners.

Lower down on the page was an additional notation: *A. Jamison, 4 p.m.* Jo knew that Arthur Jamison was her father's banker. *Did Papa go to the bank that day to withdraw the thousand dollars?* she wondered.

She looked at the page for the following day, September 17. At the bottom, she saw something that *was* unusual—the very last entry: *Kinch, VHW, 11 p.m.*

VHW stood for Van Houten's Wharf, the site of the shipping firm's docks. Her father always abbreviated it that way. But Kinch? That name meant nothing to Jo. It was so odd-sounding. Maybe it wasn't a person but a ship. That would make more sense, considering the *VHW* notation. Then again, why would her father be boarding a ship at all, never mind at such a late hour? Van Houten's partners didn't inspect cargo; their clerks did.

She flipped to the day before her father died, September 15. The same notation was at the bottom of that page, too: *Kinch, VHW, 11 p.m.* But there was additional writing underneath it. The letters were large and loopy, as if scrawled in haste: *Eleanor Owens, b. 1874.*

"Who's Eleanor Owens?" Jo whispered. She wasn't a friend or family member—Jo had never heard her name mentioned. She wasn't an employee, either. Van Houten only had one female employee—the woman who cleaned their offices—and her name was Tillie Polk. If Eleanor Owens wasn't a friend or an employee, who was she?

Then the answer came to Jo and she gasped. "Dear God," she said aloud, "Papa had a mistress."

➤ CHAPTER EIGHT ➤

Jo had seen those sorts of women. They drove flashy carriages through the park, wore too much jewelry, and rouged their cheeks.

She wasn't supposed to know they even existed, but Trudy had told her about them. They'd had a friend at school, Jacinta Smyth, who left one day without any explanation.

Trudy did some digging and found out that Jacinta's father had a mistress who'd had his child. When he refused to support the baby, the woman paid a visit to his home—during a dinner party. The resulting scandal was so terrible that the family had to move to Cleveland.

"But why would Mr. Smyth *do* such a thing?" Jo had asked Trudy.

"Because Mrs. Smyth's a cold fish. You can tell by looking at her. Men have to be kept satisfied. They have needs."

"Don't women?" Jo had asked.

"Only the bad ones," Trudy replied.

Jo looked at the notation again. *What does the* b *before 1874 stand for?* she wondered. *If it stands for* born, *then Eleanor Owens couldn't be Papa's mistress because she'd only be sixteen years old. At least, I hope she couldn't be his mistress.*

Then she had an even more chilling thought: Maybe Eleanor
Owens was the *child* of her father and his mistress—a child who
had come of age and wanted money. Maybe she was blackmailing
him and that was why he had all that cash.

"Maybe I'm losing my mind," Jo said out loud.

Her father was an upstanding man. He went to church every
Sunday and dined at home most every night. He sent her mother
flowers every week. He was as likely to have a mistress as he was to
vote Democrat.

The more she thought about the whole thing, the more outlandish it sounded.

Why was I so quick to believe Eddie Gallagher? she asked herself.
*He's probably one of those reporters who'll do anything to get a story—
even if it means making one up. The notations could have something to
do with papa's work and his death might truly have been an accident.*

Even as she thought these things, Jo didn't quite believe them.
Yet, if her father *had* killed himself, there had to be a reason. What
was it?

She paged back, reading every entry for the months of September
and August, but saw nothing else unusual. She paged forward, too,
looking at her father's future appointments. Again, nothing jumped
out at her—until she got to October 15. *Kinch, VHW, 11 p.m.* was
written on the page.

What does it mean? Jo wondered.

The clock downstairs struck the hour—three a.m. Jo knew she
would be wrecked tomorrow if she didn't get some sleep. She put
the money back in the secret hollow, tucked the agenda into a
pocket in her robe, and replaced the floorboard. As she picked up
her candle, she heard a noise from the street—a loud, metallic crash.

Curious, she walked to the windows to see what had caused it.
The glow from the streetlamps revealed a woman righting an up-
ended garbage can. She was a ragpicker—Mad Mary. Jo knew her.
Everyone did. Mary roamed the city day and night, muttering to

herself as she dug through trash and ashes, looking for bones to sell to glue factories, rags used in paper-making, or anything else that might bring a few pennies.

Jo's father, kind to a fault, had always made sure that Mrs. Nelson wrapped up leftovers for Mary if Mary came by during daylight hours. It had irritated Jo's mother, because Mary would sit on their stoop while she ate, then linger to watch the children play in the park. Friends coming to call had to step around the piteous figure in her dirty, threadbare clothing.

Mary finished digging and put her finds in her small wooden cart. There were bells on it and they jingled softly as she went on her way. Jo turned to go back to her room, but as she did, something else caught her eye—a man.

He was standing directly across from her house, staring up at her father's window—at *her*.

Startled, Jo blew out her candle and shrank into the draperies, hiding from view. She stood frozen for a few seconds until she worked up the nerve to peer out again. The man was still there, standing in the gaslight. He was smoking. His clothes were rough. His dark hair was gathered and tied at the nape of his neck. And his face . . . it must've been a trick of the light, but it seemed to be streaked with something. Dirt? Ash?

As Jo watched, her heart pounding, he flicked the remains of his cigarette into the gutter and walked away. She tried to tell herself that he was only a vagrant, but she knew it wasn't so. He'd been staring directly at the windows—the same windows where her father used to stand night after night, gazing out into the darkness. Watching. Waiting.

In that instant, Jo became certain that Eddie Gallagher had told her the truth. The names in her father's diary and the dark figure staring at her house . . . they had something to do with his death. She felt it in her bones.

She slipped back to the desk, lit her candle again, and returned to her bedroom. After hiding her father's agenda inside a fur muff in her closet, she crawled back under her covers, feeling dispirited. She had found the agenda, but it had given her no answers, only more questions.

With mounting dread, Jo realized she would have to ask her questions of the living, not the dead.

She would have to go to her uncle.

➤ CHAPTER NINE ◄

Admiral William Montfort gazed down at Jo with eyes as gray as flint and every bit as hard.

The fearsome admiral had been painted aboard his warship in 1664, only days before he'd taken the colony of Nieuw Amsterdam from the Dutch and renamed it New York. His portrait now hung in Phillip Montfort's front hall. The Montfort coat of arms, with its Latin motto, appeared in the canvas's bottom left corner.

"'*Fac quod faciendum est,*'" Jo read aloud. "Do what must be done."

William Montfort had lived by that motto, and his descendants were expected to as well. Montfort children learned to say it while still in their cradles. Jo took strength from the words now. If the admiral could confront the entire Dutch navy, she could confront her uncle. She had no choice.

People didn't just kill themselves; they did so because they were distraught. If something had been troubling her father so deeply that he wished to end his life, Phillip might know why. The two brothers had been very close.

The decision to speak with him was a daunting one, though;

Jo knew it would lead to trouble. Asking questions, demanding explanations—these things *always* led to trouble. The moment a girl learned how to talk, she was told not to.

"This way, please, Miss Josephine," said Harney, her uncle's butler. He'd gone to Phillip's study to announce her and had just returned.

"My darling Jo! What a lovely surprise!" Phillip exclaimed as she joined him. He rose from his chair by the fireplace and enfolded her in an embrace.

He looks so much like Papa, Jo thought, with a stab of pain. Phillip Montfort was older by two years—forty-six to her father's forty-four—and a little taller, but the gray eyes, the shock of black hair, and the smile were the same. And like her father, Phillip had a certain courtly formality about him. He was wearing a three-piece suit even though he was alone in his own study on a Saturday.

"Come and sit down," he said. "Your timing is perfect. I've just had Harney bring a fresh pot of tea. May I offer you a cup? I'm afraid you've missed your aunt and cousin, though. They're out visiting Madeleine's mother."

Jo knew that Madeleine and Caroline always paid social calls on Saturday afternoons. That was why she'd picked this time. Caroline's brother, Robert, was away at school.

"I'm sorry to miss them, but to be truthful, I came at this time because I want to speak with you alone," Jo said, settling herself across from him.

Her uncle's smile turned to a frown of concern. "Is everything all right?" he asked.

Jo decided not to beat around the bush. She took a deep breath, then said, "No, Uncle Phillip, it isn't. I'm afraid I have a difficult question to ask you. . . . Did Papa kill himself?"

Phillip blinked, taken aback. "Of course not! My goodness, Jo, where did you get such a dreadful idea?"

For a second, Jo was tempted to fib, but she knew better. Like her father, her uncle was no fool. He'd see right through her lie and she'd only get herself into more trouble. She bravely plunged ahead.

"After I delivered Papa's bequest to Reverend Willis, I delivered Mr. Stoatman's," she explained. "While I was there, I overheard some reporters talking. They said that Papa committed suicide."

Phillip's cheeks flushed. *Here it comes*, Jo thought grimly. And it did.

"Josephine Montfort, what the devil were you thinking?" he thundered. "Cavorting through the city unescorted! And to *Park Row*, of all places! What if someone had seen you? Bram or Addie or Grandmama?"

"Grandmama wouldn't have seen me at the *Standard*. She only reads the *World*," Jo said, trying to soften her uncle's anger with a bit of levity. Grandmama Aldrich was as likely to read the *World*—much less visit its offices—as she was to wear red garters.

"That is *not* funny, Josephine. I'm far too angry for jokes at the moment. In fact, I'm livid!"

Jo flinched. "Please don't shout, Uncle Phillip. I only went to Park Row because I didn't want to go home. I can't bear it there anymore."

Phillip was unmoved. "That's hardly an excuse!" he said.

"But you don't know what it's like!" Jo argued. "Papa's gone and Mama barely comes out of her room and the blinds are drawn all day and I feel like I've been shut up in a tomb!" A frightening thought suddenly gripped her. "You won't *tell* Mama I went to the paper, will you? She'll never let me out of the house again."

"That is *just* like you to worry more about having your wings clipped than about the wrongness of your actions," Philip said, still fuming. "You've always been a headstrong girl, and you've never heeded a scolding. Not about climbing too high in trees—"

"Caro's cat was stuck!"

"Or swimming out too far from shore—"

"I had to rescue Aunt Maddie's hat!"

"Or knocking the Beekman boy off his bicycle!"

"He deserved it! He was bullying Robert!"

Phillip closed his eyes. He pinched the bridge of his nose. "What am I going to do with you?" he said. After a moment, he opened his eyes again. "I won't tell your mother. Not this time. Partly because I feel she is somewhat to blame for this, keeping you as confined as she does. But on one condition—you must promise me you will never, *ever* do it again."

"I promise," Jo said. "And I'm sorry." She truly was. She felt terrible for upsetting him. His burdens were heavy enough without her adding to them. "I know I shouldn't have gone, but I did, and then I overheard the reporters talking, and . . . well, I have to know if they're right. I *have* to, Uncle Phillip. I think about Papa all the time. His death makes no sense to me. He knew better than to clean a loaded gun. *I* know better than to clean a loaded gun."

Phillip looked away. "We all make mistakes. Perhaps he was preoccupied. Perhaps he only *thought* he had unloaded the chamber," he said.

He was lying. Jo could hear it in his voice; she could see it in his face. "Tell me the truth, Uncle Phillip. That's why I came to you. Because I want to know the truth."

"The truth can be a hard thing, Jo. It's often best left hidden," Phillip said quietly.

"I can cope with hard things. I'm not a child anymore. I'm grown. I'm seventeen years old."

"Yes, I suppose you are," Phillip allowed, looking at Jo again. "But when I look at you, I still see the child you once were and I want to protect that child. From grief. From pain. From all the ugliness of the world."

"Please, Uncle," Jo begged.

Phillip's eyes filled with sadness. He suddenly looked old and weary. "My dearest girl," he said. "How I hoped I would never have to have this conversation. Yes. Charles killed himself. I'm sorry, Jo. I'm so very, very sorry."

❧ CHAPTER TEN ❧

Although Jo had steeled herself, her uncle's words still hit her hard.

Oh dear God, it's true, she thought. *Eddie Gallagher was right.*

"I blame myself entirely," Phillip said, his voice ragged with grief. "I saw Charles on the day of his death. We, the partners, had a meeting in his study about a ship we wanted to buy. There was something wrong; Charles wasn't himself. He and I talked after the others left and he admitted he was troubled. He was talking wildly."

"What did he say?" asked Jo.

"That he felt hopeless. That he was despondent."

"*Papa* said such things?" Jo said, bewildered. That didn't sound like her father at all.

"He did, and I became angry with him for saying them. I reminded him of his family, his many friends. We argued. How I wish to God we hadn't. I begged him to tell me what was troubling him, but he refused, so I took my leave. I went to the kitchen on my way out. We'd had a luncheon before the meeting, and I wanted to give Mrs. Nelson my compliments. I spoke with her and left, and that night my brother shot himself."

Phillip covered his face with his hands. "I saw him. Lying dead on the floor of his study. I'll never get that image out of my head. Never. I relive that day over and over again, knowing I might have prevented Charles's death if I hadn't argued with him. If I'd persuaded him to share his worries with me. How could I have failed him so badly?"

"It's *not* your fault," Jo said fervently, her heart aching for her uncle. "If there was anyone he would have confided in, it was you."

Phillip lowered his hands. He nodded, but Jo could see he didn't believe her. If only she could find the reason for her father's death, she could convince him that he wasn't to blame.

"Something drove Papa to do what he did," she said. "Could it have been money worries? His business? Did he have a disagreement with one of the partners?"

"Your father's finances are *not* a suitable topic of discussion," Phillip said. "But to answer your questions—no, they were sound, and as far as I know, he had no disagreements with anyone."

Jo took her father's agenda from her purse. "I found this in Papa's office," she said, thinking it best not to explain *how* she'd found it. Her uncle didn't approve of snooping. "Papa made some puzzling notations in it. Do you think they might have anything to do with his death?" She showed him the page for September 15 and pointed at the notations *Kinch, VHW, 11 p.m.* and *Eleanor Owens, b. 1874.* Then she showed him September 17, with *Kinch, VHW, 11 p.m.* repeated.

Phillip peered at them, then shook his head. "I'm afraid those names don't mean anything to me," he said.

Jo's heart sank. She felt certain that Eleanor Owens had some role in her father's death and had hoped her uncle could tell her who she was.

"If you'd like to leave the agenda with me, I could ask the other partners," Phillip offered, reaching for it.

But Jo was loath to part with it. "I'd like to hold on to it. It reminds me of Papa," she explained. "I'll write the names down for you."

Phillip nodded. "Very well," he said.

Jo pressed on with her questions. "Do you know why Papa would have seen his banker the day he died?" she pressed, pointing at the words *A. Jamison, 4 p.m.* written under September 16. "He'd withdrawn money. It was tucked inside the agenda. I thought it best to leave it at home."

"No, but it doesn't strike me as unusual. He often met with them," Phillip replied. "As for the money, he'd been talking about buying a new pair of carriage horses."

"Did he leave a note behind?" Jo asked hopefully.

Phillip shook his head. "Jo, I think that's quite—"

Enough. Jo knew what he was going to say. He wanted to end this discussion, but she didn't let him.

"I don't know if this has anything to do with Papa's death," she quickly cut in, "but there was a strange man outside our house late last night. He had something on his face, some sort of markings. Did Papa know such a man? Did he ever mention him to you?"

"No, he didn't," Phillip said, visibly alarmed. "What was this man doing? Was he trying to break in?"

"No, he stood by the streetlamp and stared up at the windows to Papa's study. Then he left."

"He was probably only a vagrant," said Phillip, relaxing a bit. "But if you see him again, have Theakston fetch the police."

Jo had to work up her courage to ask her next question. "Did Papa . . . Did he have someone? Someone else, I mean."

Phillip looked confused. "I don't understand," he said.

"Someone besides my mother. Could Eleanor Owens be that someone?"

"Good God, Josephine!" Phillip exclaimed, upset again. "How does a well-brought-up young lady know to ask such a thing? There certainly was *not* someone besides your mother!"

Jo winced at her uncle's sharp tone, but she was relieved to know her father had not kept a mistress.

"I've had quite enough of these questions," Phillip warned. "I know why you're asking them, but you must stop. It's not healthy. You won't find a reason. I've already tried. All you'll do is torture yourself."

Jo started to protest, to tell him she was sure they *could* find the reason, if only they kept looking, but he held up a finger, silencing her.

"Don't speak. *Think*, Jo. Think of what you've just said. You've talked about disagreements with the partners and the possibility of your father consorting with strange-looking men and inappropriate women. Does any of that sound like him? Does it explain why he took his life? No. All it does is dishonor his memory," Phillip said angrily.

Jo didn't reply; she just looked down at her hands, folded in her lap. Her uncle's words, she knew, were intended to make her feel ashamed of herself. That was what people did when they wanted to stop a girl from doing something—they shamed her.

Don't fill your plate; it's greedy. Don't wear bright colors; you'll look fast. Don't ask so many questions; people will think you bold.

"Think, too, of how irresponsibly you behaved," Phillip continued. "You're lucky you were not seen at Park Row. Not by anyone who matters, I mean. We're *all* lucky."

"What do you mean *all?*" Jo asked, lifting her eyes to his.

Phillip didn't reply right away. When he did, Jo sensed he was choosing his words carefully.

"I've worked very hard to keep the truth of your father's death out of the newspapers. Had I not, your chances of making a good match would've been ruined. There was talk in the days following his passing and I don't want it stirred up again. When you go places you shouldn't, and speak with people you shouldn't, you risk doing just that. I know how deeply you're grieving, Jo, but don't let that grief be your undoing. That's the last thing your father would've wanted."

Eddie was right about that, too, Jo realized. *Uncle Phillip* did *pay the authorities to say Papa's death was accidental.*

Phillip reached for her hand. "A woman's entire happiness depends on her marriage and I intend for you to make an excellent one."

Jo nodded, feigning acquiescence. She knew her uncle only wanted the best for her, but she couldn't do what he was asking—she couldn't stop trying to find answers, and she couldn't put her feelings in a neat little box. Her father had taken his life. Something had driven him to it, and that something must have been terrible.

He was gone, but his ghost lingered—in the quiet streets of Gramercy Square, in the hushed rooms of her house, in the hollows of her heart. It would haunt her forever unless she could find out *why.*

Phillip, still holding her hand, said, "I've treated you as an adult, Jo, and now I expect you to behave like one. Your mother has not guessed the truth and I'm glad of that. Likewise your aunt and cousins. I implore you to carry on bravely and be a comfort to your family, not a source of further distress. Will you do that for me?"

"Of course, Uncle Phillip," Jo said, forcing a smile.

He gave her hand a quick squeeze. "That's my good girl," he said, releasing it.

Jo rose to leave and Phillip walked her to the foyer. As Harney held her coat, her gaze once again met that of her ancestor. There was a challenge in the admiral's hard gray eyes.

Fac quod faciendum est. It seemed to Jo as if he'd spoken the words aloud.

"Oh, Jo, I've just remembered something," Phillip said. "I saw Mrs. Aldrich yesterday. She invited Caroline and Robert to Herondale next weekend. Gertrude Van Eyck and Gilbert Grosvenor, too.

She wondered if your mother might be persuaded to allow you to join them. Would you like that? If so, I'll have a word with Anna. It would only be a small gathering of close friends—nothing to offend the proprieties—and I think a change of scenery would do you good. The country's just the thing to rid the mind of morbid thoughts."

"I would like that very much. Thank you, Uncle," Jo said. She kissed him goodbye, then walked down the stoop to her carriage.

But it wasn't Herondale she was trying to figure out how to get to as Dolan opened the door for her.

It was 23 Reade Street.

❧ CHAPTER ELEVEN ❧

"How *does* one get inside these things with no bell and no butler?" Jo wondered aloud.

She was standing at the door of a boardinghouse, looking through its glass panes. Gas light from a single sconce flickered in the shabby vestibule, illuminating a rusty radiator and some empty milk bottles. A narrow staircase led to the upper floors.

Jo raised her gloved hand and knocked, but no one answered. As she was about to knock again, a man on the sidewalk behind her bellowed so loudly, she jumped.

"Hey, Tommy! Tommy Barton!" He waited for a few seconds, then cupped his hands around his mouth and yelled. "Barton, you lazy bastard! Open up!"

Above Jo's head, a window was raised. "Chrissakes, Al, what do you want? I'm asleep!"

"Not anymore. Press is down at the *Trib*. Chief says get your ass over there on the double!"

Additional profanities were uttered, the window was slammed shut, and Al trotted off. A minute later, a young man—bleary-eyed and tousled—hurtled down the stairs. He flung the door open and barreled past her. Seeing her chance, Jo caught the door before it could close.

"Excuse me, sir!" she called after him. "I'm looking for Edward Gallagher. Could you tell me on which floor I might find his apartment?"

Tommy Barton stopped and turned. He looked her up and down. She was wearing a matching slate-gray jacket and skirt. The suit was from two seasons ago. It was plainly trimmed but cut well. Her hair was in a simple twist, anchored with a jet comb.

"Me, I gotta go all the way over to Della McEvoy's to get a girl, and no matter which one I pick, she don't look nothing like you," Barton said. "Whose house you from, sister?"

What an odd question, Jo thought. "My own, of course. In Gramercy Square," she replied.

Tommy Barton let out a whistle. "Uptown girl, eh? They must pay 'em well at the *Standard*."

Jo blinked at him, puzzled. "I wouldn't know anything about Mr. Gallagher's financial arrangements. If you would be so kind . . ."

"Second floor. Second door on your right. Go easy on him."

Jo nodded uncertainly. "I shall," she said. She stepped into the vestibule and looked around. The walls were dingy, the linoleum worn. The sour reek of cabbage wafted through the air. Someone was shouting.

Go home. Now, a voice inside her said. *This is insanity.*

And it was. She'd taken a dreadful risk. Earlier that day, she'd removed her father's house key from his desk and a hundred-dollar note from the hollow in the floor. Then she'd had her maid, Katie, run to the bank to change the large note into smaller ones. Half an hour ago, at ten p.m., she'd left her home without an escort, to visit a man. She'd had to outwit Theakston to do it. No well-bred girl walked the streets of the city alone after dark. Were she to be found out, her reputation would be ruined.

Jo knew she should listen to the voice. Only two days ago, her uncle had told her how important it was that her conduct be above reproach. As she recalled his dire warnings, she almost lost her nerve.

If I'm seen here, if anyone finds out about this . . . , she fretted, anxiously eyeing the staircase.

She was just about to leave when she thought of Nellie Bly. Bly had faked insanity to get herself committed to a madhouse so she could write about the terrible treatment its inmates endured. If Bly was brave enough to endure ten days of abuse in pursuit of the truth, then she, Jo Montfort, could walk up a staircase.

Gathering her skirts in one hand, she took hold of the banister with the other. Halfway up the stairs, she heard a door slam above her. Footsteps pounded across the landing, and then a young man came careening toward her. He was wearing twill trousers and a tweed vest and jacket. She immediately recognized the handsome face, the too-long hair, the astonishing blue eyes.

"Mr. Gallagher! I've found you!" she said excitedly.

Eddie came to a stop a few steps above her. His eyes widened. "You've *got* to be kidding me. What are you doing here, Miss Montfort?"

"Paying you a call."

"At ten-thirty on a Monday night? Does your mother know you're out?"

"I certainly hope not," Jo said earnestly. "I paid my maid to put on my nightclothes and get into my bed in case my mother checks on me."

"How clever of you, Miss Montfort."

"That's a rather charitable interpretation of my behavior, Mr. Gallagher. I see it as highly deceitful, truth be told, but I could find no other way to speak with you."

Eddie shook his head. "Can't talk now. Sorry. Got a lead on a story."

"Really? How *exciting*!" Jo exclaimed, thrilled to be in the company of a real reporter following a real lead. She was envious, too. She wished it were her striding along the city streets in pursuit of a story. "May I walk with you? I could tell you the reason for my visit on the way."

"It's a free country," Eddie said with a shrug.

Jo was delighted with this concession. They left the boarding-house and walked to Broadway. Eddie set a fast pace. She nearly had to trot to keep up with him. As they walked, she told him about her father's agenda, the mysterious notations inside it, and the strange man she'd seen gazing up at his window. She also told him about the conversation she'd had with her uncle.

"That's why I came to your home," she explained. "Because my uncle's banned me from Park Row."

"That's all very interesting, Miss Montfort, but what's it got to do with me?"

"I need your help," Jo said. "You're a reporter. Reporters find things out. I need to find out why my father took his life. Will you help me? I'll make it worth your while."

Just then, Jo stumbled over a jutting cobblestone and nearly fell on her face. Eddie caught her in the nick of time.

"Mr. Gallagher, is it truly necessary to walk so fast?" she asked crossly, embarrassed by her clumsiness, and by the fact that one of Eddie's hands was on her waist.

"Yes, Miss Montfort, it is," Eddie said, steadying her. "I got a tip on a story just before you showed up. I need to check it out. I'm not dabbling here. This is my job I'm talking about."

"I'm not dabbling, either," Jo said heatedly. "This is my father I'm talking about. I've risked a great deal to come to you tonight. A very great deal."

Eddie removed his hand from her waist and offered her his arm. Jo took it. She had no choice. Cobblestones, ruts, and trolley tracks made a diabolical obstacle course.

When they reached the sidewalk, Eddie stopped. He didn't take his arm away. Jo didn't remove her hand. "You'll risk more if you pursue this," he said, his tone softening. "A lot more. Like I told you, suicide's an ugly thing."

"I'm prepared for all eventualities, Mr. Gallagher," Jo said.

"Are you?" Eddie asked, looking at her as if taking her measure. "All right, then, Miss Montfort, here's the deal: A man went missing two days ago. His body was found tonight behind a Cherry Street warehouse. Turns out his wife left him for someone else. She wanted a divorce, but he wouldn't give her one. Now the dead man's parents are accusing the wife's boyfriend of murdering their son. The boyfriend's been arrested. The dead man's at Bellevue."

He gave her a challenging smile. Jo swallowed. Her hand tightened on his arm.

"B-Bellevue?" she stammered. "As in—"

"As in the morgue. *That's* where I'm going. Still want to come?"

➤ CHAPTER TWELVE ⤺

"If it isn't Eddie G.! Guess you got my message. Good thing, because I'm starving. Where are you taking me?" asked the young man in the black leather apron.

He was round-faced, bespectacled, and covered in blood. As Jo watched crimson drops fall from the hem of his apron to the floor, she felt a surge of nausea. For the first time in her life, she blessed her upbringing, with its tight corseting of the emotions. It helped her keep her feelings in check and her supper in her stomach.

"It's almost eleven, Osk. Most places are closing down," Eddie said. "I'll take you out tomorrow."

"Better be somewhere good," Oscar said. "You owe me. Guys from the *Herald* and the *World* came by. I sent them packing."

"How's Moretti's sound?"

"Ate there last night."

"Donlon's?"

"I'm sick of oysters."

"Mook's?"

"Monsieur Mouquin's! Now you're talking." Oscar held up a bloodied finger. "But only if they're serving bouillabaisse."

Dear God, Jo thought. *We're in a morgue. How can they talk about food?*

"Who's that?" Eddie asked, pointing at a mangled body splayed out on a white ceramic table. Jo didn't look at it. She knew she'd run out of the place screaming if she did.

"A John Doe. Carriage accident. Cops just brought him in. Who's that?" the aproned man asked, pointing at Jo.

"Oh, her?" Eddie said. "That's . . . that's our new cub. Josephine . . ."

"Jones. Josie Jones," Jo quickly interjected, grateful for Eddie's fib. She could not let it become known that Miss Josephine Montfort of Gramercy Square frequented the morgue in her spare time. "Very pleased to meet you, Mr. . . ."

"Oscar. Oscar Rubin. A girl cub? Guess every paper wants its own Nellie Bly now." He extended a hand. It was covered with gore. Jo stared at it, horrified. "Oh, sorry," he said.

He wiped the gore off—most of it—then held it out again. Jo had no choice but to take it. Eddie was watching her, waiting for her to crumple. She knew he was testing her—and that she'd better not fail if she wanted his help.

"The *morgue?*" she'd repeated, when he told her where he was going.

"Yes, the morgue. You game?"

"Yes, Mr. Gallagher, I am," she'd replied, bluffing madly. "In fact, there is no one more game than I."

When they'd reached Bellevue Hospital, her hands had started to shake. By the time they'd walked into the morgue, her legs were trembling.

The room was cavernous and cold. Long white ceramic tables stood in rows. Bodies lay upon them—four men, two women, a little boy. The tables had channels in them to catch blood and other bodily fluids, as well as the water that dripped continuously upon the corpses from sprinkler heads suspended from the ceiling. Saws, drills, scissors, and forceps, laid out in a neat rows, rested on an empty table. The smell was unspeakable—a mixture of rotting flesh, the rusty tang of blood, and the tarry bite of carbolic soap.

The cold and damp went right through Jo, but the worst thing about the place was its sadness. The people here hadn't died where they should have—at home, surrounded by their loved ones. They'd died violently in the street like John Doe, or behind a warehouse, forsaken and alone.

"I suppose you want to see him?" Oscar asked now.

"Dying to," Eddie said.

Oscar rolled his eyes. "Hope Mook's bouillabaisse is fresher than your jokes."

Eddie and Oscar had an almost jovial way around the dead. The bodies, the blood—none of it seemed to bother them.

"He's over here," Oscar said, leading Eddie to a table by the far wall. Jo followed.

A man lay upon it. He was slight, with thinning hair and a wispy mustache. A white sheet covered him from his waist down. He had a shrunken look. His chest was narrow, pale, and hairless. Jo had never seen a man's naked chest before. A faint odor of garlic hung over him. Dried saliva coated his lips and chin. His hands had a blue tinge. His eyes were open.

"Meet Oliver Little," Oscar said.

It was too much. The poor man's chest, so bare and vulnerable. His sad, empty eyes. The sound of dripping water. The smell. Jo felt faint. She clenched her hands, driving her nails into her palms. The pain brought her back.

"Why the water, Mr. Rubin?" she asked, desperate to look away. To look at Oscar. Or Eddie. Anywhere but at Oliver Little.

"It's cold. Helps delay decomposition," Oscar said.

"So did the boyfriend do it?" Eddie asked.

"That's what the cops thought. But they were wrong. As usual," Oscar said.

"What happened?"

"Oliver Little killed himself with an arsenic-based rat poison."

"How do you know that, Mr. Rubin?" Jo asked, anxious to talk, to think, to do anything but feel.

"It's Oscar. And I know because of forensic medicine."

"Forensic medicine?" Jo echoed. The words were new to her.

"The science of death."

"Oscar's a medical student," Eddie explained. "He works nights at the morgue. Days, too, when he doesn't have class. He's putting himself through school. I don't know why. He's already smarter than most of the doctors in this town."

"How does one practice forensic medicine?" Jo asked, her curiosity overcoming her revulsion.

"Through rigorous observation, my dear," Oscar said in a professorial voice. "One notes the position of the victim's body, as well as its stiffness, color, and state of decay. One looks for blood spatter. Determines the absence or presence of powder burns. Differentiates between the cuts of a hatchet and those of a carving knife. Recognizes the chemical actions and reactions of poisons, acids, and solvents. And"—he smiled sheepishly—"goes through the stiff's pockets." He held up six empty packets of rat poison and a flat brown whiskey bottle. "I posit that Little drank some whiskey for courage, dumped the poison into what remained, then downed it."

"Could the wife or boyfriend have poisoned him and then planted the evidence in his pockets?" Eddie asked. "Arsenic is tasteless, isn't it? Maybe one of them slipped it into Little's whiskey without his knowing."

Oscar shook his head. "Arsenic's only tasteless in small doses. Six packets of rat poison in a fifth of whiskey counts as an acute dose, and in acute doses, you get a bitter, metallic taste. One slug and Little would've known something wasn't kosher. At that point, the poisoner would have had to force the whiskey down him and the struggle would have left signs—cuts or abrasions around his mouth at the very least. In addition, the symptoms he does display—the dehydration, the blue hands and feet, the hypersalivation and the garlic odor—are all consistent with acute arsenic poisoning. And I'm sure when I cut him open, I'll find lesions in the stomach and intestines, and clots in the heart. Arsenic leaves tracks."

"The wife and boyfriend—" Eddie cut in.

"—have alibis," Oscar finished. "Cop I know told me they were seen together in a restaurant from half past five until seven o'clock, and then at a theater. A shopkeeper remembers selling Mr. Little the poison around six o'clock, and a bartender sold him the whiskey a few minutes later. His body was found just after eight, and the show the wife and boyfriend attended let out at nine."

"How remarkable," Jo marveled. "You've solved the case!"

"And saved the boyfriend's neck," Eddie said.

Oscar nodded. "The boyfriend goes free, he gets Oliver Little's wife, and Oliver gets a pine box. The real killer here? A broken heart."

Oscar moved off to tend to another body. Eddie followed him, asking more questions about Oliver Little and jotting down the answers on a notepad.

As they walked away, Jo pulled Mr. Little's sheet up around his neck. *How dreadful*, she thought, *to be naked and dead and have strangers stare at you*. Had her father been laid out here? She imagined him in this place, set out on a slab like a cut of meat, and her composure suddenly broke.

"Mr. Ru—*Oscar*," she said loudly, interrupting Eddie midquestion. "Would you know if Charles Montfort's body was brought here?"

"It wasn't," Oscar said. "We were called to the house to investigate, but no autopsy was requested."

"*You* went to the house?" Eddie said. "You didn't tell me that."

"You didn't ask," Oscar replied.

Jo was relieved to know her father hadn't been brought here. "He was a suicide, too," she said under her breath, her eyes still on sad Oliver Little.

But Oscar heard her. "No, he wasn't," he said.

Jo turned to him. "What did you say?"

"I said Charles Montfort wasn't a suicide."

Jo couldn't believe what she was hearing. She shot Eddie a look. "So his death *was* an accident?"

"No, Miss Jones."

"But if it wasn't one and it wasn't the other—"

Oscar gave Eddie a look. "This one's going to have to sharpen up or Park Row will eat her alive," he said.

"Oscar, *please*," Jo pressed.

"Charles Montfort didn't kill himself," Oscar said, looking at Jo over the top of his glasses. "Charles Montfort was murdered."

❧ CHAPTER THIRTEEN ❧

"Miss Montfort? Miss Montfort, where are you going? Stop. *Stop*," Eddie said, worry in his voice.

"Home, Mr. Gallagher," Jo said, staggering like a drunk. "I'm going home."

"That's not the way to your home. It's the way to the East River."

Jo stopped. She turned around and started walking in the opposite direction. She'd stumbled out of the morgue only moments ago. Eddie had hurried after her.

"You can't go home. Not like this. You're in shock," he said now.

"I'm fine," Jo said.

But she wasn't. Her face was as white as chalk. Her body was freezing cold. She hardly knew where she was. She'd just been told a terrible truth and it had shattered her.

"How do you know Charles Montfort was murdered?" Eddie had asked Oscar back in the morgue.

"Dr. Koehler—my boss—got called to the Montforts' house. I went with him. Koehler glanced at the body, opened the gun, and ruled the death a suicide," Oscar had said contemptuously. "Then Phillip Montfort arrived. He collapsed when he saw his brother.

Koehler got him up and took him into another room, which gave me the chance to do my own exam. There were a couple of cops hanging around. I told them I needed to take notes. They didn't care what I did. They were too busy chowing on the coffee and doughnuts the butler brought them."

"What made you want to do your own exam?" Eddie had asked.

"A lot of things didn't look right," Oscar had replied. "The entry wound was in the right temple, and Charles Montfort was right-handed—"

"Which makes sense," Eddie had cut in.

"Yes, but it's the only thing that did," Oscar had countered. "The gun was still in Montfort's hand and suicides usually drop it. The entry wound itself was wrong, too. Most suicides press the muzzle of a gun right against their heads. When the gun's fired, gases and bits of gunpowder are driven into the skin, causing it to char and rip. Sometimes you can see the muzzle's imprint, too. Montfort's wound showed no imprint, no charring, no ripping. It didn't show any tattooing, either—which is a kind of stippling that happens when gunpowder particles hit the skin from a short distance, maybe six inches to two feet. That means the bullet was fired from farther than two feet."

"Which is tough to do if you're shooting yourself," Eddie had said.

"Exactly. Also, the exit wound was at the back of the skull, at a pretty sharp angle to the entry wound—which again suggests the bullet was fired from a distance. I'd expect a straighter trajectory and an exit wound on the left side of the skull if Montfort fired the gun himself," Oscar had explained.

Jo had had to steady herself against a table; her legs had begun to shake again. Eddie hadn't noticed. He'd been scribbling in his notebook. Oscar hadn't either; he'd kept on talking.

"After I looked at Montfort's wounds, I opened the cylinder of his revolver. The markings on the bottom of the casing from the bullet that killed Montfort didn't match those of the unfired bullets. They were all .38 longs, but the bullet that was fired was marked UMC—which means it was made by Remington. The others were marked W.R.A. Co. That's Winchester's mark."

"Did you tell anyone this?" Eddie had asked, his voice grave.

"I told Koehler after we left. I've learned not to offer my opinions during an exam. I told him I believed that the lethal bullet was from a different gun. He didn't agree. He said he'd seen the different markings but didn't think they were relevant. He said Charles Montfort had simply loaded his revolver with two different makes of ammunition. Maybe there was only one bullet left in his box of Remingtons, so he opened a box of Winchesters."

"It's possible," Eddie had said.

"Yes, but there was no empty box of Remingtons. Not in the cabinet where Montfort kept his ammunition. And not in his garbage can, either. I looked."

"What did Koehler say to that?"

"That Montfort might've loaded the gun days ago and tossed the box. Or he might've loaded it at a shooting range. Apparently, he liked to practice. He told me that Charles Montfort's death was a suicide, plain and simple, but that after speaking with Phillip Montfort, he'd decided to rule it an accidental shooting to spare the family further pain." Oscar snorted. "And to ensure himself further gain. I bet Phillip Montfort paid him a bundle to rule the death accidental, and Koehler didn't want me to screw it up for him. In fact, he told me I was free to disagree with his decision . . . and free to seek employment elsewhere if I did."

Oscar's story had had a terrible effect on Jo. She'd thought she would break down while he told it. She had managed to hold herself together through sheer force of will, knowing that if she suddenly became emotional, he'd want to know why. When he'd finally finished, she had managed to smile and say goodbye, and then she'd lurched out of the morgue and into the street.

"He was murdered," she said to Eddie now. "My father was *murdered*. Someone fired a bullet into his head and left him to die. I have to go to the authorities, Mr. Gallagher. Right away."

"First let's find a bench so you can sit down for a minute," Eddie said, trying to calm her.

"If you could just tell me where the nearest police station is," Jo said. She stumbled over a pile of horse manure. Once again, Eddie caught her before she fell.

"Come on," he said, putting an arm around her. "We're going to take that cab over there to my place. I'll fix you something hot to drink, then get you home."

Jo shook her head. "I don't think it's a good idea, Mr. Gallagher."

"None of this is a good idea, Miss Montfort. I tried to tell you that."

"Yes, you did. I'm sorry," Jo said weakly.

"I'm sorry, too," Eddie said in a gentle voice. "Now, please come with me before you faint in the street."

"I'm fine. Really. I just stumbled, that's all," Jo protested.

Eddie's expression was grim. "You sure did," he answered. "Into something a lot worse than horse manure."

➤ CHAPTER FOURTEEN ↤

Eddie's apartment—twenty feet square, with an alcove for his bed—was small, Spartan, and full of books.

"Have a seat," he said, pulling a rickety chair out from under a wooden table. He took off his jacket and hung it over the back of a second chair.

Jo sat, but as soon as she did, Oscar's voice was in her head again. She stood up and paced around, desperate to distract herself.

Eddie tried to make his bed without her noticing, then filled a kettle with water and carried it to the small fireplace, where coal embers glowed. He poked them to life, set a trivet over them, and placed the teakettle on it.

"I don't have a stove. The landlady does our cooking," he explained. "But I can boil water. Would you like a cup of coffee?"

"Tea, please."

"Uh, how about coffee?"

Jo nodded. "Cream, please. Two sugars."

While Eddie ground some coffee beans in a small wooden hand grinder, Jo looked around his room, searching for something— anything—to occupy her attention. She'd never been in a boy's room before, except her cousin Robert's when they were little.

Besides a bed, the alcove contained a night table and a reading lamp. There was a small sink in the room. A shelf above it held mugs, glasses, and a bottle of whiskey. Under the single window, on an empty fruit crate, was a typewriter. A dresser stood against one wall. Cuff links, a penknife, and coins were scattered across it. *Leaves of Grass* by Walt Whitman lay on top of it as well as *Walden* by Henry David Thoreau. Jo was intrigued to see *Ten Days in a Mad-House* by Nellie Bly.

She picked up Bly's book and paged through it, remembering how Bly's articles on the abuse she endured while an inmate at the Women's Lunatic Asylum on Blackwell's Island sparked a huge amount of public outrage. Because of her work, changes had been implemented in the way the mentally ill were treated.

"Miss Bly is impossibly brave, isn't she?" Jo said, putting the book back.

"*You* read Nellie Bly?" Eddie asked.

"Everything she writes," Jo said. "I try to write like her, too. A little," she added shyly.

Eddie, fiddling with a coffee press now, turned to look at her. "Seriously?"

Jo nodded. "I wrote a piece for my school newspaper on the abuses suffered by local mill girls. I interviewed several of them."

"Miss Montfort, you are full of surprises. I'd love to read it."

"I shall have to send you the original, then," Jo said with a sigh, "for I doubt it will ever be published. Our headmistress is more interested in poems about cats than the welfare of mill workers."

"You read Julius Chambers? Jake Riis?"

Jo nodded eagerly. Like Bly, they represented a new breed of journalist who wrote about social ills in the hopes of rectifying them.

"I read everything of theirs I can," she said, "but it's difficult. Mama doesn't permit newspapers in the house. I have to get Katie, my maid, to smuggle them in when I'm at home, and a delivery boy to do it at school. I have Riis's *How the Other Half Lives*, though. I keep it under my bed."

Eddie laughed. "I keep it next to mine. I really admire his work. He tells stories that never get told. I hope to do the same one day."

"Why not now?"

Eddie snorted. "At the *Standard*? Please."

The kettle whistled. He wrapped a dishrag around its handle, took it off the coals, and poured the steaming water into his coffee press. "How about no cream, no sugar?" he asked. "I haven't got either."

"Black is fine," Jo said. She sat down again, looking forward to a warming drink.

Eddie carried the press to the table. He took two mugs off the shelf over the sink, checked them to make sure they were clean, then set them on the table, too. "You'll have to forgive Oscar," he said. "He didn't know who you really are. If he had, he might've softened his words. Then again, knowing him, maybe not."

Jo nodded. She didn't want to talk about it. She'd managed to pull herself together but could easily fall apart again.

"The Adirondacks," she said, picking up a schedule for the New York & Central that was lying on the table. "Do you go there often?" she asked, hoping to change the subject.

"As often as I can," Eddie said.

"We do, too," Jo said. "Every August. We have a camp on Saranac Lake. My father takes me fishing in his canoe. We row out to . . . rather, we *did* row out—" Water splashed onto the schedule. Jo touched her cheek. It was wet. She realized she was crying.

"Forgive me," she said. She pulled a handkerchief out of her jacket pocket, dabbed at her eyes, and tried to stop, but her tears only fell harder. Mortified, she got to her feet. "Th-thank you. . . . I'll be on my w-w-way," she said, her voice hitching. She had to get out of there. *Now.* Before she made a spectacle of herself.

"Miss Montfort," Eddie said. "I really think you should sit for another minute."

"I—I can't. I have to go," Jo said, her head down so he couldn't see her tears. "I have to get back into my house and Theakston might be up and—" She stopped midsentence and raised her face to his. "It was bad enough that I'd lost my father, but now . . . *now* . . ." She looked at him helplessly. "Someone *killed* him, Mr. Gallagher. . . . *Why?* Why would someone kill my papa?"

And suddenly she was sobbing like a child. She hadn't cried for her father once since Bram and Addie had broken the news to her. She hadn't been able to. The tears wouldn't come. But they came now. In an agonizing torrent.

In an instant, Eddie was out of his chair. He pulled her to him. She buried her head in his neck and wept.

Eddie held her tightly, and let her.

➤ CHAPTER FIFTEEN ⬅

"Drink it," Eddie said. "You have to."

"I can't. It smells terrible."

"Down the hatch. All in one go."

Jo, sitting down at Eddie's table, took the shot glass he was holding out to her and downed it. The whiskey burned her throat. Her eyes watered and her cheeks turned pink as its fire spread through her chest.

"It only hurts for a second," Eddie said.

"But does it help, Mr. Gallagher?" she asked in a raspy voice.

"Yes. And it's Eddie. I think we're on a first-name basis now."

"We are, aren't we? I'm sorry. I don't know what came over me," Jo said, mortified for breaking down in front of him.

"It's called grief. And there's no need to apologize," Eddie said. The coffee had finished brewing. He pushed the plunger down on the press, poured its contents into the mugs, then handed one to Jo.

Jo thanked him and wrapped her hands around the hot mug, warming them. She felt as if she'd been gutted, as if there were nothing left inside her. The shocks kept coming, one after another. Tonight's had overwhelmed her.

"I could never quite believe his death was an accident," she said, "Suicide made no sense to me, either—despite what my uncle told me about my father being despondent. I kept asking myself, who could've upset my father enough to make him kill himself? But I couldn't come up with an answer. Murder makes sense, though. It's the only thing that does, as odd as that must sound." She took a sip of her coffee, then put the mug down. "I'm going to the police. First thing in the morning," she said resolutely.

"I wouldn't do that. Not until you have evidence," Eddie said.

"But isn't that what the police do?" Jo asked, confused. "Gather evidence?"

"In this city, they gather money. Your uncle paid them off to call the death an accident. They won't allow anyone to come along after the fact and challenge their findings. If they do, they'll look like fools."

"I could ask Oscar to help me," Jo said, trying another tack. "He could tell a judge what he told us."

"A judge would dismiss him just like Koehler did. All he has to offer is his opinion. I trust it a hundred percent, but I'm probably the only one who does. Other people think he's crazy. Most people have never heard of forensic medicine, and—" Eddie stopped talking abruptly.

"And what?" Jo pressed.

"And most of your evidence is now six feet under. I'm sorry to be blunt, but your father's body has been decomposing for more than two weeks now."

That was not an image Jo wanted to dwell on. "I'll go to my uncle. He'll know what to do," she said. Then she shook her head. "No, I won't. Going to the *Standard* on my own was bad enough. If he finds out where I've been tonight—well, you can't imagine the trouble I'd be in. I'd risk his anger if I had proof, but as you point out, I don't. And I don't know how to get any."

"I'll help you get it," Eddie said.

"You will?" Jo said, surprised. She was pleased by his change of heart but puzzled by it, too. He'd been noncommittal on their way to the morgue.

"We'll work as a team," Eddie continued. "I'll ask around. Drop the names in your father's agenda here and there. You keep your ears open around your father's friends and business associates. At dinners, dances, the races."

"I don't attend the races."

Eddie rolled his eyes. "At tea parties, then. Whatever you hear, tell me."

"I'll have to stay in town if I'm to find out anything," Jo said, thinking out loud. "I'll tell my mother I don't feel strong enough to return to school. I'll say I'd like to stay home through the holidays. But, Mr. . . . But, Eddie . . ."

"Yes?"

"What made you decide to help me?" she asked.

"I need to make my name and this story could help me," he replied.

Jo understood then—ambition, that was what was behind his change of heart. For a moment, she'd thought it might be because he'd been touched by her plight, but no. She was surprised to find that she felt hurt but quickly told herself she was being silly. Eddie Gallagher's help was all that mattered, not his motivations.

"I want a new job," he explained. "I can't work at the *Standard* much longer. Stoatman's nothing but a puppet. Your family tells him what stories to run and what to kill. I started a story on your father when I thought his death was suicide and Stoatman killed *that*. But the story's bigger now. It could really garner some attention."

"But Mr. Stoatman would never run it. You just said as much," Jo said.

Eddie sat forward in his chair. "I'd take it to another paper. Use it to get myself hired there. I write for other papers even though I'm on staff at the *Standard*. They pay me by the article. Stoatman doesn't know. I use a pseudonym. The Oliver Little story? That one's for the *World*."

"I see," Jo said.

"Big stories lead to big jobs," Eddie continued. "Charles Montfort's death turning out to be murder? That would be huge. I'm sorry to put it like that, but it's true. No one cares much about the Oliver Littles of the world—he'll get a few inches on page three and then he'll be forgotten. But Charles Montfort—rich, well-connected, a pillar of society? He's a different matter entirely. If we could get some solid proof, the case would *have* to be reopened and investigated. Even Phillip Montfort couldn't get it hushed up."

"He wouldn't want to," Jo said, defending her uncle.

Eddie raised an eyebrow.

"You don't know him. He hushed up my father's suicide, yes, but he had his reasons."

Eddie nodded, then said, "As I told you earlier, this could get ugly. And I don't quit on a story. I do whatever it takes. We have an agreement?"

"Yes," Jo said, grateful to have his help. "We have an agreement." The circumstances of her father's death had changed, but her need for answers hadn't.

Eddie held out his hand and they shook on it. Jo, never having made an agreement before, kept shaking.

"You can let go now," Eddie said.

"Oh," she said, embarrassed. "All right." She self-consciously picked up her mug again, the coffee cooler now, and sipped from it. "When can we start?" she asked.

"Right now, but—"

"Right now?" Jo said eagerly, banging her mug down. "Really?"

Eddie held up his hands. "Yes, but hold on. . . . Before we can find any answers, we need to ask a new question. It's no longer *Who upset Charles Montfort enough to make him kill himself?* It's *Who did Charles Montfort upset enough to make that person kill him?*"

CHAPTER SIXTEEN

Eddie fished his notebook out of the breast pocket of his jacket.

"After the news of your father's death broke, I had a look at the police report," he said. "That was before we talked to Oscar, of course, but the information I got from it might still be helpful."

"What did it say?" Jo asked, keen to know.

Eddie flipped his notebook open. "It said that all the Van Houten partners were at your house earlier that day for lunch and a meeting. Your butler, Mr. Theakston, let them in and let them out again—except for Phillip Montfort, who exited through the servants' door under the stoop because he went to the kitchen to compliment the cook."

"Yes," said Jo. "That's what my uncle told me."

"Theakston also said that before your uncle went to the kitchen, he and your father argued. Theakston heard their raised voices."

"They did. My uncle told me that my father was despondent. My uncle tried to make him see reason. The discussion became heated," Jo explained.

Eddie frowned. "Which makes sense if your father was a suicide, but it turns out he wasn't."

"I think it makes sense either way," Jo ventured. "Perhaps the person who killed him made him so miserable that he wished to take his own life."

Eddie weighed her words but didn't comment on them. His eyes went back to his notes. "Theakston also stated that everyone was gone by four p.m. and that he locked the house at nine p.m.—front door, servants' door, garden door. He was awakened at approximately midnight by the sound of a gunshot, as were the other servants: Ada Nelson, Katharine McManus, Pauline Klopp, and Greta Schmidt."

"I'm sure they all would have heard the shot," Jo said. "Mrs. Nelson's room is off the kitchen. Theakston's, too. The three maids live on the top floor. Only Dolan, our driver, wouldn't have. He lives behind Gramercy Square over our carriage house."

"Mr. Theakston and Mrs. Nelson stated that they immediately ran upstairs and met your mother at the door to your father's study. She'd come down from her bedroom on the third floor. The maids were on the staircase. Your mother was knocking on the door and calling to your father, but got no answer. All six stated that the door was locked from the inside. Theakston tried to break it down but couldn't. He ran to fetch Dolan. They met a patrolman on the way back. The officer—his name was Buckley—broke the door down. Once inside the study, he saw your father's body and said that the women should not enter. He noted that neither Theakston, Dolan, Mrs. Nelson, the maids, nor your mother had any blood on their clothing."

It took a few seconds for Eddie's meaning to sink in. "You're not saying that Theakston, the rest of the servants, and my *mother* were suspects?" said Jo, appalled.

"I'm not saying anything. The police were the ones asking the questions. But even if it weren't for the absence of bloodstains on their clothing, the locked door ruled them out."

"How about the absence of any desire whatsoever to do my father harm? Did *that* rule them out?" Jo asked sharply, angry at him for even suggesting such a thing.

Eddie continued, ignoring her tone. "The officer ascertained that your father was dead. A revolver identified by Theakston as belonging to your father was found in his right hand. The officer didn't touch the gun. When Dr. Koehler arrived, he removed the revolver from your father's hand and opened the chamber. It contained one spent casing and five live bullets," Eddie said, glancing up from his notebook. "Your father kept his revolver loaded?"

"He did. He was very protective of us. Always worried about our safety," Jo said. Her eyebrows knit together in concentration. "Oscar said the manufacturer's mark on the casing from the bullet that killed my father didn't match those of the other five bullets."

"Which apparently didn't trouble Koehler, as Oscar told us. Or the cops," Eddie said.

"Does it trouble you?" Jo asked.

Eddie nodded. "Sportsmen tend to have favorites. Favorite fishing rods. Favorite lures. Favorite gunmakers and ammunition. Why would your father switch from one make of bullet to another?" He looked at his notepad again. "Koehler didn't think the different markings were important. The cops didn't even record them in their report. But Oscar thinks the presence of a different casing means the killer used a different gun."

"But if that's so, how did the casing from the killer's gun get inside my father's revolver?" Jo countered.

"Good question," Eddie said, frowning. He flipped a page in his notebook. "Oscar said the casing was marked UMC .38 S & W and the unfired bullets were marked W.R.A. Co. .38 LONG."

Jo drew a sharp breath. She knew that last mark. She'd seen it very recently.

Eddie's eyes darted to her face. "What is it?" he asked.

"I just remembered something," she said. "I should've thought of it back at the morgue, but I was too upset. The day of my father's funeral, I went to his study and found a bullet. It was on the floor, tangled up in the carpet's fringe. At the time, I thought Papa might've left some bullets loose on the desk while he was cleaning his gun and knocked them off after he shot himself. And that someone—Theakston, maybe—had kicked one across the room."

Eddie sat forward in his chair, his gaze intense. "Do you remember the mark on that bullet?"

"Yes. It was W.R.A. Co. .38 LONG," she said, her gaze equally intense. "Eddie, what if—"

"The killer fired the lethal shot from his gun, then found your father's loaded revolver," Eddie said.

"He replaced one of the bullets in the chamber with the spent casing, and then put the revolver into my father's hand! It makes sense, doesn't it?" Jo asked, excited that they'd come up with a plausible explanation for the presence of two different bullets.

But instead of echoing her excitement, Eddie frowned again.

"What?" Jo asked.

"How could the killer be smart enough to replace a bullet with the spent casing, but stupid enough to drop the bullet on the floor?" he asked.

"Maybe something spooked him. Maybe he heard footsteps or shouting," Jo offered.

Eddie nodded but didn't seem convinced. He turned back to his notes.

"When Buckley declared your father dead, your mother—who was still outside the study—became distraught. Mrs. Nelson took her to her room. Theakston told Miss Klopp to fetch Phillip Montfort, and the other two maids to fix a pot of coffee. Buckley stopped him. He said he needed one girl to go to the station house to tell his captain what had happened. Miss McManus went. Miss Schmidt went to the kitchen. They all went back to their rooms first, though, to get dressed."

Eddie paused to take a sip of his coffee, then continued.

"Buckley sent Dolan for Dr. Koehler. He then asked Theakston to show him all possible exits from the house. They tested the servants' door and the door that leads from your kitchen to your back garden. Both were locked. Theakston had run out of the front door to fetch Dolan but said he had to unlock it first. There are four master keys to the doors. Buckley stated that he was unable to search for them right away because the coroner arrived, followed by the police captain and Phillip Montfort, and he had to brief them, but he confirmed the keys' whereabouts before he left. One was your father's and was found in his desk. One was your mother's and was in her bedroom. Theakston's was in his vest pocket. The fourth, Mrs. Nelson's, was hanging on a hook by the pantry."

Eddie stopped speaking. His frown deepened.

"What is it?" Jo asked.

"Mrs. Nelson stated that she hadn't been able to find her key when she went to bed that night. Buckley noted that she was distressed because she was worried the killer had used it to get inside the house. Theakston was able to calm her down when he confirmed that her key was, in fact, hanging in its usual place." Eddie looked at Jo. "That sounds odd to me."

"Not if you know Mrs. Nelson. She's very absentminded. Always misplacing things," Jo said. "Maybe the shock of my father's death made her think she'd lost her key when she hadn't."

"That could explain it," Eddie allowed. "The last thing the report mentions is your uncle's arrival. Miss Klopp went to his house to fetch him. He rushed to your house, accompanied by Miss Klopp. When he saw his brother's body, he collapsed. Dr. Koehler and one of the officers helped him up and took him out of the room. Dr. Koehler wanted him to lie down, but Mr. Montfort said he was fine, he just needed a glass of water. He went to the kitchen. Koehler and the police captain—Perkins—went with him."

Jo's heart ached for her uncle. He'd never told her that he'd collapsed. Which was just like him, stoic and protective. He must've been devastated when he saw his brother's body, yet his first thought had been to guard the family from scandal.

Eddie suddenly slapped his notepad down on the table, startling Jo.

"This makes no sense," he said, frustration in his voice. "How did the killer get in, fire a shot, and get out again totally unseen? The doors to your house were all locked. The door to your father's study was locked, too, from the *inside*. The whole scenario's impossible."

Jo's heart sank. She'd hoped they were getting close to an answer.

Eddie ran a hand through his hair. "We're missing something here. We must be. Do any of the Van Houten partners have a key to your house? Could one have come back later that night?" he asked.

"Are you suggesting that one of my father's *partners* killed him? After your ridiculous suggestion that my mother might have?" Jo asked, incredulous.

"It's a possibility," Eddie said.

"No, it's *not*," Jo retorted. "None of them has a key to our house, and even if they did, they're not murderers. My father grew up with these men, Eddie. They are all from old and fine families. It's inconceivable that they'd harm him. And I'm sure they all accounted for themselves on the evening of his death."

"Yeah, they did," Eddie said, paging through his notes. "They were all at home—Scully, Beekman, Brevoort, Tuller. What about your uncle? Does he have a key?"

"My uncle," Jo said flatly. "My father's only brother. The man who is a second father to me."

Eddie nodded.

"You yourself just told me that he was at home when my father was killed. Pauline Klopp, a maid, was sent to fetch him. She saw him there. But even if he hadn't been at home, the mere idea of him killing my father is completely absurd."

"How about rivals? Business competitors?"

Jo raised an eyebrow. "Can you really see elderly Mr. Woolcott Sloan of Sloan and Thorpe Shipping *shooting my father*? Who do you think these people are? Pirates?"

Eddie drummed his fingers on the table, then picked up a pen that was lying there. "Can I look at the names and notations you told me about on our way to the morgue? The ones from your father's agenda?" he asked.

Jo took the agenda out of her skirt pocket and handed it to him.

He copied down the notations for September 15—*Kinch, VHW, 11 p.m., Eleanor Owens, b. 1874*, and noted that September 17's and October 15's were identical—*Kinch, VHW, 11 p.m.*

When he was finished, he said, "What if your uncle's wrong? What if Eleanor Owens *was* your father's mistress? She tries to blackmail him. He refuses to pay her. She comes to the house late one night. He lets her in, takes her to his study, and she brandishes a gun, maybe just to scare him. It goes off accidentally. She puts it in his hand and—"

"Runs out of the house through two locked doors?" Jo offered.

"What about the study's windows?" Eddie asked. "The police didn't mention anything about them in their report. Were they locked?"

"No. The locks are old and don't work anymore, but they don't need to."

"Why?" Eddie asked.

"Because the windows themselves are quite high above the ground. I would guess twenty feet or so, which would make for a long, dangerous drop."

Eddie sighed. "Fine. The logistics don't work, but she's still a suspect. How about the name Kinch?" he said. "Had you ever heard your father mention it?"

"No, but since it's a single word I wonder if it might be the name of a ship instead of a person."

"What could a ship have to do with this?"

"I have no idea," Jo admitted. "What about the man I saw looking up at my father's window? What if *he's* the murderer? He certainly looked like one."

"He could be a suspect, but we still have the same problem. How'd he get in and back out again?"

"We don't have anything, do we?" Jo said, discouraged. "Only a murderer who must be a phantom because he can move through locked doors, or make himself invisible, or . . . *Oh*. Oh dear God."

Jo felt as if an icy wind had just blown through her.

"What is it?" Eddie asked, his eyes fastening on hers.

"He was *there*, Eddie," Jo said. "In the study. The killer was there the whole time!"

➤ CHAPTER SEVENTEEN ◄

"Slow down, Jo. Start at the beginning," Eddie said. "You're talking so fast I can't follow you."

Jo took a deep breath, let it out, then tried to speak slowly. "The curtains," she said. "The killer was hiding behind the curtains."

Eddie leaned back in his chair; he gave her a skeptical look.

"They're wide and puffy and they puddle on the floor. I often hid behind them as a child. My entire household could hide behind them. And *that's* where I found the bullet. . . . Don't you see?"

Eddie sat up straight. His gaze was electric. "Yes, I do," he said.

Suddenly they had a piece of the puzzle in their hands, and they both knew it.

"The killer came into my father's study late at night—" Jo began.

Eddie cut her off. "How did he get into the house?"

"He got hold of a key somehow."

"Unlikely. Maybe your father let him in. Because he knew him."

"Or her," Jo said darkly.

Eddie nodded. "They go to your father's study. The killer shoots him. He finds your father's revolver and puts it in his hand. He hears footsteps overhead. Your mother's. He panics. He knows he can't leave the study—he'll be seen."

It was hard for Jo to imagine the scenario of her father's death, but Eddie didn't spare her. He made her work. He made her think. It was not what she was used to from a man, and she liked it.

"He locks the door to give himself some time," she said, "and hides behind the curtains. In his haste, he tries to put the bullet he took out of my father's revolver into his pocket, but he misses and drops it. He doesn't *know* he's dropped it, though, because it hits the edge of the carpet and makes no noise."

"And then he waits. Barely breathing. Standing perfectly still. So still, the curtains don't even rustle."

"Listening to my mother weep and my uncle collapse," Jo said bitterly. "And then, once it's quiet and the police are gone, he leaves."

"Only maybe he *didn't* wait all that time to leave," said Eddie.

"But he couldn't have left any earlier. My mother was there, and the servants, and Officer Buckley," Jo countered.

"Not the entire time," Eddie reminded her. "After Buckley declared your father dead, everyone left the study. Dolan went to get Dr. Koehler. Mrs. Nelson took your mother to her room. The maids went back upstairs to get dressed. Theakston and Buckley walked through the house, checking doors. The killer would have had a few moments to escape, if he was bold enough to take them."

They both fell silent then but continued to stare at each other. No man had ever looked at Jo that long or that intensely. *It's not proper. He ought to stop*, she thought. But then she realized she was doing exactly the same thing to him.

"Well, now we have a theory, at least," she said awkwardly, breaking the silence and Eddie's gaze.

"And at least two suspects," Eddie said. "Eleanor Owens and the strange man who was staring at your house." He picked up Charles Montfort's agenda again and paged through it. Pointing at the notation under October 15—*Kinch, VHW, 11 p.m.*—he said, "I'm going to go down to Van Houten's Wharf on the fifteenth to sniff around."

"But my father's dead. He won't be boarding the *Kinch*," Jo said, confused.

"But the ship will still be there, presumably. Maybe someone on it knows something."

"I'll come with you," Jo announced.

"No, you *won't*," Eddie said. "The waterfront's not a nice place."

"But how will I know what happened?" Jo asked, disappointed—and annoyed. A moment ago, they'd been equals, and working to solve a crime together. Now he was forging ahead without her. "How will we communicate?" she continued. "I can't suddenly have visits or letters from a young man my mother doesn't know. And I can't send letters to your home with my name on them. What if your landlady gossips?"

"We'll write each other, but we'll use false names on the return addresses," Eddie said. "I'll tell you everything I find out."

"I suppose that would work," Jo said, somewhat mollified. It wasn't what she wanted, but at least she wouldn't be totally left out of the proceedings. "I'll be . . . Joseph. Joseph Feen. You can be Edwina Gallagher. I'll even have to explain *that*—a letter from a *girl* my mother's never heard of. I'll say you're a dressmaker my friend Trudy told me about."

The clock on Eddie's mantel chimed the hour—one a.m.

"I had no idea it was so late. I have to get home," Jo said, daunted by the task of getting back into her house without being detected.

"I'll take you," Eddie stood.

"But there's no need," Jo protested.

"Save it, Jo," Eddie said, and Jo saw there would be no arguing with him.

Eddie stood. He took his jacket off the back of his chair and shrugged it on. Jo didn't need to do the same, as she hadn't removed hers. She cast a last glance around the room, sorry to leave it. It was small, yet it didn't feel confining. Just the opposite.

I can breathe here, she thought. *Instead of suffocating among the potted palms and porcelain.*

They found a cab on Broadway. Jo told Eddie that she was getting out on Irving Place and that he wasn't to follow. If she got caught coming in through the kitchen, she might be able to explain herself by saying that she couldn't sleep and let herself outside with her father's key to get some air, but she'd never be able to explain him. Eddie reluctantly agreed. He tried to pay the cabbie, but Jo wouldn't let him. She paid the man for Eddie's return trip as well.

"Every time I see you, it's an adventure, Jo Montfort. You're a very unusual girl," he said as she got out of the cab.

"Oh, not really. Most girls are a lot like me. Wanting answers to their questions," Jo replied. "They usually don't seek them at the morgue, however. I'll give you that."

Eddie smiled, but then turned serious. "It was a very hard night for you. I'm sorry for that. I hope you know what you've gotten yourself into. What's coming won't be easy. I doubt tonight will be the last time you cry for your father."

Jo looked up at him, into his incredible blue eyes. She'd seen annoyance there on several occasions. Arrogance. Amusement. Even anger. For the first time now, she saw something else—a deep, abiding kindness.

"No, it won't," she said sadly. "But it was the first."

❧ CHAPTER EIGHTEEN ❧

"Girls, bitches, and mares . . . it all comes down to the same question: *Will she catch?*"

"Grandmama . . . ," Mrs. Aldrich said, a warning note in her voice.

"Take my Lolly, here. . . . She's a sturdy little bitch and keen in the field, but she *won't* catch. I've tried stud after stud. She's a pretty thing. Smart, too. But if a bitch won't breed, she's useless."

Jo looked at Trudy and Trudy looked at Jo. Their eyes grew large in their faces. They were standing in the foyer of Herondale, outside the closed doors to the drawing room, waiting for Addie, Bram, Gilbert Grosvenor, and Jo's cousins, Caroline and Robert. Neither girl had realized anyone was in the drawing room, but then they'd heard Grandmama's voice. Trudy, grinning, had crept close to the doors, motioning for Jo to follow. They knew they shouldn't eavesdrop but couldn't resist.

"You are far too used to having your own way, Grandmama, but you are going to have to allow Anna Montfort to have *her* way in this," Mrs. Aldrich said.

Trudy grabbed Jo's arm. "They're talking about you and Bram!" she whispered. She made a kissy face. Jo elbowed her.

"We'll see about that," Grandmama said. "If Anna's unwilling to make a match, there are plenty of others who will. Let's not forget that she was a Schermerhorn before she was a Montfort."

"Meaning what, exactly? The Schermerhorns are a very fine family."

"Anna's from a cadet branch of the family and their women don't exactly throw off pups," Grandmama said. "She only had two babies and lost one a few days after its birth. Pity, too. It was a boy. What about that pretty Harriet Buchanan for Bram? She has a fine figure and she's one of seven herself. *Her* mother was one of eight. Though Hannah Buchanan, Harriet's grandmother, was as crazy as a loon. That sort of thing passes down, you know."

"What about Bram? Does he get a say in this? He doesn't wish to marry Harriet Buchanan. He doesn't care for her," Mrs. Aldrich said heatedly.

"Passion is for the lower orders," Grandmama sniffed. "We Aldriches are not clerks and shopgirls. We make matches with our heads, not our hearts, in order to preserve our families and our fortunes. Love comes in time. And if it doesn't . . . well, we have our dogs and gardens to console us."

There was a pause in the conversation while a spaniel was admonished; then Grandmama spoke again. "My son is failing," she said. Jo could hear the sadness in her voice.

"I don't wish to speak of it," Mrs. Aldrich said.

"But we *must* speak of it," Grandmama insisted. "Peter has a year left at most and then Bram will become the head of the family. How is the boy to live? As a bachelor in some dreary city apartment? How is he to shoulder the burdens of business with no helpmate? How is the Aldrich name to endure with no new sons? He might've proposed already if this dreadful business with Charles hadn't happened. How long are we to wait?"

Jo caught her breath, afraid of the answer. She tried to leave, but Trudy pulled her back.

"I've sounded Anna on this topic. She's not for a proposal yet. She feels it would be premature," Mrs. Aldrich said.

Jo exhaled with relief.

"Premature my foot. What Anna Montfort wants is time to solicit better offers. She means to see her daughter well provided for and she's only going to entertain the highest bids."

"Grandmama! What a *dreadful* thing to say!" Mrs. Aldrich's voice rose with indignation.

Jo was mortified. Grandmama's words made her feel like a sack of flour or a bolt of cloth.

"It's also true," Grandmama said. "The Montforts have money, but not as much as we do. What they have in abundance, however, is breeding. Their bloodlines are some of the best in the country. All the money in New York can't buy *that*, and Anna knows it. My grandson is a fool if he dillydallies. He should snap that girl up before someone else does."

"Jo is only seventeen. Anna feels eighteen is the correct age for an engagement."

"Fiddlesticks! There's far too much delicacy in the proceedings these days. I was married at sixteen. My mother at fifteen. Girls have lost sight of their first duty: marriage and motherhood. How do you get up a good-sized family unless you start young? Bram should take Jo to the Young Patrons' Ball."

Mrs. Aldrich burst out laughing. "Jo's in mourning for her father. She can't go to a *ball*!"

"She can if she doesn't dance."

"Says *who*?"

"Me."

The Young Patrons' Ball was the social event of the season. Held at the Metropolitan Museum of Art, its ostensible purpose was to raise funds for acquiring art. Its actual purpose was matchmaking. Girls were given dance cards, and they sold their dances to boys.

The monies collected went to the museum. Many engagements were announced in the weeks following the ball.

"Have Bram buy Jo's entire card, even though she can't dance. It'll make a statement—that Miss Josephine Montfort is spoken for," Grandmama said. "She can wear a black gown and sit to one side of the room. That way the gossips will have nothing to say about it."

"Anna will never permit it."

"She will. I intend to speak with her myself," Grandmama said ominously. "Come on, Lolly, jump down. We've a new foal to visit."

Jo and Trudy heard Grandmama get up. They hurried out of the foyer and into the music room before they could be discovered.

Trudy plunked down on a settee, giggling. "If a bitch won't breed, she's useless!" she said, mimicking Grandmama.

Jo, not giggling, walked to a mirror, where she adjusted the brooch at her throat. "She makes the whole business sound like something that happens in a kennel," she said crossly.

"If Grandmama gets her way, you'll be married next year, and a mother the year after," Trudy said. "What a catch Bram Aldrich is. He's smart. Handsome in his way. And even richer than Mr. Gilbert Grosvenor."

"Yes, he is," Jo said distractedly.

"You'll have a stylish wedding, so you'd better whittle down that waist."

Jo stuck her tongue out in the mirror.

Trudy saw it. "Do you *want* to look like a beer barrel in your wedding dress?" she asked.

"A twenty-inch waist *hardly* makes me a beer barrel," Jo retorted. "And besides, being too thin isn't healthy. All the dress reformers say so."

"Yes, they do. And they're all spinsters," Trudy shot back.

Trudy's waist was seventeen inches around. Jo knew that she tight-laced, wearing and even sleeping in a corset so close-fitting that it was painful, to give herself an hourglass figure. Jo refused to tight-lace, much to her mother's chagrin.

"You'll honeymoon in Europe, too," Trudy continued, excited, "and live in a smart new mansion on Fifth Avenue. Right next to mine. You'll spend summers at Newport and have loads of dresses and jewels. Oh, Jo . . . this is such *good* news after you've suffered such a terrible loss. You must be the happiest girl in the world!"

"Yes, I must be," Jo said. She knew she *should* be. The thought of a proposal from Bram Aldrich, one of New York's most sought-after bachelors, would make most girls giddy, even if they were still in mourning.

Trudy eyed her closely. "Why, Jo Montfort, you're *not* happy, are you? Why on earth not?"

Jo, still looking in the mirror, didn't reply. *Yes, Jo, why not?* she asked herself. Mrs. Aldrich had invited her to the country for the weekend to lift her spirits. Her uncle had prevailed upon her mother to let her go. She'd arrived yesterday evening—Friday. It was only Saturday morning, and all she wanted to do was go back to town. The company of old friends, the excitement of a possible proposal—these things should have been enough to gladden her heart. Once they would've been, but not anymore.

Everything had changed after her visit to Reade Street. She'd wanted the truth about her father's death and she'd gotten it, and now her life was divided into a Before and an After. She was restless and unsettled and couldn't stop thinking about her trip to the morgue and what she'd learned there. About Oscar Rubin and his science of death, Eleanor Owens, the ship *Kinch*, the strange man staring up at her father's windows . . .

. . . and Eddie Gallagher.

She'd wept in his arms. She'd ruined his shirt. She'd never cried like that in front of anyone. Not even her mother. She didn't understand why she'd shown her heart to a boy she barely knew. Or why, after she'd taken her jacket off in her room that night, she'd pressed it to her face just to inhale the scent of him again.

"Josephine Montfort, the son of one of the richest men in New York is going to propose to you. *Why* aren't you happy about that?"

"*Because*, Trudy," Jo said testily.

"Because why?"

"Because I'm not a spaniel! And I don't want my whole life to be about"—she lowered her voice—"*breeding!*"

"It won't be, silly girl. There will also be parties and outings. Wallpaper. China patterns. And upholstery."

Jo groaned.

"Well, if those things don't suit you, either, what *do* you want?"

"Something other than three puppies—I mean, *babies*—before I'm twenty!"

"It won't be so bad. You just pop them out and hand them to the nanny."

Jo sighed.

Trudy gave her a searching look. "Are you having your monthlies, my darling?" she asked.

"No!" Jo said, reddening.

"Then what is it? Oh! I bet I know."

"You do?" Jo said, alarmed. She and Trudy were sharing a bedroom. Had she talked about Eddie in her sleep?

"It's about your scribbling, isn't it? You don't want to give it up."

"No, I don't, Tru," Jo said, relieved to admit it. "And it's not *scribbling*. It's journalism."

"You may not have to. See if Bram would let you do a column of some sort. On flower arranging or decorating. Under an assumed name, of course," Trudy advised.

Jo flopped down on the settee and leaned her head on her friend's shoulder. "What do you think it's like? Do you think it's *very* dreadful?"

Trudy patted Jo's hand. "Getting married? Of course not. A bit nerve-racking, perhaps, with all the preparations, but not dreadful," she said.

"No, not getting married. The thing that makes all those babies Grandmama's so eager for me to have."

"Ah, *that*. Is that what's bothering you?"

"Among other things."

"I'm afraid I don't have an answer for you, as I have kept myself pure for Mr. Gilbert Grosvenor. Below the waist, at least."

Jo raised her head and looked at Trudy. "What do you mean by that?"

Trudy giggled. "That dreamy boy who delivers the apples at school? Well, his lips aren't the only thing that's nice about him. His hands are nice, too. I let him touch me. Under my blouse."

"Trudy, you didn't!" Jo whispered, shocked. She bit her lip. "What was it like?"

"Wonderful," Trudy sighed. "If only *his* last name were Grosvenor." She lowered her voice and said, "I've asked around a bit about the rest of it. The woman who does our laundry says you just close your eyes and say Hail Marys until he finishes his business. But Maggie, our scullery maid, says if you fancy the boy—if he's handsome and he washes—then it's the loveliest thing ever."

Jo tried to picture it, but all she saw in her mind's eye—thanks to Grandmama—were two dogs, one on top of the other, and it didn't seem lovely at all.

"What if you *don't* fancy him? Can you imagine it? Being naked in a bed with a man you don't like?" she said.

"All the time," Trudy replied, grimly eyeing her engagement ring. Gilbert Grosvenor had proposed to her a week ago. Their wedding was set for May.

"Oh, Trudy," Jo said. "How will you—"

"I don't know. *Somehow*," Trudy said briskly. "But you *do* fancy Bram. How could you not? So it won't be a problem for you."

"No, of course not," Jo said quickly, looking away. She stared into the fireplace. "But I'm not talking about me. I'm talking about you. What if you broke off your engagement?"

Trudy snorted. "To do what? Marry the apple boy and live shabbily ever after? No, thank you. I won't be poor. Or a spinster. Or some bluestocking in a bow tie. Apples and kisses are nice, but this is nicer," she said, gesturing to the music room with its painted ceiling, silk upholstery, and priceless statues.

It's a business transaction for Trudy, Jo realized. She was a stunning beauty, and would trade that beauty for money—Gilbert Grosvenor's money. Love was not part of the bargain. The understanding chilled Jo a little. The chill deepened as she recalled Grandmama's assertion that her mother was doing the very same thing for her.

"What if we had our own money, Tru?" she asked, suddenly gripped by a sense of the unfairness of the whole arrangement. "What if *we* were the ones with jobs and bank accounts and investments? Can you imagine how different things would be?"

"What a strange girl you are today," Trudy said. "Stop talking rot." She took Jo's hand. They were both staring into the empty fireplace now. "And don't fret so much over the wedding-night proceedings. I'm going first. I'll tell you all about it so you'll know exactly what to expect. You can come see me in my new and very grand home as soon as I'm back from my honeymoon. We'll have a delicious luncheon, just the two of us. Prepared by my cook and served by my maid."

Jo squeezed Trudy's hand. "And just where on Fifth will this grand house be? The Seventies? Eighties?" she asked.

"I'm not sure yet, but you'll be able to find it," Trudy said ruefully. "Just look for plenty of dogs and some rather large gardens."

❧ CHAPTER NINETEEN ❧

There were footsteps in the doorway of the music room, and then a man's voice said, "Found you!"

Jo turned around and smiled. It was Bram. He, Addie, and Gilbert had just walked into the music room. Caroline and Rob were behind them.

"Is Grandmama about? I thought I heard her," Addie asked, looking worried.

"She's gone to check on a foal," Jo said.

"Good. Let's get out of here before she asks to see your teeth, Jo. Or picks up Trudy's leg to look at her hoof," Bram said mischievously.

Everyone laughed except Gilbert. He had made it known just yesterday that he found references to anatomy made in mixed company unseemly.

The group of friends made their way out of the mansion to the front lawn. The early-October morning was sunny and clear, and still warm enough to walk outside with only a wrap. Everyone was high-spirited and chatty—except Trudy. In the few minutes it had taken to exit the house, she'd changed utterly. She was no longer her fun, lively self. She was quiet and demure, deferring to Gilbert constantly, echoing his every opinion.

A nodding, smiling monkey, Jo thought crossly.

Trudy had told Jo that she wouldn't let Gilbert ruin her fun, but Jo wasn't sure about that. Gilbert was a dark cloud who could dampen anyone's spirits. What would Trudy be like a few months after she'd married him? A few years? *Defeated,* Jo thought. *Dull.* The very idea depressed her.

Bram offered Jo his arm and she took it. Gilbert offered one arm to Trudy and the other to Caroline. Rob squired Addie. The party set off toward the river.

"You look lovely today," Bram said to Jo as they walked.

"Why, thank you, kind sir," she replied.

He covered her hand with his own, a forward gesture from him. "There's color in your cheeks again and I'm glad to see it. You're still not yourself, though. You seem so distracted. I hope your stay will cheer you up."

"It already has," Jo said, smiling at his concern. "Did you, Gil, and Rob have a nice ride this morning?" she asked. The three had gone out early in a trap.

"We did. I showed them the site of our ferry dock at Kipp's Landing. Gil agrees that it should be enlarged and that the fees from the additional vessels a bigger dock could accommodate would recoup the building costs in no time."

Jo looked at Bram as he spoke. Twenty years old, tall and slender, he was a man who inspired admiration rather than passion. A recent graduate of Columbia Law School, he was intelligent and accomplished. A high forehead and receding hairline made him look older than he was, but Trudy was right: he was handsome in his way. He had a wide smile and warm brown eyes, and he moved with a loping, patrician grace. He was always in command of himself and completely at ease in the world—probably, Jo thought, because his family owned so much of it.

As the group crossed a meadow, he talked about ferries, trains, and subterranean railroads. The Aldriches owned thousands of acres

in the Hudson Valley, a good chunk of Manhattan, and large swaths
of the Bronx. They were currently cutting wide avenues through
Bronx farmland with the idea of luring people out of Manhattan's
crowded tenements to new homes the Aldriches intended to build
there. With Peter Aldrich, Bram's father, bedridden, the duties of
maintaining the family's fortune lay squarely on Bram's shoulders.
It was a heavy burden for one so young, which was why Grandmama was so impatient for him to marry.

As Jo continued to gaze at the young man who might well become her husband, Trudy's words came back to her: *But you do
fancy Bram. How could you not?*

Do you? a little voice inside her asked.

Jo quickly reassured herself that she did. In fact, she loved Bram.
He was one of her dearest friends. They'd known each other since
they were tiny children.

But do you fancy *him?* the voice persisted.

And Jo found she didn't have an answer. She loved Bram, yes,
because he was kind and decent and upstanding. Because he held
doors and chatted with deaf aunties and never used a salad fork
when a fish fork was required. But she loved her cousin Rob, too,
for all the same reasons.

Fancying someone, though—that was a different thing altogether. It was what made Trudy risk expulsion from school for a
few kisses from her apple boy. It was what singers crooned about
in the songs Mrs. Nelson was always singing, like "Oh Promise Me."
It was mad, bad, and dangerous, and though Jo didn't know what
it felt like, she suspected it had nothing to do with old aunties or
fish forks.

"I must be boring you to tears," Bram said now, after he finished
telling her about a new apartment building under construction just
above Central Park.

"Not at all!" Jo protested. Though she'd been lost in her thoughts, she actually found the rapid changes taking place in the city, and the forces that propelled them, fascinating.

"What a shameless fibber you are. You can't possibly find my work interesting. No girl could. Let's find a subject more pleasing to the feminine sensibilities—the weather. Is it not the most beautiful fall morning you've ever seen? And is Herondale not the best possible place to spend it?"

Jo was disappointed at the turn of topic, but she smiled and agreed that it was. *Who's the monkey now?* she asked herself.

"I love this place, Jo. So much. Its borders seem to me like high walls that keep us safe from the outside world."

"Yes, they do," Jo said. "I've always thought so, too."

And she had, but now, for the first time, she found those walls confining. They kept the world out, but they kept her in, too. She looked down at her gloved hand resting placidly on Bram's arm and remembered that same hand knotted in Eddie's shirt, and suddenly she felt achingly lonely. She wished she could confide in Bram and tell him about her father. She couldn't, though; he wouldn't understand.

But Eddie did.

She pictured him now—rumpled and brash, with his teasing tone, fast gait, ink-stained cuffs, and lively blue eyes. He was so different from the boys she knew, with their practiced smiles, their crisp suits and pressed shirts. So different from Bram.

Jo wished she were with Eddie now, in his room. Drinking his coffee. Looking at his things. She wished she could rest her head on his shoulder again, and feel his arms around her. These were wishes she knew she shouldn't be making, but she was, and it scared her.

Rob called to Bram. He was pointing to a boat out on the river. Bram excused himself and walked back to see what he wanted.

Rob's call broke Jo's reverie. She found herself standing alone near Herondale's high cliffs. She hadn't realized how far they'd walked. The edge was only ten yards away. They used to dare each other to go close when they were children—she, Addie, Bram, and her cousins. She'd always gone the closest.

What am I doing? she wondered. I'm here, walking with Bram, but thinking about Eddie. *If Bram* knew . . . *If he knew I'd snuck out of my house at night, that I'd gone to the morgue, and to Eddie's room* . . .

Jo shivered at the thought. Just one of those transgressions could ruin her. Theakston had nearly caught her coming back into the house from her visit to Reade Street. She'd only just made it up the back stairs ahead of him. What if he *had* caught her?

Looking out now at the broad, majestic Hudson, Jo felt as if she were on the verge of a more dangerous precipice. She took a few more steps and peered over the cliff, into oblivion. The river seemed to rush up at her. For a second, she felt as if she might actually step off the edge. It felt terrifying—and exhilarating.

"Jo!" a voice called. "Be careful!"

It was Bram. He was hurrying to her.

"You're scaring me," he said, taking her hand. "Come back, Jo. Please. You're far too close to the edge."

❧ CHAPTER TWENTY ❧

The drunk man swayed alarmingly. He straightened his filthy jacket, wiped his snotty nose, and smiled. "How much, pretty miss?" he asked. For the third time.

Jo, standing in the doorway of the Van Houten Shipping building, on South Street, was losing her patience. She wished he would just go away. The darkness made it hard enough to see who was coming and going along Van Houten's Wharf without him blocking her view.

"Please, miss," the man said, slurring his words. "You're the loveliest thing I ever saw. Can't a man have a lovely thing just once in his life? How much will it cost to get you to take a stroll with me?"

"To take a *stroll* with you?" Jo said, bristling at his cheek. "Sir, *no* amount of money, no matter how vast, could induce me to stroll, perambulate, promenade, or engage in any form of locomotion with you whatsoever. Good evening."

"My money's not good enough for you? Is that it?" the man cried. "It's as good as any other man's! Here, it's yours!" He pulled a handful of coins from his trouser pocket and threw them on the ground.

"Oh, for goodness' sake," Jo huffed. She knelt down, glad she'd thought to wear old clothes again, picked up the coins, and handed them back to him. "Instead of flinging your money about, you might consider spending some of it on a cup of coffee," she advised. Then she took her leave. She'd spotted her quarry. He was wearing twill trousers, his trademark tweed jacket, and a collarless shirt open at the neck.

"Mr. Gallagher!" she called out, hurrying across South Street to the docks.

Eddie, who'd just trotted down the narrow plank walkway between two massive ships, spotted her. His expression turned thunderous.

My word, Jo thought. *He's even handsome when he's angry.*

"I was about to say 'It can't be you.' But I know from experience that it can," he said. "What are you doing here?"

"Looking for you," Jo said, giving him a smile. She hoped it would soften him.

"I thought you were safely tucked away in the country at the Aldrich estate. That's what the social pages said."

"I returned."

"How did you know I was here?"

"It's October fifteenth. You said you would be."

"You shouldn't be here," he said, still angry. "We had a deal. You were to keep your eyes open for information about your father. I was to come to the docks."

"We *did* have a deal, but I'm finding it impossible to hold up my end. I've learned *nothing* new about my father. No one will speak of anything important in my presence. Not my uncle, nor anyone else. When I enter a room, the talk turns from ships and spices to ponies and petunias," Jo said with a sigh.

"Do you have any idea where you are?"

"Well, that's a silly question."

"You're on the waterfront."

"Am I? I guess that explains all of these," said Jo, gesturing to the ships in dock, their soaring masts silhouetted against the night sky, their prows nosing out over the street.

Eddie was not amused. "It's not funny, Jo. You're in one of the most dangerous places in the entire city."

"It's not so bad," Jo said dismissively. "The people here are actually quite kind. While I was waiting for you, a man tried to give me all his money. Before that, a woman complimented my dress and invited me to her house. She said her friend Della would find me work."

Eddie was saucer-eyed. "Promise me you will never, *ever* come down here on your own again," he said, his voice rising. "Promise me, Jo. *Now*. Or this whole thing's off."

"You're awfully dramatic tonight," Jo said. "Why are you so upset?"

"Is there *any* way I can convince you to get in a cab and go home?" Eddie asked, exasperated.

"You cannot. You can, however, tell me if you've found the *Kinch*."

Eddie sighed, resigned to her presence. "I haven't, and I've been up and down the entire wharf," he said.

"I wonder if it's a chartered vessel. Van Houten uses them at busy times—tea and spice harvests, for example—if it doesn't have room enough aboard its own ships to bring its cargo into port. If the *Kinch* was one of ours, I'm sure I'd have heard about it. Papa rarely spoke of business in front of me, but he did talk about his ships and even took me aboard a few. He was very proud of them," Jo explained. "I've seen this one before." She nodded at the graceful vessel looming above them. "The *Emma May*. She's a tea clipper."

As they were looking up at the *Emma May*, a man suddenly appeared on her deck. He walked down her gangplank carrying a burlap sack over his shoulder. Three black-and-white terriers, bright-eyed and keen, followed him.

Eddie recognized him. "Bill!" he shouted. "Bill Hawkins!"

The man waved and when he reached the dock, he joined them. "Good to see you, Eddie! And who's this pretty thing? You from Della's, dolly?" he asked Jo.

"She's a cub. I'm showing her the ropes," Eddie answered before Jo could respond. "Bill Hawkins . . . Josie Jones."

"Pardon me, miss! I didn't mean to . . . Well, never mind!" Bill said awkwardly. "Pleased to meet you." He doffed his hat. He had curly red hair, a beard to match, and teeth that were chipped and yellowed.

"Likewise, Mr. Hawkins," Jo said. *Who* is *this Della?* she wondered.

"How's the catch?" Eddie quickly asked. Jo felt he was desperate to change the subject.

Bill opened his sack and Jo looked inside, thinking it odd that anyone would fish at night. But instead of the silvery glint of scales, she saw a black, squirming mass—rats. Dozens of them. Some were dead. Others were alive—writhing and squealing, vicious with fear. She stifled a cry.

"Bill's a ratcatcher," Eddie explained. "He and his dogs clear the holds of ships at night."

"I gathered," Jo said, determined not to show the revulsion she felt.

As Eddie spoke, Bill tied a rope around the top of the sack and chucked it into the water. The dogs watched it sink, whimpering. "Quit yer whining, boys!" Bill bellowed. "There's plenty more to be found. New York's full of rats!"

"Bill, we're looking for a ship called the *Kinch*. Do you know if it's in dock?" Eddie asked.

"If it is, I don't know about it. It's not a name I've ever heard," Bill replied, spitting a gob of chewing tobacco into the water.

Jo felt crestfallen at what seemed to be yet another dead end, but then Bill said, "Tell you who might know—man by the name of Shaw. Jackie Shaw. He's an old-timer. Sailed on dozens of ships."

"Where can I find him?" Eddie asked.

"Walsh's."

Eddie groaned. "Not that dive."

"'Fraid so. If Jackie's in town, he's there," Bill said. He whistled for his dogs. They left the pile of fish guts they'd found on the dock and joined him.

"Thanks, Bill."

"My pleasure. Night, all," Bill said. He strode off to the next ship, his dogs trotting behind him.

Jo wanted to find out what a dive was, but she had another question first. "Who's this Della I keep hearing about? And where is her house?" Jo asked Eddie.

"*Della,*" Eddie said. He cleared his throat. "Della . . ."

"Yes, Della," Jo said impatiently.

"She's a . . . She, um, keeps a *house* . . . a house for *girls*," he explained awkwardly. "Bill just assumed . . . it being late and you being on the docks . . ."

"A house for girls?" Jo echoed. "Is it some kind of finishing school?"

"Yes, that's exactly what it is. The girls there are finished. And how."

"You're being awfully cryptic," Jo said, growing annoyed.

"This is a mistake. A big fat one," Eddie said, shaking his head. "You shouldn't be here. You should be home. In your nice house. Having milk and cookies."

"I only asked—"

"Let's get back to business, shall we?"

"All *right*," Jo said, wondering at his brusqueness. He seemed to be very embarrassed by the conversation. She had no idea why. "I suppose our next stop is Walsh's. What's a dive?"

"A rathole bar in the basement of a building," Eddie said absently. He was frowning up at the *Emma May.*

Jo followed his gaze. "What is it?" she asked.

"It's strange that Bill hasn't heard of the *Kinch*. He's been catching rats on the wharves since he could walk. He knows every ship that comes in and out of the harbor. If the *Kinch* was here, if it had *ever* been here, he'd know it."

Jo thought about this. "Perhaps we're mistaken and *Kinch* isn't the name of a ship," she said. "Perhaps it's a person's name. When I first saw the word in my father's diary, I assumed it was, but the more I thought about it, the more it seemed too odd a name for a person."

"But your father jotted down the letters *VHW* for *Van Houten's Wharf* next to the word *Kinch*. Why would he hold a meeting with a man on a wharf at this hour?" asked Eddie.

"Perhaps he didn't mean the actual wharf when he wrote *VHW*," Jo said. "He always referred to both the firm's docks and its offices as Van Houten's Wharf since they're just across the street from each other."

Eddie nodded at the Van Houten building. "I don't suppose you have keys to the offices?"

"No. Why?"

"Do you have any money on you?"

"Yes," Jo said guardedly. She continued to use the money she'd taken from her father's agenda. She felt guilty about it, but how else could she pay for cab rides to Reade Street or the waterfront? Her mother gave her no money of her own; young ladies who carried cash were thought common. "Why do you ask?"

Eddie didn't answer her. "Wait here for a minute," he said.

He loped off down the street to a saloon called Sullivan's. A small boy was standing outside it. A thin girl, perhaps sixteen or seventeen years old, was with him. Eddie exchanged a few words with them, then returned to Jo, accompanied by the boy.

"This is Tumbler," he said.

Before Jo could ask why Eddie had fetched him, Tumbler said, "Two dollars."

"Nice try," Eddie said.

"A dollar, then."

"How about fifty cents?"

"How about you kiss my ass, you cheap son of a bitch."

Jo blinked, appalled. The boy couldn't have been more than ten years old.

"All right. A dollar," Eddie said grudgingly. "For getting us in *and* back out again."

Tumbler held out his hand.

"You get paid when the job's done," Eddie told him.

Tumbler spat, then crossed the street to the door of Van Houten's offices.

"Come on. He works fast," Eddie said to Jo.

Tumbler glanced around, then took from his pocket a button-hook and a slim piece of metal bent at an angle at one end, like an L. He inserted them both into the door's lock.

Jo grabbed Eddie's arm. "He's breaking in!" she whispered.

"Yes," Eddie said with a grim smile, "he is."

❧ CHAPTER TWENTY-ONE ❧

"Eddie, this is wrong," Jo objected, upset.

"Sometimes you have to do wrong to do right," Eddie said. "Nellie Bly lied to get inside an insane asylum so she could expose abuse. We're not breaking in to steal things, we're breaking in to solve a crime. If Kinch *is* a person, and your father met with him here on September fifteenth—like the entry in his agenda suggests—then there could be notes from that meeting. Something that might tell us who he is."

Jo hesitated, unnerved by the thought of committing a crime, regardless of the reason.

"Look, I told you, I do whatever it takes to get the story," Eddie said. "You don't have to be a part of this."

But I am a part of it, Jo thought. *I became a part of it the moment I opened my father's agenda.*

She heard scraping as Tumbler worked, then a few clicks, and then the lock's tumblers turned. When the door swung open, she was the first inside.

"Lock it behind us in case a patrolman's around. He might try the knob. Then stay close," Eddie told Tumbler. "We'll knock on the glass when we want to come out."

Tumbler nodded, and Jo heard the door lock behind her.

Light from the streetlamps, shining in through the windows, illuminated the foyer. Framed, hand-colored maps of all the faraway places where Van Houten did business hung on the walls. Whenever Jo's father had brought her here as a child, a clerk had served her tea and cookies. She'd memorized the maps as she'd sat nibbling shortbread.

There were photographs on the walls, too, including one of her father and uncle taken many years ago. They were standing on a bustling dock, handsome in their linen suits. Their faces were bronzed and smiling. A sign behind them read ZANZIBAR. Jo knew it was an island off the coast of East Africa and an important base for Van Houten's spice trade. Her heart ached as she looked at the image of her father, so young and full of life.

Eddie glanced at the photo. "We shouldn't linger," he said softly.

Jo turned to him. "What can I do?"

"We need to look for minutes of meetings," Eddie replied. "Where would they be?"

"I don't know," Jo said.

"Guess."

Jo thought for a moment. The building had two floors. The clerks' workspace was on the ground floor. It contained tall shelves stuffed with ledgers; long, broad wooden tables; and an iron stove. The upper floor was where her father and the other partners worked. Meetings, she reasoned, had likely taken place there.

"Upstairs, I think," she said.

"Let's go," Eddie said.

It was dark on the second floor. The windows—three of them, facing the street—were higher than the streetlights, and only a little of the lamps' glow shone through them. The floor's front half was open, with a rectangular table and chairs in its center. The back half contained the partners' offices, accessed via a short, narrow hallway.

"Let's try the offices first," Jo said.

Eddie smacked into a coat stand and Jo tripped over a stool as they made their way through the room. They didn't dare turn on the gas lamps in case someone saw the light through the windows and became suspicious, but they needed something to illuminate their way.

"There has to be a kerosene lamp somewhere," Jo said. "Look over by the—"

A sound downstairs silenced her. She froze. It was the door. Someone had just closed it. A key turned, locking it. Next they heard voices. Men's voices. Two of them. Jo recognized one. "Richard Scully," she whispered to Eddie. "One of the partners."

Eddie swore under his breath. "I bet the guy with him is a cop. Somebody must've seen us and figured us for robbers."

"They can't find me here!" she hissed, frantic.

"Maybe they'll just check around downstairs and leave," Eddie whispered.

But that didn't happen. Instead, they heard footsteps, heavy and solemn, on the stairs. Scully and whoever was with him were coming up.

Jo and Eddie were trapped.

➤ CHAPTER TWENTY-TWO ◄

Jo had only seconds to find a hiding place—seconds before Richard Scully discovered her in a dark room, late at night, with a strange man.

Panic set in. Eddie was trying the doors to the offices, but every one was locked. The footsteps were coming closer. Scully and his companion had to be halfway up the stairs. Jo looked wildly around the room, and then she spotted it: a broom closet, just to the left of the stairwell.

She grabbed Eddie's hand and they sped across the room. Jo prayed that the men were too intent upon their conversation to notice the creaks and pops of the floorboards. There was no knob on the closet door, just a latch. Eddie grabbed it and yanked the door open. The closet was about as deep as a coffin. A cleaner's smock hung on a hook at the back. A mop stood in a pail, taking up almost all the floor space.

"Get in!" he hissed. "I'll find another place."

The two men were on the landing now. They'd be in the room at any second.

"There's no time!" Jo whispered. She stepped into the bucket and pulled Eddie in after her. They got the door closed just as the lights came on in the room. Jo couldn't get her footing; she lost her balance and fell against Eddie. By some miracle, she managed not to rattle the bucket.

"I can't stand up in this thing!" she whispered, her hands clutching at him.

"Lean on me!" he whispered back.

He took hold of her arms to steady her. One of his shoulders was jammed up against the back wall of the closet. The other was only inches from the door. Jo was so close to him, she could feel his heart beating. The smell of him—soap, beer, and cigarettes—was so new, so strange and overwhelming, that for a few seconds she forgot to be scared.

Then Richard Scully started talking and she remembered. She could hear him perfectly. The latch hadn't caught, leaving a narrow crack between the door and its frame. Jo could see part of the table through the crack and the wall behind it, but not the men.

"Whiskey?" That was Scully.

Jo heard no reply, but Scully's companion must have nodded, because the next thing she heard was the sound of a glass stopper being removed from its bottle, and then liquid pouring into a glass.

"Sit down," Scully said.

As the second man walked into Jo's view, then sat at the table, she stifled a gasp.

"What is it?" Eddie whispered, his lips against her ear.

"It's *him*," she said.

"Who?"

"The man who was outside my house, staring up at my father's windows!"

➤ CHAPTER TWENTY-THREE ⭇

The long hair, gathered back; the facial marks—they were all exactly the same. Jo had thought the marks were dirt or ash, but now she saw that they were tattoos, sinuous and spiky. She leaned as close to the crack as she dared to get a better view of him.

"Kinch, is it? A new face, a new name," Scully said.

Jo inhaled sharply. She squeezed Eddie's arm. Eddie squeezed back.

"I could hardly go by my old one," Kinch replied.

"What happened to you? The markings—"

"Pirates. The captain was a Lascar. The crew were Africans and Arabs. They use tattoos to tell their stories. They told mine."

"Your aspect is greatly altered. I would not know you but for your eyes."

"Seventeen years without the company of another Christian soul. Without kin. Without comfort. Seventeen years of hunger, scurvy, and fever. My *aspect*"—he spat the word—"is as you have made it. Look upon me and see the monster you have wrought."

"You . . . you don't believe I *knew*, do you? I didn't! Not until five minutes ago, when you yourself told me. I swear it!" Scully said. He sounded scared.

Knew what? Jo wondered, desperately hoping that Scully would say more, but Kinch didn't let him.

"I didn't come here for conversation," he said. "I came for the money Charles Montfort promised me when I met with him. He said he would give me a thousand dollars. He promised to help me find her."

"Yes," Scully said as he hurriedly moved across the room. "Poor, poor Charles. Most unfortunate. What a terrible accident."

"Montforts don't have accidents," Kinch said darkly. As he downed his whiskey, his eyes traveled over the portraits of Van Houten's partners hanging on a wall—five living, two dead.

"Charles Montfort, Phillip Montfort, Richard Scully, Alvah Beekman, Asa Tuller, John Brevoort, and Stephen Smith," Kinch said, raising his glass. "Cheers, gentlemen." He turned back to Scully. "You look pale, Richard. Don't worry, I won't tell anyone our secret." He placed his hand on his chest. "It's written on my heart, and that's where it will stay. As long as you cooperate."

"I'll do what I can," Scully said. "But you must be reasonable. There are limits."

Kinch brought his fist crashing down on the table. "You speak to me of limits, Richard? To *me*? Was there any limit to what Van Houten took from me?" he shouted.

Scully quickly apologized. "I didn't *know*," he said again, weakly.

"You knew about the *Bonaventure*, though," Kinch said.

"Those were hard times. For the firm. For all of us. We—"

Kinch cut him off. "Enough talk," he said. "I want my money. *Now.*" He grabbed the whiskey bottle, poured himself another glass, and downed it.

Jo heard chair legs scraping over the floorboards, then footsteps. Scully flashed into her view, then out again.

Kinch laughed bitterly. "The partners' safe. Empty once, but no longer, eh? They say money talks, but I don't believe it. If it were true, those notes would wail. They would scream."

There was the sound of a metal door closing, then footsteps again. Scully walked back into view. He placed a stack of banknotes on the table in front of Kinch.

"One thousand," he said.

"It'll do. For now," Kinch said, pocketing the money.

"How much more do you want? There must be recompense, of course. But what you're asking is impossible. Charles made promises he shouldn't have," Scully said. "Surely we can come to terms."

"I want *everything*, Richard. Those are my terms. I want to destroy Van Houten as it destroyed me," Kinch said.

"This . . . this is *outrageous*!" Scully sputtered. "I'll do nothing more for you. Not until I consult with the others."

"Consult all you like. There's proof. There are manifests, signed and stamped," Kinch said menacingly. "Do as I ask and I'll leave New York the moment I've found her. You'll never hear from me again. Refuse me and I'll make every one of those manifests public. Not only will Van Houten be ruined, its partners will be, too."

"So you say. But it was so long ago, and nothing has ever come to light," Scully countered, desperation in his voice. "What if you're bluffing?"

Kinch chuckled. It was a low, sinister sound. "*Pray* that I'm bluffing, Richard. If you still know how." He stood.

"Where can I find you?" Scully asked.

"I'll find you," Kinch replied. "Goodbye, Richard."

"You'll need this to get out," Scully said, handing Kinch a key. "Leave it in the lock."

Kinch took the key and Jo heard his footsteps echoing down the stairs. After the door opened and closed again, Richard Scully got up and moved into Jo's line of sight. She saw him put the whiskey bottle away. He put on his hat and started walking toward the stairwell; then suddenly he stopped and stared straight ahead.

At her.

Jo shrank against Eddie. Scully had seen them, but *how*? The crack was narrow. The closet was dark inside. He strode toward them, a furious expression on his face.

"We're done for," Eddie whispered, his hands tightening on Jo's arms.

What would she say to Mr. Scully? To her mother when he marched her up the steps to her house and rang the bell? Life as she knew it was about to end. She'd never be able to show her face in New York again.

Scully reached the closet and stopped. "Damn that lazy woman!" he growled. "I've told her a thousand times to keep doors *closed*."

He kicked the door hard. It slammed shut. The sound startled Jo, but she didn't move. She and Eddie stayed perfectly still until they'd heard the downstairs door open and close once more.

"He's gone," Jo breathed, her body sagging with relief. "Thank God."

Eddie pushed on the door. It didn't budge.

"Eddie, are we—" Jo started to say.

"Yeah. Looks like we are," Eddie replied.

Jo and Eddie were locked in the closet.

❧ CHAPTER TWENTY-FOUR ❧

"Try the door again!" Jo said frantically.

Eddie pushed on the door but nothing happened. The latch was on the outside, and it had clicked into place.

"I want to tail Kinch," Eddie said anxiously. "I'm going to lose him if we don't get out of here and he might be tough to find again."

"I'm going to lose my reputation if we don't get out of here and that will be *impossible* to find again," Jo said.

"I have a penknife in my pocket. Maybe I can jimmy the latch," said Eddie. "I have to let go of you. Can you steady yourself against the wall?"

"I think so," Jo said. Eddie got the knife out of his pocket and carefully opened the blade. He inserted it into the crack between the door and the frame and jerked it upward. It snagged in the soft wood of the doorframe and promptly snapped off.

"Maybe I can break the door down. Stand back," Eddie said.

"Stand back?" Jo asked. "How? I'm in a *bucket*!"

Eddie threw his shoulder into the door as hard as he could, which wasn't very hard at all, since he had little room to maneuver, but it was hard enough to knock him off balance and into Jo. His head smacked against hers. The bucket tipped. She fell backward into the wall.

"Ow!" she cried. "That really hurt!"

"Sorry! Are you all right?" he asked, reaching for her.

"I'm fine. But I won't be if we don't get out of here," she said when she was upright again. "What are we going to do?"

"Maybe I can push against the door with my feet."

Eddie braced his back against the wall behind him and tried to lift his feet, but the space was so tight, he couldn't raise them high enough to get any leverage. He swore under his breath and stood straight again.

"I have to get out of this bucket. My feet are cramping," Jo said.

"Step out and twist yourself sideways," Eddie said. "It'll be a tight squeeze, but you can wedge your feet between mine."

Jo did so. Before, they'd been standing face to face. Their shoulders had nearly touched the door and back wall of the closet, but there had been a bit of room at their backs. Now Eddie turned to face the door, his back against the back wall, and Jo wedged herself in front of him, with her back against the door, and there was no room between them at all. Her eyes were blind in the darkness, but her sense of touch was heightened. She could feel every point of contact with his body. One of her legs was between his, and one of his was between hers. Her hips were pressed against his and her breasts were jammed into his chest. Her cheek touched his jaw.

Jo found that she was suddenly warm and light-headed. She tried to tell herself it was because she couldn't draw a proper breath in the small space, but it wasn't. It was because of Eddie.

Only days ago, she'd asked Trudy what it was like to want a man, and Trudy had told her but she hadn't understood. Now she did. Eddie flooded her senses. He made her giddy. He made her ache. He filled her with a hunger that was new and deep and dangerous.

"Well, this is cozy," he said. "How are your feet?"

"My what?" she said, dazed.

"Your feet?"

"Oh, my *feet*. Much better, thank you," Jo replied.

She suddenly felt something graze her lips. *His lips*. She was sure of it. Was it an accident or had he done it on purpose? There was only one way to find out. She stood stock-still, her face upturned in the dark. Waiting. Hoping. Fearing that he would, and that he wouldn't.

"Jo," he said, his voice low.

Her heart was pounding so hard, she thought it would burst. She closed her eyes. Wanting him to kiss her. To touch her. Feeling as though she would die if he didn't.

"Jo, I think I . . ."

"Yes, Eddie?" she whispered.

". . . hear something."

And then the door was wrenched open and she was hurtling backward. She hit the floor with a painful thud. Eddie fell on top of her, breaking his fall with his hands to avoid crushing her.

"Hidin' out in a closet, eh?" an angry voice said. "I *knowed* you'd try to gyp me, you sneaky bastard. Gimme my dollar right now. Or I'll set the Tailor on you."

Jo and Eddie looked up.

It was Tumbler.

✥ CHAPTER TWENTY-FIVE ✥

"Everything all right?" a willowy blonde asked. She was the girl who'd been standing outside the bar with Tumbler. Now she was outside Van Houten's.

Nothing was all right. Jo's backside hurt from the fall she'd taken. Her feet ached from standing in the bucket. She was flustered by what had happened in the closet, and what hadn't.

"I found 'em, Fay," Tumbler said as he relocked Van Houten's door. "They was hiding in a closet."

"We weren't *hiding*," Jo clarified. "We got locked in."

"Where's his money?" Fay asked. Her dress, made of sprigged cotton, was faded and worn. Her face was fine-featured and pretty.

Jo pulled a dollar note from her skirt pocket and handed it to her. Fay's eyes, hard and predatory, lingered on Jo's pocket.

"Don't do it," Eddie cautioned.

Fay gave him a dirty look. She was about to say something when a piercing whistle sounded from up the street. Her expression changed. For a second, she looked like the hunted instead of the hunter.

"Come on, boy. He wants us," she said to Tumbler.

Jo heard the lock's bolt shoot home. Tumbler pocketed his tools; then he and Fay hurried off into the night.

"Who's that girl?" Jo asked, staring after them.

"One of the best pickpockets in the city. She works for the Tailor. Tumbler does, too. You shouldn't keep your money in your pocket, by the way. Put it down your . . . your . . ." He pointed to his chest, reddening slightly. "To keep it safe."

Jo was not about to unbutton her jacket in front of him. She tucked her money into her boot. "Who's the Tailor?" she asked, straightening again.

"New York's very own Fagin," Eddie replied. "He takes in orphans and teaches them how to thieve. He's called the Tailor because he makes clothing for his army of little pickpockets so they blend in with their victims. Some of it's really sharp."

"But Fay's dress wasn't sharp, it was shabby," Jo said.

"She dresses for the neighborhood she's working. First rule of picking pockets: don't stick out."

Two beggar women were walking toward them. One was agitated and the other was trying to calm her. Jo recognized the woman who was upset; it was Mad Mary, the ragpicker. She was whimpering about some fearsome ghost come back from the dead to haunt her.

"Here, Mary, take a slug of this," the other woman said, handing her a bottle. "It kills ghosts dead."

Jo's eyes lingered on them. It was a chilly night, and neither was dressed for it. They were both so thin. Impulsively, she went to them and gave them each a dollar. Mary, still upset, asked her if she'd seen the ghost.

"I haven't, Mary. I'm sorry," she said.

The other woman offered Jo a slug from her bottle if she'd give her another dollar. Eddie stepped in then, took Jo's elbow and steered her up South Street. Mary said a forlorn goodbye as they left.

"That was a lucky break we caught," he said, nodding back at Van Houten's. "Did you see Kinch's face?"

Jo nodded.

"Any idea who he is?"

"No," Jo replied. "Mr. Scully knew him, though, but by another name. 'A new face, a new name,' he said. She paused, then said, "Do you think Kinch did it? According to my father's agenda, he saw Kinch the night before he died." A shiver ran through her at the thought of being in the same room with her father's murderer.

"No, I don't. It doesn't make sense," Eddie replied. "Your father had plans to see Kinch again. On September seventeenth and tonight. He had a thousand dollars in his agenda. It was for Kinch. Kinch said as much to Scully. Why would Kinch kill a man who was going to give him a thousand dollars? Maybe more?"

"You're right," Jo said. She was half relieved and half disappointed. The mystery of her father's death only ever seemed to deepen.

"We need to find out who Kinch is, though, and what the partners of Van Houten did to him," Eddie said as they skirted a drunk passed out on the sidewalk and continued uptown.

"I have difficulty believing anyone at Van Houten did anything to him," Jo said. "They are all upstanding men."

Eddie rolled his eyes.

"What was that for?" Jo asked indignantly.

"You better get used to the idea that maybe *someone* at Van Houten isn't so upstanding."

"Why?" Jo countered. "Because a strange, shadowy man shows up and says so?"

"Because Scully would never hand over a thousand dollars of the firm's money unless he absolutely had to. No one would. Kinch has dirt on Van Houten. Scully knows it. Sounds like your father did, too."

Eddie's reasoning made sense to Jo, but it was hard to accept. She'd known the partners her entire life. They'd come to her home for dinners and parties; she'd gone to theirs. And now, according to Kinch, they'd done something very wrong.

"If the firm *did* do something to Kinch—and I still don't entirely believe they did—I'm certain my father was trying to put it right," she said. "Scully said so. 'Charles made promises he shouldn't have.' It's just the sort of thing he would have done—promise to help."

Eddie gave her a doubtful look and pressed his point. "Kinch talked about manifests and something called the Bonaventure. A ship, maybe? He also said, 'He promised to help me find her.' A ship is referred to as *she* and *her*. If the *Bonaventure* is a ship, could Van Houten have taken it from him somehow? Did your father or uncle ever mention it?" he asked.

"Not to me."

"Maybe they had some sort of business deal and it went sour. Maybe the *Bonaventure* was indeed a ship and Van Houten sold it to Kinch and it was no good. Or maybe the ship belonged to him and they did him out of it somehow. Maybe—"

Jo groaned with frustration. "Maybe we should try to come up with some facts. Because all of our theories are just that—*theories*," she said impatiently. "If we want answers, we have to find Kinch."

"No, *I* have to find him," Eddie said. "*You* will not, under any circumstances, attempt to find him. It's too dangerous. I'll ask the Tailor about him. He knows every shady character in the city. After I ask Bill Hawkins and Jackie Shaw about the *Bonaventure*."

"And what do I do? Twiddle my thumbs?" Jo asked.

Eddie thought for a bit, then said, "We still don't know who Eleanor Owens is. Her name was in your father's agenda, too. Maybe you could track her down."

"Where do I start?" Jo asked, thrilled by the idea.

"At the Bureau of Vital Records. If she was born in the city, her birth records will be there. You might be able to find an address and—"

"Eddie!" Jo said excitedly, stopping dead on the sidewalk. "I just thought of something! Could Eleanor Owens be Kinch's *her*?"

"What do you mean?"

"Maybe when Kinch said, 'He promised to help me find her,' he was talking about Eleanor Owens!"

"I hadn't thought of that. Nice work," Eddie said admiringly.

Jo flushed with pleasure at his praise. They'd made progress tonight. She wanted to make even more. "Let's go to Walsh's to see if Jackie Shaw is there," she said. "We still need to find out what the Bonaventure is. If it *is* a ship, maybe he knows about it."

"Uh-uh. The only thing we're going to find tonight is a cab so I can get you home," Eddie said, looking around for one. "You can't come down here again, Jo. I'm dead serious. This is no place—"

His words were cut off when a door opened two houses up from them. Light, laughter, and perfume spilled out of it. A few seconds later, two young men spilled out of it as well, and stumbled into the street. Women crowded into the doorway, at least a half dozen of them, giggling and waving. They were wearing nothing but thin silk chemises, stockings, and garters. Their hair was loose; their lips were rouged. One was drinking champagne out of the bottle. She looked no older than Jo.

"What *is* this place?" Jo asked, appalled.

"That's . . . um, well . . . that's Della's," Eddie said, flustered. "It's her house. One of them."

"Bye-bye, Georgie!" one of the women cooed.

"Come back soon, Teddy!" another called.

Jo looked at the men and froze.

"What's wrong?" Eddie asked.

"That's George Adams and Teddy Farnham," she said in a choked voice. "I know them!"

George and Teddy were walking backward down the street, blowing kisses to the girls. It was too late to make a dash for it. They were only a few feet away. Any second now, they'd turn around and see her.

Eddie grabbed Jo's hand. He pulled her into the shadows of the neighboring stoop and spun her around so that her back was toward the two young men. Then he took her in his arms and kissed her. It was not the soft graze of lips she'd longed for inside the broom closet, but a hard, hungry smash of a kiss that took her breath away.

"Hey, fella, get a room!" George bellowed as he passed by.

Teddy hooted, and the two of them staggered off singing. As soon as they were gone, Eddie released her.

Jo stumbled backward. She pressed a hand to her chest, trying to catch her breath. "How dare you!" she sputtered, blushing furiously. "How *could* you?"

"Hey, you're welcome," Eddie said.

"*What?*"

"I just saved your backside. I think a thank-you's in order," he said.

Jo advanced on him, intending to give him what for, but his slow, teasing smile and his eyes, so deeply blue, stopped her cold.

She grabbed his lapels, pulled him to her, and kissed him back.

➤ CHAPTER TWENTY-SIX ✦

"Bram *knows*."

Jo's breath caught. She dropped the teaspoon she was holding. It clattered to the floor.

"He . . . he does?" she said, her voice barely a whisper.

"Of course he does," Addie Aldrich said, picking up the teaspoon.

"But how? Who told him?" Jo asked, panic-stricken.

"No one, silly. It's written all over your face. Bram *knows* how upset you are at having to miss the Young Patrons' Ball. We all do. Just look at you. You look so unhappy."

Jo laughed, weak with relief. "Oh, Addie, you know me too well. I can't hide anything from you," she said.

For a few heart-stopping seconds, she had been terrified that Addie meant Bram knew about Eddie. All she'd thought about for four days straight was Eddie and the kisses they'd shared at the waterfront. She remembered the thrilling feeling of his arms around her and the taste of his lips—and the terror she felt right afterward.

"I . . . I shouldn't have done that," she'd said, breaking away from him. "I'm sorry."

"Are you?"

"Yes! Aren't you?"

"No."

"Well, you *should* be, Mr. Gallagher."

"It's Eddie, remember? And why should I be?"

"Because I . . . Because you . . . Because—"

Eddie had pulled her back to him and kissed her again. Slowly and deeply.

"Still sorry?" he'd asked, his voice husky.

"Yes," Jo had said.

He had kissed her cheek, and then all along the delicate line of her jaw.

"Still?"

"Yes."

He'd kissed her neck and the soft hollow just below it.

"Oh, Eddie, *no.* Not a bit."

She hadn't wanted to find a cab. She hadn't wanted to be parted from him. So they had walked to Gramercy Square hand in hand. They hadn't said a word until they'd reached the square and then Jo had spoken first.

"Eddie, I have—"

"Bram Aldrich. I know. Will Livingston and Henry Jay are sweet on you, too. I read the social pages."

"And I can't—"

"I'm not asking you to."

"Then what—"

"I don't know, Jo. I don't know."

He'd taken her face in his hands then and kissed her again, and his body was so warm, and his lips so sweet, and the beat of his heart under her hand so strong, that the questions hadn't mattered. He'd let her go and then waited outside in the street until she'd snuck into her house and up to her room, and had lit a candle and held it in the window so he'd know she was safely inside.

As she'd undressed for bed, she'd glimpsed herself in her mirror and seen a girl both familiar and unfamiliar staring back. This girl looked rumpled and flushed from her adventures. Inquisitive. Determined. Jo had known she wasn't that girl, not yet, but she wanted to be. And Eddie had showed her that she could be. She was so different when she was with him. Bolder. Better. Alive.

She had lain in her bed, staring up at the ceiling, for more than an hour, trying to name what she was feeling. Bram had never made her feel the way Eddie did—desperate for his touch, his kisses. Was this how Trudy's apple boy had made *her* feel? No, it couldn't be, because she'd discarded him faster than last season's hat when Gilbert proposed.

And then, right before she fell asleep, Jo had realized what the feeling was. "I think I'm falling in love with him," she'd whispered to the darkness.

It was Sunday afternoon now, and Jo and her mother were receiving some close friends and family members. Jo was sitting with her cousin Caroline and a few other girls. More visitors were standing by the mantel or milling about the room. Most everyone was chatting about the ball, which was to be held two weeks from yesterday.

Jo smiled and tried her best to be a good hostess, but she didn't want to be there. She wanted to be with Eddie, walking the streets of the city, meeting Bill Hawkins and Fay and Tumbler, hiding out in a broom closet. She felt like a fairy-tale princess woken by a kiss to a new world, new people, new emotions. *Leave your sleep,* this new world said. But how? Heads would turn if she so much as left the room.

"It's these mourning ensembles that make you look so miserable, Jo," Caroline said now. "Black makes any girl look like a sour old maid."

Jo was dressed as etiquette dictated—in a black day dress, simple and dull. Katie had styled her hair in a plain knot. A jet brooch was fastened at her throat.

"Elizabeth Adams ordered a gown from Paris especially for the ball. Edie Waring saw it and says it's spectacular," Jennie Rhinelander gushed.

Jo had been looking forward to the Young Patrons' Ball before she'd lost her father—and found Eddie. Now she wanted no part of it.

"I don't care what Elizabeth's doing. I think any girl who doesn't put her Paris dresses away for at least a year is vulgar," Addie sniffed.

"You know she's wearing it for one reason only—to turn Bram's head," Jennie said. "She's after him. She wants him to escort her to the ball. Anyone with eyes can see it."

"Jennie, dear, you have a talent for saying the most inappropriate things," Caroline scolded.

"It's not inappropriate, it's true!" Jennie protested.

"You are *such* a child. The truth is usually inappropriate," Caroline said. "That's why we avoid speaking of it."

"Elizabeth's wasting her time. Bram's sweet on someone else," Addie said, squeezing Jo's hand. "And do you really think Grandmama would allow her grandson to take up with an Adams? Elizabeth's father made his money from *shoe polish*, for goodness' sake. She's only invited to the ball because the organizers had no choice— her father donated ten thousand dollars to the museum."

"It's such a shame you can't go, Jo," said Jennie. "Isn't there some way?"

"Aunt Anna would never allow it," Caroline said. "Not so soon after Uncle Charles's death."

"Oh, we'll see about that," Addie retorted smugly.

"What do you mean?" asked Caroline.

"Anna Montfort follows the rules, but Grandmama makes them. And when it suits her, she breaks them," Addie said. "She's here and she means to have a word with Mrs. Montfort about the ball."

With a sense of dread, Jo remembered the conversation between

Grandmama and Mrs. Aldrich that she and Trudy had eavesdropped on. Grandmama, it appeared, meant what she'd said.

No! Jo thought, alarmed. *She mustn't speak with Mama. I don't want to encourage Bram.*

Jo looked for her mother, trying not to show the sense of urgency she felt. If she could sit down next to her before Grandmama did, perhaps she could thwart any talk of balls. Finally, Jo spotted her. She was sitting with Phillip and Madeleine in a corner of the room Jo called the jungle because it was dominated by four giant palm trees in pots. There was an empty chair next to her.

"Oh, dear. Uncle Phillip hasn't been offered any lemon wafers and he's so partial to them. Where *is* that maid? I'll have to bring him some myself. Do excuse me," Jo said to her friends.

She hurried to the sideboard, where the refreshments had been set out. As she did, she spotted Grandmama by the piano—only a few feet away from her mother. Jo would have to move fast. She quickly arranged some cookies on a plate and was just about to take them to her uncle when Bram stopped her.

"Are these Mrs. Nelson's lemon wafers? I have to have one before Grandmama feeds them all to Lolly," he said. He took a cookie off the plate and swallowed it in one bite.

"Greedy thing. At least Lolly *sits* for a cookie," Jo scolded, smiling and polite even when she was desperate.

Bram winked and moved off. As he did, guilt—heavy and nauseating—descended on her. *He has expectations,* she thought, staring after him. *He shouldn't. Not anymore. I have to tell him.*

Tell him what? a voice inside her asked. *Tell him you've fallen for a penniless reporter whom you barely know? That's a brilliant idea, Jo. As soon as you've told Bram, you can tell your mother. I'm sure she'll be delighted.*

Jo watched Bram bend down to speak with ancient Mrs. De-Peyster, who had terrible arthritis in her legs and was sitting by the fire to warm them. He took her thin, wrinkled hand and said something that made her laugh. Her eyes sparkled and color came to her cheeks. She patted his hand fondly.

The exchange made Jo's heart ache. Bram was so *good*. He was a solid, honorable man who would always take care of her and make certain she lacked nothing, but she also knew that were she to become his wife, he would never allow her to write stories for newspapers. Or let her go to the morgue. Or kiss her the way Eddie did, with everything inside him—and she knew she would never kiss him back with everything inside her.

What am I going to do? What on earth am I going to do? she wondered.

I don't know, Jo. I don't know, Eddie had said. Neither did she, and it frightened her. She *did* know that she had to avoid the Young Patrons' Ball, though. At all costs.

She started toward the empty seat by her mother, when she saw, to her horror, that it had been taken by Grandmama. *Blast!* she thought. She couldn't join her mother's group now. There was no place for her to sit and to hover would be rude.

The withdrawing room was actually two rooms, each with its own doorway and a fretwork arch between them. Jo ducked out of one door, hoping no one noticed, trotted down the narrow hallway that ran alongside the rooms, then reentered through the second doorway. She was behind her mother's group now, shielded by the palm trees. She couldn't see much from this vantage point but she could hear everything.

"... a flighty girl, Anna, and restless. A girl full of passions," Grandmama was saying.

She's talking about me, Jo realized, her trepidation growing.

"It's best to nip that sort of thing quick, before she takes up painting, or smoking, or, God forbid, writing. Addie tells me she already dabbles in her school's newspaper."

"She doesn't *dabble*," Phillip said, leaping to Jo's defense. "She's a good writer. Which is not a sign of flightiness, by the way. It's a sign of intelligence."

Jo felt a rush of gratitude toward her uncle. He was always in her corner.

"I suppose a facility with words can serve a girl well," Grandmama allowed. "After all, one must communicate with tradesmen to save one's husband the task, but that should be the end of it. That queer Edith Jones was overfond of books," she added darkly. "But Teddy Wharton cured her of it. The Whartons are sporting people, you know. They don't go in much for books. Edith was lucky to snare him. She was lucky to snare *anyone*. She was twenty-three when she married. Twenty-three! No children yet, and it's been five years. If you ask me, the best way to settle a girl is to marry her off young and make her a mother before there's time for any odd ideas to take hold. I see it in my bitches. The longer bad habits are indulged, the harder they are to break."

"Grandmama, *do* come and say hello to Mrs. DePeyster. She's asking for you." That was Bram's mother. She'd just walked over to the group.

"Why can't Theodora come here?" Grandmama asked petulantly.

"Because her knees are paining her."

Jo heard Grandmama get to her feet. "Bad breeding," she said smugly. "Theodora was a Montgomery. They *all* have weak bones."

"She's intolerable!" Jo's mother hissed, after Grandmama had left. "How dare she compare my daughter to a spaniel!"

"Perhaps you should have Mrs. Nelson put out marrow bones for the young ladies present instead of lemon wafers," said her uncle mischievously.

Jo bit back a laugh.

"Do *not* make jokes, Phillip. Can you believe that she wants Jo to go to the Young Patrons' Ball? It's completely out of the question."

Jo felt relief wash over her. She was out of the woods.

"Grandmama's worse than usual, I agree, but there's a reason for it: Peter had a terrible spell last week. He recovered, but only barely. The doctor says he won't survive another such attack. She's desperate to see Bram married," her uncle said solemnly.

Oh, no, Jo thought, upset by the news of Mr. Aldrich's bad turn—and by what it might mean for her.

"I'm very sorry to hear it, but Jo can't accept a proposal now," her mother insisted. "The Aldriches must wait until her mourning has ended."

Phillip was silent for a moment; then he said, "And if they do not? You know as well as I do that Bram's the most suitable match for Jo. The Aldriches will attend the ball, as they always do. Bram wishes to escort Jo. If he cannot, he may take another young lady."

"And *you* know that Jo's the most suitable match for Bram. There *is* no other young lady," Jo's mother said haughtily. "Not in her league."

"There *is*, Anna."

"Who?"

Jo knew the answer.

"Elizabeth Adams," her uncle said.

Anna laughed dismissively.

"She may not be in Jo's league socially, but she's very determined, and determination can carry a girl a long way. I'm out and about during my mourning, as men must be. I frequently run into Bram, and I've noticed that Miss Adams has begun to keep him company. . . ."

Phillip lowered his voice and Jo could no longer hear what he was saying. She risked parting the palm fronds and saw her mother give her uncle a curt nod. Her heart sank. She didn't need to hear more to know what had happened.

Thanks to Grandmama, that old battle-ax, she was going to the Young Patrons' Ball.

✈ *CHAPTER TWENTY-SEVEN* ✦

Jo, standing on the stoop of a tenement on Varick Street, tried not to stare at the large, naked breast in front of her. Pale and blue-veined, it spilled out of its owner's grimy blouse and hung down to her waist.

She'd never seen such a large breast. She had never seen any breasts except her own, which were nowhere near as generously sized. A small baby was attached to the breast, sucking greedily.

"*I'm* Eleanor Owens. What's this about?" the woman whose breast Jo was staring at asked. Two small children peeked out shyly from behind her skirts.

"Good morning," Jo said, lifting her eyes to the woman's face. She had rehearsed her story carefully. "I'm looking for an Eleanor Owens who was employed as a cleaner by Van Houten Shipping. Would that happen to be you?"

"No, it wouldn't. And I don't know nothing about no Van Houten Shipping," the woman said anxiously. "Is this other Eleanor Owens in some kind of trouble? Are there going to be coppers coming to my door?"

Jo felt discouraged but forced herself to smile. "Not at all. Miss

Owens recently left the firm's employ but failed to collect her last week's wages," she fibbed. "She gave no forwarding address. We are trying to track her down and give her the monies owed."

The woman looked relieved. "Wish I *was* her. I could use the money."

Jo looked at the two children, still hiding behind their mother. They were barefoot. Their clothing was ragged.

"As it happens, the firm has authorized me to recompense any persons inconvenienced by their inquiries," she said.

She hadn't rehearsed this part of the story, but the words came out smoothly nonetheless.

"Beg your pardon?" The woman looked confused.

"I can pay you a dollar for taking up your time," Jo said. She handed the delighted woman the money, bade her good day, and returned to the hansom cab she'd hired. It was a small, two-wheeled carriage pulled by a single horse. Enclosed at the sides and open at the front, it was light and maneuverable. Its driver sat above and behind the passengers.

"One Twenty-Six East Thirty-Sixth Street, please," Jo told him as she climbed back in.

Katie, her maid, was waiting for her.

"You'll come to a bad end, miss, if you carry on with unsuitable men," she said in her heavy Irish brogue. "My cousin's husband's sister Maeve? *She* stepped out with an *actor*. He put her in the family way then skipped off. When Maeve's father found out, he threw her into the street. She had to go into a workhouse. Lost the baby and bled to death. Wound up in a pauper's grave at eighteen. Dug it herself, she did, and her fancy man handed her the shovel."

"Why, thank you for that very uplifting story, Katie," Jo said, giving her a look. "However, I am *not* carrying on with an unsuitable man."

"Then why are you sneaking off at night? During the day, now, too. Telling your mother you'll be one place, then going somewhere else."

"To gather facts for a story I'm working on," Jo replied.

Katie raised an eyebrow. "What's the story about?" she asked.

"I can't tell you. Not yet."

"Because there is no story, is there now, Miss Jo?" Katie asked.

"Of course there is. Would I be going to such lengths if there weren't?"

Katie's look of skepticism deepened to one of worry. "This foolishness all started with Mr. Montfort's passing. You haven't been the same since you lost him," she said. "Everyone says so. Cook. The other maids. 'Miss Jo's not herself,' they say. 'Miss Jo's acting very odd.'"

"Do you want that black velvet coat in the window of Lord and Taylor's or not?" Jo asked, fed up with Katie's ominous pronouncements.

"I'd trade a seat in heaven at the right hand of God for that coat."

"Then keep quiet or you won't get the extra dollar I promised you."

Katie pantomimed locking her lips and throwing away the key.

"We'll see how long *that* lasts," Jo said.

Katie glared. She smoothed her skirt. Inspected her boots. Straightened her hat. Finally, the words burst out of her. "Why do you have to get up to such tricks—"

"Ten seconds. A new record."

"—when you have the ball coming up and a dress to decide on and new shoes to buy? Who could want more than that?"

"Anyone with a brain," Jo replied.

"You should have stayed at Miss Addie's. With Miss Jennie and Miss Caroline. That's where you told Mrs. Montfort you'd be," Katie said reproachfully. "I was to walk you there, wait for you, and see you home. Mrs. Montfort didn't say anything about gallivanting through the city."

"I'd hardly call this gallivanting. And besides, I couldn't stay at the party. It was too dangerous. I nearly died."

"From what?"

"Boredom."

Addie Aldrich had invited Jo, Caroline, and Jennie for tea. The purpose of the gathering was to talk about the Young Patrons' Ball and what everyone would be wearing.

Her mother had been of two minds about letting her go to Addie's tea, but as usual, her uncle intervened. He'd said young ladies in mourning needed time with friends, and her mother had relented. Jo had been glad. She didn't care about the tea, but she was very excited at the thought of leaving it—early.

After spending an hour talking about ball gowns, which interested Jo not at all since she couldn't wear one and had to go dressed in black, she'd excused herself, saying she felt fatigued. Her friends had traded anxious glances. Jennie said maybe she ought to see a doctor. Jo thanked them for their concern and assured them all she needed was a rest. As soon as she and Katie turned the corner, though, she'd hailed a cab. She had three hours until she was expected home and intended to put them to good use.

"Headstrong girls *always* end badly," Katie said now.

"Headstrong is just a word, Katie—a word others call you when you don't do what they want," Jo said.

She reached for the notebook that was resting beside her on the seat and flipped it open. She'd had Katie buy it for her at Woolworth's. It was just like Eddie's. Six addresses were written on the notebook's first page. Four had been crossed out. Jo drew a line through *84 Varick Street* now. That made five dead ends.

Eleanor Owens b. 1874, Jo's father had written in his agenda. She assumed the *b.* stood for Eleanor's birth year, which would make her sixteen, but wasn't positive, so she decided to pursue every Eleanor Owens in the city, regardless of age, to see if they had any connection to Van Houten. She'd found some of the addresses in a city directory Theakston kept in the butler's pantry, and a few more during an outing that was supposed to have been made to the Metropolitan Museum to contemplate the statuary but had been secretly diverted to the Bureau of Vital Records.

After leaving Addie's house and crisscrossing the city all afternoon to knock on doors, Jo had determined that none of the Eleanor Owenses whose addresses she'd written down was the one she was after. One of them was fifty, one was seventy-eight, one was six, one was two, and the woman she'd just interviewed looked about thirty. Jo had used her cleaner story with all of them, except the two children. None had any connection to Van Houten.

Now Jo had one last address to try. She'd found information for this last Eleanor at the Bureau of Vital Records. According to her birth certificate, her parents were Samuel Owens and Lavinia Archer Owens, and they lived on Thirty-Sixth Street. At least, they had in 1848, the year of Eleanor's birth. Hopefully, they were still there. The address was in a genteel section of Murray Hill. Jo knew that no cleaning woman would live there. She'd have to devise another story.

"Mr. Theakston knows you're up to something," Katie said, interrupting her thoughts. "I heard him tell Mrs. Nelson. You're lucky he didn't catch you the last time you snuck out. He will sooner or later, though. He'll go straight to Mrs. Montfort, and *then* you'll be in for it!" She narrowed her eyes. "What did you do that night, anyway?"

What didn't I do? Jo thought, thinking back a week ago to her trip to the waterfront. *I went to the waterfront, met a lock picker and a pickpocket, broke into Van Houten, and kissed Eddie Gallagher.*

The memory of the kisses they shared still warmed her, but she frowned now, recalling something Eddie *hadn't* shared with her. Something that still puzzled her.

"Katie, have you ever heard of a woman called Della McEvoy?" she asked.

Katie turned white. "God in heaven, miss, is *that* where you went? Please tell me it wasn't."

"It wasn't. I told you, I'm working on a story. Della's name was mentioned by one of my sources. Who is she?"

"I can't tell you," Katie said. "It's not proper. I wouldn't feel right about it."

Jo took a dollar note out of her pocket and dangled it in front of her maid. "Would this ease your troubled conscience?"

Katie snatched it. "Della McEvoy sells girls," she said. "To men."

Jo remembered the scantily clad women in the doorway of Della's; she remembered George Adams and Teddy Farnham stumbling down the stoop.

"What do you mean *sells* women?" she asked, mystified. "To work for them?"

"No, not to work for them. At least, not in the way you're thinking. Della sells girls for the night."

Jo thought of Theakston and the many jobs he did after dark. "To do what? Polish silver?" she asked. "Wind clocks?"

"No! Della keeps a disorderly house."

"I don't care how messy she is," Jo said, growing irritated. "What does she *do*?"

"For goodness' sake, miss," Katie said, exasperated. "Della McEvoy is a procurer. A madam. A female pimp. She runs a brothel. The girls who live in it have sex with men for money. They're called prostitutes. Does that explain it plainly enough?"

Jo sat back in her seat, shocked. "How do you know this?"

Katie snorted. "How could I not? Della's only one of many. Disorderly houses are all over the city. You'd know that if you had to walk everywhere instead of taking a carriage. Stroll through the Tenderloin sometime. The girls are practically hanging out the windows—and their corsets. They'll come right up to a fellow on the street, bold as brass."

Jo recalled a conversation she'd had with Trudy. "Are they like mistresses?" she asked.

"A mistress has it easy. She's only got to contend with one man. He pays her rent. Pays her bills. Some do quite well for themselves. Della's girls, they go with whoever wants them," Katie explained.

"But what becomes of these girls? After they . . . they . . ." Jo wasn't sure how to say what she meant.

"After they lie down for every Tom, Dick, and Harry with a dollar in his pocket? They don't last long, most of them. They catch diseases," Katie said.

"How *awful*," Jo said, shuddering. "Why do they do it?"

Katie looked at Jo as if she were an idiot. "Because they've got no choice, miss. Maybe someone's abused them—a funny uncle or stepfather. Maybe they're hungry and can't find a proper job. Maybe they're addicted to drink or dope, and the madams give it to them. There are hundreds of reasons. As many reasons as there are girls."

Jo was suddenly embarrassed that she'd ever asked Eddie about Della. Her embarrassment deepened as she remembered the man at his boardinghouse who'd thought she was from a house like Della's. He'd assumed she was a prostitute simply because she was walking on her own in the city at night. Men could walk the city at night and no one thought the worse of them, but a woman walking alone . . . that was scandalous enough to get oneself labeled a prostitute.

Jo bristled at the unfairness of it, but then her cab arrived at Thirty-Sixth Street and she had to put her feelings aside. The Owens house was situated midway between Lexington and Third Avenues on the south side of the street. A narrow alley ran between it and the house next door. After telling the driver to wait and Katie to stay put, Jo alighted, climbed the stoop, and knocked.

A few seconds later, the door opened. "May I help you, miss?" inquired a smiling butler.

"I hope so," Jo said. "I'm looking for Eleanor Owens."

The butler's smile curdled. "There's no one here by that name," he said brusquely, closing the door.

"Wait, please!" Jo said, stopping it with her hand. "Can you tell me where she's gone?"

"I must ask you to release the door," the butler said coldly.

"Mr. Baxter, is everything all right?" A maid carrying a coal scuttle had stopped on her way through the foyer. She looked Jo up and down.

"Perfectly fine, Sally. Go about your business," the butler ordered.

"What's going on, Baxter?" another voice said. It belonged to a well-dressed, gray-haired man who'd appeared in the doorway.

The butler took a step back and Jo saw her chance. She quickly pulled a calling card from her pocket and handed it to the gray-haired man. It was a terrible risk using her real name, but she had no choice. An Eleanor Owens had lived here. Maybe *her* Eleanor Owens. She had to find out where she'd gone.

"Mr. Owens, I presume? My name's Josephine Montfort. I'm searching for an Eleanor Owens, and I wondered if perhaps—"

The man's face darkened. "There's no Eleanor Owens here," he said.

"Samuel? Who's that at the door?" a woman's voice, tremulous and thin, called from within.

"Mr. Owens, if I may—" Jo started to say.

"You may not. Good day," the man said. He tore up her calling card, threw the pieces on the floor, and slammed the door in her face.

Jo stood there, blinking at the brass door knocker, flabbergasted. "You're lying, Mr. Owens," she said. "I know you are. What I don't know is *why*." She turned, still smarting from the rude treatment she'd received, and walked down the stoop.

"I guess *that* line of inquiry is cut off," Katie said archly as Jo climbed back inside the cab. "Where to now, Nellie Bly?"

"Home," Jo said with a sigh.

"Thank goodness."

Jo sank down in her seat, despondent not to have found Eleanor Owens. *Eddie would have found her,* she thought. *He's a real reporter, not a pretend one like me.*

She pictured his handsome face and wondered what he was doing now, on a Wednesday afternoon. Sitting at his desk at the *Standard* typing madly, she imagined. How lucky he was, she thought, to be able to do something important with his life. Something that mattered.

The cab made its way east, then turned onto Park Avenue and headed south. To Gramercy Square. And her house. And a long, dreary evening full of nothing that mattered.

❧ CHAPTER TWENTY-EIGHT ❧

Jo stared up at her bedroom ceiling and counted the number of squares in the pressed tin. It was eight a.m., time to start her day, but she didn't want to get out of bed. If she did, she'd have to look at it—her gown for the Young Patrons' Ball.

It had arrived from the dressmaker's yesterday. It was black, of course, with a high neck and long sleeves. Katie had hung it over the door of her wardrobe so the creases would fall out. It floated there now, at the edge of Jo's vision, like a specter.

Jo turned on her side, away from her wardrobe, so she couldn't see the gown. She was still annoyed with Grandmama for insisting she attend the ball. She didn't want to go in the least.

Except maybe she did.

Because Eddie Gallagher was a cad. And she was an ungrateful wretch who should be thanking her lucky stars that a decent man like Bram Aldrich wanted to take her to the biggest social event of the season.

It had been nine days since she'd seen Eddie, since he'd kissed her in the shadow of Della McEvoy's, and she hadn't heard a word from him. He couldn't pay a visit, of course, and they didn't have a telephone—her mother thought them vulgar—so he couldn't call. But he hadn't even sent a note. Every time the post arrived, Jo had eagerly sifted through it, looking for something from Edwina Gallagher, and every time she'd been disappointed.

She told herself he hadn't written because he had nothing new to tell her, and she tried her best to believe it. But he could've written for another reason—to tell her that her eyes were like limpid pools of moonlight and her lips were as soft as rose petals, or whatever it was that sweethearts wrote to each other.

The day after he'd kissed her, all she could think of was how wonderful those kisses were. Now, convinced he didn't care for her, she wondered why he'd kissed her at all. And why she'd kissed him back. What had she been thinking? She'd never kissed Bram on his lips, and she'd known him her entire life. Why had she been so forward with a boy she barely knew?

Jo groaned, suffering an agony of remorse, and pulled her pillow over her head. She would have stayed that way all day, but a knock on her door got her going. It was Katie with her morning tea.

"You'll want to drink up quickly, miss," she said. "There's a girl here to see you. She says it's urgent."

Jo sat up, intrigued. "It's a bit early for visitors. Who is she?"

"A Miss Sally Gibson. She apologized for the early hour, but said she's out on an errand for her employer and can't stay long."

"How strange. I don't know anyone by that name. What does she want?"

"She wouldn't tell me. All she would say is that she has something *you* want."

Jo threw back her covers and got out of bed, eager to meet the mysterious Miss Gibson.

"Where's Theakston? Where's my mother?" she asked, tugging at her nightgown. "Help me get this thing off."

"Mr. Theakston's at the florist's ordering the weekly arrangements. Mrs. Montfort is at the cemetery. She left half an hour ago. After she visits your father's grave, she plans to call on your aunt Madeleine," Katie said, lifting Jo's nightgown over her head.

"Good, I should have at least an hour before Theakston returns. Longer for Mama," Jo said.

She stood naked as the day she was born as Katie handed her a pair of bloomers. She felt no self-consciousness in front of her maid. Someone—a nanny, a maid—had been dressing her her entire life. Jo stepped into the bloomers and buttoned them at the back. Next, she pulled on a cotton chemise. A stiff silk corset went over that. Jo held it in place as Katie tightened the laces. Finally, a dress—one made of black crêpe—went over her head.

"I can manage the buttons," Jo said. "Do my hair, would you? Then take Miss Gibson into the drawing room."

Katie brushed Jo's hair, pinned it up, and hurried downstairs. Jo finished with the long row of buttons, brushed her teeth, and followed her.

Sally Gibson, small and sly-looking, was standing by the piano holding a silver vase as Jo entered the drawing room. She was inspecting the hallmark on its base.

"Are you an admirer of Louis Tiffany's work, Miss Gibson?" Jo asked archly.

Sally turned to Jo and Jo realized she *did* know her—at least, she knew who she was. "You're the Owenses' maid," she said.

"Yes, I am," Sally said.

"Why are you here?" Jo asked.

Sally gave Jo a cunning smile. "To tell you about Eleanor Owens," she said, putting the vase down. "If you make it worth my while."

✈ CHAPTER TWENTY-NINE ✦

Jo's pulse leapt like a highly strung horse, but she quickly reined it in. She was excited by this unexpected turn of events, but wary, too.

"How did you find me, Miss Gibson?" Jo asked.

"I picked up the pieces of your calling card. The ones his lordship threw on the floor," Sally said sarcastically.

Jo remembered handing Mr. Owens her calling card when she visited his home two days ago, and Mr. Owens tearing it up.

"I'm going to get right down to business, Miss Montfort," said Sally. "I know all about Miss Eleanor, and I'll tell you everything— for twenty dollars."

"That's a good deal of money, Miss Gibson," Jo said coolly.

"For some, maybe," Sally said, taking in Jo's well-appointed drawing room.

"I'm looking for information on Miss Owens because I want to solve a crime. Perhaps you should tell me about her not for money, but because it's the right thing to do," Jo suggested.

Sally snorted. "As far as I'm concerned, the right thing to do is to get a bit of cash together so I can go to Coney Island next summer."

"Five dollars," Jo offered. "Your Eleanor Owens may not be the one I'm seeking."

"Fifteen."

"Ten."

"Done."

"Please sit down, Miss Gibson. I'll be back in a moment," Jo said.

She hurried to her bedroom to get the money. On her way, she saw Katie and asked her to bring refreshments to the drawing room. A few minutes later, with ten dollars in her purse and a cup of tea in her hand, Sally started to talk.

"Eleanor was Mr. and Mrs. Owens's only child," she said. "She grew up at the house on Thirty-Sixth Street, but she went away."

"Why wouldn't Mr. Owens tell me that?" Jo asked.

"He never talks about her. No one else is allowed to, either," Sally explained. "It all started when Miss Eleanor fell in love with a man her parents didn't approve of. He was divorced. He had no children, but the Owenses wouldn't allow Eleanor to even consider a divorced man. At least, that's what Mrs. Kroger said."

"Who's Mrs. Kroger?" asked Jo.

"The Owenses' cook," Sally replied, helping herself to a lemon wafer. "Or rather, she *was*. She died two years ago. She's the one who told me Eleanor's story. She said that Eleanor got engaged secretly. Her fiancé had to travel for his work—to Zanzibar in Africa—but promised to marry her when he returned."

Jo's ears pricked up at that. Van Houten had offices in Zanzibar. Her father and uncle had spent time there as young men, overseeing the firm's eastern base of operations.

"Her fiancé bought her a ring with sapphires and diamonds in it," Sally continued, "and he gave her a pendant in the shape of half a heart with his name engraved on it. The other half, which he kept, had her name on it. They met secretly at night in the weeks before he left. In a bower in the Owenses' garden. The house has an alley running along one side, as you might've noticed. There's a brick wall between the alley and the garden. It has a wooden door in it that bolts from the garden side. Eleanor would unlock it at midnight and let him in."

Sally brushed cookie crumbs off her skirt. "One thing led to another and Eleanor ended up in the family way. She didn't find out until after her beau had left. She wrote him immediately, but mail takes a long time to get from New York to Zanzibar and it was well over a month before he received her letter. And then it took another month for his reply to arrive. He told Eleanor that she was not to worry, that he would come for her. But by then she was showing, and her father was furious. He and Mrs. Owens told everyone that Eleanor had gone away on a tour of Europe, but really they'd locked her up in her room. All she could do was read and make things for the baby—clothes and toys. And wait for her beau. But he didn't come. When it was her time, she was taken to Darkbriar in the dead of night."

"Darkbriar?" Jo echoed, confused. "Why? That's an insane asylum."

"Eleanor became difficult," Sally explained. "She tried to break out of her room several times. She insisted on keeping the baby. She flew into rages and had weeping fits. The Owenses said she was not in her right mind and had her committed."

Jo knew Darkbriar; she'd seen it countless times. It had been built in the early 1800s as a place for the wealthy to hide family members who heard voices or saw things that weren't there. It was situated on the edge of the East River, between Thirty-Fourth and Forty-Second Streets on what had once been brambled farmland. The city had long since pushed up to its gates, but behind them, Darkbriar brooded, its stone buildings blackened with soot, its cemetery dotted with headstones, its shady grounds sheltering well-dressed, hollow-eyed men and women.

"And did Eleanor have her baby there?" she asked, grimacing at the idea of being forced to deliver a child in an asylum.

"She did. It was a girl. Mrs. Kroger saw her. She said she was pretty, with blond hair and blue eyes. The delivery was hard, though. Eleanor took ill with a fever. The baby died."

"How awful," Jo said, saddened. She hadn't expected a story as grim as the one Sally was telling her.

"I suppose it was," Sally said, as if the thought had never occurred to her before. "A Mr. Francis Mallon, one of the orderlies, had the baby buried on the grounds. He gave the death certificate to Mrs. Kroger but instructed her not to tell Eleanor the truth. Her rages were getting worse, Mr. Mallon said, and her doctor didn't think she could cope with the death of her baby."

Jo poured more tea into Sally's teacup. Sally shoveled sugar into it, stirred in some milk, and reached for another cookie—as comfortable in Jo's drawing room as if it were her own.

"When Eleanor recovered, she asked for her child," Sally said. "She had to be told something, so Mr. Mallon told her that the baby was well and had been taken to an orphanage, along with all the pretty things Eleanor had made for her, and that she'd be placed in a good home with loving parents. He'd hoped that would calm her, but it didn't. A few days later, she broke a window, attacked him with a shard of glass, and escaped."

"My word," Jo said, amazed by Eleanor's courage. "Where did she go?"

"To search for her baby. She went to every orphanage in the city, begging for the child. But of course no orphanage had her; she was dead. When Eleanor's parents heard she'd escaped, they asked the police to find her, but Eleanor eluded them. Mrs. Kroger saw her once. She tried to talk to her but Eleanor ran away."

"Is she still on the streets?" asked Jo hopefully. If Eleanor was in the city, perhaps she could be found.

"No, she's dead," said Sally, dashing Jo's hopes. "Her body was pulled out of the East River two months after she escaped from Darkbriar. A fisherman found her off Corlears Hook. It wasn't possible to identify her properly. By her face, I mean. The fish . . . well, you can imagine. The authorities identified her by the jacket she was wearing and a piece of jewelry—a pocket watch her parents gave her for her eighteenth birthday. Her pendant was gone—the one with her fiancé's name on it. So was her engagement ring. The police said she was probably robbed and then pushed into the water by the thieves. In their haste, they missed her watch."

"When did this happen?" Jo asked, remembering that her father had written down a date by Eleanor Owens's name in his agenda.

"Eleanor had the baby in 1874," Sally replied.

Jo sat back in her chair. She couldn't believe it. She'd actually found the Eleanor Owens in her father's agenda, and had learned that 1874 was not *Eleanor's* birth year but her *child's*. Jo was elated, but the feeling dissipated as she realized that she still didn't have the answer to the most important question: *why* did her father make the notation in his agenda? Who was Eleanor Owens to him?

An ugly thought had gripped her when she'd first seen the notation, and it came rushing back at her now. Could *he* have been the father of Eleanor's child? And if so, did that have something to do with his death?

Jo did some quick calculations in her head. Her father had been in Zanzibar in 1874, just like Eleanor's fiancé. Jo felt a sickening dread in the pit of her stomach. Had he been with Eleanor Owens before he left? He'd been married to Jo's mother then. Had he been carrying on with Eleanor at the same time? Had he told her some ridiculous story to hide that he was married?

"What about the baby's father? Did he ever return from Zanzibar?" she asked apprehensively.

"No, he didn't," Sally said.

Jo tried to keep her voice steady. "Do you know who he was? Do you recall his name?"

"He was a partner in . . . Oh, what's that big shipping firm called? Van Houten! That's it."

Jo felt sick. "Please, Miss Gibson," she said. "You must tell me his *name.*"

❧ CHAPTER THIRTY ❧

"Stephen Smith."

Jo closed her eyes and exhaled raggedly, immensely relieved.

"Are you all right, miss?" Sally asked, peering at her closely.

"Quite," Jo said, regaining her composure.

"Stephen Smith, it turns out, died at sea," Sally explained. "Seventeen years ago. Shortly before he was due to return to New York."

Jo knew that. The first time she'd ever seen Smith's portrait, during a trip to Van Houten's, she'd asked her father who he was. She knew the faces in the other six portraits, but not his.

"Mr. Smith drowned," her father had replied. "A long time ago. His ship was lost in the Indian Ocean during a storm." She'd wanted to know more, but his tone had been forbidding, so she hadn't pressed him.

"Mrs. Kroger didn't think that Eleanor ever knew Mr. Smith had drowned," said Sally. "She was in Darkbriar by the time his death made the papers here. It might've been a comfort to her to know she hadn't been abandoned. He was a nice man, Mrs. Kroger said. Mrs. Kroger always felt bad about what had happened. *Unsettled.* That's the word she used."

"Unsettled? Why?" Jo asked.

Sally refilled her teacup. "Because Stephen Smith had a se-cret. At least, that's what Mrs. Kroger said. He found something out about his firm. Something terrible. And he felt he had to set it right. He sent Eleanor packets. They contained some kind of pa-pers having to do with the secret. Manifests, I think they're called. Mr. Owens wouldn't allow correspondence from him to enter the house, so Mrs. Kroger would meet the postman, take anything from Mr. Smith, and smuggle it in to Eleanor. Mr. Smith wanted Eleanor to keep the papers safe until he returned."

The hair on the back of Jo's neck stood up.

Kinch had also talked about manifests—with Mr. Scully at Van Houten's. *There's proof. There are manifests, signed and stamped,* he'd said.

Kinch, like Smith, had a secret. He'd been on a ship with African crew members. Had he been in Africa, too? And he knew Scully. He called him Richard. And Scully knew Kinch, despite his tattoos. *Your aspect is greatly altered. I would not know you but for your eyes,* he'd said.

And Kinch, like Smith, had lost a *her.* Maybe a woman, not a ship, just as Jo had suspected when she and Eddie talked about Kinch at the waterfront.

Could it be? she wondered, with mounting excitement. *Could Kinch be Stephen Smith?*

He has *to be,* she thought. *Africa, manifests, Van Houten, a secret— there are too many similarities for it to be coincidence. It makes sense. It fits together perfectly.*

Except for one rather inconvenient fact, a voice inside her coun-tered. *Stephen Smith is dead.*

Jo racked her brain, desperate to see if there was something she was missing, something that could make the impossible possible. If there was, it eluded her. She decided to take a different tack.

"Miss Gibson, did Mrs. Kroger ever tell you what terrible thing Stephen Smith discovered?" Jo asked bravely. She feared the answer to her question as much as she'd feared learning the identity of Eleanor Owens's lover.

"No. Miss Eleanor never told her," Sally replied.

"Mrs. Kroger had *no* idea what was in those papers?"

Sally shook her head. "She questioned Miss Eleanor about it. She even asked to see the papers, but Miss Eleanor refused. All she ever said about them was 'The letters are safe under the heavens. The gods watch over them. And us.'"

"The letters were never found?"

"No. After Miss Eleanor went into the asylum, Mrs. Kroger looked everywhere for them. She thought if she could get Mr. and Mrs. Owens to read them, they might see that Mr. Smith was an upstanding man and change their opinion of him. But she never found them. And then Miss Eleanor died and there wasn't a reason to keep looking."

Jo gripped the arms of her chair, electrified by that last piece of information.

"This next question is very important, Miss Gibson," she said urgently. "Did a man with very marked facial tattoos—black swirls and spikes—ever visit the Owenses?"

"*I* never saw such a person," Sally replied. "And I can't imagine Mr. Baxter opening the door to a man who looked like that."

"Did Mrs. Kroger ever mention such a man visiting?"

"No, and she certainly would have mentioned it. She was the talkative type."

"Was the Owenses' house ever broken into?" Jo asked.

"Not to my knowledge," Sally said.

Jo sat back in her chair, her mind working over what Sally had just told her.

Kinch and Stephen Smith are the same man—I don't know how

they are, but they are—and that man is a liar, she realized. *He bluffed Richard Scully, and probably my father, too. He doesn't have the manifests. They're still wherever Eleanor Owens hid them.*

Jo knew what her next step was: she had to find those manifests. They would certainly tell her what terrible thing Van Houten was accused of doing.

Jo regarded the opportunistic Sally. "I'm told Atlantic City is much nicer than Coney Island," she said.

"I'm sure it is, Miss Montfort. And a damn sight more expensive," Sally retorted.

"I shouldn't think that would be a problem for an enterprising girl like you."

Sally raised an eyebrow. "Have something in mind, do you?"

Jo smiled. "As a matter of fact, Miss Gibson, I do."

✵ CHAPTER THIRTY-ONE ✵

Letter from Miss Edwina Gallagher to
Miss Josephine Montfort

October 24, 1890

Dear Jo,
Writing in haste . . . Bill Hawkins never heard of the
Bonaventure *and Jackie Shaw's not in town, but I got myself*
into Van Houten's office twice with the help of Tumbler. I've
worked my way through half of the firm's ledgers but haven't
found anything on the Bonaventure *yet. I'm going to keep going*
back until I've gone through everything. I'm telling you this to
keep you in the know, but you're not to come downtown. Don't
even think about it. Sit tight. I'll keep you apprised.

Yours,

EG

Letter from Mr. Joseph Feen to Mr. Edward Gallagher

October 24, 1890

Dear Eddie,

I'm sorry to hear that your time at Van Houten has not proved fruitful. You might be interested to know that Eleanor Owens is dead, but she had a daughter with Stephen Smith in 1874. Sadly, the child is also dead. Mr. Smith, it appears, believed something untoward took place at Van Houten's. Just as Kinch does. In fact, there are many similarities between the two. Smith sent documents to Eleanor. Could they be the manifests Kinch spoke of? They contain answers we need, I'm sure of it. I'm going to try to find them. I'm telling you this to keep you in the know, but you are not to come uptown. Don't even think about it. Sit tight. I'll keep you apprised.

Yours,

JM

→ CHAPTER THIRTY-TWO ←

"The Phillip Montforts, ma'am," Theakston said, handing Anna Montfort a calling card.

He bowed and left the drawing room. A few minutes later, Jo's uncle, aunt, and cousin came in, all ruddy-cheeked. Phillip was rubbing his hands together and exclaiming about the crisp autumn air. Madeleine and Caroline had cashmere shawls wrapped about their shoulders. They joined Anna near the fireplace as Jo poured tea. It was a blustery Tuesday afternoon.

Jo greeted her relatives so warmly, they never would have guessed she was miserable.

Thirteen days had now elapsed since she'd last seen Eddie Gallagher, and she'd had only one very businesslike note from him. She was more worried than ever that she'd badly misjudged what occurred between them, and that the kisses they'd shared were nothing more than a pleasant diversion for him. Why hadn't he written a more intimate note? Why hadn't he tried to see her?

"Mrs. Nelson's lemon wafers! My favorite!" Phillip exclaimed as Jo's mother passed a plate of the delicate, buttery cookies. He ate one, then said, "Anna, I have some good news for you. Charles's lumber mills are all but sold."

"Oh, Phillip, that *is* good news!" Anna said, smiling.

Jo smiled, too, feigning enthusiasm for the conversation.

"The buyer is serious, and I expect to finalize the sale before year's end," Phillip added.

"And Van Houten?" Anna asked. "How is that proceeding?"

"The transfer of Charles's shares to the remaining partners is under way. The paperwork should be completed next month."

"I can't thank you enough," Anna said. "I'm so grateful to you for handling Charles's affairs."

Phillip held up his hands. "Don't thank me yet, Anna. There's still the *Standard* to be gotten rid of, and that's proving trickier."

Jo was no longer feigning interest in the conversation. She looked at her uncle over the top of her teacup.

"How so?" Anna asked.

Phillip took a sip of tea and placed his cup back in its saucer. "The newspaper business had become a tawdry one, I'm afraid. No matter how hard I try to enforce a civilized tone at the *Standard*, I fail. The sooner we're rid of it, the better," he said.

Anna sat forward in her chair, a concerned expression on her face. "Surely Mr. Stoatman isn't following the lead of the *Herald* or the *World*," she said.

"No," Phillip replied. "It's not Stoatman who worries me, but rather the quality of reporter he employs."

Jo refreshed her uncle's tea. She was listening raptly now.

"What do you mean, my dear?" Madeleine asked.

"I went to see Stoatman yesterday—we meet once a week—and he was on the telephone when I arrived, so I waited. And while I was outside his office, I overheard a pack of reporters talking, and by God, they *were* a pack—a wolf pack!" Phillip said, his face flushing with anger. "One of them, a strapping, dark-haired boy—Gleeson or Gilligan, some sort of Irish name—was bragging to the others about a story he was writing. He talked about a young woman who was helping him with the story in a most disparaging way. She was doing so because she fancied him, he said. And he, it was quite clear, was encouraging the poor girl for his own ends." Phillip shook his head. "I tell you, I had half a mind to knock the arrogant young fool right on his backside!"

Jo froze, teapot in hand. She felt as though she couldn't breathe.

"Papa!" Caroline scolded.

"I did!" Phillip said indignantly. "I want the *Standard* sold as quickly as possible. Journalism is no longer a business with which this family should be involved. The breed of man who now practices it wants only to claw his way to the top and doesn't care who he steps on to do it. You wouldn't understand, Caro. You either, Jo. You're not parents yet. But I have a daughter and a niece, and to think that someone in my employ would talk about a young woman so makes my blood boil."

Jo forced herself to take a breath. She placed the teapot back on its tray. Eddie had agreed to pursue information on her father because he knew the story of his murder would be a big one and could help him get a better job. Was *he* the reporter her uncle had overhead? Was she herself the poor girl?

"Papa, you're turning into an old curmudgeon!" Caro teased. "Just like Grandmama."

Phillip softened. He patted his daughter's hand. "I suppose I am. I'll have to get myself a walking stick and a dozen spaniels."

Everyone laughed. Everyone, that is, except Jo. She felt sick inside. She was a fool. An impulsive little idiot who knew nothing of men.

"Speaking of Grandmama . . . I hear there's to be a small birthday supper for her soon. Just family and close friends. Here in the city," Madeleine said. "A fortnight after the Young Patrons' Ball."

"I'm sure we'll all be summoned," Anna said archly. "Mourning makes no difference to her."

"Will you go?" Madeleine asked.

Anna gave her a look. "We will *not*. I still can't believe I agreed to let Jo go to the ball."

"She'll only be sitting, not dancing. It will all be very proper," Madeleine said. She turned to Jo. "Has your gown arrived, Jo, dear?"

But Jo, staring into the fire, didn't hear her.

"Jo? What's wrong?" Madeleine asked.

Jo realized she was being addressed. "Nothing, Aunt Maddie. Nothing at all," she said, her voice strained.

Anna and Madeleine traded worried glances.

"I've upset you, Jo, haven't I?" Phillip said unhappily. "I shouldn't discuss untoward topics in front of young ladies. I'm sorry."

"Our Jo is such a sensitive soul," Madeleine said soothingly. "Let's talk of more civilized subjects, shall we?"

Jo pasted on a smile. She nodded agreeably. But Phillip's words echoed in her head:

. . . and he, it was quite clear, was only using the poor girl for his own ends. . . . A strapping, dark-haired boy—Gleeson or Gilligan, some sort of Irish name—

No, Uncle Phillip, not Gleeson or Gilligan, she thought miserably. *You got the name wrong. It's Gallagher.*

❧ CHAPTER THIRTY-THREE ❧

The beautiful girls in their silk dresses looked like a living garden as they whirled across the dance floor. From the chair in which she was sitting, Jo saw the pale pink of peonies, the dusky red of late summer roses—and the vivid larkspur blue of Elizabeth Adams's sensational Paris gown.

"I'm just *waiting* for her to inhale," Caroline Montfort said cattily as she watched Elizabeth waltz with Teddy Farnham. "The second she does, her bosom will burst right out of her bodice. Won't *that* be a sight!"

"You are a wicked girl, Caro," Trudy Van Eyck said. "If you have nothing nice to say"—she paused, then grinned devilishly—"then say it to me."

"Her waist is only sixteen inches around. She told me so," Jennie Rhinelander said. "Just look how that dress fits her!"

"It *is* a beautiful dress," Jo said wistfully, eyeing Elizabeth's magnificent gown. "It's so long since I wore one. All of you look so fetching tonight, not just Elizabeth. Like rare birds of paradise. And me? I look like a sooty old pigeon."

"You don't, Jo. Not at all," Addie said kindly.

"Addie, dear, I look like a serving girl and you know it."

"Oh, miss, would you fetch me some punch?"

It was Bram, holding an empty cup. The waltz had ended. He'd danced it with his mother and had come over to join them.

"Aren't you a funny boy?" Jo said, pretending to be put out.

"I'm only teasing you, Jo," Bram said. "Black suits you."

"Black suits *no one*," Jo retorted.

"It suits a chimney sweep. Or a governess. Or a penguin," Trudy said.

Bram swept a deep bow, took Jo's hand in his, and kissed it. "Or a rare and brilliant star, sparkling brightly against a night sky," he said.

"My word, what's *in* that punch, Bram Aldrich?" Trudy asked. "And where can I get some?"

They all laughed at Trudy's comment. Jennie left to join the dancers, and Bram and the three remaining girls sat out the next waltz to keep Jo company.

Addie, Caro, Trudy—they're all so wonderful to me, Jo thought, surrounded by her friends. *And Bram took pains to tell me I look nice, even though I don't. They're so good, so kind, and I'm so lucky I came to my senses before it was too late. Before I threw away everything for Eddie when he doesn't care for me. Let him find Kinch. Let him solve the murder. Let him bring the whole ugly thing to the attention of the authorities. It's not my place to do so. It never was.*

Jo had been telling herself these things ever since she'd heard her uncle's story about his trip to the *Standard,* and she was at the point now where she very nearly believed them.

Another waltz ended. The conductor announced there would be a quick break, followed by a quadrille. As he did, the couples left the dance floor to seek refreshments. Jennie returned to the group, trailed by Elizabeth Adams. Elizabeth's cheeks were flushed prettily. The blue of her gown set off her cobalt eyes. She said hello to everyone but saved her warmest smile for Bram. Addie caught it and glowered. Caroline rolled her eyes. Jo felt an unwelcome twinge of jealousy.

After a few minutes, the orchestra began to tune up. A Roosevelt and a Van Alstyne swooped in and asked Caroline and Jennie to dance—promising to pay handsomely for the privilege. Caro and Jennie marked their cards and followed the boys to the dance floor. Trudy drifted off to find Gilbert, who did not like balls. Or punch. Or museums. And Jo, Bram, Addie, and Elizabeth stood chatting awkwardly. Bram, a gentleman, did the polite thing and asked Elizabeth to dance since he couldn't ask Jo.

"Don't worry about Elizabeth," Addie said as they headed off. "Bram's only being courteous. He bought out all your dances, didn't he? The museum will make a bundle! Why, I wouldn't be at all surprised if in a few months he were to—"

"Addie Aldrich, there you are!" It was James Schermerhorn, a relation of Jo's. "I've been looking all over for you. Caro needs a fourth couple for her quadrille. Would you honor me with a dance?"

"Oh, Jim, I can't," Addie said. "I don't want to leave Jo all alone."

"Go, Addie," Jo said to her friend. "I couldn't bear the look on Jim's face if you turned him down."

Addie hesitated. "If you're sure you won't be lonely . . ."

"I'll be perfectly fine."

Jo smiled as Jim led Addie to the dance floor. He bowed; she curtsied. They disappeared into a sea of swirling skirts.

The Metropolitan Museum's enormous foyer, with its graceful arches, marble pillars, and soaring ceiling, served as a ballroom tonight. It glowed with the light of a thousand candles. Porcelain vases containing hothouse blooms stood on marble pillars. Waiters in white jackets served cups of punch on silver trays as an orchestra played.

And though Jo could not be part of the ball, she enjoyed watching the dancers. The scene they made was so breathtakingly beautiful, she wished she could press it between the pages of a book and save it forever, just like she used to do with flowers when she was little. The girls were so lovely with their hair swept up, jewels at their pale necks, arms lithe and graceful in white kid gloves, and the boys were dashing and courtly. Her heart filled with emotion because she knew that tonight many of her friends were pairing not only for a dance but for life.

Propose. That's what Addie was going to say earlier, Jo thought. The knot of dread in her stomach—present ever since she'd overheard Grandmama talking about her wish for Jo and Bram to marry— tightened.

What if Bram does ask me someday? What will I say? she wondered.

A streak of blue caught her eye. It was Elizabeth, flashing by with Bram. Jo's eyes lingered on them. They made a handsome couple, and again she felt a stab of jealousy. Her feelings confounded her. One minute she was frightened of encouraging Bram's interest, the next she was scared of losing it.

"You might want to watch out for Miss Adams," her mother had advised as Jo left for the ball. "I understand that she's a girl who has no scruples about taking what doesn't belong to her."

"I shall be certain to guard my watch, then," Jo had cheekily replied.

"You know *exactly* what I mean, Josephine," her mother had said. "It was your uncle's idea that you go to this ball. I was unsure about it at first, but I now believe he's right. It's not wise to be absent from the market too long or you might be left on the shelf."

"You make me sound like a pineapple, Mama. And anyway, haven't you heard? Bram's not taking me. He's taking Annie Jones," Jo had said, mischievously referring to a bearded lady in the employ of Mr. Barnum's circus.

"An overfamiliarity with the amusements of the lower orders does not become a young lady," her mother had retorted frostily.

Jo shuddered at the memory. She'd earned her mother's chilly disapproval with a mere joke. She could only imagine what would've happened if she'd actually told her about Eddie. Thank goodness she hadn't.

Eddie doesn't care. You know that now, she said to herself. *And instead of dreading Bram's proposal, you should be doing everything you can to encourage it. Because he* does *care. And if you don't start acting like* you *do, you'll lose him to Elizabeth Adams.*

Jo's dark thoughts had put a scowl on her face; she could feel it. Certain that girls who scowled did not receive marriage proposals, she smiled brightly and focused once more on the lovely scene before her.

As the orchestra played on, however, the music began to overwhelm her. The scent of the hothouse flowers became cloying, and the dancers, whirling and smiling through the quadrille's complicated steps, seemed like clockwork figures. She glimpsed something dark in the beautiful scene. It showed through the surface like base metal under badly plated jewelry.

The glittering ball, Jo realized, was a symbol of her life. Everything was lovely and perfect as long as each person knew the steps and executed them. The women must only ever watch and wait. The men were the ones who would decide. They would choose. They would lead. And the women would follow. Tonight and forevermore.

Despite her resolutions, Jo's fake smile slipped. She suddenly wanted out—out of this room, out of the ball, out of the small, gilded parakeet's cage she lived in. The feeling was so strong, it was all she could do to stop herself from running for the door.

She wanted a bigger world—the world that Eddie had shown her. She wanted freedom, but what happened to the parakeet once it was free? She knew. Every once in a while, she saw the colorful little bodies of birds that had escaped captivity lying on the ground in Central Park, dead of hunger or cold. And she knew that she had no more idea of how to survive outside her cage than those pretty, fragile, foolish birds.

"Hey, miss," said a voice at her elbow, startling her. "How 'bout a glass of punch?"

What a dreadfully rude waiter, Jo thought. "No, thank you," she said, not even bothering to glance at him.

"It's really good. Have some."

Jo couldn't believe the impertinence of the man. "I am not thirsty at present," she said coldly.

"For Pete's sake, sister, take the punch."

Jo turned, ready to give the insolent fool a piece of her mind. Her sharp words died in her throat, however, as she recognized the blue eyes, the tousled hair, the broad smile.

It was Eddie.

❧ CHAPTER THIRTY-FOUR ❧

"What are you *doing* here?" Jo hissed, glancing around to see if anyone was watching them. Luckily, all eyes were on the dancers.

"Pretending to be a waiter so I could talk to you."

"But how did you—"

"Take the punch, will you?" Eddie said, holding the tray he was carrying out to her. "Before the maître d' who's staring at me realizes I'm *not* a waiter."

Jo did so. She took a sip, then held up a finger, as if asking him to wait for her to empty her cup.

"Nice touch," Eddie said, handing her a napkin.

"Why are you here?" Jo asked, her voice still cold. She hadn't forgotten the story her uncle had told about the callous reporter, or that Eddie had written her only a single terse note since she'd last seen him.

"I'm here because Jackie Shaw's in town," Eddie replied.

Jo's eyes widened, her anger toward him momentarily forgotten. "He's the one Bill Hawkins mentioned, isn't he? The one who might know about the *Bonaventure*," she said.

Eddie nodded. "It's going to cost and I'm broke. Had to pay the rent yesterday. I was hoping you might have a few bucks."

"I do, but not with me. I'll have to—" Jo abruptly stopped speaking. She'd spotted her uncle out of the corner of her eye. He was watching her—and Eddie. She finished her punch, then put the empty glass back on Eddie's tray. Phillip started walking toward them.

"Dip your head," she whispered.

"What?"

"You're a servant. I've just dismissed you. Acknowledge it before my uncle thinks something's amiss."

Eddie did so.

"Meet me upstairs in the sculpture gallery in five minutes. By Cicero."

"But—"

"*Go.*"

Only seconds later, Phillip arrived at her side. "Are you all right, Josephine? Was that man bothering you?" he asked, staring at Eddie's back.

"Not at all, Uncle Phillip," she said. "In fact, he was very kind to me. He noticed I was flushed and brought me a drink."

Phillip frowned with concern. "Are you unwell?"

"Just a little overheated. It's grown so warm in here. I'm going to go and pat some cold water on my cheeks. Please excuse me."

As she walked out of the foyer toward the ladies' lavatory, Jo congratulated herself on her quick thinking. She'd managed to buy herself a few minutes away from the ball and establish an excuse for the premature exit she was already planning. She'd say she was feeling light-headed and wished to go home. It wouldn't be a total lie. She *was* feeling light-headed. Only it wasn't overheatedness that was causing it.

She told herself any excitement she felt was over Jackie Shaw, and the lead he might possibly provide—not Eddie.

But she knew that was a lie. The mere sight of him made her forget herself. He was a flame and she'd gotten burned, and the pain was terrible, yet it didn't make the fire any less alluring.

As soon as she was out of her uncle's sight, she turned right toward a flight of stairs, grabbed her skirts in her hands, and hurried up the steps. She knew her way around the Met. She visited often, but only during daylight hours. The upper floors were dark and deserted now, and it was hard to get her bearings. Moonlight slanted across the statues, giving them a ghostly look. A bench had been moved across the doorway to the sculpture hall to prevent people from entering. Jo didn't see it until it was too late. She barked her shin against it, paused to rub it, then made her way down the long hall to the statue of Cicero.

Eddie was standing behind it, in a shaft of moonlight, still wearing his waiter's garb.

"That jacket is two sizes too big," Jo coolly observed. Her traitorous heart was beating faster than it should, but he didn't have to know that. She would not make a fool of herself again.

"I sneaked in and gave a guy my last dollar to let me borrow it," Eddie said. "There was no other way to speak with you. Seems my invite got lost in the mail."

"How did you know I'd be here?" Jo asked, her tone still unfriendly.

Eddie smiled. "It's the biggest social event of the season. Where else would Miss Josephine Montfort of Gramercy Square be?"

Jo didn't return the smile. She was in no mood to be teased. Not by him.

Eddie grimaced. "Is it just me or is it chilly in here?" he said.

Jo looked away.

"Did I do something wrong?" he asked. "Look, I'm sorry I came here. I probably put you in a bad position. I didn't want to, but there was no other—"

Jo looked at him. There was confusion on his face and hurt in the depths of his eyes. Could her uncle have been mistaken? Could he have overheard some other reporter? She bit her lip. What she was about to do was foolish, but she couldn't help herself.

"Eddie, are you sorry?" she asked.

"I just said so, didn't I?"

"I meant for the other night." Jo hated herself for asking, but she had to know. "I . . . I haven't heard from you for a good two weeks. Except for a rather businesslike note. Is that why? Because you're sorry? About what happened between us, I mean?"

"No, Jo. That's *not* why. Work is why. I'm at the *Standard* all day, and at night I'm working any lead I can find on Kinch and . . ." He trailed off. He sighed deeply. "Just, um . . . forget it."

Jo looked at him quizzically.

"Look, everything I just said is a load of horse— It's total bunk. The truth is, I've barely slept since I last saw you. I think about you all the time. I never wanted . . . I didn't . . . Oh hell, Jo!" he said, throwing his hands up. "I shouldn't be saying these things to you. I mean, you're not here with me tonight. You're with Bram Aldrich, and I have no right—"

Eddie didn't get to finish his sentence. Jo took his face in her hands, pulled him to her, and kissed him. With her lips, her breath, and her body, she gave him his right.

Her uncle *was* wrong. She was, too, for doubting Eddie. The reason he'd kept his distance was because he thought she was spoken for. He cared for her, as she cared for him. And the knowing of it made her wildly happy.

It was Eddie who finally broke their kiss. He smoothed a piece of hair off her cheek and said, "This is going to sound like a line from a dopey song, but you look beautiful in the moonlight."

He leaned in for another kiss, when they both heard it—a crash. It came from the doorway. They froze.

"The bench," Jo whispered. "Someone walked into it. Someone's there."

They both peered around the statue. The bright shaft of moonlight that illuminated the back of the statue also fell across the bench—and the man who'd stumbled into it. Jo glimpsed close-cropped hair, hard eyes, and a long, livid scar running across his right cheek.

The man stepped over the bench, into the gallery. Eddie pulled Jo back behind the statue. They crouched down, out of the moonlight. Neither could see the man now, but they could hear him. He was walking toward them, his footsteps echoing in the dark.

Jo hardly dared to breathe. Her heart was thumping. She was scared of being discovered here alone with Eddie, just as she had been when they'd hidden in Van Houten's broom closet, but this time her fear ran deeper. There was something about the man she'd just seen—a brutal, predatory air—that made her feel afraid of him.

Eddie put his mouth against her ear. "Is there another way out?" he whispered.

Jo nodded.

"Run on three," he said. "I'll stop him."

Jo shook her head.

"Yes!" Eddie hissed.

Closer and closer the man came, his pace slow and measured.

"One . . . ," Eddie whispered.

A few more steps and he would see them. All he'd have to do was turn his head to the left.

"Two . . ."

Jo could feel her heart hammering against her ribs now. Her back was against the statue's base. Her face was buried in Eddie's chest. She knew he was trying to save her. If she could get out of the gallery and back to the ball, no one would ever have to know she'd been anywhere other than the lavatory. But what would happen to him? She tensed, dreading what he was about to do.

And then, miraculously, the man stopped. For a few long seconds, they heard nothing, and then only the sound of his footsteps receding. A moment later, he was gone.

Jo exhaled raggedly. "A guard?" she whispered.

"Must've been," Eddie replied. "Where's that other way out?"

"There's another doorway at the far end of the hall," Jo said, taking his hand.

She led him through it, then down a stairway that emptied into a gallery of Renaissance paintings. It, too, was deserted, but it was on the ground floor of the museum and opened onto the foyer. Light spilled into it, and from where Jo and Eddie stood, they could see the dancers, and beyond them, the orchestra. A waltz was playing.

"I can rejoin the festivities from here," Jo said. "Hopefully, no one will see me do it. You'll have to do the same, but don't follow too closely lest we give anyone the wrong idea."

"Or the right one," Eddie said.

He pulled her close and kissed her again. In his arms, she no longer knew where she was or who she was, only what she wanted—him. The strength of her feelings frightened her. This passion was the wind that would push her off the cliff and leave her broken on the rocks.

This time it was she who broke their kiss. She took an unsteady step back, her chest heaving. From the look in his eyes, she knew he felt the same way.

"My God, Jo," he said. "What are you doing to me?"

They heard the swelling of violins. The waltz was almost over. "I have to get back to the others," she said. "I'll make my excuses and leave right away. After I arrive home, I'll pretend to go to bed, get the money, and sneak back out."

"No, you won't."

"I'm going with you."

"You are *not*. Walsh's is in Mulberry Bend, and the Bend makes the waterfront look like the Ladies' Mile."

"Meet me at Irving and Nineteenth in an hour."

"Jo, I swear to God . . ."

"I want to hear what Shaw has to say," Jo said stubbornly. "It's your story, Eddie, but it's my father. You take my money, you take me."

"You don't belong in the Bend," Eddie protested. "You could spook the source. You'll wreck everything!"

The last notes of the waltz rose. On the far side of the room, Elizabeth Adams and Bram were executing a final twirl. Bram led with elegance and Elizabeth followed him gracefully. Her color was high. Her eyes were sparkling. As the music ended and the applause began, Bram bowed to her. She curtsied. They were both smiling.

"Too late, Mr. Gallagher," Jo said. "I already have."

⤞ CHAPTER THIRTY-FIVE ⤝

Jo stared in horror at the dirty rag Eddie was holding. "I'm not wearing *that*!"

They'd just gotten out of a cab. Eddie had asked the driver to drop them at Mulberry and Bayard, but he'd refused to cross Canal Street. "Not at this hour, pal," he'd said.

"You *are* wearing it or you're not going," Eddie said, handing the rag to her.

"What *is* it?" she asked, holding it between her thumb and forefinger.

"A workman's apron. I found it as I was leaving the museum. Put it around you, like a shawl."

"But it stinks of turpentine!"

"Good. It'll block the other smells."

Jo, grimacing, gingerly draped the apron around her shoulders.

"No. Like this," Eddie said, pulling it up so it covered her head. "Keep your eyes on the ground. Don't look anyone in the face." His tone was hard; he was worried. "We're in the Bend now. It's dangerous here."

"I *know* that. I've read Jacob Riis."

Eddie snorted. "Riis was a tourist. Let's go," he said, taking her arm.

"And you're not?" Jo shot back.

He didn't answer her, but set off at such a brisk pace, she had to trot to keep up. *Maybe this wasn't the best idea after all*, Jo thought. But she had no intention of turning back.

Ever since she'd left the museum, nearly two hours ago, time had rushed by in a mad, breathless dash. At the ball, she'd told both Bram and her uncle that she was feeling unwell. Phillip had been concerned; he'd offered to ride home with her, but she refused. She made the same excuse to her mother when she arrived at her house, then hurried to her bedroom. Katie had followed her upstairs to help her undress, and it was she who was in Jo's bed now. Another crisp dollar had bought her cooperation.

As soon as her mother had retired and Theakston had disappeared into his room, Jo—wearing Katie's work clothes—had hurried from the house with five one-dollar notes and two five-dollar notes in her skirt pocket. She'd met Eddie on Irving Place and given him the singles, and then they'd taken a cab downtown. The dark, enclosed cab would have been the perfect place to steal another kiss if either wanted to, but they'd been too busy talking. Jo told Eddie all about her visit with Sally Gibson and what she'd learned.

They continued that conversation now as they crossed Canal and started down Mulberry, past darkened shops and gas-lit bars, past overflowing ash cans and empty beer barrels. They avoided stumbling drunks, stray cats, and a wizened old lady selling baked potatoes out of a basket. "Ever since I spoke with Sally, I've been convinced that Kinch is Stephen Smith. He has to be. There are just too many coincidences otherwise," Jo said, clutching both ends of the nasty rag Eddie had given her under her chin. She was certain she'd never get the smell out of her hair.

"Yeah, but there's a problem with your theory. . . . Smith's dead.

He drowned. His ship went down in the Indian Ocean, somewhere in the Seychelles," Eddie said.

"The Seychelles? How do you know that?" Jo asked. She knew that Smith had died in the Indian Ocean, but not that his death had occurred in the Seychelles.

"I looked it up after I got your letter. The *Standard* did a story on it back in '74. A reporter filed it from Zanzibar. He interviewed your uncle, who told him that in late 1873 Smith sailed to the Seychelles on a ship called the *Gull* to see if any of the smaller islands were suitable for growing nutmeg. He never came back. Nor did the crew. The ship was never seen again, either. There were storms in the area where Smith was sailing—reported by the crews of other ships in the same waters—and it was thought that one of them destroyed the *Gull.*"

"Smith could have survived," Jo ventured.

Eddie gave her a skeptical look. "It's a real long shot. No other crew members survived."

"Maybe they did."

"Where did they go? They didn't come back to Zanzibar. None of them was seen again."

"They could have made it to one of the islands," Jo persisted.

"If they made it to a big island, other people would have seen them. The smaller islands are uninhabited. How would they have survived on one?"

"By eating coconuts," Jo said.

Eddie snorted. "For seventeen years?"

Jo racked her brain, trying to come up with an answer. There *was* one, she was sure of it. Kinch was Stephen Smith. He *had* to be. She thought back to Van Houten's and the conversation between Kinch and Scully, sifting through every word. And suddenly she had it.

"Pirates, Eddie!" she exclaimed. "He said so himself! Remember? Maybe they found him on an island and took him aboard their ship."

"Ships can't even get near a lot of those islands."

"They could've found him after the storm, floating on some wreckage. Maybe he drifted to an island and sent up smoke signals. Maybe he made a raft and got off the island and the pirates spotted him in the ocean."

Eddie raised an eyebrow. "Maybe someone's been reading *Robinson Crusoe*."

"I'm right about this," Jo insisted. "I just *know* it."

"Knowing is not enough. We need proof. I can't write my story without it and you can't go to the police without it, and we don't have it."

"*Yet*," Jo said stubbornly.

She and Eddie were now well down Mulberry Street. Jo, determined to see the infamous slums of the city's Sixth Ward, disregarded Eddie's order to keep her eyes down and looked around.

She saw squat wooden houses, soot-stained tenements, and a one-cent coffee shack. She dodged a small child carrying a jug of beer, a dead dog lying across the sidewalk, and a tramp asleep on a warm grate. Sounds rose all around her—shouts, a baby's wail, the jingling bells on a ragpicker's cart. As they turned onto Bayard, a stench rose, too—a stench so strong, that walking into it was like walking into a brick wall.

"Eddie! Oh my word," Jo said, gasping. "What *is* that?" The foul smell was in her nose and throat, gagging her. Her eyes were tearing from it.

"Outhouses. Hold the apron over your face."

Jo did so. The turpentine smelled like perfume in comparison. She wondered how the poor people who lived here could breathe. They walked another half block and then Eddie stopped.

"Here we are," he said, pointing at a steep set of steps that led from the sidewalk to the basement of a pawnshop. They ended at a narrow doorway. A faint yellow glow emanated from it. Snatches of a bawdy song drifted up. "I don't suppose I can convince you to go home *now*, can I?"

Jo shook her head. Eddie started down the steps. She followed him, and a minute later found herself inside a room with an earthen floor and a low ceiling blackened by cigar smoke. The air reeked of sweat, mildew, and gin, and the walls oozed dampness. Men, dirty and ragged, smoked and drank, and Jo made out two women sitting on the floor, their backs against the wall. One was passed out with a sleeping baby in her lap. The other stared at her drink as if it were the only thing in the entire world.

Jo understood now why places like this were called dives: because the ruined souls in them had descended to the lowest possible depths.

Rickety tables and chairs were strewn around the room. A plank stretched across two barrels served as a bar. The two men who stood at it eyed Jo boldly as she and Eddie approached. One said something under his breath; his companion laughed. Jo nervously looked around for another way out. Just in case. But there wasn't one that she could see.

The bartender glanced at them. "No rooms for rent here," he said.

Eddie colored. "We don't want a room, Mick."

The bartender gave him a closer look and grinned. "Eddie Gallagher, as I live and breathe! It's been ages. How are you, boy?"

"Well. Yourself?"

"Never better. What can I do for you?"

Eddie pushed one of Jo's dollars across the bar. "We're looking for someone," he said quietly. "Man by the name of Jackie Shaw."

The bartender pocketed the dollar and nodded at a man hunched over a table in a corner.

Eddie thanked him; then he and Jo crossed the room. Jo wondered how Eddie knew the bartender but didn't have long to dwell on the question as a fight broke out only a few feet away from her. Words were exchanged; then one of the combatants grabbed the other's head, pulled it down, and rammed a knee into his face. Jo heard a sickening crack, and saw blood gush from a broken nose. She stifled a cry and clutched Eddie's arm.

Mick picked up a baseball bat, slammed it on the bar, and loudly threatened to bash both men's heads in if they didn't take it outside. His violent threats made Jo feel oddly safe. She doubted any of the dive's patrons would bother her or Eddie after Mick's warning.

"Jackie Shaw?" Eddie said as he and Jo reached the corner table.

The man sitting there picked his head up. "Who wants to know?" he asked blearily. He looked to be in his fifties. One eye was clouded by a cataract. His teeth were rotten.

Eddie pulled up two chairs and sat down in one. Jo took the other. He had a story prepared. "My name's Eddie Gallagher. I'm a reporter. I'm working on a story about the Montforts and New York's shipping industry. And I was wondering if—"

"Piss off," Shaw said in a surly voice.

"Eddie, I think he's *drunk*," Jo whispered.

"I might be, sister, but I'm not deaf," Shaw snarled. "And I'd have to be blind drunk to talk about the Montforts. To you or anyone else." He gripped his glass tightly as he spoke.

Hearing the man say her family's name made the hair on the back of her neck stand up. He knew something, Jo was sure of it. She looked at Eddie and could see by his expression that he felt the same way. They couldn't let this chance get away. She decided to take a risk. "Mr. Shaw, my name is Josie Jones. I'm also a reporter."

"I don't give a fiddler's fart who you are," Shaw said.

Jo pressed on. "Allow me to be candid. My colleague and I are not working on a story about shipping. We're investigating the death of Charles Montfort. We think he was murdered. We're trying to find out why," she said.

"Murdered, eh?" His clear eye took on a haunted look. "If you're going to bury the past, bury it deep, girl. Shallow graves always give up their dead." He touched the bill of his cap. "Good night, all."

Shaw moved to get up, and Jo traded frantic glances with Eddie. "Mr. Shaw, can I buy you a drink?" Eddie asked.

Shaw shook his head. "It'd take more than one, son," he said, making to leave once more.

"How about the whole bottle?" Jo offered, desperate to keep him there. "Plus this." She placed one of her five-dollar notes on the table, keeping it half hidden under her hand. Five dollars would be a small fortune to Shaw—and to everyone else in the room.

Shaw turned and looked at her, and she could tell he was battling with himself. She wasn't sure what would win—his fear or his need for gin. "Where the hell'd you come from, sister? You for real?" he finally said.

"Yes. I am, in fact, very much for real," Jo said, hoping he'd change his mind and sit back down.

He did. Jo slid the money to him while Eddie quickly went to the bar. He returned a minute later with two more glasses and a dirty brown bottle. After pouring three shots, he held up his glass. "Cheers," he said, taking a sip—and wincing.

Jo only pretended to sip hers. It smelled like kerosene.

"That mine when we're done talking?" Shaw asked, nodding at the bottle.

Eddie assured him that it was, as long as he answered their questions. "Do you know of a ship called *Bonaventure*?" he asked.

Shaw looked as if Eddie had just doused him with cold water. He downed two more shots, and then, when Eddie threatened to take the bottle away, he started to talk.

"The *Bonaventure* sometimes docked in Zanzibar. She had Portuguese papers and a Portuguese crew. Cutthroats, every one. Kill you as soon as look at you. They were only there for the money, and the *Bonaventure*'s cargo brought cash. A lot of it."

"Tea? Spices?" Eddie said, shooting Jo an excited glance. She could barely hold back an excited smile.

Shaw stared at his glass. It was as if he hadn't even heard Eddie. Jo silently urged him to speak, to tell them what he knew.

"There were rumors about the *Bonaventure*. Some said it wasn't Portuguese at all, but a Van Houten ship. Of course, no one ever proved it. And you'd have to be crazy to try. The Montforts, Charlie and Phillip . . . they weren't men you wanted to cross," he said.

Jo knew her father and uncle could be tough negotiators and stern taskmasters. She knew, too, that in a commercial enterprise, one's partners and employees were not always happy with the terms of every deal. Sailors and captains often complained they hadn't been paid enough. Listening to Shaw now, Jo assumed the dig he'd made at her father and uncle was simply more such sniping.

Eddie poured more gin. Shaw watched the alcohol flow into his glass. "All the gin in New York couldn't drown the memory of the sounds that came from the ship," he said.

"Sounds? What sounds?" Jo asked, puzzled. Tea and spices didn't make noise.

"I was aboard the *Albion*, a tea clipper," Shaw continued. "This was nearly twenty years ago. We were off the coast of Mozambique. It was night, and a thick fog had come down. Out of nowhere, the *Bonaventure* came at us. Our captain was mad as hell. He hailed her but she didn't answer. She passed within yards of us, as quiet as a ghost ship. I heard it then. We all did. Some nights, I still hear it." He passed a trembling hand over his face. "The fog closed around her again and we kept going. What else could we do?"

"Mr. Shaw, what was on that ship?" Jo pressed, anxious for an answer.

Shaw didn't reply. He looked past Jo, toward the bar, and it seemed to her as if he was working up his courage. Then suddenly his eyes widened; he jumped to his feet, startling her.

"Hey! Where are you going? We had a deal!" Eddie said.

"Sorry, son. A bottle of gin's not worth my life."

"Mr. Shaw, *please* don't go," Jo begged.

Shaw was about to bolt, but the desperation in Jo's voice stopped him. "Follow the *Nausett*," he said tersely. "Follow the *Nausett* and you'll find the *Bonaventure*. God help you if you do."

He stumbled across the room, climbed the steps to the sidewalk, and was gone. Jo, bitterly disappointed, looked toward the bar to see what had spooked him. A man was hurrying out of Walsh's, close on Shaw's heels. He shielded his face with his hat, but Jo still managed to glimpse close-cropped hair, hard eyes . . .

. . . and a cheek puckered by a long, livid scar.

➤ CHAPTER THIRTY-SIX ◄

"It was *him*, Eddie, I know it was!" Jo said. She was turning in a frantic circle out on the sidewalk, looking for the scar-faced man, but he was gone.

"*Who?* What are you talking about?" Eddie asked, catching up to her. She'd run out of the dive as if she were on fire.

"The man who just left Walsh's! He's the same man we saw at the museum. The one in the sculpture gallery."

"Are you sure, Jo?"

"I'm positive. Is he following us? Who is he?" she asked.

"I don't know," Eddie replied. "But he sure spooked Shaw."

Eddie started back to Mulberry Street; Jo fell in step beside him.

"What was on that ship?" Eddie asked, frustration in his voice. "What did Van Houten trade besides tea and spices?"

"Coffee, quinine, and cocoa. But we're not even sure it *was* a Van Houten ship. Shaw himself wasn't sure," Jo said.

Eddie gave her a sidelong glance. "You *still* believe no one at Van Houten is involved in any wrongdoing? Your father is murdered. A strange man shakes down Scully. A weird ghost ship carries suspicious cargo. Oh, and I almost forgot—some scar-faced tough might be following us."

His sarcastic tone stung, and Jo—smarting from it—didn't immediately answer him. Shaw's words echoed in her mind: *If you're going to bury the past, bury it deep, girl. Shallow graves always give up their dead.* An uneasiness had descended on her, as cold and ominous as a winter night.

"I don't know what to believe," she admitted.

Eddie applauded. "Finally!" he said.

"*Must* you be so condescending?" Jo asked, annoyed.

"Do forgive me," Eddie said, with mock contrition. "I meant to goad, not condescend."

Jo glared at him. Was it only a few hours ago that she so desperately wanted to kiss him? Now she felt like throttling him. She was used to polite deference from young men and kept forgetting that Eddie was not terribly polite or deferential. They started to argue more heatedly, but the sound of another voice stopped them.

"Eddie. Eddie Gallagher."

Eddie came to a standstill. He held a hand out, staying Jo.

A girl stood on the sidewalk just ahead of them, at the corner of Bayard and Mulberry. She was wearing a striped silk dress, a velvet cape, and a plumed hat. It was an ensemble Jo herself would have been pleased to own, and the girl wore it well, but her sudden appearance had an unsettling effect on Jo. The girl was beautiful and so incredibly out of place, but no one seemed to notice. People passed her by without a second glance. Jo felt as if someone had dropped a magnificent jewel on the dirty street, but no one was bold enough to pick it up.

"Fay," Eddie said, looking at the girl. He didn't sound happy.

The girl nodded and Jo suddenly recognized her. She'd seen her at the waterfront with Tumbler, but the girl looked very different tonight. Not only were her clothes far better than what she'd been wearing then, her face was rouged, and her hair was auburn, not blond.

"He wants you, Newsie," she said.

Eddie quickly glanced up Mulberry. As he did, Tumbler emerged from the shadows. Two other boys stepped out of doorways; two girls sitting on a stoop stood up. They were all beautifully dressed, just like Fay. With their pale, expressionless faces, they reminded Jo of sinister porcelain dolls, suddenly come to life.

"I wouldn't run if I were you," Fay advised. "Tumbler and Ashcan have knives."

Eddie swore. His hand tightened on Jo's arm. For the first time that night, Jo was not just nervous or anxious, but genuinely afraid.

"Just me, Fay," Eddie said. "Not her. I'll go with you, but she goes home in a cab."

Fay shook her head. "Sorry, Newsie," she said with a regretful smile. "He wants you both."

❧ CHAPTER THIRTY-SEVEN ❧

The alley Eddie led her down was so narrow and so dark that Jo could hardly see where she was going, but she had glimpsed its name as she'd entered it. Someone had scrawled it on a wall: *Bandits Roost*.

Eddie held her hand tightly as they walked. His steps were quick and sure; he knew his way. Fay, Tumbler, and the four other children trailed them.

"Where are we going?" Jo whispered.

"To see the Tailor. We've been summoned," Eddie replied.

"He's the man for whom Fay works, isn't he? New York's very own Fagin?"

"The one and only," Eddie said grimly.

"Should I be scared?"

"You should be home. Why did I let you come here? If we get out of this, I'm never taking you with me anywhere again. *Ever.* I swear to God."

The *if* worried Jo. "What does he want with us?"

"To talk. At least, I hope that's what he wants."

The alley opened into a rectangular yard bordered by ramshackle wooden buildings, each three stories high. Thin, hollow-cheeked men wearing little more than rags sat around the yard smoking pipes or drinking from cracked mugs. Jo glimpsed a room through an open door. Women and children lay sprawled on the floor of the small space.

"Almost there," Eddie said, leading her toward the most decrepit house in the yard. Its ground-level windows were dark and its door was shut tight, but its second floor boasted a balcony. Eddie looked up at it. As he did, a young man who was loitering in the yard walked up to him.

"Why, if it isn't Eddie Gallagher," he said. "Slumming tonight, are we, Newsie? Who's yer fancy lady?"

Jo stiffened. The man seemed to know Eddie, just as Mick Walsh had, but there was a menacing tone to his voice. Like the other men in the yard, he wore an old bowler hat pulled low across his brow. His left eye was covered by a patch.

"Pretty Will," Eddie said. "It's been a long time. Sorry I can't chat, but I've got business with the Tailor."

The young man stepped directly in front of him.

"I don't want any trouble," said Eddie, holding his hands up.

"Doesn't mean you won't get none," Will said. "I'll have them cuff links off you, for starters. That jacket, too. Plus whatever's in your pockets." He looked at Jo leeringly. "And then I'll have her."

Eddie pushed Jo behind him. He raised his fists.

"Whatcha gonna do, Newsie? There's one of you and ten of us," Will said, gesturing to the men in the yard.

"Never mind what *he's* going to do," Fay said. She'd pushed past Jo and Eddie and was now in Will's face. "It's what *I'm* going to do that should worry you." She pointed at the balcony. "I'll tell *him*. When he hears you've interfered with his guests, he'll come down here with his scissors. He sharpens them every night." She touched Will's eye patch with a gloved finger. "But I don't have to tell *you* that, do I?"

Fear flickered in Will's remaining eye. Seeing it, Tumbler grinned and made a stabbing motion with his hand.

"Watch yourself, you little shit," Will growled, moving away from them.

Tumbler put his fingers in his mouth and blew a shrill whistle. Seconds later, a ladder was lowered from the balcony. He climbed it.

Fay nodded at Jo. "What were you thinking, bringing her here?" she asked Eddie.

"It's a long story," Eddie replied.

Fay shook her head. "You're a fool, Newsie. She'll be the death of you." She started up the ladder.

"You're next," Eddie told Jo, keeping a watchful eye on Pretty Will.

Jo put her hands on a rung, took a deep breath, and started to climb.

➤ CHAPTER THIRTY-EIGHT ➤

Jo expected fierce-looking villains. Guns and knives. Piles of money. Bottles of gin.

She never expected lace.

As she stepped through the window into the Tailor's rookery, she nearly landed in a basket of it. Bolts of fabric leaned against the walls—delicate chintzes, watered silks, rich brocades. Coffee tins overflowed with buttons and beads. On the far side of the room stood several dressmaker's dummies. One sported a mauve gown so exquisite it could have passed for a Worth. Jo walked to it and touched a sleeve. She couldn't help herself.

"It would look divine on you, my dear," a voice said.

She turned and saw a man sitting at a wooden worktable. He held a long pair of scissors in one hand. He was slight, with a narrow, angular face, a high forehead, and deep-set eyes. They glittered darkly in the lamplight. His hair, dark brown and streaked with gray, was pulled back and tied with a ribbon. He wore a grimy white shirt, a gray wool vest, and matching narrow-cut trousers. A pincushion was strapped to one wrist.

"Jacob Beckett, high-class tailor, at your service," he said, dipping his head.

Something in his smile frightened Jo, but she knew better than to show it. She met his eyes and said, "Josie Jones, reporter. I'm pleased to meet you."

Just then, a small, dirty hand came up over the top of the table and closed around a jeweled button. In one swift, fluid motion, the man stabbed his scissors into the wood. Jo gasped, certain he'd also driven the blades through the child's flesh, but he'd only pinned its shirt cuff. The child, a little blond boy with vacant eyes, whined as he tried to pull free.

The tailor put a hand on the boy's head. "You steal *for* me, Noggin, not *from* me, remember? If you *bring* me something, I . . . ," he prompted. "I what, boy?"

"*Feed* Noggin," the boy said.

"And if you *take* something I . . . what? Come now, say it. . . ."

"*Beat* Noggin."

"Very good. Off you go." The man pulled his scissors out of the table, releasing the boy's cuff, and turned back to Jo. "Simple as an apple, that one, but he has a face like an angel. He's so pretty in the sailor suit I made him, ladies stop dead in their tracks to coo over him."

"And never feel a thing when Fay moves in," Eddie said. He'd just crawled in through the window, after having pulled the ladder up behind them.

The Tailor ignored his remark. "Do have a seat," the Tailor said, motioning Jo and Eddie to two empty chairs at the table. "Fay, my dear, some coffee for our guests."

Jo's eyes followed Fay as she moved across the room to a large black stove. She saw more children—dozens of them. They were thin and wary and wouldn't meet her gaze. Some had bruises on their arms or faces. The youngest were asleep in wooden bunks. Older ones were wearily polishing silver, cleaning jewelry, or sorting coins.

It hit Jo then, how big the Tailor's operation was. All these orphans were being brought up to lead a life of crime. She was so deeply distressed by the sight of the children, she spoke without thinking.

"You're running a factory here—a factory of little thieves. The Artful Dodger would feel right at home."

"Jo . . . ," Eddie warned.

But the Tailor smiled. "I thank you for the compliment. Dickens's work is an inspiration to me, Fagin a hero."

"I wasn't paying you a compliment, sir," Jo retorted. "Dickens wrote *Oliver Twist* as a deterrent to crime, not a spur to it. You're exploiting innocent children. You've made criminals of them. Doesn't your conscience trouble you?"

"Life's black-and-white uptown, but here in the Bend, it's a dirty gray," the Tailor said. He wasn't smiling anymore. "I've kept throwaway children alive—that's what I've done. See Jakes over there?" He nodded at a little boy. "I found him abandoned in the outhouse where he was born. And Muttbait"—he pointed at a tiny girl with livid scars on her face—"she was left in an alley and attacked by dogs. I found Snow"—he gestured at a girl of about ten—"freezing to death on Mott Street. Her mother turned her out. She had no choice. She has seven more at home and earns less in a year than what you spend on one bonnet. I house them and feed them, and they, in turn, must earn their keep. So no, Miss Montfort, my conscience does not trouble me. Does yours trouble you?"

Jo blinked. "How did you know my—"

"I make it my business to know who enters my home."

Jo was taken aback but not ready to concede her point. "There are orphanages where these children could go. There are mission houses."

"Indeed there are," the Tailor allowed. He turned his glittering eyes on Eddie. "And most would rather starve on the streets than live in them. Isn't that right, Mr. Gallagher?"

Eddie gave him a deadly look. "Are we going to chitchat all night?" he said. "What do you want?"

Before the Tailor could reply, Fay, still in her elegant suit, came up behind Eddie and Jo and placed mugs of black coffee before them. Then she walked around to where the Tailor stood and dropped a handful of heavy silver buttons on the table.

His eyes lit up. "Very nice! Where'd you get them?" he asked her.

"Pastor's Theatre," she said. "I snuck into the cloakroom and cut them off."

As Jo watched, astounded, Fay divested herself of the evening's gleanings. Two wallets and a gold watch came out of pockets cannily stitched between the pleats of her skirt. A silver cigarette case was pulled out of one boot, a money clip from the other. Five silver dollars came out of her corset, followed by a gold ring with a diamond in it.

The Tailor gave an admiring whistle as he examined the ring, and Fay proudly related how she stumbled outside the theater and took it off a man's hand as he helped her up.

"Well done," the Tailor said, beaming at her.

"Wait," Fay said. "There's one more thing. . . ."

With a taunting smile, she held out a gold ladies' watch. And a five-dollar note.

Jo recognized the watch. She felt in her skirt pocket; it was empty. "Those are mine!" she cried.

"Not anymore," the Tailor said happily.

"Give them back," Eddie demanded.

"I could," the Tailor mused. "Or I could keep them, beat you both silly, and toss you off the balcony."

Eddie rose from his chair. Immediately, a dozen children surrounded them, each brandishing some sort of weapon—scissors, kitchen knives, ice picks, a wrench.

Jo put a hand on Eddie's arm and pulled him back down. She

was very scared now, but she knew she must not lose her head. The portrait of Admiral Montfort flashed before her eyes. She heard his stern voice telling her that a Montfort does what needs to be done. What needed to be done now was to figure out how to get herself and Eddie out of there. Alive.

"Why are you down here?" the Tailor asked. "I don't like reporters. I especially don't like them in my backyard."

"We're working on a story. An exposé of living conditions in the Bend," Eddie lied.

The Tailor shook his head. "I want the *truth*, boy," he said. And then, in one swift, fluid motion, he arched across the table and drove his scissors into the wood again—this time only inches from Jo's hand.

"God *damn* you!" Eddie shouted, ready to lunge at the Tailor, but Muttbait stopped him.

She'd come up from under the table, as silent as a viper. She was wedged between Eddie and the table now, still holding the ice pick she'd brandished earlier. Only now she was holding it directly under Eddie's left eye. The tip had nicked his skin. A drop of blood slowly made its way down his cheek.

"You might have left, boy, but I'm still here," the Tailor hissed. "You forget me? Forget who I am? Some cheek, to come nosing around in the Bend, *my* Bend, without so much as a by-your-leave. Talk. *Now*. Or you'll be feeling your way home."

It wasn't Eddie who started talking, but Jo. She was terrified. Not for herself, for him. She was so scared, she babbled like a lunatic.

"My father was murdered. I'm trying to find who did it. Eddie's helping me. That's why we're here," she said.

The Tailor raised an eyebrow. "Keep going," he ordered.

Jo did. Without looking at Eddie. She knew if she so much as glanced at him, she'd come apart. She told the Tailor about her trip to the morgue. About Kinch, Eleanor Owens, and the *Bonaventure*.

She said they'd just come from Mick Walsh's, where they'd spoken to a man named Jackie Shaw.

"What did Shaw tell you?" the Tailor asked. "The truth, girl."

"Not much. Shaw doesn't know who Kinch is," Jo said, trying hard not to give in to her fear.

"What about the ship?"

"He said the *Bonaventure* docked in Zanzibar," Jo explained. "He led us to believe that it carried some kind of mysterious cargo, but he didn't tell us what it was. I think he might've, but someone spooked him. A man. He had a scar on his face. Dark eyes. Short hair. Shaw saw him and left Walsh's as fast as he could."

The Tailor pondered her words, then nodded. "Down, Muttbait," he said.

The little girl lowered her ice pick and disappeared back under the table, and Jo felt her heart rate return to something approaching normal. Her fear ebbed, and anger took its place. The Tailor was a bully, and she despised bullies. He lived off the backs of children and kept them, and his visitors, in line using violence.

Eddie wiped the blood off his face with the heel of his hand. "She gave you what you want. Let us go," he said.

"Before you do, I would like to have my watch back," Jo said.

The Tailor sputtered laughter. "I'm sure you would," he said.

Jo was seething, but she kept her expression calm and her voice level. The Tailor, she saw, understood two things—brute force and money. She had no access to the former, but she could leverage the latter.

"I'm afraid you don't understand," she continued. "My mother will notice that I no longer have the watch and will want to know what became of it. I don't want to raise her suspicions. It's difficult enough as it is for me to get out of my house at night. You may keep the five dollars."

The Tailor looked as if he simply could not believe what he was hearing. "Oh, I may, may I? How very kind of you," he said sarcastically. "I'm tempted to follow my original idea, however, and throw you off the balcony."

Jo leaned toward him, her gray eyes hard and calculating. "That would be an unfortunate choice."

"Very unfortunate," the Tailor agreed. "For you."

"No, sir. For *you*."

"How do you figure that?"

"If you take my things and kill me, you forfeit a lucrative business arrangement," she explained. "The watch is only gold plate. It's from Woolworth's. Would I be foolish enough to wear anything of value to the Bend? Of course not. I've already paid for Tumbler's services. I'll pay you again for similar services, or for any information pertaining to Kinch or the *Bonaventure*." She gestured to the room and all of its occupants. "These children go everywhere, do they not? One of them might spot Kinch. My proposal will bring you more profit than what you'd make selling a trinket."

Eddie blinked.

The Tailor snorted. "You're a Montfort through and through, aren't you?" he said. Then he gave Fay a curt nod. She handed Jo her watch back but gave the five-dollar note to him.

"How am I supposed to get her a cab home with no money?" Eddie asked.

"You're a clever lad. You'll think of something. But do be careful, my dears. It's dangerous in the Bend," the Tailor said with a baiting smile.

Jo didn't care about a cab, or how far she had to walk. All she felt was relief that they'd survived their interview with this dangerous man. She stood, wanting only one thing: to get far away from him.

As she and Eddie rose from their seats to leave, she saw Fay—who'd removed her face paint—grasp her wig and pull it off. Her blond hair was coiled close to her head. They stared at each other.

Jo was angry at Fay for leading her here and picking her pocket, but at the same time, Fay intrigued her. Jo guessed they were about the same age, but that was the only similarity between them.

"You look very different now," she said.

"That's the idea," Fay replied.

"She's as fair as the wee people. That's why I call her Fairy Fay. She came to me as a tiny girl. She'd been left in a stairwell by her gin-fiend mother. She was starving and sick, and lucky I came along when I did. She's brilliant, my Fay. Learned the trade quick. With that face and the dresses I put her in, she can mix anywhere, but alas, she's getting known. Despite the rouge and the wigs," he said, sighing. "Her pickpocket's career is ending and another awaits her. She has something even more valuable under her skirts than wallets or buttons."

Fay looked away, but not before Jo could see the hopelessness in her eyes.

The Tailor caught it, too. "Oh, come now! That's no way to repay my kindness," he scolded. He rose and walked behind her. "I took you in, girl. Taught you a trade." He skimmed his hands over her waist to her hips. She stiffened but didn't move away. "And when the time comes, Madam Esther will teach you another. Only the rich can afford to be idle," he said, looking pointedly at Jo.

Jo's skin crawled at the way the Tailor put his hands on Fay.

"Who's Madam Esther?" she asked, aiming the question at Fay.

Fear flickered in Fay's eyes. She walked away without answering and busied herself at the stove.

Jo wanted an answer. She turned to the Tailor. "Who's Madam Esther?"

Eddie took her arm. "Forget it," he said. "We're leaving. *Now.*"

The courtyard was empty as they climbed down the ladder. As soon as it was hauled up again, the Tailor stuck his head over the balcony.

"You're not quite the clever negotiator you think you are, Miss Montfort," he said tauntingly.

"I'm not?" Jo said, looking up at him.

"Next time, I'll expect a tenner for any information I give you. And I'm doubling Tumbler's rate, too," he gloated. "You want my help, you'll pay for it."

"Yes, I suppose I shall," Jo conceded. "Still, I didn't do so badly," she added. "Do you recall that Woolworth watch you returned to me?"

The Tailor nodded.

Jo smiled. "It's really Cartier."

➤ CHAPTER THIRTY-NINE ◀

Eddie and Jo stood on the corner of Baxter and Canal, gasping for breath. They'd run all the way there from the Tailor's roost.

"*Cartier?* You came down here with a Cartier watch? Are you insane? I can't believe he didn't come after us. He still might. Put it down your corset—*now*," Eddie ordered.

"*What?* How? I can't!" Jo protested.

"Put it in your underwear or I will."

Jo saw that he meant it. She unbuttoned the top of her jacket, then her blouse, and dropped the watch down her corset.

"His eyes must be getting bad. Or maybe it was the light," Eddie said as she buttoned herself back up again. "If he'd seen what that watch really was, he *would* have thrown us off the balcony. I can't believe you got it back. Where'd you learn to negotiate like that, anyway? Your father?"

"Certainly not," Jo said. "He never talked business around me. I learned it from Katie, my maid. We haggle all the time."

"Over what?"

"The cost of her services. I pay her to sneak things into the house that my mother doesn't approve of, and to help me sneak out.

These past few days, I've paid her a small fortune. She's in my bed yet again, pretending to be me. And probably wondering where on earth I am."

Eddie checked his own watch. "It's late. If we walk at a good clip, we should get you home before two." He took her hand and they started walking east on Canal. It's been a very interesting evening in your company, Miss Montfort. As usual," he said. "But once again, it seems we've ended up with more questions than we started with."

"Speaking of questions," Jo said, "no one ever answered mine. What was the Tailor talking about when he said Fay would have to learn a new trade? Who's Madam Esther?"

"You should probably ask your mother about that," Eddie said. Then he shook his head. "What am I saying? Whatever you do, *don't* ask your mother about that. She'll never let you out of the house again."

"What do you mean?" Jo said.

"Esther is . . . well, she's like Della McEvoy."

Jo remembered her conversation with Katie. "You mean she's a pimp?"

Eddie nearly choked. "Um, *madam* is generally how such women are referred to. Where did you learn *that* word?"

"Does that mean Fay will work for Esther? As a prostitute?"

"It looks that way," Eddie said grimly.

"Because the Tailor's making her?"

"Yes."

"But that's terrible!" Jo exclaimed, outraged. "She's not a slave, to be bought and sold. We have to stop him, Eddie."

"I wish we could."

"We could tell the police what he's doing. They'd arrest him."

Eddie shook his head. "No, they wouldn't. He *owns* the police. At least, the ones in the Sixth Ward. He pays them to turn a blind eye to his activities."

"We could tell them about Madam Esther, then."

"She probably pays the cops more than the Tailor does."

"Eddie, this isn't *right*," Jo said, upset.

"No, Jo, it's not."

"How can the police allow such a thing to happen? They're supposed to protect people!"

"Fay's not a person to them. She's a throwaway girl. One of thousands in this city."

"There must be a way to help her," Jo said, unwilling to accept defeat. "There must be *something* we can do. I could—"

"Go to your mother? Your uncle? Tell them you met a pickpocket who's about to become a prostitute and you'd like to help her out?" Eddie suggested.

Jo saw the impossibility of the situation. She fell silent, remembering how scared Fay looked when the Tailor talked about Esther. How young she looked underneath all the rouge. Jo remembered something else, too—how Fay had spoken to Eddie, warning him that Jo would be the death of him. Her tone had been familiar and knowing.

Another question surfaced, demanding an answer—one that had been gnawing at her ever since they'd encountered Mick Walsh. "Eddie, how do you know all these people in the Bend?"

"Work," he replied quickly. Too quickly.

Jo looked at the side of his face. His expression had become unreadable.

"No, I don't think so," she said slowly. "Mick Walsh was surprised to see you. He said it had been a long time. He wouldn't have said that if you were around here all the time scaring up stories. Fay knows you, too, doesn't she? Pretty Will. The Tailor. He said you'd left this place. He said—"

"Hey, Jo?" Eddie cut her off. "Just because you're playing reporter doesn't mean you are one." His tone was cold.

Jo stopped dead. She felt as if he'd slapped her. "That was rotten, Eddie. And mean. And not like you at all," she said, wounded.

Eddie laughed, but it had a hollow sound to it. "Not like me?" he echoed. "And what makes you think you know me? You *don't* know me, Jo. Not at all."

He closed his eyes for a few seconds, then opened them again and looked around. As if he was seeing the Bend in a new way.

Or perhaps, Jo thought, *an old one.*

❧ CHAPTER FORTY ❧

"You know these people because you used to be one of them."

As Jo said the words out loud, she knew them to be true.

Eddie nodded. "I fought Pretty Will. Played with Fay. Filched Mick's gin. Stole for the Tailor."

He turned his eyes to hers, and she saw why he'd hidden them—they were filled with sadness.

"This place was my home," he said.

"You lived in an apartment here?" Jo asked. "In the Bend?"

"We weren't that posh," Eddie said. "We lived in one room of an apartment." He nodded at a tumbledown building on the corner of Canal and Mott. Its front door hung crookedly from its hinges. "In a house just like that one. My parents and five kids, but two died when they were babies." He was staring at the building, but Jo felt he was seeing something else—his past.

"I want to go inside," she said.

"No, you don't."

But Jo didn't listen. She walked up the stoop and pushed the door open. The smell was eye-watering—unwashed bodies, urine, and smoke. A small gas lamp sputtered in the dank, airless hallway, illuminating the crumbling walls. A man was sprawled on the dirty staircase in a drunken stupor. Two filthy children sat on a step above him, prodding him with a stick and laughing.

Dead cockroaches crunched under Jo's feet as she made her way to the backmost room. Live ones disappeared into cracks in the walls. The room's door was partly open, too. In the yellow glow of a kerosene lamp, she could see that it was small, no more than ten feet by twelve. Children lay on the floor sleeping. A thin woman stood by the only window, silhouetted in the moonlight. She was rocking a wailing baby in her arms. A man sat on a chair, his head in his hands. He told the woman to shut the brat up or he would.

Jo had never seen poverty like this, or people so helpless against it. She turned and walked out of the house, grieved to know that Eddie had suffered such poverty himself, amazed that he'd survived it.

He was in the shadow of the building, looking up at the night sky, when she rejoined him.

"Have a good look?" he asked.

Jo ignored the edge that had crept back into his voice and took his arm. They started walking east again. "This place is why, isn't it?" she said. "It's why you became a reporter."

Eddie nodded. "I want to tell the stories of the people in that house," he said. "The ones that never get told. I want to tell the world that these people exist. Nellie Bly's doing it. Riis and Chambers are doing it. They're changing things. I want to change things, too. That's why I want to leave the *Standard*."

Jo realized she had tears in her eyes. She blinked them back, not wanting Eddie to see them. He was proud and would think they were tears of pity, not sorrow.

"Where are they now? Your brothers and sisters? Your parents?" she asked.

"I haven't seen my father since I was six. He left us. My mother died when I was ten. Two days before she passed, she took us—me, my brother, and sister—to Saint Paul's, a church orphanage. We didn't want to go, but she said the Tailor wasn't getting her children. She didn't know it, but he already had me. Sometimes the only money we had were the coins I'd earned thieving for him. The church took us in. They fed us, educated us, and beat us silly. My sister Eileen lost the hearing in one ear after a beating. She was only eight."

Emotion choked off Eddie's words. He got hold of himself, then said, "She's a maid for a family in a big house now. They're good to her. Tom, our brother, he's in a big house, too," he added bitterly. "He's in prison. For manslaughter."

"He *killed* someone?" Jo said, wide-eyed.

"He went after the priest who beat Eileen," Eddie explained. "Tom punched him in the face. The priest fell and hit his head on the altar step. Cracked his skull and died. Tom got twenty years. Turns out it's a life sentence, though. He caught tuberculosis in prison. He doesn't have long."

"Oh, Eddie," Jo said, her heart breaking for him. "I'm so sorry."

He looked at her and she saw more than sadness in his eyes; she saw regret.

"Why am I telling you all this? I shouldn't be," he said. "You know something, Jo? You're right to be sorry. Not for me, for yourself. And I should be, too. Because I have no right to take you to a place like this—"

"You didn't *take* me. I came here."

"—and I have no right to drag you into the Tailor's lair, or Walsh's, or my past. I *am* sorry, Jo. I really am."

Jo took his face in her hands and stopped his words with a kiss. "You weren't sorry a few hours ago. In the museum," she said.

"Don't," he warned. "This isn't a joke."

She kissed him again. "Are you really sorry? Because I'm not."

"More than you'll ever know."

She kissed his cheek, the smooth spot under his ear. "Still sorry?"

"Jo . . ."

She kissed his chin, his neck, and then his mouth once more. "Are you sorry, Eddie?" she whispered.

He pulled her to him and held her tightly. "No. God, no. But you will be, Jo. And when that day comes, it'll kill me."

➤ CHAPTER FORTY-ONE ◄

"Where's the money?" Sally Gibson hissed, opening the servants' door under the stoop of the Owenses' brownstone.

"Lovely to see you, too, Miss Gibson," Jo said, handing her a ten-dollar note.

Sally glanced up and down the street. "Come inside. Hurry up!" she said, tugging on Jo's arm.

Jo was dressed like a servant. She'd borrowed one of Katie's work dresses again. A battered straw bonnet covered her head. She and Sally Gibson had arranged this meeting during Sally's visit to Jo's home.

"Come on Sunday afternoon when no one's home," Sally had said. "The servants have the day off and the Owenses go to Mrs. Owens's sister's for an early supper."

Jo had told Eddie of the plan last night as he'd walked her home after their visit to Mulberry Bend. She'd asked Sally to smuggle her into Eleanor's room and Sally had agreed. Jo planned to search it from top to bottom, hoping to find the letters and manifests Stephen Smith had sent her.

"Be careful, Jo. The Owenses aren't the Tailor. They'll call the police if they catch you. This is a dangerous game you're playing," Eddie had warned.

A dangerous game? She was playing so many, it made her head spin. And none more dangerous than the one she was playing with him. Yet she couldn't let him go. After their night in the Bend, after learning about his past and what he'd overcome, her feelings for him had only deepened. The thought of a day without him in it— that was the most frightening thing of all. More frightening than the scar-faced man or even the Tailor.

It had taken some doing for Jo to get herself to the Owenses' house. Her mother had been up and about so Jo hadn't been able to simply leave a note and disappear. Instead, she'd told her she had a headache and wanted to go to Central Park to get some fresh air. Katie would accompany her.

Anna had allowed it and Theakston had offered to call for the carriage, but Jo declined, telling him she planned to walk. She and Katie set off together, but the minute they turned off Gramercy Square, Jo hailed a cab, making sure its passenger seats were enclosed instead of open. Once they were inside it, she pulled the shades down and switched clothes with Katie. Then she'd had the driver drop Katie at Saint Mark's Place, where Katie's mother lived, and Jo continued on to Murray Hill.

Katie had instructions to meet her on Thirty-Sixth Street in two hours' time. They'd hail another cab there, change clothes again, and return home. Jo found the machinations required just to take a trip of a few blocks exhausting.

"How nice to be Bram or Cousin Rob and go where you wish when you wish," she'd grumbled to Katie, but Katie hadn't responded; she'd been too busy counting her money.

"Don't make any noise," Sally said now, leading Jo up the back stairs of the Owenses' house. "You have to be quiet in case someone returns home early." She led Jo to a room on the second floor and unlocked the door. "I'll fetch you in two hours. The cook and butler usually return first, at six-thirty. You have to be out by six," she said.

Jo nodded, unnerved by the task ahead of her. She felt like a thief. Eddie's words came back to her: *Sometimes you have to do wrong to do right*. Taking a deep breath, she opened the door to Eleanor Owens's bedroom and stepped inside.

➤ CHAPTER FORTY-TWO ❧

The air was heavy and sad and carried the faint scent of violets. Jo felt as if she'd entered a tomb.

Nothing of Eleanor's had been touched, it appeared, since the day she'd been taken to Darkbriar. A pair of silk slippers stood by the bed. A pile of books lay on the night table. A clock ticked. Jo moved around the room slowly, painfully aware that she was trespassing.

The furniture was all of good quality but dated. A faded rug covered the floor. A slipper chair stood in a corner. No dust was to be found anywhere; the maids had obviously been told to keep the room clean but to leave everything as it was.

Why? Jo wondered. *Do Eleanor's parents come in here for solace? Or to punish themselves?*

The vanity table was covered with silver-backed brushes, perfume bottles, and framed photographs. Most of the photos were of pets—a cat with a ribbon around its neck, two small dogs, a horse. One was of a pretty young woman with delicate features, light hair, and smiling eyes. She was wearing a style of dress that had gone out of fashion years ago. Jo reminded herself that Eleanor had died in 1874. Things had changed. The world had moved on.

Next to the photo was a jewelry box. Jo lifted its cover. Inside was a string of pearls, several pairs of earrings, some bracelets, and a few brooches. There was also a gold pocket watch, ruined, it appeared, by water.

A shiver ran up Jo's spine as she realized she was looking at the watch that had been on Eleanor's body when it was found. She remembered Sally telling her that, and also saying that the gold pendant Eleanor had worn—one half of a heart, engraved with the word *Stephen*—and her sapphire-and-diamond engagement ring had likely been stolen.

Jo turned the watch over. *For Eleanor, on her 18th birthday. Love from Mother and Father,* read the inscription.

Her parents loved her, yet they imprisoned her in this room, Jo thought. *They hoped to save her reputation, to protect her; instead they destroyed her.*

Eleanor had made her own choices—or tried to. She'd chosen a man. She'd chosen to sleep with him before they were married. She'd chosen to keep their child. She'd broken the rules and she'd paid for it—with her life.

Jo thought of Eddie and imagined telling her mother about him. She wouldn't end up locked in her room, but she'd undoubtedly find herself on a train to Winnetka to visit her maiden aunt for a good long time.

Because that's what happens to girls who break the rules, she thought.

The porcelain clock on the mantel chimed. Four-fifteen, its hands said. There was no time to waste. Jo put the watch back in the jewelry box, ready to begin her search.

The draperies were drawn over the room's two windows. Wanting more light, Jo walked to one and opened the heavy silks. She glanced into the Owenses' large back garden as she did. The flowers were dead and the leaves had turned. White marble statues lined the perimeter of the yard. In its center was a bower, presided over by two more statues—one of a man, the other of a woman. Jo couldn't make out who they were.

She turned away from the window and faced the room. "Where do I start?" she whispered.

The bed seemed like a good place. Moving quickly, she ripped the bedcovers, shams, and sheets off it and felt the mattress for lumps but found nothing. Next, she pulled the carpet up, sounded the floorboards, knocked on the baseboards. After that, she removed all the drawers in the vanity and the bureau and felt around inside the frames. She lifted pictures off the wall to see if anything had been attached to their backs. Undeterred, she opened the closet and went through muffs and valises. She tapped the mantel, listening for a hollow place. She went into Eleanor's bathroom and looked inside the medicine cabinet, under the tub, and behind the toilet's water tank.

And then, nearly two hours after Jo had started her search, she gave up. She'd found nothing. Wherever Eleanor had hidden the letters, it wasn't in this room.

They could be anywhere in the house, she thought despondently. *She could've hidden them inside the piano or the grandfather clock. Up in the attic or behind the coal bin. I need two months to search, not two hours.*

Jo glanced at the mantel clock. It was nearly six. Sally would be coming to fetch her any minute now. She'd been careful to put everything back in its place, but a last glance around the room revealed that she'd forgotten to close the draperies. As she reached for the heavy silk panels, her eyes strayed to the garden, and she froze.

A man in rough clothes with tattoos on his face was standing in front of the bower. He must've sensed her, for he looked up, and his eyes, dark and vengeful, met Jo's.

It was Kinch.

❧ CHAPTER FORTY-THREE ❧

"He was *here*! I swear it! I *saw* him!" Jo said, standing by the bower in the Owenses' back garden. "He was *right here*! A man with black hair and marks on his face. How did he get in?"

She was breathless. Eager to corner Kinch, she'd run from Eleanor's room down the back stairs to the kitchen and then outside, with Sally hot on her heels.

"I don't *know* how he got in and I don't care," Sally said. "You have to leave, Miss Montfort. *Now.*" She looked back at the house anxiously. "It's past six. If anyone sees you here, I'm done for!"

Jo took a last look at the bower. She was close enough now to see the two marble figures flanking it: Selene, goddess of the moon, and Helios, the sun god. "How could he have just disappeared?" she asked, bitterly disappointed that he'd gotten away.

"If you don't come along, miss, I'll lock you out here and pretend I have no idea how you got in, and you can explain yourself to Mr. Owens," Sally threatened. "Or you can fly over the wall, just like your make-believe man did."

"That's *it*!" Jo exclaimed. "Didn't you tell me that there's a door in the garden wall? And that it opens onto an alley?"

"Yes, but it's locked. Would you please leave?" Sally said, desperation in her voice.

But Jo didn't. Her eyes played over the garden's alley-side wall, searching for the door. The bricks were heavily overgrown with ivy, but in one place, the undersides of several leaves were showing, and the vines were hanging loosely, as if they'd been disturbed. Jo dashed to the spot and immediately saw the door underneath it. Its wood was old and weathered, its hinges rusted. A sliding bolt was fastened to the door, but its keep was missing. Jo looked down and saw it lying on the ground.

"Kinch kicked it open," Jo whispered. She turned to Sally. "Didn't you say that's how Stephen Smith used to meet with Eleanor? By using this door?"

At that second, a light went on in the parlor. Sally saw it. She grabbed Jo's hand and pulled her into the shadows of the house. "Mr. Baxter's back!" she hissed. "Come *on!*" She ran into the kitchen, dragging Jo after her. They hurried past the butler's pantry to the front of the house and the servants' entrance. Just as she put her hand on the doorknob, the door was wrenched open.

"My goodness, Sally!" A small, red-haired woman stood in the doorway with her hand on her chest. "What a start you gave me!"

"I . . . I'm sorry, Mrs. Clarkson," Sally stammered.

Jo remembered Sally telling her that Mrs. Clarkson was the Owenses' current cook.

"Who's this?" Mrs. Clarkson asked, eyeing Jo suspiciously.

"Josie Jones. Sally's cousin," Jo said, thinking quickly. "Pleased to meet you, ma'am."

"You know you're not to receive visitors here, Sally," Mrs. Clarkson said sternly. "I'll have to inform Mr. Baxter."

"I'm not visiting, ma'am. I only came by to give Sally some news. Our grandmother has taken ill. The doctor says she only has a few days left. I had to let her know. She's Gran's favorite," Jo said, surprising herself with how easily the lie came to her lips.

Mrs. Clarkson softened. "Oh. Well, I suppose that's all right, then," she said. "I'm very sorry to hear it."

"I'll be on my way," Jo said. "Goodbye, Sal. Try not to be too upset."

"I'll try, *Josie*. Thanks for coming by," Sally said, glaring.

A few seconds later, Jo was back on Thirty-Sixth Street. Kinch's voice was in her head, and his threat to Scully echoed in her mind: *There is proof. There are manifests, signed and stamped.*

There are manifests. Not *I have the manifests.* Because he *didn't* have them. But he needed them if he was going to continue extorting money from Van Houten's partners.

In her mind's eye, Jo saw his face again. She saw his fearsome eyes and, though the evening was not a cold one, she shivered. Ever since she'd first spoken with Sally, Jo had been certain Kinch and Stephen Smith were the same man. They'd even used the same method to gain access to the Owenses' garden. But now, having seen Kinch again, doubts gnawed at her. In the portrait hanging at Van Houten's, Smith looked like a kind, mild man, and Kinch looked like anything but.

He'd seen her at her father's window; he knew who she was. And now he'd seen her at Eleanor's window. Did he know she was searching for Stephen Smith's letters, too?

From the second Jo had laid eyes on Kinch, he'd struck her as a ruthless man. She doubted he would let much stand in the way of what he wanted.

Not a garden wall.

And certainly not a girl, either.

❧ CHAPTER FORTY-FOUR ❧

Letter from Mr. Joseph Feen to Mr. Edward Gallagher

November 3, 1890

Dear Eddie,
I searched for the manifests in Eleanor's bedroom but didn't
find them. Kinch appeared in the back garden. I saw him.
Which is a positive development. He saw me, too. Which is not.
                                                    JM

Letter from Miss Edwina Gallagher to
Miss Josephine Montfort

November 4, 1890

Dear Jo,
You're kidding me.

EG

Letter from Mr. Joseph Feen to Mr. Edward Gallagher

November 5, 1890

Dear Eddie,
I do not "kid," though on occasion, I jest. This, however, is
no such occasion. Meet me at the Met. By the Etruscan pots.
Tomorrow at 3 p.m. I shall, as usual, be wearing black.
JM

❧ CHAPTER FORTY-FIVE ❧

Jo sat on a tufted bench inside the antiquities wing of the Metropolitan Museum of Art, staring at a cracked clay pot.

She'd chosen this particular gallery because it was always empty. No one ever came to see the Etruscan pots, and why would they? The Etruscan pots had nothing to say. The Etruscan pots were deadly.

Jo looked around, recalling the last time she'd been here—five days ago, for the Young Patrons' Ball. She'd not heard from Bram since, but she *had* heard he'd been seen chatting with Elizabeth Adams at a party three nights ago. Elizabeth tended to get what she wanted and Jo knew she should try to counter the girl's efforts; instead, she hoped they succeeded. Jo's emotions were still contradictory and confusing to her, but one thing was clear—she could not accept a proposal from Bram. Not when she had such strong feelings for Eddie.

"Where *are* you?" she whispered impatiently. It was three-fifteen. He was late, and she was bursting to tell him everything she'd learned since she'd last seen him.

She heard footsteps behind her and her heart quickened. She turned around eagerly, but it was only the guard. A few minutes later, she heard another set of steps, brisk and determined. She turned again, and this time her heart did more than quicken; it nearly leapt out of her chest.

How can any man be so handsome? she wondered. Eddie could have used a shave, and his too-long hair had only gotten longer. His clothing was rumpled and ink-stained, as always. Yet somehow, an old tweed jacket, a badly knotted necktie, and wrinkled trousers looked better on him than the finest hand-tailored suit did on any other boy. His color was high. He was frowning. He smiled when he saw her, but his eyes retained their intensity.

"Sorry I'm late. There's been a development," he said, sitting down next to her.

"You can't sit there!" she whispered. "Sit on the other side of the bench with your back to me. In case someone sees us!"

Eddie looked around. "But there's no one here," he said.

"Eddie!"

He moved to the other side of the bench, and his back touched hers as he sat.

"I have *so* much to tell you," Jo said. "About Eleanor Owens and the letters and—"

"I know you do, but—"

Jo cut him off. "Kinch wants those letters, Eddie. So he can keep on blackmailing Van Houten," she said. "We need to determine conclusively that Kinch is Stephen Smith, and I've figured out a way to do that: we follow Mr. Scully. Kinch is going to try to get Mr. Scully to pay him more money. If we follow Scully, we'll be there when Kinch shows up and we can—"

"Jo, *listen* to me," Eddie said urgently. "We *can't* follow Scully."

She turned to face him, forgetting she wasn't supposed to. "Why not?" she asked.

Eddie had turned to her, too. He looked troubled. "Because Richard Scully was found earlier today at Van Houten's Wharf," he said.

"That's hardly surprising. He works there," Jo said.

"He wasn't found at the office, Jo. He was found in the water. Dead."

❧ CHAPTER FORTY-SIX ❧

Jo stared at the dead man lying on his back. His lips were parted, as if in protest.

"Couldn't we at least close his mouth?" she asked.

"Not without breaking his jaw," Oscar said matter-of-factly. "The muscles are too stiff. Rigor's set in. It'll release in a few hours. Don't worry. The undertaker will pretty him up for his funeral."

I hope so, Jo thought, upset to see an old family friend, a man she'd known her entire life, stretched out on a cold ceramic table in the city morgue. The shock of Eddie's news still hadn't worn off, and she wondered now, as she looked at the corpse, if Scully's death had anything to do with her father's.

"The cops say Scully drowned," Eddie had explained to Jo, back at the museum. "He was at Van Houten's working late, and it was foggy when he started for home. They think he became disoriented and fell into the river."

Jo had found that impossible to believe and had told him so. "Richard Scully walked to Van Houten's every day of the week except Sunday," she'd said. "He could've navigated the waterfront blindfolded."

"I have a bad feeling about this, Jo. The body's at the morgue. I'm heading over there to see what Oscar thinks," Eddie had said.

He'd tried to dissuade her from accompanying him, but there was no way she wasn't going. She'd left the museum a few minutes after he did to avoid being seen with him and had hailed a separate cab.

"Take your notes fast, kids," Oscar advised now. "The undertaker's on his way. The cops brought Phillip Montfort and Alvah Beekman here to ID the body. When they finished, Beekman went to the undertaker's and Montfort went to notify the family."

Poor Uncle Phillip, Jo thought. *First he loses my father and now Mr. Scully.*

As Eddie pulled out his notebook, Jo leaned over Richard Scully's body and peered at it. Scully was a waxy gray, except for some purple blotches on his face, torso, and the tops of his legs. His eyes were half closed, and the skin around them was badly swollen with blood so dark, it looked black. His fingers were curled into his palms. Silt from the bottom of the East River streaked his forehead. A towel had been placed over his groin by Oscar, when Jo and Eddie arrived, to protect Jo's sensibilities.

But Jo found that her sensibilities didn't need protecting. The last time she'd come to the morgue, she'd been overwhelmed by horror and sadness. Those feelings were still there, but they'd been eclipsed by an intense desire to find out exactly how Richard Scully had ended up in the East River.

"Any idea when Scully drowned?" Eddie asked. "This morning? Last night?"

"He didn't drown," Oscar said.

"C'mon, Osk. He was found in the water," Eddie countered. "The cops fished him out. There were multiple eyewitnesses."

"I didn't say he wasn't found in the water. I said he didn't drown."

"Are you telling me—"

"—that Richard Scully was murdered? Yes, I am."

Eddie let out a low whistle.

Jo's entire body went cold. She'd found it hard to believe that Mr. Scully had simply fallen into the water, but it was difficult to hear the word *murder* again.

"How do you know, Oscar?" she asked.

"To start with, there's no froth in the airway," Oscar said, pointing at Scully's nose and mouth.

"Froth?" Jo echoed.

"It's a mixture of water, air, mucus, and sometimes blood that gets churned into foam as the drowning person tries to breathe. Its absence suggests Scully *wasn't* trying to breathe when he went into the water. Which means he was already dead. And then there's this," he said, turning the body onto its side.

Jo grimaced as she saw the gaping laceration on the back of Scully's head. His skull had been fractured. The bone was cracked like an eggshell.

"Blunt instrument trauma," Oscar said. "The weapon was curved, I'd say. A baseball bat. Or a billy club. The blow fractured both the parietal and occipital bones, and caused the periorbital ecchymoses—"

"In English, Osk," Eddie said, writing like mad.

"—the raccoon eyes. Blood from the fracture leaked into the sinuses and the tissue around the sockets and discolored the skin. The man who hit him—"

"How do you know it was man?" Jo interrupted.

"Because strength is required to crack a man's skull wide open. Confidence, too."

Jo wondered at that. "One needs confidence to kill?" she asked.

"It helps," Oscar said. "Anger gets the job done, too, but it's messy. This was quick and clean. The killer swung hard and accurately. Men are generally better at the motion of swinging than women because they get more practice. They swing sledgehammers and axes. Cleavers. Scythes."

"Did Dr. Koehler see this?" asked Eddie.

Jo remembered that Dr. Koehler was the coroner, and Oscar's boss.

"Yes," Oscar said, frustration in his voice.

"And he's still calling it a drowning?"

"He says Scully hit his head on a piling as he fell into the water."

"Is that possible?" Jo asked.

Oscar looked at her over the top of his glasses. "Not unless he was in the habit of walking backward." He ran his hand over Scully's back. "See this?" He tapped a patch of dark purple. "It's livor mortis. After the heart stops beating, blood settles in the lowest part of the body and produces this discoloration. Scully was in a shallow area, and the sailor who spotted him said he was lying on his back. And as we can see, there is indeed livor on his back."

"I thought dead people floated," Eddie said.

"That happens later, as the body decomposes. Bacteria inside it release gas, causing it to bloat and rise. Most of the time, a fresh body will sink first. Especially if it's wearing a heavy wool overcoat like Scully was," Oscar explained. "The cops who pulled him out of the water corroborate that he was on his back. *But*"—Oscar eased the body back down on the slab—"we have signs of livor here, too." He pointed to the faint purple markings on Scully's right cheek, and on his chest, belly, and legs.

"Which means?" Eddie prompted.

"Which means he fell forward when he died and stayed that way for some time. At least half an hour, probably three or four. When the body was put into the river and came to rest on its back, the blood resettled dorsally. The fact that the dorsal livor is well developed indicates that the body remained that way for at least ten hours. Since he was discovered at noon, that means he went into the water sometime around two a.m. Back that out by three hours to allow for the livor to develop on the front of his body, and we get a time of death of approximately eleven p.m." He prodded Scully's thigh like a housewife prodding a cut of meat. "The advanced degree of rigor confirms my hypothesis."

"You say he was killed at eleven but not dumped in the river until two a.m. . . . Where was he in the meantime?" Eddie asked.

"Good question," Oscar said. "Usually in cases like this—well-dressed gentleman whacked on the back of the head at night—it's a robbery."

"You don't think this was?" said Jo.

"I did before I saw the livor on Scully's front. No robber's going to hit him, leave him on the street for several hours, then come back and throw him in the river. And then we have the fact that nothing of Scully's appears to be missing. A robber would've taken his billfold, watch, and wedding ring. Probably his coat and shoes, too. It makes no sense. Nor does the river."

"The river? Why not?" Eddie asked. He was still scribbling.

"As I said, the waters around Van Houten's Wharf are relatively shallow, particularly where Scully was dumped. And with the waterfront being such a busy place, chances are good his body would be seen. Why would a killer who wanted to cover up his crime hide a body in plain sight?"

Jo knew. And the knowledge frightened her. She looked at Eddie. He'd stopped writing. He knew, too; she could see it.

"Oscar—" he started to say, but his words were cut off by a booming voice. It was coming from the hallway, outside a set of swinging doors.

"It's the boss," Oscar said. "He doesn't like me entertaining visitors. Make yourselves scarce."

Eddie took Jo's arm and hurried her out of another set of swinging doors. As soon as they were out in the street, Jo started talking.

"It's Kinch, isn't it? He's the killer. He didn't want to hide Scully's body. He wanted it found," she said. "Just like my father's.

He wanted both murders to look like accidents. That way, the authorities don't go looking for the murderer, and he can remain at large and threaten the rest of the partners. He's going to kill them one by one."

Eddie nodded. "I think you're right. Back when we eavesdropped on Kinch and Scully, I thought Kinch wouldn't kill your father because he was going to give him a thousand dollars. But maybe that's *all* your father was going to give him. Maybe he balked. Scully certainly did."

"So Kinch killed them both. Which is what he'll do to the rest of the partners if *they* refuse to meet his demands."

"It's very possible, Jo," Eddie said solemnly.

Jo's fear bloomed into terror. "Dear God," she said, "what if my uncle's next?"

❧ CHAPTER FORTY-SEVEN ❧

A fine dappled gray pulled Phillip Montfort's spacious and comfortable brougham up Madison Avenue. The horse was carefully controlled by the carriage's driver—a man who knew that being too free with the reins resulted in undesirable behavior.

Inside the carriage, its occupants, en route from Richard Scully's burial to a funeral reception at his home, just as carefully reined in the emotion they felt at the loss of yet another member of their close-knit circle.

Except for Jo, who was wringing her hands—hidden inside her muff—in an agony of indecision.

She needed to tell her uncle about Kinch and the threat he posed, but she knew that by doing so, she might get herself into a great deal of trouble and be forbidden to leave the house, and jeopardizing her ability to pursue her father's killer was the last thing she wanted to do.

"I have to tell my uncle. I *have* to," she'd said to Eddie two days ago, after they'd left the morgue.

"What are you going to say when he asks you how you know?" he'd countered. "That you went to the morgue to personally inspect Scully's corpse?"

Jo didn't have an answer. Not then, and not now, but she knew she had to protect her uncle no matter the consequences. If Kinch had taken two lives, he'd have no qualms about taking three.

"It's so senseless, Richard's death," her aunt Madeleine said, bringing Jo's mind back to the present. "Being taken in the prime of his life. All because of a misstep."

Jo suddenly saw her chance—a way to warn her uncle without revealing what she'd been up to.

"What if they're wrong?" she asked, choosing her words carefully so as not to give herself away.

"What if who's wrong, dear?" asked her aunt.

"The police. What if it wasn't an accident? What if Mr. Scully was murdered?"

Jo's aunt looked taken aback. Her mother looked downright shocked. "Josephine Montfort, what a *dreadful* thing to say!" she scolded. "Where do you get such ideas?"

"He could have been," Jo insisted. "They say he could've been killed and then thrown into the water."

"Who, may I ask, is *they?*"

"The papers, Mama," Jo fibbed.

Her mother looked scandalized. "Are you reading the newspapers? You know I forbid it," she said sternly.

"I heard the newsies crying the story," Jo answered quickly, covering her tracks.

That much, at least, was true. Newsboys for the *World* and the *Herald* had not stopped shouting about the double tragedy that had befallen Van Houten. First Charles Montfort, then Richard Scully. Gossips wondered how two such terrible accidents could have befallen the partners of one firm in such rapid succession. The more lurid papers had suggested that Van Houten was cursed.

"They are *such* nuisances!" Madeleine said.

"Maybe Mr. Scully was hit over the head," Jo pressed. "What if he was? And what if this awful man is still skulking around the waterfront just waiting to attack someone else? Uncle Phillip could be in danger. Any of the partners could."

"Josephine, that is *enough*," Anna warned. "That you are overwrought is understandable, but still, you must contain yourself. Murder is not a suitable topic of conversation for a young lady."

Jo looked directly at her uncle. "You must be careful coming and going from Van Houten's, Uncle Phillip. And everywhere else. You must avoid anyone who looks strange and dangerous. You *must*. Promise me you will," she demanded, her voice rising.

Jo's mother and aunt traded worried glances; she saw them. Phillip leaned forward and patted her hand. "I shall take extra care. You have my word, Josephine. Now please stop worrying."

He smiled at her, but she could see that his mind was elsewhere. On Richard Scully, no doubt, Jo thought. He'd just seen him— one of his oldest friends—buried. He hadn't dismissed her worries, but he hadn't given them his full attention, either, and Jo was not satisfied. She decided to tell him the whole story. There was no other way.

The group drove on in silence until the carriage stopped outside of the Scullys' town house. Phillip and Rob stepped out, then helped the women alight. As her uncle started for the steps, Jo heard a tinkling sound. She looked down and saw coins on the sidewalk.

"My goodness," Madeleine scolded, "Phillip, you're dropping money all over the place."

Phillip sighed. "There's a hole in my coat pocket," he said wearily, not bothering to pick up the coins. "I keep forgetting to tell the valet."

Jo's heart ached for him. He was fastidious about his appearance, so much so that the whole family teased him about it. The fact that he'd forgotten to have his coat fixed was a small but telling sign of how heavily the burden of grief was weighing on him.

"The beggars will have a field day, Papa," said Rob as he took his mother's arm and led her up the Scullys' steps to their front door.

Phillip followed, escorting Jo's mother. Jo and Caroline brought up the rear. Though Caroline was busy prattling about what sort of punch the Scullys were likely to serve, and that plump little Araminta Scully oughtn't to have too much of it, Jo could still hear her mother and uncle talking.

"I've told you repeatedly, Anna, she's a very sensitive girl. These sorts of shocks prey heavily upon such types and lead to morbid imaginings. You must either send her back to school, or perhaps for a long visit to your sister in Winnetka . . ."

Jo caught her breath. That was exactly what she *didn't* want.

". . . or at least allow her more freedom to visit with friends, walk in the park, take trips to the shops, and do all the things girls her age do."

Her mother nodded at his last suggestion and Jo exhaled, relieved not to have been banished to her aunt's. Still, Phillip's words only reinforced her desire to speak with him. He hadn't taken her worries seriously; he believed she was only imagining the threat to his safety. But how would she get him alone? And what, exactly, would she say?

For the next hour, Jo bided her time. She moved through the Scullys' home, offering her condolences to Mrs. Scully, making small talk with her friends, observing Bram carry a drink to Elizabeth Adams, avoiding Grandmama, and all the while keeping an eye on her uncle's whereabouts.

When she saw him leave the drawing room—presumably to use the lavatory—she made her move. She coughed a few times, then excused herself from a conversation on the pretext of finding a servant to get her a glass of water. Out in the Scullys' long hallway, she spotted her uncle. He was headed back to the drawing room.

"Uncle Phillip?" she said. "Do you have a moment?"

Phillip smiled. "For you, Jo, I have hours."

A streak of unseasonably mild weather had continued, and the Scullys had opened a pair of doors that led from the back of the first floor to an enclosed porch, and from that down into their garden. Jo had seen the open doors earlier, and she led him through them now. She'd figured out a way to tell him what she knew without telling him how she knew it.

"This is all very mysterious," Phillip said bemusedly as she led him under an archway of bare branches into a gazebo near the garden's back wall. "Have you news to tell me? Shouldn't Bram be asking my permission first?" he teased.

"Oh, Uncle Phillip," Jo said brokenly. He was hoping for a bit of happy news, and she was about to give him a very terrible truth.

Phillip's smile faded. "What's wrong, Jo?" he asked, worry in his voice.

Jo took a deep breath.

And told him.

➤ CHAPTER FORTY-EIGHT ◄

Phillip turned as gray as a corpse.

Jo had told him everything that had happened since they'd last spoken about her father's death, with one important omission—her own role in uncovering the information. She didn't want him to know she'd been sneaking out of her house at all hours. He'd certainly put a stop to it.

When she finished, her uncle was silent. He didn't lecture or scold or threaten to send her away. Instead, he sat down heavily in a garden chair and closed his eyes. When he opened them again, he looked wearier than she'd ever seen him. Heartbroken. Hollow.

Jo understood his reaction; he was in shock. She'd felt the same way when she'd first learned the real cause of her father's death.

"I'm sorry, Uncle Phillip. It's a very hard thing to have to accept. I know it is. I was devastated when I found out."

Phillip looked at her searchingly. "Josephine, what you're saying . . . It's . . . well—"

"I know it must sound crazy, Uncle Phillip—"

"Yes, it does."

"—but I swear it's all true."

"How in God's name did you learn of these things?" he asked, almost fearfully.

Jo was ready for that question. She hoped the answer she'd come up with would keep her out of trouble. "I hired a private investigator."

"An investigator?" Phillip said skeptically. "What's his name?"

"His name is . . . is Oscar. Oscar Edwards," she replied, having made it up on the spot.

"I'd like to meet him."

"It's not possible at the moment. He's out of town," Jo fibbed.

"I see. How are you funding his efforts?"

Jo hesitated; she hadn't anticipated that question. "With some money that I . . . that I have tucked away," she replied.

"And you believe the things this Mr. Edwards told you?"

"As if I'd witnessed them myself," Jo replied, sitting down across from him. "Can you understand now why I'm so worried about you?"

Phillip nodded. Emboldened by this, Jo decided to press her luck. Maybe he himself could provide the information she and Eddie still needed.

"I know I've blindsided you, Uncle Phillip, and I'm sorry, but I need to ask you a few things. Your answer might help Mr. Edwards. The ship Kinch mentioned . . . the *Bonaventure* . . . does Van Houten own it?"

"No. I've never even heard of it."

"What about one called *Nausett*?"

"Yes, we owned her," Phillip said.

Jo was on the edge of her chair. She thought of Jackie Shaw's words: *Follow the* Nausett *and you'll find the* Bonaventure. *God help you if you do.*

"She was ours all too briefly," Phillip continued. "We bought her back in 1871. After the war ended. Planned to run her out of

Zanzibar, but never got the chance. Winds pushed her onto the rocks as she was coming around the Cape of Good Hope. She broke up. Lost most of her crew, but a few made it to shore."

Jo's heart fell. *Shaw's wrong: the* Nausett *doesn't lead to the* Bonaventure, she thought. She tried a different line of inquiry. "Is there any substance to Kinch's claims? Was the firm ever implicated in any wrongdoing?" she asked.

"Of course not, Josephine!" Phillip said, offended.

"Is it possible that Kinch could be Stephen Smith?"

"How? Smith took one of our ships, the *Gull*, to explore in the Seychelles. He never returned. None of the crew did. The *Gull* was never seen again. Our business is a risky one. Ships are lost all too frequently."

"But *could* he have survived? Kinch spoke of pirates. Could a pirate ship have rescued him?"

"*Pirates?*" Phillip echoed in disbelief. "Men with earrings and eye patches and parrots on their shoulders? Jo, surely you see that all these theories of yours are . . . well, preposterous," he added gently. "If Smith *had* survived a shipwreck and had somehow been rescued, he would have returned to Zanzibar."

Jo felt her conviction that Kinch was Stephen Smith weakening once again. Maybe her theory *was* preposterous. Her uncle certainly thought so.

"Smith had rooms in Zanzibar and possessions," Phillip continued. "And, as you just informed me, he had a fiancée in New York, Eleanor Owens, who was expecting their child. I can't imagine that he would have willingly abandoned her."

"Did he have any family?" Jo asked.

"He'd been divorced and had no children. His mother was still living—she was in Boston. I had his things sent to her. And that was the end of it," Phillip said. He regarded Jo levelly. "The greatest proof, to me, at least, that Stephen perished is that there has been no word of him all these years. In Zanzibar, New York, or anywhere else. He was an upstanding man, one who would never turn his back on his obligations—whether they were to his partners or his intended."

They both went silent; then Phillip said, "I must be frank with you, Josephine. I'm having a great deal of trouble accepting what you've told me—that my brother was murdered. Richard, too. That a mysterious tattooed man is behind it all—"

Jo cut him off. "You *must* believe it, Uncle Phillip. Your life and the lives of the other partners may depend on it," she insisted.

She thought she'd convinced him that Kinch—whoever he was—posed a real threat and was dismayed to find she had not.

Phillip held up his hands. "Please don't get upset. I promise I'll be on my guard and that I'll warn the other partners about this man Kinch. But you must make *me* a promise, too—that we'll keep this between ourselves for now. I'll tell the others that *I* learned of these things. I don't want them to know you did. They might talk, and I—"

"—don't want my sterling character tarnished," Jo said, exasperated. Even at a time like this, her uncle worried about her marriage prospects. It infuriated her, but touched her, too.

"Yes. Exactly. If something untoward is going on, I'll get to the bottom of it—believe me. But you must keep an eye on the future, Josephine. What may or may not have happened cannot be allowed to destroy your prospects. Or Caroline's and Robert's. Do you understand?"

Jo knew he was referring to Bram Aldrich. She didn't have the heart to tell him that she'd probably already destroyed those plans. Instead, she assured him she would say nothing to the remaining partners.

She was glad her uncle hadn't asked more questions about Oscar Edwards. She'd been worried that he would try to cut off her investigation, but he hadn't done that, either. Things had gone well. Better than she'd expected, in fact, and she was deeply relieved. Yet as she looked at her uncle's face, still so pale and worn-looking, her heart clenched.

"It'll be all right, Uncle Phillip," she said, taking his hand. "You're prepared for Kinch now, should he choose to visit you. And Mr. Edwards is busy tracking down Kinch's whereabouts and trying to gather proof of his doings. And when we have all of those things, we can pursue justice. For Papa and Mr. Scully."

"I'm so sorry for all of this," her uncle said. "For your father. And Richard. I'm sorry that such slight shoulders as yours have had to carry such a heavy burden of grief. It's too much for one so young and delicate."

His eyes met hers. She saw concern for her in them, and something else that was harder to define. Was it sorrow? Pity?

"I'm *fine*, Uncle Phillip, I promise," Jo said.

They stood then, and Jo took her uncle's arm. He covered her hand with his own, and together they walked out of the gazebo and under the bare branches to rejoin the mourners.

➤ CHAPTER FORTY-NINE ➤

Jo hurried up the steps to the Metropolitan Museum of Art, excited to see Eddie.

She'd written him Saturday afternoon, after she'd returned home from the Scullys', asking him to meet her by the Etruscan pots at ten a.m. today, Monday, so she could tell him how things had gone with her uncle and see if he'd turned up any new information.

Her mother had let her go to the museum without any discussion this morning. Her uncle's advice—to allow her more freedom—had obviously sunk in.

"Miss? Please, miss . . . ," a voice said as she reached the top of the steps.

It was a beggar boy. He was standing by the museum's door. Jo was about to give him a few coins when a guard advanced on him. "Get lost, street rat," he growled.

The boy darted away and Jo reached for the door.

"Miss Jo, *wait*!" the boy shouted.

Jo stopped and turned around. *How does he know my name?* she wondered.

"It's me, Tumbler!" the boy cried, dodging the lumbering guard. His face was flushed. He looked upset.

As soon as he said his name, Jo recognized him. She hurried to him, put an arm around his shoulders, and walked back down the steps, away from the guard. "What is it? What's wrong?" she asked.

"Fay sent me. We was at the morgue this morning, her and me. Muttbait was with us. . . ."

Tumbler was talking so fast, Jo could hardly keep up. "Slow down!" she said.

The boy took a big gulp of air. "Some fool got hit by a carriage," he said. "Me and Fay and Muttbait was pretending to be his family. Oscar usually chucks us out, but he was busy and he didn't see us, so we got the stiff's tiepin and pocket watch. We couldn't get his wallet, though. That's why we need you."

Jo was horrified. "You need *me* to help you rob a body?"

"No! Listen, will you? On our way home, we walked past an alley that runs alongside the morgue," Tumbler said. "Fay heard strange noises coming from it. She went down to see what was making them and found Eddie Gallagher crumpled up in a heap."

Jo's heart lurched. She grabbed the boy's shoulders. "What happened?" she asked.

"He was on his way to see Oscar about a story, but he never made it. Someone came out of the alley after him. He's beat up real bad. We got him to his room. He's scared the same man who came after him might come after you."

"Who was it?" Jo asked.

"Dunno, miss. Fay told me to say that he needs a doctor and she can't pay for one cuz her and me and Muttbait didn't get the stiff's wallet and she don't have any cash. You got any, miss?"

But Tumbler got no cash and no answer, because before he even finished speaking, Jo was down the museum steps and on the sidewalk, running for a cab.

❧ CHAPTER FIFTY ❦

Jo was more afraid than she'd ever been in her life. She'd been so worried Kinch might attack her uncle, she'd never even imagined that he might go after Eddie.

When she got to Reade Street, she saw that there was blood on the sidewalk outside Eddie's building. It was on the front door of the building, too, which was slightly ajar. She rushed inside the vestibule and up the stairs and pounded on Eddie's door.

"About damn time!" Fay said as she opened it. "Here, take this." She tossed Jo a bloody rag. "I'm going for a doctor. He's coughing up blood. I sent Muttbait back to the morgue to get Oscar, but he hasn't showed." She grabbed her jacket and hat and ran out of his room, slamming the door on her way.

There was a bowl of red-tinged water on the floor by Eddie's bed. Jo nearly stepped in it as she hurried to him. She sat down on the bed and gently took one of his bloodied hands in hers.

Eddie's left eye was swollen shut. His lip was cut. His nose was bruised and bleeding. More blood stained his once-white shirt. Jo couldn't tell if it had dripped from his face or if it was coming from an injury on his chest.

Eddie opened his good eye. "Jo?" he said. "Thank God you're all right. I was worried about you."

"I'm fine," Jo said. She wasn't concerned about herself, only him. "Are you bleeding anywhere besides your face? Does anything feel like it's broken?" She dropped the rag Fay had tossed to her into the bowl of water, took off her jacket, and rolled up her sleeves. She'd been required to take a first-aid course at school. Her lessons came back to her now.

"Ribs, maybe. He got me on the ground and landed a few good kicks."

Jo unknotted his tie and pulled it off. She unbuttoned his shirt and opened it.

"Nice poker face," Eddie wheezed.

Jo shook her head, too upset to speak. His chest was a patchwork of scrapes and bruises. She could see from the way his ribs flared that it hurt him just to breathe. This was all her fault. Kinch had beaten Eddie because Eddie was pursuing him—at her request. Blinking back tears, she picked up the bowl on the floor, walked to the sink, and dumped out the bloodied water. She refilled the bowl with clean water and rinsed out the rag Fay had tossed at her, then got to work cleaning Eddie's wounds.

"It was Kinch, wasn't it?" she said, trying to keep her voice steady.

Before he could answer, the door burst open and Fay tumbled back inside, dragging Oscar Rubin behind her. He was carrying a black leather bag. A little girl with a face marred by scars followed them in and closed the door behind them. She saw the small fireplace and sat down by it to warm her hands.

"I found him and Muttbait coming up Reade Street," Fay said breathlessly.

Oscar's eyes fell on his friend. He let out a low whistle. "What, exactly, have you done to earn yourself such a thorough beating?" he asked, putting his bag on the table.

Jo stood up so that Oscar could sit down on the bed.

"I'd like to know that, too," said Fay. She was looking at Eddie with a mixture of worry and anger.

"Nothing," Eddie replied, glancing at Jo. She knew he was trying not to say more than she might want him to.

"Of course not," Oscar said sarcastically. He was wearing a stethoscope around his neck. He leaned over now and pressed it to Eddie's chest, holding a finger up for silence. Next he looked up Eddie's nose and made him open his mouth wide. He examined Eddie's swollen eye and the rest of his cuts and bruises, then sat back.

"The good news is that your lungs are fine," he said. "The blood you're coughing is coming from a burst vessel in your nose. It's dripping down your throat and triggering a reflex. Should stop soon. The damage to your eye's only external, and you still have all your teeth. The bad news is that two of your ribs appear to be cracked, you may have a concussion, and the cut on your temple needs stitches."

He took a bottle of laudanum—a morphine solution—and a shot glass from his bag. He filled the glass half full and handed it to Eddie, who drank it down.

"So what happened?" Oscar asked as Eddie handed the glass back.

"I was heading up to the Met but decided to see you on the way," Eddie explained. "To see if anyone interesting died a terrible and violent death."

"Slow news day?"

"Very." Eddie coughed. "A man came up behind me. He shoved me in the alley just south of the morgue and beat the tar out of me," he said.

"Just one man? Are you sure? He did a lot of damage."

"He was strong. And fast. I threw a punch; he deflected it. I threw another; he grabbed my hand and bent my fingers back. Whipped me around and got me in a choke hold."

Jennifer Donnelly

Oscar paused at that; then he rummaged in his bag and pulled out a clean white linen towel and placed it on the table. "Any idea who he is?" he asked, neatly laying out bandages, iodine, scissors, a wad of cotton, a needle, and black thread on the towel.

Jo waited to hear Eddie say the name Kinch.

"Unfortunately, yes. I don't know his name, but I recognized his face. I've seen him before," Eddie said. He turned to Jo. "It was the man with the scar on his cheek. The one who followed us in the Met. And who spooked Jackie Shaw at Walsh's."

Fay, who'd been standing still, arms crossed, swore under her breath. Eddie looked at her. His eyes narrowed. He was about to ask her something, but Jo cut him off.

"Eddie, are you *sure?*" she asked. She'd been so certain it was Kinch.

"Positive. I got a good look at him. He leaned over me when he was done and said that this was only a warning. He told me that this time I'll wish I was dead, but next time I *would* be if I didn't mind my own business. He knew my name. He knows yours, too, Jo. He said it. That's why I sent Tumbler to warn you. We may have been after the wrong man all this time. Scarface might be our killer, not Kinch."

"Your *killer?*" Oscar echoed, looking from Eddie to Jo.

Eddie didn't answer him. Neither did Jo. They were too intent on their conversation.

"But how does he know our names?" Jo asked.

"From Jackie Shaw?" Eddie offered. "Maybe Scarface caught up with Shaw outside of Walsh's. Worked him over the same way he worked me."

"But I gave Shaw a false name, remember?"

"Yeah, you did. I forgot," Eddie said.

"Wait . . . you're not Josie Jones? A cub?" said Oscar.

Jo shook her head. She regretted giving Oscar a false name.

When she'd first met him at the morgue, she hadn't known if she could trust him; she knew now. "My real name's Josephine Montfort. I'm Charles Montfort's daughter," she said.

Oscar let out a low whistle. "That explains a few things, but I still feel like I'm missing something." He looked from Jo to Eddie to Fay. "Who's Scarface? And how does he know you?"

"That's the big question, Osk," Eddie said.

"I wish we knew," said Jo.

Fay said nothing. However, she looked distinctly uncomfortable. Eddie picked up on it.

"Fay, you know something, don't you?" he said. His gaze was piercing, but Fay didn't flinch from it.

"It can't get back to the Tailor. If he finds out I told you, I'm dead," she said. Her voice was steady, but fear flickered in her eyes.

"What is it?" Eddie asked.

"I know how Scarface knows your name," she said to Eddie. She nodded at Jo. "Hers, too. And her whole damn story."

"How?" Jo asked.

Fay turned to her. With an expression that was part pity, part contempt, she said, "You told him."

⇝ *CHAPTER FIFTY-ONE* ⇜

Eddie sat up, a furious expression on his face. "Son of a *bitch*!" he yelled, startling Jo.

"Did you forget what the Tailor's like, Newsie?" Fay asked harshly. "He played you like a fiddle. And you let him."

"Scarface was *there*, wasn't he? Why the *hell* didn't you tell me, Fay?"

"What was I supposed to do? Shout it out?" Fay yelled. She ripped off her jacket and unbuttoned the top of her blouse. Bruises mottled her neck. "*These* are because I was short the other night. What do you think he would've done to me if I'd told you—and right in front of him, no less?"

Eddie's anger evaporated. Sorrow took its place. Jo could see it in his eyes. The sight of Fay's bruises seemed to hurt him more than his own wounds did.

"You got out, Newsie. *You*. Not me," Fay said, buttoning her shirt back up.

"I'm sorry," Eddie said softly.

Jo was upset by the marks of violence on Fay, shocked by Eddie's sudden outburst, and lost by their exchange. "Can one of you please tell me what's going on?" she asked.

"Tell me, too, while you're at it," Oscar said, scrubbing his hands in Eddie's sink.

Eddie explained. "The man with the scar on his face was at the Tailor's when we were there, Jo. He heard every word you said."

"Where was he?" Jo asked, horrified to think she'd been in the same room with such a violent man. And that Fay and the Tailor's other orphans had. It scared her to think that he'd contrived to find out Eddie's name, and her own, and that he now knew the details of her father's death as well.

"There's a curtained alcove at the back of that room," Fay said. "It's where the Tailor sleeps. Scarface was there the whole time. Sitting on his bed."

"Who is he? How is he involved in this?" Jo asked.

"I don't know," Fay replied. "The Tailor didn't say his name, and I didn't hear much of what passed between them." Her mouth hardened into a tight smile. "I *saw* what passed between them, though—a twenty-dollar note. Scarface told the Tailor what he wanted: to find out what the two of you were up to. And the Tailor took it from there. I've never seen the man before and I've been at the Tailor's almost all my life, but I get the feeling they know each other well."

Oscar moved from the sink back to Eddie's bedside. Fay and Jo stepped aside.

"Oh, don't mind me," Oscar said as he sat on the bed and began to tend to Eddie's wounds. "I'm only here to clean you up and make sure you don't die of a septicemia or gangrene." He turned to Jo. "Since no one seems to want to enlighten me, could you at least heat some water?"

Jo felt bad. Oscar had given them information they would never have gained from anyone else, and now he was taking care of Eddie. It was only right to tell him why. She looked at Eddie, silently asking him if it was safe to.

"I trust him with my life. Fay, too," he said, as if reading her mind.

"What about her?" Jo asked quietly, pointing at Muttbait, who was still sitting by the hearth.

"Don't worry about her," Fay said. "She won't say a thing to the Tailor. He's not the one who holds her when she wakes up screaming from her nightmares. Same thing every time, isn't it, girl? Dogs in an alley."

Muttbait nodded silently.

Still, Jo hesitated. She wasn't used to sharing secrets. At school, and even with most of her friends here at home, the less people knew about you, the better. Gossip was a deadly weapon, and the girls in her circle knew how to wield it.

Fay gave Jo a withering look. "So *that's* how it is?" she asked. "Eddie took a beating over this. If the Tailor finds out what I've done, I will, too. Oscar's involved now. He doesn't even know why. And you won't tell him."

Jo realized that Fay was daring her—daring her to confide, to trust them. All of them. And she realized something else: she very much wanted to. She filled the kettle with water, as Oscar had asked, and set it on the hearth to warm. Then she sat down at Eddie's table and told her story, start to finish. Oscar listened attentively. Fay did, too. Some of it was news to her, as there had been developments since Jo's visit to the Tailor.

"So there you have it," Jo said when she was done. "I'm sorry to have made you a part of it, Oscar, and you, too, Fay, but I'm grateful to you both for the help you've given me."

Oscar said nothing in reply. His gaze had shifted from Jo to Eddie's window. He was frowning.

Jo looked at Eddie. "Is he angry with me?" she whispered anxiously.

"No. That's how he thinks," Eddie said. "Give him a minute. He'll be back."

"I'll keep my eyes peeled for Scarface. Let you know if I see him,"

Fay said. "The Tailor's already got us looking for Kinch. Scarface wants *him* found, too. But it seems Kinch doesn't want to be found. He's lying low. Probably in some flea-ridden dump where no one asks too many questions. Problem is, the city's full of those."

Oscar suddenly took a deep breath, as if he were surfacing from some watery depth. He looked at Eddie over the top of his spectacles. His eyes were sharp and focused now.

"He's a cop," he said. "A cop or a hospital worker."

"Who is?" Eddie asked. "Kinch?"

"Scarface."

"How do you know that?"

"Because of that move he used on you. The one where he grabbed your hand and bent your fingers back. Cops use it to take down unruly prisoners. I've seen orderlies at Bellevue use it on violent patients, too. If you want to find him, sniff around precinct houses and hospitals."

"I will. Thank you, Osk," Eddie said.

Oscar frowned. He grabbed Eddie's chin and turned his head. "This thing's still dripping," he said, pointing at the cut on Eddie's temple. He threaded his needle, and rubbed it—and the thread—down with alcohol.

"I'm sure it'll stop," Eddie said, eyeing the needle nervously.

"No, it won't. You won't feel a thing. You've had laudanum."

"Not enough," Eddie said.

Jo turned away as Oscar started stitching.

"Ow, Osk. Ow, ow, ow, *ow*!" Eddie yelled as the needle pierced his skin.

"Pipe down, sissy-boy," Oscar said.

When he finished stitching, Oscar pulled Eddie's bloodstained shirt off and cleaned his wounds using soap and the water Jo had heated. As he was placing his implements back into his bag, his stomach growled loudly.

"Charming," Eddie said.

"It's the perfectly natural result of muscle contractions moving chyme through the alimentary canal," Oscar said cheerfully.

"Chyme?" Eddie repeated. "What kind of disgusting substance is that?"

"It's the liquid mix of food and digestive juices. The rumbling noise itself is caused by pockets of gas getting squeezed through the tract along with the slurry on its way to the anus. It tends to be louder when the stomach is empty. Which mine is. I missed my lunch to come here. What've you got to eat?"

"Nothing."

"Figures," Oscar said. "I'm off, then. Got two autopsies this afternoon. Can't do them on an empty stomach."

"How can you do them on a full one?" Eddie asked.

"We have to go, too," Fay said. "We have work to do, since we didn't get the nice fat wallet we were after earlier," she added, giving Oscar a pointed look.

"Don't you ever feel bad about robbing corpses?" Oscar asked her.

"Don't you ever feel bad about cutting them open?" Fay asked him.

"No, because they're dead," Oscar replied.

"Exactly," Fay said.

She called for Muttbait, then patted Eddie's cheek on her way out. "You take care, Newsie."

Eddie caught her hand. "I will. Thanks, Fay. I'd still be in that alley if you hadn't shown up. I owe you."

"Hardly," Fay said, suddenly shy. She pulled her hand free and headed for the door. Then she stopped short, turned, and pointed at Jo. "*Don't* get him killed, Jo Montfort. Or you'll have me to worry about, as well as the Tailor and Scarface and Kinch and any other murderous lunatics who might be after you."

"Out of all of them, you scare me the most," said Jo.

Fay smiled. "I'll take that as a compliment," she said. And then she was gone.

"I'll come back tonight to check on you. Maybe bring you some dinner," said Oscar, picking up his bag. "You like goulash?"

"I'll eat anything. Thanks, Osk."

Jo closed the door after Oscar left and leaned against it.

"There's an old shirt in the top drawer of my dresser, Jo," Eddie said. "Would you mind?"

Jo opened the drawer. A faded band-collar shirt, made of dungaree, was on top of a neatly folded pile. Under it were two pressed white shirts, the kind one wore to an office. Something about the meager collection of clothing made her heart clench. When she was little, her father used to let her pick his shirt for him while he was shaving. He had shelves upon shelves of shirts, far too many to count. Eddie had so few.

"Did you find it?"

Jo quickly turned around. "Is this the one?" she asked, holding it up.

Eddie nodded. She helped him lean forward, buttoned him into it, then eased him back against his pillow. He closed his eyes.

"Fay likes you. I can tell," he said.

"Really? I'm scared to think how she'd treat me if she hated me," Jo said. She sat on the corner of the bed, careful not to jostle him.

"It's just a front. She's not that bad." He opened his eyes again.

Jo remembered the bruises on Fay's neck. "The Tailor . . . he beats her?"

"He beats them all if they don't bring him enough swag," Eddie said. "He used to beat me silly."

Jo winced at that. "I'm sorry," she said. "For you and Fay. For all those children."

"I'm fine. Fay's the one to worry about. She's the oldest. She bears the brunt of the Tailor's temper."

Jo looked down at her hands. Something had occurred to her

when Fay warned her not to get Eddie killed—something that made her feel quite jealous.

"You know Fay well, it seems," she said. "Back when you lived in the Bend, were you two . . . um . . . close?"

"Are you asking me if we were sweethearts? We weren't," Eddie replied. "Fay's like a sister to me. We both survived the Tailor. So far, at least. That forges a pretty deep bond."

Jo nodded, relieved, but upset about something else. Though she tried to hold them back, her tears came. They rolled down her cheeks and splashed onto her hands.

"Hey, what's the matter?" Eddie asked. "I'm telling you the truth about Fay. I swear it."

"It's not that." Jo raised her head. "This is all my fault, Eddie. I'm to blame for what happened to you," she said. "If I hadn't gotten you involved in my affairs, you wouldn't be here, all bloodied and bruised and—"

"Hey, stop," Eddie said, cutting her off. "If you hadn't gotten me involved in your affairs, *you* wouldn't be here. And that would hurt even more than Oscar's bad sewing job."

Jo wiped her cheeks with the back of her hand.

"It hurts to sit forward. Otherwise I would. So I could kiss you," he said.

"I suppose I shall have to kiss you, then," Jo said. Her heart beating wildly at her own forwardness, she leaned close, meaning to kiss his mouth.

But he shook his head. "Not there," he said. "Too sore."

She tried for one cheek, but it was bruised.

"Not there, either."

The other cheek had a trickle of blood on it from the cut Oscar had stitched. "This is impossible!" she said.

"Yeah, it is," Eddie said. His voice carried a note of sadness that made Jo realize he meant more than their kiss.

She picked up his hand, turned it over, and kissed his palm. Then she held it against her cheek, eyes closed, wanting to show him how she felt, to show him that maybe there was a way after all. All they had to do was find it.

"Is it, Eddie?" she whispered. "Is it impossible?"

But Eddie didn't answer her.

His eyes were closed. His breathing was deep.

He had fallen asleep.

❧ CHAPTER FIFTY-TWO ❧

Jo gently smoothed a stray lock of hair from Eddie's forehead and stood up quietly. He was exhausted from his ordeal. He'd probably be hungry, too, when he woke. There wasn't any food here, and it would be hours before Oscar came back with his supper. She meant to make sure he had everything he needed.

A floorboard squeaked as she crossed the room. Eddie stirred. "Don't go," he murmured.

"I'm just going out to fetch a few groceries," Jo answered. "I'll be right back."

Jo rolled her sleeves down, put her jacket on, and, for the first time in her life, went shopping for household things. It was a daunting prospect, dealing with tradesman, but exhilarating, too. Out on Reade Street, she found a chemist's and bought a cake of soap, bandages and iodine, and a bottle of laudanum.

Fruit was bought from an Italian pushcart man, as was a willow basket to carry her purchases. Something called a delicatessen, run by Germans, provided her with bread, cheese, sausages, coffee, a bottle of milk, chicken soup in a tin pail—which she'd had to promise to return—and a thick slab of butter cake.

When she returned to Eddie's room, he was still asleep. She tiptoed around, putting the soup on the hearth so it would stay warm; the bread, coffee, and cake on the table; and the perishables on the cool windowsill. When she was done, she realized that she was exhausted, too. Distress over what had happened to Eddie had wiped her out.

I'll just rest for a moment, she thought, *and then I must go home before I'm missed.*

The only problem was there was nowhere to lay her head—only the bed, which was occupied by Eddie, or the hard table in the center of the room. There was a cushion propped against the footboard. She decided to rest there.

She curled up at the end of the bed, careful not to disturb Eddie, and nestled into the pillow. As she relaxed, she looked around the little room—at Eddie's coat hanging on the back of the door, his fishing rod, typewriter, and books.

What is his life like, lived in this small room? she wondered. *What would mine be like, living here with him?*

Precarious, exciting, frugal, bohemian—all these words flashed through her mind, but one flashed more brightly than all the rest: *happy*.

We wouldn't have much, she thought, *but we'd have each other. He'd get the job he wanted at the* World *or the* Tribune. *I'd get a job, too. He'd never stop me from writing stories—real ones—about mill girls, or the Tailor, or Fay. We'd eat breakfast together every morning at that little table, and that would be wonderful. And we'd fall asleep in each other's arms every night in this very bed, and that would be wonderful, too*, she thought, blushing. She was certain that with Eddie it *would* be wonderful. It would be romantic and tender and nothing at *all* like Grandmama's blasted spaniels.

There has *to be a way. If Mama would only consent to meet him, she would see what a good, honest, hardworking man he is. If she would only give him a chance. But she never will*, Jo thought.

Nor would her uncle. They wanted Bram for her. She realized

she would have to choose between Eddie and her family. And that choosing one would mean losing the other, and either way, she'd break her own heart.

"It *is* impossible. It's a fantasy," she whispered. "One I should never have allowed myself to indulge in. And it's time to give it up."

She looked longingly at the man sleeping next to her, then closed her eyes.

"If only I knew how."

❧ CHAPTER FIFTY-THREE ❧

"You snore, Miss Montfort."

Jo groggily opened her eyes.

"Like a dog," Eddie said, gazing at her.

"I do *not*!" Jo retorted, mortified. She'd only meant to rest, not fall asleep.

"An old dog. With a bad cold. It's very attractive."

Jo burst into laughter. "You're hardly one to talk about what is and isn't attractive, Mr. Gallagher. Not with blood leaking out of your nose."

"Ugh. Really?" Eddie said. He wiped his nose on his sleeve. It came away red.

"I'll get you a handkerchief." Jo rose, dug around in his bureau, and found one. As she handed it to him, she sat down again. "How are you feeling?"

"The laudanum helps," he replied.

"I brought you more. Plus soup and bread and all sorts of tasty things to tide you over until Oscar gets here with your supper."

Eddie smiled. "That was very kind of you. Thank you," he said, then turned serious. "Speaking of Oscar . . . as soon as I'm able to,

I'm going to nose around the city's hospitals like he suggested, to see if I can spot our man."

"Please be careful. Promise me you will," Jo said.

"I promise."

"I'm going to try a new tack, too," Jo said. "I thought about it while I was out shopping."

"What is it?" Eddie asked.

"Ernst and Markham, Maritime Insurers. They're the firm that guarantees all of Van Houten's ships and most of the rest of the vessels that come in and out of New York. When I spoke with my uncle, he said he didn't know anything about the *Bonaventure*. He told me that Van Houten didn't own her. But I wonder if perhaps she belonged to Geert Van Houten, the man who sold the firm to my father and my uncle. He's dead, but Mr. Markham would know. I just have to come up with a good excuse for going to see him."

"I'm sure you will," Eddie said. "I've also been mulling a visit of my own to the Owenses' house. Maybe Eleanor didn't hide the manifests in her room. Maybe they're in the basement, or the attic."

"And just how do you plan to get into their house?" Jo asked.

"Haven't quite figured that out yet," Eddie admitted.

A nearby church bell tolled the hour.

"Two o'clock?" Jo exclaimed. "Is it *that* late?" She started to get up, but Eddie caught her hand.

"Stay with me, Jo," he said.

"I can't, Eddie. I've got to get home before I'm missed."

"No. I meant stay with me today. And tomorrow. And every day after." His voice was serious; his eyes were, too.

"If I did, my mother would send the police, if not the army, to fetch me home," Jo said, trying to keep her voice light and teasing, trying to keep him from veering into dangerous territory.

"Jo, I'm not joking. I mean it. I'm in—"

"Eddie, *don't*. Please," she said, scared that he was about to say something she desperately wanted to hear and desperately didn't. She would have to make a choice if he pressed her, and she couldn't.

She kissed his lips, sore as they were, stopping any more words. Words would make whatever was between them real. And as soon as it was real, it was over.

"I've got to go," she said. "I'll write you. And I'll try to get back here if I can."

She gathered her things, kissed him one last time, then headed for the door.

"Eddie," she said, her hand on the doorknob. "You promised me you'd be careful. Don't forget that."

"I won't."

"The man with the scar . . . What if he comes after you again?"

"I'm not afraid of him."

"After what happened, maybe you should be," Jo warned.

Eddie shook his head ruefully. "He can only break my ribs, Jo," he said, "not my heart."

❧ CHAPTER FIFTY-FOUR ❧

Letter to Mr. Reginald Markham, Ernst and Markham, Maritime Insurers, 116 Fulton Street, Brooklyn, from Miss Josephine Montfort

November 10, 1890

Dear Mr. Markham,
Please allow me to introduce myself. My name is Josephine Montfort. I am the daughter of the late Charles Montfort. I am writing to ask a favor of you. I have decided to write a history of Van Houten Shipping and wonder if I might pay a call at your premises to ask you a few questions about some of the firm's more illustrious ships.

With the recent loss of both my father and Mr. Richard Scully, I wish to preserve the story of the firm, and the contributions of its founders, for future generations. I hope you will agree with me that this is a fitting tribute to the memories of both men.

Yours sincerely,
Josephine Montfort

Invitation to Miss Josephine Montfort from
Mr. Abraham Aldrich

MR. AND MRS. PETER ALDRICH
CORDIALLY INVITE YOU TO A BIRTHDAY SUPPER
IN HONOR OF MRS. CORNELIUS ALDRICH III
SATURDAY, NOVEMBER 15, 1890,
AT SEVEN O'CLOCK IN THE EVENING
1 EAST 65TH STREET

Note on invitation written by Abraham Aldrich

November 10, 1890

My dear Jo,
Your mama's already been sent an invitation to Grandmama's
party, but I'm sending one especially to you. Do come. It's only
meant to be a small affair, so the etiquette police won't arrest
you. Ask your mother. If she says no, ask your uncle Phillip. If
he says no, ask Mr. Theakston. But come.

Yours,
B.

Letter from Miss Edwina Gallagher to
Miss Josephine Montfort

November 11, 1890

Dear Jo,
I took a page from your book and flimflammed my way into
the Owenses' house. Told Chuckles the butler that I was an
inspector for the gas company. Searched the entire basement.
Got soot in my eyes and spiders down my shirt, but I didn't get
the letters. They may be safe under the heavens, but they're not
in the basement.

EG

Letter to Miss Josephine Montfort from
Mr. Reginald Markham

November 11, 1890

Dear Miss Montfort,
Please accept my condolences. Your father was not only my
client, but also my friend, and I deeply mourn his loss.
I think a history of Van Houten is a most worthy project and
would be happy to assist you in any way that I can. Would
Thursday at eleven a.m. be convenient?

Cordially yours,
Reginald Markham

➤ *CHAPTER FIFTY-FIVE* ◄

Brooklyn isn't very lovely, Jo Montfort thought, *but it* is *exciting.*

From her vantage point on the deck of the Fulton Street ferry, she could see scores of ship's masts poking up through smoky skies, as well as train tracks and boxcars, delivery wagons, barrels of beer, sides of beef, tea crates, fish, flowers, and furniture.

She smelled the salt of the ocean on the breeze. Black pepper wafting from a warehouse. Tar. Pickles and pretzels. Coal smoke. And the sharp scent of roasting coffee.

As the ferry nosed into its slip, her fellow passengers hurried toward the exit, eager to disembark and get to their destinations. Jo, however, lingered, not wanting her first trip across the East River to end, happy as always to be smack in the middle of all that was exciting, instead of shut away from it.

She wasn't supposed to be here. Her mother never would have allowed her to take a ferry to Brooklyn. She was supposed to be at the Astor Library back in Manhattan. That was where she said she was going. And she *had* gone there—Dolan had driven her—but she'd left as soon as he'd departed and hailed a cab to the waterfront.

That she'd gotten out of the house at all was due entirely to the plan she'd recently cooked up—that she would write a history of Van Houten Shipping. It was a brilliant idea, if she said so herself, and had been found acceptable by her mother, though she'd needed some convincing.

"A history of Van Houten?" she'd said with a frown, after Jo had broached the idea. "Why?"

Jo had explained how she wished to write down the firm's origins before all recollection of them was lost. Her father's and Mr. Scully's memories had been lost with them. She wanted to make sure their contributions were not.

"And when I'm finished with the history," she'd said, "I intend to make a gift of it to the remaining partners and their families, but I'd first like to present it as a special gift to Uncle Phillip. He's done so much for us since we lost Papa. I don't think we can ever adequately thank him, but I hope this will be a start."

Her mother had softened at that, as Jo had known she would. Like Jo herself, she thought the world of Phillip and was grateful to him and to Madeleine for their many kindnesses since her husband's death.

"Well, you *do* have a facility with words," her mother allowed, "and I'm sure your uncle and the other partners would be very pleased to receive such a gift."

Jo had been thrilled but hadn't wanted to show it in case her excitement spooked her mother and caused her to change her mind.

"Eventually, I'll interview Uncle Phillip and the other partners," she said evenly, "but I'd like to introduce the history with some background on the rise of New York as a port city. May I go to the Astor Library to do a bit of research?"

"But that's all the way downtown. And it's Katie's day off. You'd be by yourself," her mother protested.

"It's a library, Mama, not a saloon," Jo pressed. "I need some work to do. I'll go mad otherwise."

A shadow had crossed Anna's face at the word *mad*. Jo had said it on purpose, hoping to remind her of Phillip's warning about morbid thoughts undoing sensitive minds. The plan worked, for her mother had responded immediately.

"All right," she'd said. "But be certain to sit in a well-lit area. I don't want you to develop a squint, Josephine; it's most unbecoming. Dolan will drive you there, and he'll fetch you back at four sharp."

Jo had been so glad she could have danced around the room. Getting out of the house, at least during the day, had become a little easier.

Jo disembarked from the ferry now and walked up bustling Fulton Street, checking the numbers on the buildings. She walked for a few minutes before spotting Ernst and Markham's premises. As she entered the building, a clerk greeted her, then told her that Mr. Reginald Markham had been called to a meeting in his partner's office but would return to his own momentarily. In the meantime, Master Clarence Markham, his grandson, would be glad to escort her upstairs.

Clarence Markham appeared then, as if on cue. He was about twenty-five, Jo guessed. Plump and blond, with a bristly mustache, he reminded her of a walrus.

"Miss Montfort, what a pleasure it is to meet you," he said, ushering her upstairs and into his grandfather's office. "My condolences on your father's passing."

Jo thanked him and allowed him to take her coat and hang it on a wall hook. She was shown to one of two chairs in front of the large walnut desk. Tea was brought by the clerk who'd greeted her; then Clarence sat down next to her.

"Now, Miss Montfort, tell me all about your little project," he said. "Perhaps I can be of some help. I can explain the insurance business, if you like. It's very complicated."

"That's very kind of you," Jo said, endeavoring to move her chair back slightly, as their knees were almost touching. "But I was rather hoping to speak with your grandfather, as my questions pertain to the acquisition of Van Houten ships made quite a few years ago."

Clarence leaned forward and patted her hand. "You can ask me. I work on Van Houten's policies. I'm familiar with all their vessels."

Jo was annoyed by the pompous Clarence, but it looked as if she was stuck with him until his grandfather arrived. She forced a smile, removed her gloves, and took a fountain pen and notepad from her bag. "If I'm not mistaken, the very first ship was the—"

"Before we begin," he interrupted, "may I say how well your dress becomes you?" Clarence's eyes traveled over Jo's body and came to rest on her chest.

Jo blushed, embarrassed. She'd worn her best black day dress and had taken a great deal of care with her hair. Now she wished she had not. "Thank you, Mr. Markham," she said, trying to mask her discomfort.

"One doesn't get to admire many of the fairer sex here at the docks."

"I'm sorry to hear it. I believe the firm's first ship was called—"

"Insurance is a demanding taskmaster, Miss Montfort," Clarence said earnestly. "My duties afford me little time to cultivate friendships with young ladies. I imagine you have just the opposite problem. A girl as pretty as you are must have many beaux. Are you engaged?"

Jo was mortified. "No, Mr. Markham, I am *not*," she said, her blush deepening. "About Van Houten's ships—"

Clarence leaned closer. "Then may I be so bold as to hope I have a chance?"

Jo flattened herself against the back of her chair. "Mr. Markham, if we might discuss a ship. Any ship."

"Of course, Miss Montfort," said Clarence, with an oily smile. "How about *court*ship?"

Jo was stunned speechless. Clarence patted her hand for a second time. His palm was damp. Beads of sweat had broken out on his forehead. His foot was touching hers. And then, to Jo's horror, he began to inch his toe up the side of her boot.

Jo didn't know what to do. Men of her world did not behave in this manner. But she wasn't in her world now. She badly wanted to call Clarence Markham a cad and leave, but she imagined telling Eddie she'd had the chance to learn about the *Nausett* and let it go because she was frightened off by an errant foot.

Two can play these games, Jo thought. She took a deep breath, raised her own foot, and stamped it down hard on Clarence Markham's toes.

Markham yelped and shot back in his chair.

"I'm so sorry," Jo said in a tone that indicated she was anything but. "Something ran over my boot. A rat, I think. How will I explain to my uncle that I made young Mr. Markham lame?"

Markham blanched. "Oh, there's no need, Miss Montfort," he said quickly. "Not on my account, I assure you." He pushed his chair back a bit. "Now, about those ships . . ."

Jo smiled, satisfied. "Yes, Mr. Markham. About those ships."

⤞ CHAPTER FIFTY-SIX ⤝

An hour later, Jo had the names and detailed descriptions of fifteen Van Houten vessels written down in her notebook, but the *Bonaventure* was not among them.

Clarence's grandfather arrived shortly after Jo put Clarence in his place, and Clarence quickly departed. The elder Markham looked to be in his seventies. He had bushy gray hair and muttonchop whiskers and wore a black suit fashionable at least two decades ago. He was courtly and well-mannered—in marked contrast to his grandson—and extremely long-winded.

He was now telling her about the *Emma May.* As he held forth, Jo surreptitiously glanced at her watch. Van Houten owned close to a hundred ships. If she didn't hurry him along, she'd be here until midnight. As she nodded and smiled and took notes, she tried to figure out how to ask for the information she actually wanted. Her purpose in coming here today was to dig up anything she could on the *Bonaventure,* but her instincts told her to tread cautiously. If that ship had been involved in some sort of dirty dealing and Markham knew of it, he might refuse to speak of her at all. Couching the question wouldn't get it answered, though. She decided there was nothing to do but ask about the ship outright.

"You're giving me such a wealth of information, thank you," she said as Mr. Markham recited the *Emma May*'s dimensions, "but there's one ship you haven't mentioned, and I'm particularly interested in her, as I heard one of the partners, I can't remember who, speak of her—the *Bonaventure*."

Mr. Markham shook his head. "Never heard of her," he said. "She definitely wasn't one of Van Houten's."

Jo felt both relieved and let down. She was glad to learn that the suspicious ship had not been owned by Van Houten. How could the partners have been involved in shadowy dealings—as Kinch claimed—if they didn't even own the ship said to have carried the suspicious cargo? But she was disappointed not to discover who *had* owned it. Neither Bill Hawkins nor her uncle had known anything about the *Bonaventure*, and they were two men who knew a great deal about ships. Markham was her last hope.

As Jo sat listening to him tell her about the *Peregrine*, another ship she couldn't have cared less about, Shaw's advice flashed through her mind once again, just as it had when she'd asked her uncle about the *Bonaventure*. *Follow the* Nausett *and you'll find the* Bonaventure. *God help you if you do.*

"The *Peregrine*, a lovely ship," she said, cutting Mr. Markham off as politely as she could. "I look forward to hearing more about her, but before I do, Mr. Markham, just to . . . um . . . keep things in alphabetical order, could you tell me about the *Nausett*?"

Jo thought she might receive a guarded response or perhaps a load of useless details. What she didn't expect was the wistful look that crossed Markham's face.

"Goodness," he said, leaning back in his chair. "I haven't thought about *that* ship in years. She sank off the Cape of Good Hope."

Jo felt her pulse quicken. Her uncle had told her a little about the ship. Perhaps Markham could tell her more.

"The *Nausett* was a Baltimore Clipper," Markham explained.

"I'm not familiar with the type," Jo said, scribbling down his every word.

"Most people your age aren't," Markham said. "There aren't many around anymore. She was a slave ship. She plied the Atlantic before the Civil War. After the slave trade was outlawed, Van Houten bought her for a good price. She was sailed to Portugal, where labor is cheap, to be refitted for the spice trade."

Jo sat up a bit straighter at the mention of Portugal. She remembered Jackie Shaw saying that the *Bonaventure* had a Portuguese crew and papers.

"Phillip told me he planned to have the chains and manacles removed," Markham continued, "as well as the decking upon which slaves were held."

Jo shuddered at the words *chains* and *manacles*, horrified to think of what the poor souls on board that ship had endured.

"Spices are a lucrative cargo, and lucrative cargo is always important, but it was especially so then because of the economic difficulties after the war," Markham explained. "Currency was devalued, and many businesses suffered, including shipbuilding." He paused. "Do you understand these terms, Miss Montfort? Finance, economics . . . they can be a bit overwhelming to the feminine mind."

"I will do my best to keep up, Mr. Markham," Jo replied. The touch of sarcasm in her voice was lost on him.

"Very well. Where were we, again?"

"The postwar economic difficulties . . . ," Jo answered.

"Right you are."

". . . caused, paradoxically, by inflation, the demonetization of silver, speculative investments, railroad bankruptcies, the Black Friday gold panic of 1869, and a rather large trade deficit," Jo said.

She'd received an A+ on her paper on the reconstruction of the South.

Mr. Markham stared, his mouth slightly ajar. "Yes. Quite so," he said. "Well, ahem, as I'm sure you *also* know, shipbuilding—rather than shipping—was your family's business for well over a century."

Jo nodded. She remembered her father once pointing out a furniture factory on the west side of the city and telling her that the original Montfort shipyards had been located where the factory now stood.

"After the war, your father and uncle saw the writing on the wall. They were young but shrewd and knew they had to get out of the shipyards and into trade," Markham explained. "So they made a bold move—they sold the shipyards and bought a shipping firm from old Geert Van Houten. The business was nearly moribund, but Van Houten's docks were spacious and underutilized—prime waterfront holdings."

Markham was telling Jo things she knew, but she didn't interrupt him to point that out, fearing that if she cut him off, she might also cut off an important detail about the *Nausett*.

"The sale of the shipyards didn't bring as much as your father and uncle would have liked, though. They needed to raise more cash, so they brought other men into the firm as partners. These men were known to them, and trusted. They kept the business afloat, so to speak, but barely. They needed one final partner, and they found one—a Mr. Stephen Smith."

Jo's excitement was building. She might be able to learn more about Stephen Smith, as well as the *Nausett*, from Markham.

"Mr. Smith was lost at sea while he was working in Zanzibar, I believe," she said.

"Yes. It was a tragedy. Stephen Smith was an asset to Van Houten. He'd lived in India for several years and had an extensive knowledge of the spice trade."

"I'd be grateful for your impressions of him for my history," Jo said, eager to keep Markham talking about Smith. "Did you know him?"

"By reputation only. He was said to be honest in his dealings, but he was a Boston man originally, and divorced—which is barely acceptable today, never mind two decades ago. I doubt Charles and Phillip would have taken him on in fatter times, but they needed funds, and I believe it was Smith's money that allowed the firm to purchase the *Nausett*. Her loss was quite a blow to the company, but of course she was insured."

Jo's hopes started to fade. She forged ahead with one last question, trying for a smooth segue. "Do you know if Van Houten ever employed a Mr. Kinch as . . . as a captain on the *Nausett*? Or any of their ships?"

Markham shook his head. "The name doesn't ring a bell," he said. "Then again, I wouldn't know the names of all the firm's employees. Now, about the *Peregrine* . . ."

Jo's heart sank. She'd run into another brick wall. Her entire trip to Brooklyn had been for nothing. Markham had told her nothing at all about the *Bonaventure*, and nothing useful about the *Nausett*, Stephen Smith, or Kinch. She gritted her teeth as he droned on, wondering how she could make a graceful exit, when the clock on the wall struck the hour—half past twelve.

"Oh, my! Is it that time already? I'm afraid I'm going to have to cut our delightful visit short, Mr. Markham. My mother is expecting me home by one-thirty."

Mr. Markham's bushy eyebrows shot up. "But I haven't finished telling you about the rest of Van Houten's ships!" he protested.

"And I would love to hear about them," Jo fibbed. "Might I return another time, if it's not an inconvenience?"

"Of course, Miss Montfort," Mr. Markham said warmly. "It would be my pleasure."

Jo rose. Markham got her coat for her. "Shall I call for Clarence to escort you downstairs?" he asked. "I'm sure he'd like to say goodbye."

"I'm sure he would," Jo said without thinking. "I—I mean, I'm sure *I* would," she said, flustered. "Like to say goodbye. But I must catch a ferry. *Now.* Or I'll be late for my . . . *piano lesson.* Good day, Mr. Markham."

She hurried out of the building, feeling dispirited. The *Nausett* didn't lead to the *Bonaventure;* it led straight to the bottom of the sea. She'd write to Eddie when she got home to let him know she'd turned up nothing. Sighing deeply, she wondered what he would do next.

As Jo made her way back down Fulton Street to the waterfront, turning questions over in her mind, deeply lost in thought, she had the sudden, unsettling feeling that someone was watching her. Unnerved, she whirled around. The crowd of people, some on their way to the ferry, others on their way to lunch, flowed around her. She scanned the faces rushing by, expecting to see the frightening man with the scarred cheek among them, but he wasn't there.

"You're being silly," she told herself, but her uneasiness remained. She turned around and quickened her steps to the docks.

❧ CHAPTER FIFTY-SEVEN ❧

"Oh, *blast*," Jo said as she watched the ferry pull away from the slip.

She was standing on the dock behind the wooden safety gate and would now have to wait until the ferry discharged its passengers on the Manhattan side and made its way back. She still felt spooked and didn't relish spending a good hour on the rough-and-tumble waterfront.

"Ferry leave without you, miss?" a kind voice called to her.

A plump, smiling woman was standing on the deck of a small barge. It was moored just to the right of the ferry slip. Her face was weathered from wind and water. Her sleeves were rolled up. She was wiping her hands on a towel.

"I'm afraid so!" Jo called back.

"We can take you, me and my husband. We've got a load of sacking going to Peck Slip. We'll let you out there. Come aboard. The dockside's no place for a decent girl. My name's Mrs. Rudge."

"Thank you!" Jo said, relieved. Just as she started toward the barge, she felt a hand close on her arm.

"Don't," a voice warned.

Startled, Jo turned to face a young woman. She had red hair and was wearing a fancy hat and a butterscotch-plaid suit. She looked like the young wife of a prosperous waterfront merchant.

"*Fay?*" Jo said.

"Don't go with her," Fay said, still gripping Jo's arm.

Jo glanced back at the barge. The kindly woman's smile had soured. "Let go of her, Fairy Fay," she said. "You've no business on this side of the river."

"Piss off, Wilma," said Fay.

"You're going to be sorry you said that, girl," Mrs. Rudge hissed. She climbed over the side of the barge onto the dock.

A razor blade appeared, as if from thin air, in Fay's hand. She pushed Jo behind her. "Come on, then, Wilma," she said, pinching the blade between her thumb and forefinger. "Let's see if your ugly face looks any better without a nose."

Mrs. Rudge stopped dead. "Hank!" she bellowed, glaring hatefully at Fay. "Get up here! *Now!*"

"What do you want, woman?" a voice bellowed from belowdecks.

Fay didn't wait for Wilma to tell him. She took Jo's arm again and hustled her back up Fulton Street.

"Where are we going?" Jo asked, breathless and more than a little worried to find herself arm in arm with a girl who'd once robbed her.

"To Manhattan," Fay said, hurrying her along.

"But the docks are that way!" Jo protested, pointing behind them.

"I *know* that. We're hoofing it." She glanced at the waterfront. "Hopefully, Wilma's decided not to follow us. So you won't get *me* killed as well as yourself."

"*Killed?* Fay, what are you talking about? I missed the ferry and Mrs. Rudge offered to take me across."

Fay smirked. "I'm sure she did. Wilma and Henry Rudge make a business out of getting unsuspecting travelers aboard their barge. They wait until they're well out in the river, away from any other boats. Then they rob them and toss them overboard. Most make it back to shore. Some don't."

Jo was shocked. She might've survived the ordeal, because she could swim, but then again, she might not have. Swimming in a sheltered cove at Newport in the summer was not the same thing as swimming in strong river currents, in a dress and coat, on a chilly autumn day.

"Thank you," she said gratefully. Fay had quite possibly saved her life.

Fay waved her thanks away. "Keep moving. We're not out of the woods yet," she said, picking up the pace.

"How do they get away with it? Don't the victims go to the police?" asked Jo, trotting to keep up with her.

"Sometimes, but it's one person's word against another's," Fay explained. "There aren't many witnesses in the middle of the East River. And Wilma fences any swag right away, so if the cops come calling, they don't find a thing."

"I'm glad you happened to be on Fulton Street," Jo said. "I had the feeling someone was watching me. It was you, wasn't it?"

Fay nodded. "I saw you come out of a building, looking all distracted. Someone else saw you, too. A pickpocket I know by sight but not by name. I followed you to make sure he didn't get too close."

"Why are you so far afield?" Jo asked.

"Things are a bit hot for me in Manhattan at the moment," Fay said. "Got caught a couple of days ago. Spent a night in the clink. Cop who took me in warned me that the next time it'd be prison, not a station house cell."

As Fay spoke, Jo noticed a faded bruise under the powder on her face. "What happened to your cheek?" she asked.

Fay shrugged. "Occupational hazard," she said.

"What does that mean?" Jo asked. Then she understood. "Did the police hit you?"

"No, the mark did," Fay replied. "The police know better than to hit anyone in the face. They go for the gut. You can't see the bruises there. Bastard cop held my arms, though."

"Why?"

"The mark was afraid to fight me fair."

Jo stopped dead. "Two *men* against a girl?"

"I'm not sure I'd call them men," Fay said, nudging her along.

"We have to report this," Jo said, outraged.

"Good idea," Fay said sarcastically. "Hey, let's call the police."

Jo saw the difficulties Fay faced. The Tailor beat her if she didn't steal for him, and the police beat her if she did. "I wish there were something I could do. I'm sorry that happened to you," she said, uncomfortably aware of how good she had it compared to Fay.

Fay smiled darkly. "Not as sorry as that mark's going to be. I know where he lives. I heard the desk sergeant asking him for his name and address," she said.

She was still holding the razor blade she'd used to scare off Wilma Rudge. As Jo watched, she put it on her tongue and pressed it against the roof of her mouth.

"Don't! You'll cut yourself!"

"Not if you do it right. Got to use the new kind. Disposables. They're thin and bendy, see?" She flexed the blade. "Want to try?"

Jo shook her head.

"You're hopeless, aren't you? As far as I can tell, you've no skills at all," Fay said. "If you're going to pay visits to Mulberry Bend and the docks, you should at least be able to defend yourself. Or the Wilma Rudges of the world will turn you inside out."

Jo liked the idea. The thought of being able to stand up for herself was appealing.

"Can you show me how?" she asked. "But without any razor blades," she added.

Fay nodded. "I can show you a few basics. But not here. Up on the bridge. It's quieter."

"The bridge?" Jo echoed.

"Yes. That giant thing above us?" Fay said, pointing at the Brooklyn Bridge.

"Of course, the *bridge*. Are we going to walk over it?" she asked eagerly.

"What else would we do? Fly?" Fay gave her a sidelong glance. "You don't get out much, do you?"

"I've never walked over the Brooklyn Bridge, and I've always wanted to. Papa said it isn't safe for young ladies to stroll across. This is exciting!" Jo said, her close call with Wilma Rudge forgotten in the anticipation of seeing the city from high up.

It was Fay's turn to stop dead. "How is a long walk across a boring old bridge exciting? Tell me, Jo Montfort, are all rich people insane?" she asked.

"Walking *anywhere* on my own is exciting," Jo said, looking up at the bridge's soaring, graceful spans.

For a moment, she forgot her companion was a notorious pickpocket, devious and dangerous, and that she herself was a proper young society lady. For a moment, they were just two girls heading off on an adventure.

"Didn't you say we had to keep moving? Hurry *up*, Fay. Let's *go*!" she said.

Fay laughed as Jo pulled her along. It was a low, rusty sound. As if she'd forgotten how.

Or had never learned.

⇥ *CHAPTER FIFTY-EIGHT* ⇤

"Okay, here's a dip called the Pretty Girl. Pretend you're a big fat man who's just finished a five-course dinner at Rector's lobster palace and now you're off to the opera to ogle the soprano," Fay said.

Jo, giggling, got off the bench upon which she'd been sitting, in a viewing area built on the Manhattan-side tower of the Brooklyn Bridge, and lumbered around like a bear. No one paid her any attention. She and Fay were two of only a handful of people there, most of whom were looking at the Statue of Liberty.

"Very good," Fay said. She started to circle Jo. Her eyes became predatory and her movements catlike. "You've a cigar in one hand and your coat in the other. Your cummerbund's too tight, you're drunk from too much brandy, and you're sore because the chorus girl you took to Rector's barely let you cop a feel."

"*Fay!*" Jo said, scandalized.

"Stay in character!" Fay scolded. "Now, here *I* come. Dressed to blend in. I don't do anything, say anything, or wear anything that makes me stand out." As she spoke, she bumped into Jo and dropped her purse. Jo picked it up and held it out to her.

"Time for the three *F*s of the female pickpocket," Fay said. "First *F: Flirtation.*" She smiled demurely, batted her eyelashes, and thanked Jo. "Second *F:* Flattery." She placed a dainty hand on Jo's arm. "Oh, how gallant you are, sir, to retrieve my purse for me!" she cooed in honeyed tones. "And finally, our third *F:* Finesse." Fay stepped back, holding Jo's pocket watch.

"I didn't even feel that!" Jo exclaimed, clapping. "Show me how!"

Fay grinned, pleased at Jo's praise. "Lifting watches is hard. We'll start you off with something easier. I have a coin purse in my skirt pocket. Try to take it," she instructed, turning her back to Jo.

Jo tiptoed up to Fay, then pounced, thrusting a hand deep into her right pocket.

Fay turned around. She shook her head. "Are you trying to pick my pocket or rip my skirt off?" she asked.

"Sorry," Jo said sheepishly.

"Try again. Use your pointer and middle finger only, not your whole hand. You need to be light and quick."

Jo tried several more times, aiming for Fay's right pocket, but Fay was walking in a slow circle, and Jo kept missing. Finally, her hand sank into the folds of Fay's skirt and her fingers scissored closed on something. "Ha!" she crowed, grinning, but her triumph was short-lived.

"My goodness!" she cried, as she realized she was holding a small silver revolver instead of a purse.

"Whoops. Wrong pocket," said Fay.

"I'll say!"

"Give it back and try again," Fay said.

"I'm afraid to. What else do you have in there? A machete?" Jo asked reproachfully.

"Don't be so silly."

Jo tried one more time and found something soft. *That must be it*, she thought, but when she pulled it out, it wasn't a purse, either. It was a small, ragged cloth doll.

The doll wore a frayed calico dress. Its hair was made of yarn that had once been yellow but was now browned with grime. Its smile was stitched in red thread, and its eyes were tiny blue buttons. It was a small child's toy, and Jo thought it an odd thing for a girl like Fay to be carrying.

"That's my good-luck charm," Fay said. She sat down on a bench. "I need a rest. I'm winded. Thirsty, too. Teaching the likes of you is hard work."

Ever since they'd reached the viewing area, about an hour ago, Fay had been showing Jo self-defense moves as well as giving her pickpocketing lessons. Jo had learned how to jab a man in the Adam's apple, and how to knee him in the groin if he was standing, or in the face if he was bending over.

Fay pulled a small silver flask and matching cigarette case from the folds of her skirt. She handed the flask to Jo, who looked at it questioningly.

"Go on, it's only gin."

Jo sat down beside her, took a swig, and coughed. "That's almost as bad as Eddie's whiskey," she said, wiping her mouth.

"The more you drink, the better it tastes," Fay said, motioning for her to take another swallow.

Jo did so. And then another. And then she handed the flask back to Fay. The alcohol warmed her chest. Its heat spread through her body, making her feel languid and loose-limbed. She liked the feeling.

Fay tongued the razor blade out of her mouth and carefully laid it on the arm of the bench. She drank from the flask, capped it, and lit a cigarette. After taking a few deep drags, she handed that to Jo, too. Jo took a puff and found herself racked by a fit of coughing.

"Is this supposed to be enjoyable?" she rasped when her coughs subsided.

"It's tolerable once you get used to it," Fay replied. "Most things are."

Jo realized she was still holding Fay's doll. "This isn't much of a good-luck charm, considering you were caught by the police a couple of days ago," she said, handing it back.

"I suppose you're right," Fay said, pocketing it. "The Tailor said he made it for me when I was little. To shut me up. He says I wouldn't stop crying when he first took me in."

Jo remembered the Tailor's story, how he found Fay in a stairwell, abandoned. "Do you remember your life before the Tailor?" she asked, curious.

"I can't remember a thing. Not a face or a voice. Not the place I was found in. Nothing. I can't even remember my own name. My real one, I mean. Can't remember anything but the Tailor. He's a shit, but I owe him everything. He's fed me all these years. Clothed me. Kept a roof over my head. That's more than many kids in the Bend have. It's more than Eddie and Tommy and Eileen had."

Jo couldn't imagine having it worse than living with the Tailor. "Eddie told me a bit about his life," she said. "It sounds like he had a hard upbringing."

Fay nodded, her eyes steely now. "The hardest," she said. "His mother used to beg scraps from restaurant kitchens—bones, corn-cobs, potato peelings—and boil them for broth. Sometimes a cup or two of that was all they'd have to eat for the day."

Jo's heart hurt at the thought of Eddie's mother having to beg in order to feed her children, and of Eddie and his siblings being hungry. "What was he like when he was little?" she asked.

Fay laughed. "A damn good thief. Tough. Ruthless. Like all the rest of us. You have to be to survive the Bend. And the Tailor." Fay took another drag on her cigarette and said, "He likes you some-thing wicked. I can tell. You like him, too, don't you?"

Jo blushed. Fay elbowed her. Her shrewd eyes locked on Jo's, and Jo found herself powerless to evade them. Or her question.

"Yes," she finally admitted. "I do."

"That's tough," Fay said. "Can't really see it happening. Him being him and you being you."

"Nor can I," Jo said sadly.

"The social pages all say Bram Aldrich is your best beau."

"You read the social pages?" Jo had trouble imagining Fay in the Tailor's lair, perusing news of balls, operas, and plays.

"Of course I do. I steal from the rich, don't I? I have to know where they are," said Fay matter-of-factly. "Anyway, is it true? Are you Bram's sweetheart?"

Jo shook her head. "I don't think so. Not anymore," she said. "I have some stiff competition, and I believe she's winning."

"You could always elope with Eddie," Fay suggested. She leaned back as she spoke, stretched her legs out and crossed one ankle over the other. Staring straight ahead now at the waters of New York Harbor, she took a puff of her cigarette.

Jo leaned back and stretched her legs, too. She felt unguarded and open, not at all like herself. *It's the gin,* she thought. She reached for Fay's cigarette, took a drag, and slowly exhaled.

"The truth is, Fay, sometimes I wish I could marry him—more than anything—and other times I wish I'd never met him," she said wistfully, looking up at the sky. "I wish I'd never gone to the *Standard* and never overheard him talking. That's how I found out about my father, you know. Ever since that day, I've been doing things I never thought I'd do. And most of them aren't good. I keep stepping out of my world, going farther away from everything and everyone I know. I'm scared, Fay. Scared I'll go too far one day and I won't be able to find my way back."

Fay was silent. Jo turned and looked at the side of her face. "Now's when you tell me it'll be fine. I'll be all right. Everything will work out," she said.

Fay smirked. "That only happens in stories," she said. She motioned for her cigarette, took a few puffs, and said, "Who would you have if they *both* asked you to marry them, right at the same time, and you had to choose?"

"But that's the thing, I *can't* choose," Jo said despairingly.

"But if you *could.*"

Jo didn't want to answer the question. Fay was digging deep. Too deep.

"Oh, I don't know," Jo finally said, trying to sound nonchalant. "You tell me. Whom should I choose? What's better—security or love?"

Fay didn't reply right away. Instead she looked out over the East River for a bit; then, in a voice raw with longing, said, "*This* is the best thing, Jo. The city stretched out before you, glittering like a sack of diamonds. Yours for the taking. A drink and a smoke and no one to please but yourself. Freedom. That's my answer. The freedom to be your own best thing."

Without any warning, tears came to Jo's eyes. Neither of them could choose their future, it was true—but Jo knew that the life she would have as Bram's wife, or the wife of any of a number of the city's golden boys, would be paradise compared to the one Fay was facing.

She reached for Fay's hand. "You're *not* going to Madam Esther's. I won't let you. I *won't.*"

"It won't be so bad," Fay said bravely. "At least I'll be off the streets at Esther's. And her heavies don't allow shenanigans. Anyone causes a ruckus and he's out."

"You speak well. Can you read and write, too?" asked Jo.

"Yes. The Tailor taught me."

"You could get a proper job, then," Jo said hopefully. "As a typist or a shopgirl."

"The Tailor said if I ever tried to leave him and go straight, he'd tell my employer about my past. I'd be fired immediately."

Fury rose in Jo. "He doesn't own you," she said. "You're not his slave."

Fay inhaled another lungful of smoke and blew it out again. "What's done is done."

"There *must* be some way around this," Jo insisted. "We just have to figure it out."

Fay stood up and stretched. "You know, you never even told me what you were doing in Brooklyn all by yourself."

"Don't change the subject. This is serious. There are diseases. You could get sick."

"Does it have anything to do with that man you're after? Kinch? I'm still trying to find him for you," Fay said. She dropped her cigarette and ground it out with her toe.

"Fay, *listen* to me—"

"I *don't* want to talk about it anymore," Fay said, angrily. "So don't make me, all right? I don't have a way out of it. We can't all marry an Aldrich, you know."

Jo winced at that.

"Look, I'm sorry," Fay said, softening. "It's nice that you care. Thank you." She hesitated, as if working up her courage, then said, "You're a friend, Jo. The only friend I've got. The only *real* one. And I know you mean well, but there's nothing you can do."

There was resignation in Fay's voice but fear in her eyes. Jo saw it and knew it would be unkind to keep pressing her. "All right," she said. "I'll stop."

"Good."

"For now."

Fay shook her head, smiling. As she did, they heard church bells on both sides of the river ring out the hour.

"*Three?* That *can't* be the time. I have to get back. My driver's supposed to pick me up at the Astor Library at four," Jo said. She felt like a slave to the clock, always having to make sure she wasn't gone too long, for fear of making her mother suspicious.

"I'll get you there. We'll make it. You can flag a cab when we get to the other side," Fay said. She grabbed her razor blade and hooked her arm through Jo's, and together they hurried off. Ten minutes later, they were standing on Pearl Street. Jo saw cabs moving up and down it, and knew she'd make it back to the library in time.

"This is goodbye," Fay said, "but listen, Jo, I meant what I said about Kinch. I'll keep looking. Somebody somewhere in this city must've seen him."

"Thank you," Jo said. "And thanks for the drink and the smoke and the pickpocketing lessons, too."

Fay laughed. She gave Jo a little wave, and then she was walking away. Jo watched her go, worried for her—this slight, brave, rough girl who'd endured so much and would endure much worse if the Tailor and Madam Esther had their way.

Fay passed a woman digging in a rubbish bin and gave her a coin. It was Mad Mary. She kissed Fay. Fay patted her shoulder and walked on.

Jo's own words echoed in her head. *I keep stepping out of my world, going farther away from everything and everyone I know.*

She thought about that world now and the people in it. They were good people, decent and upright. She thought of her friends— Addie, Jennie, Trudy, and Caro. None of them even knew who Madam Esther was, never mind what she did. They didn't know about people like Fay, Tumbler, or the Tailor.

They don't know me, either. Not really, Jo thought. *They don't know what's going on in my life and they'd be horrified if they did. They'd never offer to teach me how to pick pockets, or track down a dangerous man with tattoos on his face and darkness in his heart.*

"Fay!" she called. Too loudly. But she didn't care.

Fay, who was a good twenty yards down the sidewalk now, turned around. She gave Jo a questioning look.

Jo started walking toward her, then broke into a run. "You're the only friend I have, too," she said, catching up to her. "The only real one."

The two girls—one from Gramercy Square, the other from Mulberry Bend—hugged each other tightly, then went their separate ways.

➤ CHAPTER FIFTY-NINE ◄

Braid the raven hair,
Weave the supple tress,
Deck the maiden fair
In her loveliness. . . .

Jo stepped out of her bath and pulled the plug. As she toweled herself off, she continued to sing "Braid the Raven Hair," a song from *The Mikado*, an operetta her mother found unrefined but Jo loved.

Paint the pretty face,
Dye the coral lip,
Emphasize the grace
Of her ladyship!

She took her lacy white nightgown from its hook on the back of the bathroom door and put it on. Her own raven tresses were piled high on her head to keep them out of the bathwater. She let them down and brushed them, then opened the bathroom door and stepped into her bedroom, singing the last couplet of the song.

Art and nature, thus allied,
Go to make a pretty bride!

"Don't scream," a man's voice said.

Jo screamed.

"Now you've done it." It was Eddie. He was sitting on her bed.

Jo didn't have her dressing gown on. Her hair was loose. Her feet were bare. She was mortified.

"*I've* done it?" she said angrily, trembling from the fright he'd given her. "What are you doing in my bedroom?"

Before he could respond, they both heard footsteps coming down the hallway.

"Where's my dressing gown?" Jo said, panicking. And then she spotted it—Eddie was sitting on it. "Give it to me!" she said, tugging it out from under him.

She shrugged into it, conscious of Eddie's eyes on her. Just as she was knotting the sash, she heard a pounding on the door.

"Miss Josephine! Are you all right?"

"Miss Jo, what's wrong?"

"It's Theakston and Katie," Jo whispered. "You can't be here!" She looked around her room frantically, then said, "Get under the bed. Hurry!"

The door opened just as Eddie pulled his feet in under the dust ruffle. Her mother strode into the room, followed by the butler and maid.

"Josephine, what is going on?" she demanded. "Why did you scream?"

Jo pressed a hand to her chest. "I'm *so* sorry, Mama. It was a mouse," she fibbed. "A big one. It ran across my foot as I got out of the bath. I shouldn't have carried on so, but it frightened the wits out of me."

Her mother looked relieved. "Poor dear. How awful." She felt

Jo's forehead. "You're warm and flushed. It must've startled you terribly." She turned to Theakston and said, "Go make sure the wretched thing is gone."

"Yes, Mrs. Montfort," Theakston said, hurrying to the bathroom. He came back out again almost immediately and said, "It's gone. I have no idea how it got in. Perhaps it followed water pipes up from the basement."

"Get an exterminator here first thing in the morning, Theakston," Jo's mother said, turning to leave. "Good night, Josephine. Do get some rest."

"I will, Mama," Jo said. "Good night."

Theakston and Katie followed her mother out of the room. Jo quickly shut the door behind them and leaned against it, trying to slow the pounding of her heart. She waited until the footsteps had all receded, then said, "Come out of there!"

Eddie peeked out from the dust ruffle. "Good story," he said. "Quick thinking."

"Never mind that! How did you get in here?" Jo asked.

She was glad to see that his eye was no longer swollen and the bruises on his face had faded a little but was too angry to tell him so.

"I was across the street," he said, pulling himself out from under the bed, "figuring out how to get a note to you, when your maid came out to dump some ashes in a garbage can. I asked her to give you the note, but she said no. So I hid behind a carriage and waited. When she came back with more ashes, I snuck inside. I made my way down the hall and up the back stairs, hoping I'd find your room before someone found me. Then I heard you singing and I knew which room was yours. You have a nice voice."

"Have you lost your mind? You could've been seen!"

"I didn't have a choice. I have to talk to you," Eddie said, sitting on Jo's bed. "Tumbler found Kinch."

Jo blinked. "Are you serious?" she asked. "Where is he?"

"In a boardinghouse. But Tumbler wants twenty bucks to tell me which one."

"*Twenty dollars?*" Jo exclaimed. "That's a ridiculous amount of money!"

"If Fay finds out, she'll kick his backside for him," Eddie said. "If the Tailor finds out, he's done for. Needless to say, I don't have the money. I'm hoping you do."

Jo walked to her closet, fuming. She pulled a wad of notes out of the boot in which she'd hidden them and gave Eddie what he needed. She had no choice but to pay Tumbler his fee. They couldn't let Kinch slip away.

"Thanks. I've got to go. Tumbler's waiting for me by a bar on Irving Place," he said, starting for the door.

"Wait!" she said. "Do you know how to get back out?"

"Um, yeah. At least, I think so," he said.

Jo could not imagine how she would explain his presence in her house to her mother or Theakston if one of them found him wandering around.

"I'll show you," she said.

She opened the door, looked up and down the hall to make sure no one was in it, then slipped out of her room, motioning for Eddie to follow her.

"You'll have to go out the way you came," she whispered. "The front door's closer, but we'd need to take the main stairs to get to it, and they're near my mother's room. She might hear us."

Eddie nodded. They made their way quietly down the back stairs, Jo hoping all the while that she could sneak him out of the servants' entrance, but they didn't even get as far as the kitchen. As they rounded the last curve of the narrow, spiraling staircase, she saw that instead of being dark and empty, the kitchen was lit up.

"Theakston, blast him!" she whispered. From their vantage point by the supply closet, she and Eddie could see the butler. He was at the sink, soaking pieces of bread with rat poison.

"I've more bait than traps," he suddenly said, then started toward the supply closet. Jo grabbed Eddie's hand and pulled him into the stairwell. Neither dared to breathe until Theakston returned to the sink. Then they dashed back up the stairs.

"When does he go to bed?" Eddie asked, when they were safely back in Jo's room.

"I don't know. He goes on these missions sometimes when he can't sleep," Jo said worriedly. "Tonight he's trapping mice, thanks to you. Other nights he polishes doorknobs or refills every fountain pen in the house. He's usually at it until dawn."

"*Until dawn?*" Eddie ran a hand through his hair. "That's great. Just great. I'm totally stuck. Jeez, Jo, why'd you say it was a mouse that made you scream?"

Jo looked at him in disbelief. "You're right, Eddie. I should have said it was a man." She started to pace her room. "What am I going to do?"

Eddie pulled a cashmere throw off her bed. "I just want you to know—" he started to say.

Jo cut him off. "That you're very sorry. And you'll never do anything like this again?"

"—that you look very beautiful right now. And if I were a cad, I'd kiss you."

His voice was teasing, but his eyes told her he meant it. Jo looked away, afraid of his desire. Afraid of her own.

By the time she worked up the courage to meet his eyes again, he was no longer looking at her. He'd kicked off his shoes and was stretching out on her chaise longue. He covered himself with her throw, laid his head on a pillow, and closed his eyes.

"Eddie? *Eddie!* What are you doing?" Jo asked, panic-stricken.

"Sleeping. At least, I'm trying to."

"You're sleeping? *Here?* In my room? With me?"

"You're very fresh tonight, Miss Montfort. I'm sleeping here in your room, yes. But not with you. Let's not rush things. I'm not that kind of boy."

Jo blushed scarlet. "I didn't mean that! I—I meant sleeping, not . . . *sleeping.*"

Eddie chuckled. "Go to sleep, Jo. So I can. Maybe Theakston will give up in a few hours. I'll get a bit of sleep now, then try to sneak out again. Hopefully Tumbler will still be at the bar."

"And if you can't sneak out?" Jo asked anxiously.

"Then I'll be ruined. My honor compromised. My reputation in shreds. Turn off the light, will you? I've been running all over town today. Chasing Kinch. Sniffing around police stations and hospitals to see if I can spot Scarface. I'm whipped."

Jo reluctantly did so. Then she stood in the middle of the dark room, fretting and wringing her hands. She had not counted on a man spending the night with her. She was confident her mother would not check on her again, but how was she supposed to relax enough to go to sleep with Eddie here?

Finally, seeing there was nothing she could do about it, she got into her bed, pulled the covers up to her chin, and stared at the ceiling. She couldn't see Eddie, but she could hear him. His breathing slowed, then deepened. When she was sure he was asleep, she sat up. Katie hadn't pulled her curtains tonight, and moonlight was spilling into her room and washing over him. She leaned forward on her hands, gazing at him, liking the fact that he was asleep and she wasn't. She liked being able to study the planes and angles of his face uninterrupted. The line of his jaw. The bump on the bridge of his nose.

"Wish you *were* a cad, Eddie Gallagher," she whispered. "Wish to God you'd kissed me."

"Do you?"

Jo gave a startled gasp. "I thought you were *asleep*!"

"I was. You woke me up. Can't you ever stop talking?"

"Sorry! I—I didn't mean to," she stammered. "I just ... I wanted to—"

"If you want a kiss so badly, come and get one."

Jo got out of her bed. Her heart was hammering even harder than it had when Eddie surprised her. She sat down on the chaise. Eddie's eyes were open now. He took her hand and laced his fingers through hers. She leaned over him and kissed his lips. He tasted like cigarettes and coffee. He smelled of the crisp autumn night, coal smoke, and ink. Being close to him ... it wasn't like standing on the edge of a cliff, it was as if she were running for that edge just as fast as she could.

She broke the kiss and traced the outline of his mouth. Wonderingly, she touched his cheek. His neck. The smooth V of bare skin in his open collar.

He laughed. "I've stumbled into a den of iniquity. I'm safer with the Tailor and Pretty Will and every thief and cutthroat in the Bend than I am with Miss Josephine Montfort of Gramercy Park," he said. Then he pulled her down to him, kissed her forehead, and closed his eyes again.

Jo laid her head on his chest. He felt so warm, so strong, so strangely, wonderfully male. Folded into his arms, she could almost believe that the impossible was possible. She stayed awake for some time, blinking in the darkness; then finally she fell asleep, listening to the sound of his heart.

➤ CHAPTER SIXTY ᐊ

Anna Montfort smiled.

And Jo realized just how long it had been since she'd seen her mother do that.

"You look beautiful, Josephine," Anna said, her eyes shimmering with tears. "How I wish your father could see you."

"Oh, Mama," Jo said, surprised by her mother's sudden softness. She reached for her hand and squeezed it. "Don't. If you do, I will."

"I mustn't, then. If we dare to go to Grandmama's supper with red eyes, we shall certainly hear how badly bred we are," Anna said, squeezing back before she let go.

Jo laughed, enjoying these fond few minutes with her mother. A pretty gift box rested in her lap. They were in their carriage en route to Grandmama Aldrich's birthday supper.

Jo, who'd assumed she would not be allowed to go, had been surprised when her mother said she could, and even more surprised when her mother said she would accompany her.

"It's only a small gathering," she had explained. "Just family and close friends. There will be music, I'm told, but no dancing. I should hate for you to go alone, Josephine."

Jo was surprised again when a box arrived at the house for her just that afternoon. It was from Aunt Madeleine's dressmaker; she recognized the label. At first she thought it must've been delivered to the wrong Montfort residence, but her mother assured her it had not been.

"It's for you," she'd said. "A special present from Phillip and Maddie. Open it."

Jo took the lid off the box, parted the clouds of tissue paper, and lifted out a gown of slate-gray silk. It had a pointed bodice, a square neckline, and long sleeves that puffed slightly near the shoulders, but *only* slightly, as neither Madeleine nor Anna believed in following fashion too closely. It was plain and boasted no embroidery or lace, as that was too forward for a young woman not yet out of mourning, but it was not black, and for that reason alone, Jo loved it.

"Your uncle and aunt are rather more progressive than I, and they felt it was high time you had a change from black," Anna explained. "I allowed myself to be swayed." She held up a finger. "But just for tonight."

Jo had hugged her mother, dashed off a thank-you note to her aunt and uncle for Katie to deliver, then gone upstairs to bathe.

She'd greatly welcomed the distraction of a new dress. She'd been dreading Grandmama's party because it meant dealing with Grandmama, and she'd also been anxious about other things— Bram, mainly, and any lingering expectations he might have. She had to tell him that she did not wish to pursue a match with him. How could she, when she was in love with Eddie Gallagher?

Jo thought back to the night they'd spent together. The milkman rattling bottles all along Gramercy Square had woken them just before dawn. Eddie had sworn when he'd seen the time, knowing Tumbler would be gone, and with him, any chance of finding Kinch.

They'd hurried downstairs and raced through the kitchen right before Mrs. Nelson came out of her room to start the servants' breakfast. Jo just managed to sneak Eddie out without anyone seeing him, and he managed to steal one last kiss as she did.

Mrs. Nelson had been surprised to see Jo in the kitchen, and at such an early hour, but Jo had made up a story on the spot. She claimed she'd come down for a cup of warm milk because she couldn't sleep. Mrs. Nelson insisted on making the drink for her. Jo thanked her, took the drink to her room, and climbed back into bed, reliving every moment she'd spent with Eddie.

She remembered the sound of his breathing, the confusion on his face when he woke, and the warm smile that replaced it when he realized where he was. She remembered how deliciously strange his body felt next to hers. The sweet weight of his arm across her. His stubbled chin. She remembered how different her own body felt. For once it wasn't a thing to be tamed and contained by laces and stays, but something wonderfully lush and yielding.

As she'd lain in his arms in the darkness, listening to him sleep, she'd wanted to wake him so she could ask him a thousand questions. She wanted to know more about his childhood. What made him angry. What made him laugh. She wanted to hear about his hopes and dreams, and she wanted to tell him hers. She wanted to tell him how exciting it was to walk the streets of the night city and meet its people. And that she wished she could write a story about them all. Eddie was the only person she *could* tell. The only one who understood.

Is this love? she'd wondered, in the depths of the night. A few weeks ago, she'd thought she might be falling in love. By the time the sky lightened outside her windows, she knew that she had.

What she didn't know, though, was where things stood between her and Bram. She wanted to clear the air, to tell him the truth. She couldn't do it at Grandmama's party—it would be awful to create any awkwardness at what was supposed to be a happy event—but when she saw him tonight, she would ask him to call at her home

tomorrow. She would tell him the truth in the privacy of her drawing room, and then she would tell her family.

Bram would be a gentleman, of course. He wouldn't create a
fuss, and he might even be relieved. After all, he did seem to be
spending more time with Elizabeth Adams these days. Her mother
and uncle, however, would be very upset. By saying no to Bram
and confessing her feelings for a penniless reporter, she would be
insulting Bram's family and embarrassing her own. She would be
breaking with her world.

It was a frightening prospect, but when she felt her nerve failing her, she remembered the words Eddie had spoken to her in his
room, the day he'd been beaten up.

. . . stay with me today. And tomorrow. And every day after. . . .

She'd thought what he'd asked was impossible. But maybe it
wasn't. If only she could be bold enough, and brave enough, to claim
the things she wanted: love, a purpose, a life. But could she be?

As Dolan nosed their carriage next to the sidewalk in front of
the Aldriches' imposing Fifth Avenue mansion, Jo steeled herself.
For the next few hours it would be spaniels and small talk. She
peered out her window and saw Mrs. Livingston and Mrs. Schuyler,
both swathed in fur, walking up the mansion's wide marble steps.

Bram, tall and handsome in a dinner jacket, stood at the top of
the steps. Jo glimpsed roses in vases inside the foyer; saw Mrs. Aldrich, beautiful in satin and pearls; and heard Vivaldi being played.
The scene was elegant and fine, and for a moment, Jo's heart swelled
with bittersweet emotion at the beauty of her world and the people
in it. And yet, she felt as if she'd already left this beautiful world and
was only glancing back at it, as if from a distance.

A footman in livery opened the Montforts' carriage door and
helped Jo and her mother step out. As soon as Bram saw them,
he bounded down to greet them. Before he got to the sidewalk,
though, old Mrs. van Rensselaer waddled up.

"Anna, my dear! So good to see you out!" she bellowed, taking Jo's mother's arm. "Do help me up the steps, will you? My sciatica's troubling me terribly tonight."

Anna did so, which left Bram to offer his arm to Jo.

"Why, Jo, you're a picture," he said, smiling at her.

And she was. Her new dress fit her perfectly and complemented her gray eyes. Katie had done a wonderful job with her hair, coiling it on top of her head and tucking two mauve roses at the back. Jo's mother had come into her room just as Jo was stepping into her shoes. She'd dismissed Katie and had provided the finishing touch herself: a necklace of amethysts, pale and demure, given to her by Jo's father on their wedding day.

Jo smiled at Bram's compliment and was about to return it, when a voice, thick with a warm Southern accent, said, "Bram Aldrich, there you are, you old hound!"

Bram turned around. "Clem!" he exclaimed. He turned to Jo. "Jo, may I present Clement Codman. He's from Raleigh. We're cousins, a few times removed. Clem, this is my dear friend Josephine Montfort."

"This is Jo? Why, she's *ten* times prettier than you said, you ol' weasel, you!" Clement took Jo's hand and kissed it. "He's tryin' to keep you under wraps, Miss Montfort. He doesn't want competition!"

"I'm very pleased to meet you, Mr. Codman," Jo said, smiling at the boisterous Southerner.

Jo's smile never slipped, but she flinched inside, unhappy to hear that Bram had spoken of her to his cousin. At least he'd only referred to her as a friend. She hoped that whatever he'd said to Clement about her was old news, and that it was Elizabeth Adams he talked about now.

Clement and Bram got into a conversation about another family member, and Jo's attention wandered. Her hand was still resting on

Bram's arm, and to simply walk off would have been rude. As she waited for the conversation to finish, she watched the van Eycks arrive and waved to Trudy.

Just as she was beginning to wonder if Bram and Clement would *ever* stop talking, someone else came walking up the sidewalk, weaving between the couples and families. He was wearing a tweed jacket, not a tuxedo, and his dark hair curled out from under the edges of his cap—too long, as always. He had a smile on his face.

And a girl on his arm.

She was very pretty. She had dark hair, too. Blue eyes. And pink cheeks. The young man said something to her, and she dipped her head toward him. He covered her hand with his. She smiled up at him lovingly and kissed his cheek.

Jo didn't know the girl. She'd never seen her before.

She knew the man, though.

It was Eddie Gallagher.

➤ CHAPTER SIXTY-ONE ◆

Voices echoed inside Jo's head.

Her own: *What was he like when he was little?*

And Fay's reply: *A damn good thief. Tough. Ruthless. Like all the rest of us.*

Her uncle's: *A strapping, dark-haired boy—Gleeson, or Gilligan, or some sort of Irish name. . . .*

And finally, Eddie's: *You don't know me. Not at all . . .*

No, Mr. Gallagher, she said silently as she watched him and his girl turn the corner and disappear. *I don't.*

"Now, don't you forget old Clem, Miss Montfort! I'll see you inside!"

Though Jo's heart had just been broken and all she wanted was to run into an empty room and weep, she smiled at Clement and said, "I look forward to that, Mr. Codman."

"Sorry about all the family talk, Jo," Bram said, patting her hand. "Shall we go in?" He started up the steps, then frowned. "Jo? Are you all right? You look so pale."

"I'm fine, Bram," Jo said, summoning all her strength. "Just a bit cold, that's all."

"How thoughtless of me. Come inside and warm up."

He hurried her into the foyer and a maid took her wrap. They walked down a long hallway to the drawing room, where Grandmama sat like a pasha, surrounded by friends, family, and half a dozen dogs.

"Happy birthday, Grandmama," Jo said, forcing brightness into her voice. "And many happy returns." Jo handed her the gift box. Grandmama opened it and was delighted by what it contained: a silver pin in the shape of a spaniel.

"Thank you, Josephine. It's beautiful," she said.

"I hope you received some lovely gifts today," Jo offered woodenly.

"I did. But not what I wanted most."

"And what was that?" Jo asked.

Grandmama looked pointedly at Bram. "A great-grandson."

Bram smiled tightly. "Let's get some punch, Jo," he said, taking her arm and leading her to the refreshments table. Platters had been laid out, from which people helped themselves. There was a glazed ham, tomato aspic, several roasted chickens, pickled vegetables, salads, cheeses, and fruit compote.

"I'm sorry about that," Bram said as he poured a glass of punch for Jo. "We'd hoped for good behavior from Grandmama today, but no such luck."

Jo barely heard him. She'd barely heard Grandmama. Her aunt and uncle came over, beaming, to compliment her dress. She smiled and thanked them. She drank the punch. And all the while, she felt like a puppet. As if someone else were pulling the strings that made her head nod and her mouth smile.

A poor, foolish girl, her uncle had said some days ago, talking about a girl a reporter was using to get a story. That was her—the most foolish of girls.

She'd trusted Eddie, fallen in love with him, considered giving up her life and everyone in it for him, and all the while, he'd only been using her to get a story. And he hadn't even waited until he *had* the story before he'd moved on to another girl. Anger smoldered inside her now, pushing aside the sadness.

"Let's find a chair and listen to the music," Bram said, leading her to the drawing room.

As she walked alongside him, past flickering candles, flowers, friends in gorgeous dresses, servants with crystal glasses on silver trays, a realization broke over her like an ice-cold wave. She'd come so close to stepping off the cliff, to making the biggest mistake of her life—one that would have cost her this fine and beautiful world.

They sat down on chairs that had been scattered around the edge of the dance floor, and Jo realized her feelings were visible on her face, because Bram took her hand and squeezed it.

"Leave it behind for a few hours, Jo," he said. "The sadness and the grief. I don't want to see any frowns on that pretty face tonight, only smiles."

He's always so kind, Jo thought, looking at him. *So good. So constant.*

He let go of her hand then, but she held his fast. "Bram," she said, her voice catching.

"Yes?"

Kiss me, she wanted to say. *Put your arms around me and hold me close and kiss me. Fill up my heart and my head like Eddie did. Make me want you, not him. Make me forget him.*

"Yes, Jo?"

"I just, well . . . I wanted to say thank you."

Bram looked at her with a quizzical expression. "For what?" he asked.

"For always being so incredibly good," she said with feeling.

He laughed, clearly uncomfortable. Emotion of any sort always made him awkward. "Don't be silly," he said, turning to the musicians.

He pulled his hand free. Jo folded her hands in her lap and sat very still, a smile plastered on her face, all the while tormenting herself with memories of Eddie's every kiss, of the way her skin tingled when he touched her, of his warmth, his scent, the sound of his voice. She hated him with a passion now, but she still wanted him with all her heart.

The musicians played on. And then, after half an hour, they stopped. Grandmama was brought forth, protesting the whole while, and a cake was carried out. After a song had been sung and the candles blown out, everyone watched Lolly the spaniel get the first slice.

"I think it will be some time before we get our slices," Bram observed dryly. "There are five more dogs to be fed." And then, all in a rush, he said, "I'm tired of sitting. My mother has a new orchid. It's purple. She's given it pride of place in the conservatory. Would you like to see it?"

"Very much," Jo replied mechanically.

They walked out of the ballroom, down hallways, past withdrawing rooms, a smoking room, and a library, until they arrived at the conservatory. Jo spotted the brilliant orchid and immediately walked over to it.

"It's beautiful, Bram," she said. "The color is so pure." She couldn't have cared less about the orchid. She only wanted to go home and cry into her pillow. Her face was beginning to ache from the effort of keeping a fake smile in place.

"Jo, I'm afraid I brought you here under false pretenses," Bram said. "The orchid was only a ruse."

She turned to him, puzzled. "How very mysterious of you. A ruse for what?" she asked.

And then it hit her. She gasped. Her hands went to her mouth.

Bram, smiling, mistook her reaction for happy surprise. He went down on one knee.

"Darling Jo," he said, pulling a diamond ring from his breast pocket. "Will you marry me?"

Jo felt as if there were iron bands around her chest. She didn't know what to do. She hadn't seen this coming.

"Bram, I—I . . . ," she stammered.

"Is that a yes?"

Desperate, Jo stalled for time. "I—I can't give you my answer. I must have my mother's permission. And my uncle's."

Bram smiled. "You do. I asked them both a week ago."

Jo's stomach twisted with terror. That was why her aunt had sent the dress. Black was not suitable for receiving a proposal, but gray was acceptable. That was why her mother had been teary in the carriage and had wished for her father to be here. Why her uncle had beamed at her. Why Clem had come to this supper. And Trudy. They'd all known what Bram was planning, yet they hadn't consulted her, for they hadn't seen the need. Of course she'd say yes.

"I know it's a bit sudden," Bram said, "but I can't wait any longer." He stood then, and kissed her on the lips. Lightly. Gently. As if he were afraid to break her. "I care greatly for you, Jo. We would make a splendid pair. We've known each other all our lives. Our minds are aligned on most things, and that's the best foundation for a marriage, I think."

As Jo fought down the urge to run, Bram talked on, enumerating all the strong points of his proposal, as if he were presenting a business deal. When he finished, he slid the ring on her finger.

"I hope you like it. It sparkles so brightly," he said. "But not as brightly as you do."

"Oh, Bram," Jo said tearfully.

He smiled, then kissed her again. "Your mother and uncle are waiting for us. Can I give them both some happy news for a change? And Grandmama a wonderful birthday present? I think she wants you to marry me even more than I do," he said, laughing. "Tell me, Jo, will you be my wife?"

➤ CHAPTER SIXTY-TWO ⥽

Jo stepped out of Grace Church and onto the sidewalk.

It was a stunningly beautiful day, crisp and sunny, with a fierce blue sky, though Jo barely noticed. For the past week, she'd moved as if in a trance.

She was wearing a new gray suit, trimmed with black braid, and carrying a mink muff. Her mother, at Grandmama's urging, had continued to allow Jo to wear less severe mourning attire. The suit had arrived from the dressmaker's yesterday and was a bit snug, but Katie had pulled her corset so tight this morning that it now fit perfectly. Jo couldn't breathe all that well, but that didn't matter. If she allowed herself to breathe, to feel, to listen to what her heart was trying to tell her, she would come apart.

What have you done? You don't love Bram, it said a thousand times a day. *Why did you do it?*

To make my family happy, she would reply, trying to hush it. *Because it's expected of me. Because Bram's right, we understand each other. Because he wants me, at least. And Eddie doesn't.*

Eddie's betrayal had done more than wound her; it had broken her, heart and soul. To care for someone as much as she cared for him, she'd learned, was dangerous. It was better to marry someone whom you didn't care for too much. That way, he could never cause you so much pain.

"That was a fine sermon! A fine sermon indeed!" said elderly Mr. DeWitt to the Reverend Willis, who was shaking hands with his parishioners.

"Wonderful, Reverend, just wonderful," said Mrs. Newbold. "Ah, Josephine! There you are, my dear! I heard the news. You'll be the most beautiful bride in New York. Bram is a very lucky man."

Jo smiled and nodded and thanked Mrs. Newbold, just as she'd been thanking scores of other well-wishers. She'd accepted Bram's proposal a week ago, and already most of the city, if not the entire state, knew they were engaged, thanks to Grandmama. The wedding was planned for June. By that time she would be past her six months of mourning.

Jo looked for her mother and spotted her talking with some Livingstons. She was still wearing her full widow's mourning, including a black bonnet and veil. Jo didn't want to hear any more good wishes on her engagement, so she decided to wait for her mother in their carriage.

As she started toward it, though, she felt a tug on her hand. She turned and saw a fetching brunette, elegantly turned out in blue silk.

"Fay?" she said, surprised to see her. "What are you doing here?"

"Waiting for you," Fay replied tersely. She was smiling, inclining her head, looking for all the world like another member of Grace's upper-crust congregation.

"But how did you know I'd be here?" Jo asked.

Fay rolled her eyes. "Where else would Miss Josephine Montfort of Gramercy Square be on a Sunday morning?" she asked. She glanced around and, in a lower voice, added, "Look, I can't stand here smiling like a jackass all day. I found Kinch."

Jo blinked.

"That's it? A blink?" Fay whispered. "I said I found *Kinch*. What's with you, anyway? You look like you just stumbled out of a Mott Street opium den."

"I got engaged. I suppose it produces a similar effect."

"Damn." Fay looked up, directly at Jo. "Who to?"

"Bram Aldrich."

"I had my money on Eddie."

"Then I'm afraid you've lost it," Jo said, her heart aching at the mention of Eddie's name.

"Listen to me, Jo, snap out of whatever funk you're in. Your man Kinch was hard to find, but I've found him. This might be your only chance to talk to him."

Jo nodded and a bit of spirit came trickling back into her veins.

"He's in a boardinghouse on Pitt Street. Number Sixteen. I spotted him late last night on Canal Street and followed him. It's a rough place. Don't go there alone. Get Eddie."

Jo took a deep breath, her ribs straining against her corset. "Does the Tailor know? Does the man with the scarred face?" she asked.

"If they do, I didn't tell them."

"Josephine?" a voice interrupted.

"That's my mother," Jo said without turning around. "Thank you, Fay. I'm in your debt."

"I'll take a pack of Duke's at your earliest convenience," said Fay. Then she smiled prettily and moved off.

"Come along," Anna said, stepping up beside her. "I'm ready to go."

"Mama, would you mind terribly if Dolan took you home and then took me to the park?" Jo asked, feverishly working out a way to get to Pitt Street. "It's such a fine morning. I'd love to get some fresh air."

"A walk in the park! What a capital idea!" It was Uncle Phillip.

He was suddenly at their side, with Aunt Madeleine and Caroline close behind him.

No! Jo thought.

"Let's all go," Jo's aunt said brightly. She took Anna's hand. "I know you're in mourning, but no one will begrudge you a bit of air. It's Central Park, not Mr. Barnum's circus."

Anna hesitated. Jo silently urged her to decline.

"Do come," Phillip said. "This has been such a sad time for us all, but now Jo's given this family happiness again. You must share in it, too."

Finally, Anna relented. "You're right as always, Phillip," she said, smiling. "Let's go."

"Splendid!" Phillip said. "Our carriage is just ahead of yours. Perhaps the Aldriches would like to join us."

"I'll ask them," Madeleine said, moving off to find Grandmama.

Anna walked to the carriages with Caroline, and Phillip walked with Jo. He gave her a conspiratorial smile and Jo smiled back, though it killed her. He meant well. He'd heard her ask to go to the park and had sought to help her, but she didn't want to go to the blasted park! She'd meant to have Dolan drop her off, and as soon as he was gone, take a cab to Eddie's, then continue with him to Pitt Street, where they could confront Kinch. And what was she doing instead? Promenading! She wanted to scream with frustration.

Eddie had not contacted her since the Aldriches' party, and she'd certainly made no effort to contact him. The thought of going to him, of actually seeing him in person, was painful in the extreme, but she didn't know what else to do. Fay was right. She couldn't go after Kinch alone.

"Was that a new friend?" Phillip asked, interrupting Jo's thoughts. "I haven't seen her at church before."

"Who?" Jo asked distractedly.

"The young woman you were speaking with. A few moments ago."

"You must mean Miss Pitt. I only just met her," Jo fibbed as they arrived at their carriages. "I stepped on her hem and had to apologize to her. She's from Philadelphia. She's visiting for the weekend."

"Philadelphia? Would her family be the Horace Pitts or the Morrison Pitts?"

"She didn't say, Uncle Phillip."

Phillip frowned and was about to ask her another question when Madeleine rejoined them.

"The Aldriches will follow us," she announced. "I'm afraid the dogs will be joining us, too," she added. "Grandmama's got them in the carriage. I'm surprised she didn't bring them into the church."

"I'm sure she *tried*," Jo's mother said, suppressing a smile. She turned to Dolan, who was holding the door for her. "The park, please, Dolan. Bethesda Terrace."

Dolan helped her in, then Jo, and then he climbed back into his seat, cracked his whip, and set off. Phillip, Madeleine, and Caroline were right behind them. The Aldriches brought up the rear.

"Maddie's right. It'll be good to get some air," her mother said, smiling. "We'll have a lovely stroll, all of us. Family and family-to-be. Won't we, Jo?"

"Yes, lovely," Jo said, smiling back.

Her voice was even, her expression calm, but inside her mink muff, her hands were knotted into fists.

➢ CHAPTER SIXTY-THREE ➢

Mrs. Byrne, Eddie's landlady, looked Jo up and down.

It was quite clear from the expression on her face that she thought Jo was a shameless, scheming hussy bent on ensnaring Eddie and depriving her of a boarder.

"Sorry, miss," she sniffed. "I have no idea where Mr. Gallagher is."

"*Please*, Mrs. Byrne. It's imperative I find him," Jo said.

It was late, nearly ten o'clock at night. She'd wheedled Katie into changing places with her again and had arrived at Eddie's boarding-house moments ago, only to be told he wasn't in.

"Oh? And why's that?" Mrs. Byrne asked, folding her arms over her large bosom.

"It concerns a lead for a story he's working on. An important story," Jo said. "I should hate to be the one who cost him that lead," she added.

Worry flickered in Mrs. Byrne's eyes. "He's down the street," she said, relenting. "At Jimmy Mac's saloon."

Jo thanked her and dashed off. She had no trouble finding Jimmy Mac's; she heard the music from a block away. As she stepped inside, the smell of sweat, smoke, and beer hit her. The room was crowded and hot. People were shouting. Men in threadbare jackets and women in faded, ill-fitting dresses were drinking and laughing.

Across the room, a young black man hammered out a cakewalk tune, jangling and syncopated, on a battered upright piano. His talented hands flew across the keys. Dancers whooped and shouted as he played, their boot heels pounding against the plank floor. Jo had only been in one other bar before: Mick Walsh's dingy dive, where the patrons were bent on drinking themselves to death. Jimmy Mac's was nothing like that. It was bright, lively, and loud.

Jo searched the crowd for Eddie. Her traitorous heart leapt as she spotted him leaning against the bar. He was wearing his denim shirt and a tweed vest. His sleeves were rolled up. She could see a bit of his bare chest peeking through his open collar. His dark hair, wavy and thick, fell across his forehead. And his blue eyes were crinkled in laughter at whatever the man next to him had just said.

God, but he's handsome, Jo thought. *Handsome and heartless and cruel.*

Eddie looked up just then. His eyes found hers and widened in surprise. He cocked his head questioningly. Jo made her way to him, pushing through the crowd.

"You're very flushed, Miss Montfort. Have you been dancing?" he asked, when she reached him.

"No, I—" Jo began to say, but he cut her off.

"Would you like to?" he asked in a mocking tone. "The piano man's playing 'Good Enough.' One of my favorites. Ironic, no? Seeing as I wasn't." He smiled, feigning regret, then said, "Ah, but you can't dance with me, can you? You're betrothed now, and I doubt Mr. Aldrich would approve. All the best on your engagement, by the way. I read about it in the papers."

His tone was still mocking, but his smile was bitter.

Anger flared inside Jo. *You have no right to be bitter*, she wanted to say. *You have someone else. You were only using me.*

"I didn't come here to dance, Mr. Gallagher," she said coldly.

"No? Then why did you come? To break more hearts? Or to step on the pieces of mine?"

Jo's eyes narrowed. "That is rich coming from you, Eddie!"

"Coming from *me*? I'm not the one marrying Bram Aldrich!"

"No, you're not. Why would you? He can't advance your career," Jo said pointedly.

"What are you talking about?" Eddie asked, confused.

"Spare me the bad acting," Jo said. "I came here because I have something for you. Something you'll *truly* love—a scoop. I know where Kinch is. Fay told me. She followed him last night. He's in a boardinghouse on Pitt Street."

"You could have told me you were getting engaged, instead of making me read about it. Why didn't you?" Eddie asked.

His eyes sought hers and she saw an anger there that matched her own. And something else. Something she didn't expect to see— hurt, deep and raw. It was a sham, she was sure of it. She quickly looked away, determined never to be swayed by him again.

"We had an agreement, remember? My answers, your story," she said. She would not let him see how badly he'd hurt her.

Eddie's eyes hardened. "An agreement. That's all this was, wasn't it? I forgot," he said. He grabbed his coat and hat off a barstool. "All right, then, let's finish it."

He led the way through the crowd to the door. Jo trotted to keep up with him. It was harder, much harder than she'd imagined, to be close to him. A part of her wished that she'd never glimpsed him with his lady friend, that she was still ignorant of the sort of man he really was. At least then she could believe he still cared for her. Because see- ing him again made it painfully clear to her that she still cared for him.

A story. A way to make his name. That's all this is to him, she told herself, shoring up her defenses. *That's all you are to him.*

Eddie reached the door. He opened it and held it for her, and the two of them hurried out of Jimmy Mac's and into the night.

❧ CHAPTER SIXTY-FOUR ❧

A man sat on the stoop of Number Sixteen Pitt Street cleaning his nails with a knife. Grime had blackened the house's red bricks. Its stone steps were cracked. Its front door sagged forlornly on ancient hinges.

The man's hands were dirty, his clothing patched. As Jo and Eddie neared him, he pulled something out of his hair and crushed it between his fingers.

"Are you the landlord?" Eddie asked.

The man pointed to the door.

Jo and Eddie opened it and walked into what had once been the elegant, high-ceilinged foyer of a fine single-family house. Pitt Street had been a desirable address a hundred years ago, but its graceful homes had been sold off and turned into boardinghouses as the clamorous city pushed ever northward.

On the left of the foyer was a large withdrawing room, its tall, arched doors long gone. Eddie entered it and Jo followed. Chunks of plaster had fallen from the ceiling. What remained of the wallpaper was stippled with mildew. A few old chairs, stuffing spilling out of their torn upholstery, were scattered around the room. A tarnished gas chandelier provided a sickly yellow light.

People, vacant-eyed and broken, warmed themselves by a meager fire. A few nursed glasses of cloudy gin dispensed for a penny a shot by a man sitting in a corner. As Jo watched, another man carefully folded a piece of newspaper into the bottom of his shoe to cover the holes in its sole. A woman wearing a moth-eaten jacket applied rouge to her cheeks in the reflection of a cracked mirror. Then she reached down the front of her dress and hiked her breasts up so that they were nearly spilling out of the garment.

"Want a room, do you?" a voice said.

It was the man selling gin. He had bright eyes, greasy brown hair, and a straggly beard.

Jo stiffened, insulted by the implication. "We do not," she said.

"We'd like to pay a call on one of your lodgers. A Mr. Kinch," Eddie said.

"No one here by that name," the man said.

"Are you certain?" Jo asked.

"You think I don't know who's staying in my own house?" the man growled.

Uncowed, Jo said, "He's very unusual-looking. He has tattoos on his face."

"Oh, him," the man said. "He left. Stayed one night. Never gave his name."

"When?" Jo asked, her heart sinking.

The man worked a bit of food from his teeth with his tongue. He stared ahead of himself silently. As if he hadn't heard her. Eddie put a dollar into his hand.

The man touched the brim of his hat and said, "This afternoon. Around three."

"Have you rented his room yet?" asked Eddie.

"No."

"Can we see it?"

The man looked from Eddie to Jo, then laughed. "Sure you can *see* it. Rent's a quarter. For looking at it, or for anything else you have in mind."

Eddie gave the man a look. Then he gave him the money. The man handed him a key. "Room C. Third floor. At the back."

Jo followed Eddie to the staircase. She had to steel herself to climb it. Roaches crawled over the steps and up the wall. The smell of unwashed bodies and chamber pots was overwhelming. But there was an even worse stench underneath those—the stench of despair.

Jo's nerve was faltering by the time they finally reached the third floor. A door opened near the landing and a man came out of it, weaving and bobbing. He made his way to the bathroom. Seconds later, Jo heard him being sick. She glanced into his room and saw a woman sitting on the edge of the bed, her head in her hands.

"Do you really think we'll find anything here?" she asked Eddie.

"It's worth a look," he replied.

They reached Kinch's room and Eddie unlocked the door. He found a switch on the wall, and the room's sole gas jet sputtered to life. Jo followed him inside, her eyes widening. She'd glimpsed such rooms in the Bend, but she'd never stood inside one. A torn curtain hung from the small, dirty window. There was a filthy rug, a small fireplace, and a single bed with a stained mattress. Looking at the cracked walls and the smoke-blackened ceiling, Jo thought she would fling herself out of the window if she had to spend even one night here.

"This makes no sense. He has money. Richard Scully gave him a thousand dollars. He could stay in a decent place. Why would he come here?" she asked.

"So he could disappear," Eddie replied. "I bet he moves around constantly. Probably only spends one night in any given place."

He'd barely spoken to her, or even looked at her, all the way from Reade Street. Even now, he said as little as possible. Jo hated this new silence between them but was doing little herself to dispel it.

Frowning, Eddie crossed the tiny room to the mattress and flipped it over, then did the same to the rug, but found nothing. Jo glanced at the fireplace. There were ashes in the grate. Not from wood or coal, but the kind left after burning paper. She knelt down and peered into them. At the edge of the pile was something small and white, a scrap of paper. Most of it had burned, but a tiny bit was still intact. She picked it up. Fragments of words were visible.

cis Mallo

arkbri

Jo caught her breath. This was a clue. An important one. She was sure of it.

"Eddie, look!" she said, forgetting her anger in the excitement of her discovery. "These letters, they're parts of names—Francis Mallon and Darkbriar, I think. Mallon was the orderly Eleanor Owens attacked when she escaped from Darkbriar, remember? Kinch must be going to see Mallon. To ask him about Eleanor. Maybe to find out if she said anything to him about the manifests."

"You know something, Jo?" Eddie said.

She turned to him eagerly. "What?" she asked.

But Eddie wasn't looking at her. He was gazing out the filthy window. In a tired, hollow voice he answered her. "I don't care anymore."

❖ CHAPTER SIXTY-FIVE ❖

"That's it? We're done? It's over?" Jo said, livid.

"The driver's waiting. Get in," Eddie replied through gritted teeth. He was holding the door of a hansom cab open for her.

They'd walked out of the boardinghouse, and then from Pitt Street to Houston Street, after Eddie declared he was through—through with Kinch, Scarface, Eleanor Owens, the *Nausett*, the *Bonaventure*, and her. Especially her.

"You're just going to leave me here?" Jo asked. She was standing on the sidewalk. She'd refused to get into the cab.

"Yes, I am. I can't do this," he said, and started to walk away.

For a few seconds, Jo was speechless. First he broke her heart, and now he was leaving her in the lurch with their investigation unsolved. How could he *do* these things?

"I'm blind, I must be," she said aloud. "You really fooled me, Eddie."

Eddie stopped. He turned around. "*I* fooled *you*? What are you talking about?"

"I thought you were kind. I thought you cared. But you're not. You're cruel!" Jo shouted angrily.

Eddie spun around. "Me? *Me?* Seriously, Jo?"

"Hey, sister, you want a ride or not?" the cabdriver yelled.

"Not!" Jo shouted, slamming the cab door closed.

She stalked up to Eddie, her fists clenched. "Are you forgetting why I came to you? Because of my father. *I* haven't stopped caring. I cared then, and I care now. I want my answers."

"For God's sake, Jo, I care, too! I care about *you*!" Eddie said. His words, spoken loudly, echoed down the dark street.

Jo almost laughed out loud. "Is that so? I must say, you have a *very* strange way of showing it."

"Me?" Eddie said.

"Yes, Eddie, *you*!"

Eddie held up his hands. "I'm going now. Because this is crazy. But before I do, tell me one thing, just one thing. . . ."

Jo jutted her chin at him. "What?"

"Why did you do it?" he asked. "Why did you rip my heart out? Why did you say yes to Bram?"

Jo felt like he'd slapped her. She took a faltering step back. "Do *not* do this, Eddie. My nerves cannot withstand further assaults at the moment."

Eddie snorted. "Oh, *please.* Your nerves are as strong as steel. I know why you did it. Because I'm not good enough for you. Because no matter what I do, no matter how hard I work, I'll never be a van Rensselaer or an Astor or an Aldrich."

"What did you say?" Jo asked, her voice shaking with anger.

"I think you heard me just fine."

"Oh, is that what you think, Eddie? Let me tell you what *I* think. I think you're a *cad.* And I think your lady friend would be awfully upset if she could hear you right now."

Eddie suddenly looked confused. "My what?" he said.

Jo glared at him. "Don't play the innocent. I saw you with her. On Fifth Avenue. Outside the Aldriches' home. Just over a week ago."

"On Fifth Avenue?" Eddie echoed, looking confused. "A week ago?" Understanding broke over him. "That was Eileen. My sister. I was taking her to dinner."

Jo was stunned. "Your . . . your *sister?*" she said in a small voice.

Eddie had told her about Eileen the night they'd gone to the Bend. She'd lost the hearing in one ear when a priest beat her. Jo remembered now how the girl on Eddie's arm had leaned in close to him. It was because she'd been trying to hear what he was saying.

"You thought Eileen was my girl," Eddie said flatly. The anger in his beautiful blue eyes turned to hurt. "Is that the kind of man you think I am? You think I could kiss you, and fall asleep holding you in my arms, and then carry on with someone else?"

Jo's heart turned to lead as she realized what she'd done. *I've made a mistake*, she thought. *A terrible one.*

"I—I didn't know what to think." She stumbled over her words. "I saw you with a girl, and my uncle . . . he said he'd overheard a reporter at the *Standard*, a reporter with an Irish surname, saying dreadful things about a young woman whom he was using to get a story."

"I don't know what your uncle heard, but it didn't come from me," Eddie said. He gave her a sad smile. "Eileen and I, we look a lot alike. Didn't it even occur to you that she might be my sister? Maybe you *wanted* to think I was with another girl, Jo. It makes things easier, doesn't it? If I'm a cad, then you don't have to make a hard choice."

"That's not *true!*" Jo protested.

Eddie shook his head. "Like I said, I can't do this anymore. Meet with you. Be near you. Talk about what was, or wasn't, between us."

"Eddie, I'm sorry, I—"

"I love you, Jo," Eddie cut her off. "You're the most remarkable, beautiful, confounding girl I've ever met. I shouldn't say that to you, I know. And I'm not saying it because I want to, but because I have to. I'm telling you so that you understand why I won't see you anymore. It's not right. You're another man's fiancée now."

Jo stared at him. He looked miserable after his admission. She wanted to say something, anything, but she didn't trust herself to speak without bursting into tears.

Eddie flagged down another cab. "This time, you're getting in." He opened the door. "Irving and Sixteenth," he said to the driver.

Silently Jo climbed into the cab and Eddie closed the door behind her. The cab's window was down. She put a hand on the sill.

"Goodbye, Miss Montfort. I hope you find what you're looking for," Eddie said.

Tears welled in Jo's eyes. "Eddie, no. You can't. You can't say such things to me and then just walk off."

"Yeah, Jo. I can," he said. And then he turned away from her and headed down the street.

"Eddie, *wait*!" Jo called after him, but the only answer she got was the sound of his footsteps fading.

Distraught, she sat back in her seat and tried to collect herself. But it was no good. "Damn it! Damn you!" she yelled, pounding a gloved hand on the seat. She swallowed hard to get the lump out of her throat. "What have I done?" she said.

But she knew. She'd believed the worst of Eddie instead of the best. She'd lost faith in him because she had no faith in herself. Not in her ability to decide for herself. To choose for herself. Or even to *be* herself.

And now it was too late. She'd promised herself to Bram. The engagement had been announced. A date had been chosen. Everyone was so happy. Everyone but her.

"What am I going to do?" she whispered.

The tears that had been welling finally fell. Drops became a torrent. Sobs wrenched themselves out of her.

Jo's heart was in pieces. And she'd shattered it herself.

❖ CHAPTER SIXTY-SIX ❖

Jo sucked in a deep breath. "Pull yourself together," she hissed at herself as she walked up Irving Place.

The cabbie had dropped her at Sixteenth Street. Jo had paid him and started toward Gramercy Square, concentrating on her breathing as she walked. She had to calm herself. It wasn't easy getting back inside her house. She would need her wits about her.

It was a little after midnight and very dark. Irving had only a few sputtering gas lamps to light her way. She passed Seventeenth Street, then Eighteenth, lost in painful thoughts about Eddie.

How could she marry Bram now, knowing Eddie's true feelings for her? And knowing her own true feelings for him? But how could she break her engagement to Bram?

And the investigation into her father's murder—how would she continue it without Eddie's help? They were a team, an effective one. They'd been so close to finding Kinch. So close to confronting him face to face. Though she was frightened of the man, she wanted to look into his fearsome eyes and ask him who he was. *Was* he Stephen Smith? Had he killed Richard Scully? And her father?

He would hardly tell her if he had, but she would know anyway. His eyes would reveal the truth.

Jo, breathing easier now, thought back to what she'd learned at Pitt Street. Kinch was going to go to Darkbriar, to speak with Francis Mallon. She was sure of it. He was still searching for the manifests. If she could only find them before he did. If she had them in hand, she could see for herself what the *Bonaventure*'s cargo was, and if the ship really was connected to Van Houten.

I'll go see Francis Mallon myself, she decided. *I don't need Eddie for that. All I need to do is go to Darkbriar and ask to speak with him.*

She shuddered at the thought of walking through Darkbriar's high gates and into the asylum itself, but told herself that she was being silly. She'd be perfectly safe.

Busy concocting a story to tell her mother that would allow her to get to Darkbriar and back, Jo didn't hear the footsteps at first. By the time she did, it was too late.

A hand was clapped over Jo's mouth. Her arm was twisted behind her back. Terrified, Jo struggled against her attacker, but she was no match for him. He dragged her down a dark alley that ran between two houses and pushed her against a wall. Stars exploded behind her eyes as she hit her head. Rough bricks scraped her cheek.

Her attacker had taken his hand away from her mouth, but he still had hold of her arm. It felt as if it were being ripped from its socket. Suddenly something glinted silver before her eyes. It was a knife, its blade caught in a shaft of moonlight slanting in through the top of the alley. A whimper of fear escaped her.

"Not another sound or I'll cut you," a voice said—a man's voice, harsh and low.

Jo nodded as best she could.

The man pressed himself against her. "Such a pretty girl," he said, his breath warm in her ear. "What's she doing out by herself? She should be home, where good girls belong. Only sluts walk the streets at night. Are you a slut, Miss Montfort?"

"Please . . . ," Jo whispered. Her eyes were closed. Her body was shaking. She was out of her mind with fear.

"*Please,*" the man echoed mockingly. "Is that what you say to your paperboy?"

He kissed her neck and trailed the tip of his knife over her cheek to her nose. Jo whimpered again; she couldn't help it.

"So *very* pretty," the man said. "But you won't be, without a nose. Keep poking it into other people's business and I'll come into your house one night, into your bedroom, and slice that pretty nose off. I'll be gone before you've even stopped screaming. You think your paperboy will like you then? No one will."

The man lowered his knife. He kissed her again. His breath was rancid.

"I'm going to go now, Miss Montfort," he said. "But you're going to stay here. Right against this wall. You're going to count to ten, very slowly, and then you're going to go home and do as you're told. Like a good girl. If you do, we need never see each other again. Start counting. Nice and slow . . ."

Jo did, her eyes still closed, her voice hitching.

When she got to ten, she opened her eyes. The man was gone. She was alone.

She took a shaky, faltering step. And then another. And then she fell to her knees in the dirty alley and vomited.

➤ CHAPTER SIXTY-SEVEN ◄

"White can be so stark," Anna Montfort said. "Ivory might be a better choice with your complexion. For your dress *and* your flowers. Oh, this would all be so much easier if Grandmama weren't insisting that the ceremony be held at Herondale!"

"It's for Mr. Aldrich's sake, Mama," Jo said blandly. "He cannot attend otherwise."

They were in the dining room, eating breakfast. It had been decided just yesterday that Jo would wear white at her wedding. Somber colors were usually required for one only recently out of full mourning—as Jo would be in June—but Grandmama had declared that Jo was making a trip to the altar, not a mausoleum, and refused to even hear of mauve for her wedding gown.

"You're right, of course, Josephine," Anna said. "Peter must be a part of his son's wedding. And there's also the fact that Herondale is private. It has a nice tall gate to keep out all the dreadful reporters determined to tell the world what sorts of canapes were served."

"No," Jo murmured. "We can't have any dreadful reporters."

"But the problem remains: how do we get dozens of hothouse roses from the city to the country?" her mother continued.

Jo was barely listening. Her hand absently went to her right cheek and the cuts there, made by the brick wall when her attacker pushed her head into it.

I stumbled, Mama. In my bathroom. Just this morning. I was thinking about the wedding, not paying any attention, and I fell and hit my head against the edge of the bathtub.

That was how she'd explained the cuts. Two days after the attack, they were starting to heal. The rest of her wasn't.

She'd staggered home that night, holding back her sobs until she got to her room. Then she'd pulled her clothing off, run a scalding hot bath, and sat in it, feeling as if she'd never get clean.

She'd barely slept since the attack. She had no appetite. Her assailant had terrorized her. Hurt her. Made her feel dirty. And there was nothing she could do about it. He seemed to know that. He seemed to know that she wouldn't tell anyone, not her mother, or uncle, or the police. That she *couldn't* tell anyone. It was as if he knew *her.*

And she hadn't so much as glimpsed him. He'd made sure of that. She'd heard his voice, and she didn't think it was Kinch's, but couldn't be sure. She'd been too frightened to focus on it. *Was* he Kinch? Or was he the man with the scarred face, the one who had attacked Eddie?

His voice wouldn't go away. She kept hearing it in her ear, over and over. . . . *You're going to go home and do as you're told. Like a good girl. . . .*

Yes, I am, she thought. *I have no choice. I'm going to give up pursuing my father's killer. Give up my dream of becoming a reporter. And give up the man I love. I'm going to be a good girl and do what everyone else wants. Because if I don't, I'll find a man with a knife in my bedroom one night.*

Jo's bright eyes were dull now, her lively face a mask. Fear had dampened the fire that burned inside her to an ember. Soon it would die altogether. Maybe not today, or even in a year or two. But bit by bit, it would fade. Until the things she'd hoped for from life, and the person she'd longed to become, were only dim memories.

The world outside Gramercy Square, she'd learned, could be dark and dangerous, and one had to be strong to move about in it. Nellie Bly was strong. Fay was strong. Eleanor Owens had been, too. But Jo Montfort? She felt so weak now that lifting her teacup seemed like an ordeal.

"Whatever color we decide, the roses must come from Meeker's florists. They're the only ones I trust. . . ."

Her mother was still talking about flowers. Jo nodded listlessly, not caring about flowers or anything else. And then the door to the dining room opened abruptly and a pale and flustered Theakston hurried into the room.

"Madam, I beg your pardon, but Mrs. Phillip Montfort's maid is here," he said, obviously upset.

Anna looked at him coldly. "Why are you telling me this, Theakston?" she asked. "I'm not in the habit of receiving other people's servants."

"I'm quite aware of that, madam. But this is a most unusual circumstance. She's come to fetch you and Miss Jo to Mrs. Phillip Montfort's side. It appears—"

Theakston stopped talking. He struggled for words.

"What is it, Theakston? For goodness' sake, get a hold of yourself!" Anna chided.

Theakston nodded. He squared his shoulders. "Mr. Alvah Beekman has been murdered, madam. By a lunatic wielding a knife. It happened late last night, and it appears that the same lunatic attempted to take another life as well . . . Mr. Phillip Montfort's."

✥ CHAPTER SIXTY-EIGHT ✥

"I'm all right," Phillip Montfort insisted. "It's only a cut. It will heal. It's Alvah's family we should be thinking of, not me."

Jo, in tears, was sitting at her uncle's side. Her mother was on his other side. Her aunt Madeleine, trembling and red-eyed, was pouring tea. Jo and her mother had arrived only moments ago. They'd been met by a somber-looking Harney, who led them directly to Phillip's study. Caroline was there, too, ordering the maid to build up the fire. Robert had been called home from school and was expected later in the day.

Phillip was seated by the fire, wearing trousers, a shirt, and a dressing gown. He was ashen-faced, and there was a livid bruise on his cheek. His shirt collar was open, a bandage visible under it. A decanter of brandy and an empty glass rested on a table next to him.

Jo was extremely upset to see her uncle looking so shaken and diminished. She wanted to know what had occurred but knew better than to ask questions while a servant was in the room.

"Phillip, what in God's name happened?" Anna asked as soon as the maid left.

"Alvah and I were walking home," Phillip said. "We worked until ten last night and decided not to trouble our respective cooks with a late supper, so we dined at the Washington."

Jo knew the place. It was a hotel a few streets west of Gramercy Square. Her uncle often dined there.

"We were walking along afterward when a man suddenly came at us. He punched me in the face. I remember that, and then it gets hazy. He . . . he had a knife," Phillip said, his voice breaking. "And he went for Alvah."

Anna gasped and covered her mouth with her hands. Jo knew she ought to have been shocked as well, but she wasn't. She'd feared this very thing.

Phillip paused to collect himself. He refilled his brandy glass. Jo had rarely seen her uncle drink, and never before evening.

"I managed to get to my feet. The man slashed at me, I ducked, and the knife grazed my chest. I was able to grab his hand and I must've shouted for help, because suddenly bystanders were there, and the police, and they managed to subdue him."

"Thank goodness those officers came before he . . . he . . . Oh, Phillip!" Madeleine said, bursting into tears.

"Now, now, my dear," Phillip said.

Caroline took her mother's hand.

"What will happen to the man?" asked Jo. She had more questions for her uncle. She wanted to know what his attacker looked like, if he'd said anything, and if the police had identified him. But she couldn't ask them. Not in front of her mother, aunt, and cousin. Her uncle knew that she had worried about his being attacked—and why—but they didn't.

"He'll be charged, I imagine," Phillip replied. "The police were going to take him to the Tombs, but he was so violently out of control, they took him to Darkbriar instead."

Jo knew about the Tombs. It was the city jail on Centre Street. It had been nicknamed the Tombs because it resembled a mausoleum.

"Darkbriar was close by, much closer than the Tombs," Phillip continued, "and it has special cells to prevent inmates from harming themselves. I don't know if the police will keep him there. Perhaps they'll take him downtown if they manage to calm him."

"The police brought Phillip here just after two a.m.," Madeleine said. "I sent for the doctor right away."

"You should have sent for us, too, Maddie," Anna said reproachfully.

"Nonsense," said Phillip. "There was no need. I'm fine." But his hand shook so badly as he was speaking, he had to put his glass down.

"Papa, you're exhausted," Caroline said anxiously. "Dr. Redmond said you weren't to tire yourself. He said you needed to rest."

"I will, Caro, but I'm not finished yet. I'm afraid I haven't told you everything. Not even you, Maddie. I wanted to wait until we were all assembled." He took a deep breath, as if marshalling his strength. "The man who attacked me—Kinch, he calls himself—claims he was an employee of Van Houten's."

The hair on the back of Jo's neck stood up.

"Was he?" Madeleine asked, aghast.

"I'm not sure. He claims Van Houten took something from him. Even as the police were putting handcuffs on him, he was shouting that he'd have his revenge. And he . . . he mentioned Richard and Charles. He said they'd already gotten what they deserved and so would the rest of us."

Jo hadn't noticed until that moment how hard she was gripping the arms of her chair. It was almost a confession. Almost, but not quite. Kinch had killed Beekman; her uncle had seen him do it. Had he also killed her father and Richard Scully?

"Phillip, what are you saying? You can't mean that this man . . . that he killed Charles?" Jo's mother said. Her voice was barely a whisper.

"I don't know, Anna. The police raised the possibility, though I don't see how he could have gotten inside the house. The doors were locked, and Charles never would have let such a wild-looking man in," Phillip reasoned.

"I don't believe it. I *can't*," Madeleine said, shaking her head. "This man's a lunatic. Why should we believe *anything* he says?"

"Kinch is certainly not in possession of his faculties," Phillip said.

"Then why are you telling us this, if it's not true?" Madeleine asked unhappily. "Haven't we had enough upset?"

"Because the truth doesn't matter to the press," Phillip replied. "Reporters arrived on the scene last night before poor Alvah's body was even cold. When they hear of Kinch's ravings—and they will—they'll have a field day. Three Van Houten deaths, a madman—it's catnip to an editor. Every paper in the city will be splashing rumors about as if they were gospel, and every shoeshine boy and scullery maid will be gossiping about the Montforts. I want you all to be prepared for it. Reporters may accost us in our carriages. They may knock on our doors and camp out on our stoops. You are, of course, to say nothing to them."

As he finished speaking, a bout of coughing overtook him. He leaned back in his chair when it was over, flushed and spent.

"Papa, you're overtaxing yourself. You *must* rest," Caroline urged. "Shall I call Harney to help you upstairs?"

"Certainly not. I'm fully capable of walking up my own stair-case," Phillip said, getting to his feet. "If harassment by the papers becomes as bad as I fear, I shall look into renting a house in the country for all of us. I'm sure the Aldriches would know of some-thing suitable."

"Papa . . . ," Caroline pressed.

"Yes, Caro, I know," Phillip said wearily. "I'm going." He bade everyone goodbye, then slowly walked out of the room.

"We are so lucky, Maddie," Anna said, when he was gone. "If he'd hit his head harder, if that horrible man had been quicker . . . I can't even bear to think about it."

"We are, yes," Madeleine agreed. "But the poor Beekmans are less fortunate, and now we're all facing another funeral. It's too much too fathom."

"You don't think there's any truth to what Phillip said, do you? About this evil man having something to do with Charles's death?" Jo's mother asked, her eyes clouded with worry. "I don't think I could bear it if . . . if . . ."

Jo's heart ached for her mother. Jo had had time to get used to the fact that her father had been murdered; her mother hadn't.

"We'll have to wait and see, Anna," Madeleine said. "Hopefully the doctors at Darkbriar can figure out whether this horrible man Kinch is telling the truth."

"Perhaps once Phillip regains his strength, he could speak with Mr. Stoatman and see what his reporters have heard, if anything," Anna suggested. "To have Charles's name on the lips of every filthy newsboy, on top of everything else we've been through, is adding insult to a great deal of injury."

Jo wanted to know what Stoatman's reporters had heard, too. She didn't care about preparing for the tidal wave of gossip that her uncle feared, though. She only cared about finding out whether Kinch had murdered her father. If the doctors at Darkbriar were to get a confession out of him, the police would be the first to know, and the press a close second.

"I wish we didn't have to wait. If only *we* knew some reporters we could ask right now," Maddie said, sighing.

"Thank goodness we don't," Anna retorted.

Jo picked up her teacup and studied its contents.

But I do, she thought.

Eddie was angry with her, and he had every right to be, but hopefully he would help her. Hopefully he would see her.

Just this one last time.

➤ CHAPTER SIXTY-NINE ⮜

"Would you like a seat, miss?" the brisk young woman at the cash register asked as she totaled a patron's bill.

"Actually, I'm looking for a friend. I'll sit with him, if I may," Jo replied.

The woman nodded. She glanced at Jo, then looked her up and down as Jo made her way through the dense lunchtime crowd at Child's Restaurant on Park Row. Jo looked very different, in her expensive suit, from the other women there in their white cotton blouses and serviceable serge skirts.

Child's was a new sort of restaurant for people who worked. Jo had heard about it but had never been inside. She marveled at the immaculate white tiles on the wall, the sparkling counters with shiny metal stools under them, and the long, marble-topped tables where perfect strangers sat down next to one another and ate bowls of soup or thick sandwiches brought to them by waitresses in starched aprons.

"Eddie Gallagher? He's probably at Child's," the young woman at the front desk in the *Standard*'s receiving area had told her. "He usually eats lunch there. It's just across the street."

Jo had used the Astor Library and her history of Van Houten as an excuse to leave the house. She said the news of Mr. Beekman's death was upsetting to her and she needed to take her mind off it.

"How *is* that history coming?" her mother had asked. "I should like to read it."

"Mama, I *never* show my first drafts," Jo had said. "Let me polish it and then you can read it."

Anna had agreed, but she'd cautioned Jo to finish it quickly, for she now had other, more important things to think about than her scribbling.

Finish it? Jo had thought guiltily. *That's going to be difficult, considering I haven't even started it.*

As she moved toward the far end of the restaurant now, past reporters and their editors, clerks and accountants, typists, secretaries, and shopgirls, she finally spotted Eddie. He was seated at a table by a window with Oscar Rubin. All the chairs at their table were taken except for the one next to Oscar.

"Mr. Gallagher, Mr. Rubin, how delightful to see you both," she said as she approached them. Eddie, his hands wrapped around a mug of black coffee, looked up and groaned, but he got to his feet as a gentleman should. Oscar did, too.

"Sorry. We were just—"

Leaving, he was about to say. Jo was sure of it. But Oscar cut him off.

"About to order! Nice to see you again, Jo. Care to join us?"

Eddie looked daggers at him.

"I'd love to," Jo said. "Thank you." She sat. Eddie and Oscar did, too.

"What brings you to this fine establishment?" Oscar asked. "The corned beef? The meat loaf?"

"May I take your order?" a waitress asked before Jo could answer him.

Eddie ordered franks and beans, biscuits, and a root beer float.

"Jeez! Glad I'm not sleeping with you tonight," Oscar said. "Did you know the average human passes over a quart of gas a day? And that's without any beans in the mix."

"*Oscar,*" Eddie said, nodding at Jo.

Jo bit back a smile. Had any other man said such a thing in front of her, she would have been mortified. With Oscar, however, bodily functions were simply part of the conversation.

"Sorry, Jo," he said. "I forget you're a girl. Bring a couple spoons for the float, will ya?" he asked the waitress. Then he ordered the special. Jo had no idea what to do, so she asked for the special, too.

"Nature calls," Oscar announced, standing up. "Be right back, kids."

"That's a compliment, by the way," Eddie said as soon as he'd left. "What Osk said about forgetting you're a girl. It means he's comfortable around you."

"I'm flattered," Jo said, feeling awkward now that they were alone. She looked up at him from under her hat brim. She'd angled it down over the right side of her face so that it hid the marks on her cheek. "Eddie, the reason I came here—"

"Jo, I meant what I said the other day. I can't see you anymore," he said firmly. "Every time I do, it's like ripping a scab off a wound."

"I know. I'm sorry. It's not easy for me, either, and I wouldn't have come except—"

Eddie's float arrived. As the waitress hurried off again, he excavated a soupy spoonful of ice cream and offered it to her. She shook her head.

"Ever had a float? Try a bite," he said, his voice softening a little. "It's good."

He moved the spoon so close to her face, she had no choice. Melted ice cream dribbled down her chin. He wiped it off with his napkin, bumping her hat brim as he did. Jo quickly adjusted it, but not quickly enough.

Eddie's eyes narrowed. "What happened to your face?" he asked.

"I fell."

She pulled the hat low again, trying to hide the cuts on her cheek, but to her chagrin, Eddie reached over and removed it. She snatched it back from him and placed it on her lap.

"Where?" he demanded.

"In my bathroom. I banged my cheek on the side of my tub."

"Tub sides are smooth. You'd have a bruise, or a gash, if you'd smacked into one. Not scrapes."

"Who do you think you are? Oscar Rubin?" Jo joked, trying to deflect further questioning.

"You came here because you want something from me. Tell me what happened or you won't get it," Eddie said.

"I told you, I—"

"The truth. Now."

Jo didn't want to talk about it; talking about it meant reliving it, but she had no choice. "He came after me," she finally admitted.

Eddie stiffened. He pushed his float aside. "Kinch?" he said.

"I don't know. Maybe. Or maybe it was Scarface. I wasn't able to get a look at him."

"What happened? Did he threaten you?"

Jo didn't answer.

"*Jo,*" Eddie said, struggling to keep his voice down.

"He pulled me into an alley. He said he'd come inside my house at night and slice my nose off. With a knife. The one he was holding to my face."

Eddie got to his feet, flushed with anger. "I'll kill him. I'll find whoever did it and I will *kill* him," he said.

"Sit down!" Jo hissed, embarrassed. "You're making a scene."

"This has gone way too far. It stops. Right now," he said, pounding his fist on the table. "You are never, *ever* to go out late at night alone again. You shouldn't even have come here!"

Jo laughed bitterly. "You sound just like my attacker. He'd be happier if I stayed inside, too."

Eddie shook his head. "I can't *believe* you just said that. That is truly sh—*totally* unfair!"

"So is telling me to stay in the house!" Jo said, furious herself now.

"I only said it because I'm worried about you! What if it's *not* Kinch? What if it's Scarface and he's watching you? He threatened to murder me—"

"Are you going somewhere? Leave cash if you are. Don't even think about trying to stiff me with the bill," Oscar said to Eddie as he pulled his chair out. He looked from Eddie to Jo and grimaced. "Uh-oh. Lovers' quarrel?"

"*Oscar!*" Eddie said.

"Hey, what happened to your face, Jo?" Oscar asked. "Wait. Never mind. I'll probably get yelled at for asking *that*, too."

He picked up the second spoon the waitress had brought and slid Eddie's float across the table.

"Were you two talking about the shadowy Mr. Kinch? The guy they nabbed for Beekman's murder?" he asked.

"Yes," Eddie said. He pulled his billfold out of his back pocket and put a dollar on the table. Jo's heart sank as she realized he was leaving.

"Cops are saying he'll get the noose. If he does, they'll be hanging an innocent man," Oscar said through a mouthful of ice cream. "Innocent of doing Beekman in, at least."

Eddie shoved his billfold back into his pocket. "How do you figure that?" he asked.

Oscar licked the spoon clean and said, "Because he didn't do it."

➤ CHAPTER SEVENTY ❧

Jo and Eddie both pounced on Oscar at once.

"Oscar, Alvah Beekman is *dead*," Eddie insisted, sitting back down. "He's in the morgue. You laid out the body yourself."

"He's dead, all right. Someone cut his throat from ear to ear. Severed the carotids and jugulars, the trachea, esophagus, and even nicked a vertebrae," Oscar said.

Jo's stomach lurched, but in her heart, she felt the tiny ember—all that was left of the fire that used to burn there—glow a bit brighter.

"And Kinch was *there*," Eddie continued. "The police who arrived on the scene said so."

"I'm not saying he wasn't there," Oscar allowed. "I'm saying he didn't do it."

"But my uncle *saw* him," Jo pressed. "He was attacked by him."

"Phillip Montfort isn't a credible witness," Oscar said. "He took a blow to the head. A cop I talked to who was on the scene said he was dazed. Montfort may remember the sequence of events incorrectly. He may have confused Kinch with a possible accomplice or even a bystander. He might have blacked out."

Jo frowned, remembering her uncle's account of the attack. "He did say that part of the attack was hazy," she admitted.

The waitress brought their food. She placed a plate of franks, beans, and biscuits in front of Eddie. Jo and Oscar got grilled cheese and bowls of creamy tomato soup. She left their bill on the table.

"How do you know Kinch didn't do it?" Eddie asked as she left.

Oscar tied his napkin around his neck. "Because Beekman's killer was left-handed and Kinch is right-handed," he said. "Look at this. . . ."

He leaned over, dug in his doctor's bag, which was under the table, and pulled out a copy of the *World*. There was a grainy photograph on the front page. Jo shivered as she saw who was in it—Kinch. She was troubled to see that at least one paper already had the story and was splashing it on the front page.

"See Kinch's hand?" Oscar asked.

Jo peered closely at the photo and saw that Kinch was trying to shield himself from the blinding flash by holding up a hand—his right hand. A police officer was at Kinch's left side. At his right side was another man, wearing a white uniform. He must've been moving when the photo had been taken, as his face was badly blurred. A thin, dark shadow ran across it. The caption explained that Police Officer Dennis Hart and Orderly Francis Mallon were leading the prisoner into Darkbriar.

"Francis Mallon," Jo said. "He was the orderly in charge of Eleanor Owens. How strange."

"Not really," Eddie said. "It just means he's worked at the asylum for a while."

"I suppose you're right," she allowed. She continued to stare at the blurry image, unable to shake the feeling that there was something familiar about it, but then Oscar said, "Hey, Jo!"

She looked up to see a slice of radish come whizzing at her and batted it away with her right hand. It landed in Eddie's plate.

"See? It's instinctual. We try to protect ourselves with our domi-nant hand." Oscar picked up a triangle of grilled cheese. "You can keep the newspaper," he told Jo.

"All that tells us is that Kinch is right-handed," Eddie said, pick-ing the radish out of his beans. "Not that Beekman's killer was left-handed."

Oscar held up a finger. He was chewing a mouthful of sandwich. "True enough," he said after he'd swallowed. "You'd have to look at Beekman's corpse to know that his killer was left-handed. If you did, you'd see that the killer started the cut on the right side of his neck and pulled the knife across to the left. Allow me to demonstrate."

He picked up his butter knife with his right hand and moved to stand behind Jo. "You're my victim," he said. "If I'm left-handed, I come up behind you, grab your hair with my right hand, and cut with my left. I start *here*"—he touched the butter knife to the right side of her throat—"and pull the knife leftward. If you look at the wound closely, you can tell where the blade entered and in which direction it traveled. On Beekman it entered on the right side and moved left. Ergo, his killer is left-handed."

The way Oscar was holding her sparked a horrible memory. For a split second, Jo wasn't in Child's; she was back in the alley by her home. Her attacker had her pinned. Her right cheek was mashed into the wall. He was holding a knife to her face—with his left hand.

Oscar released Jo and put the knife down. A few diners had stopped eating, looks of concern on their faces. Oscar assured them Jo was perfectly fine and sat down again.

"You tell Dr. Koehler?" Eddie asked.

Oscar snorted. "He said the police saw Kinch holding a knife and that's good enough for them."

"But if Kinch *didn't* kill Mr. Beekman and attack my uncle, why on earth was he at the murder scene? And who *did* kill Beekman?" Jo asked.

Oscar cleared his throat. "Would you forgive an indelicacy, Jo?" he asked.

"Gee, Osk, why start now?" Eddie asked.

"The building Alvah Beekman was killed in front of sits next to one of Della McEvoy's disorderly houses. The cops say he visited Della's several times a week. There's no way that's ever going to make the papers, but it might be worth checking into. The crime scene building is abandoned; it's empty. So there's no one there who would've seen or heard anything, but maybe Della or one of her girls did."

Jo colored at this, embarrassed to think of Mr. Beekman visiting Della McEvoy's. How *could* he? He had a wife. And a daughter Jo's age. He went to church every Sunday.

"I already worked that lead," Eddie said.

"Did you?" Jo asked, curious. "Why?"

She knew that the *Standard* wouldn't run a story suggesting Alvah Beekman frequented a disorderly house, which made her wonder if Eddie was still writing up the story for another newspaper—even though he'd told her he'd quit.

"Because I was bored. Nothing better to do," Eddie replied off-handedly. "Della left town. She shut the house up tight."

"So much for that idea," Oscar said. He pointed his spoon at Jo's bowl. "You going to eat that?"

Jo looked down at the thick, reddish soup and shook her head. All the talk of sliced throats had made her queasy. She pushed it over to Oscar. Her sandwich, too.

"Oscar Rubin? Is that you?"

A young woman, her dark hair coiled into a neat bun, had appeared next to their table. She wore glasses, a brown overcoat, and a dress of navy twill, and carried a thick textbook.

"Sarah Stein!" Oscar exclaimed, standing. And grinning. From ear to ear.

Eddie stood, too. "Hey, Sarah, how are you?" he asked.

"Fine! Fine! Finish your lunch," the young woman said, motioning for the two men to sit. "I just came over to say hello."

Oscar introduced Sarah to Jo. She clearly already knew Eddie. "Sarah's a medical student, too," he explained. "She's number one in her class."

"Oh, Oscar," Sarah said, flapping a hand at him and blushing.

"I have a new cadaver for you. I'll be sending it over tomorrow," Oscar said, a little shyly. "Female. Midtwenties."

Sarah's eyes lit up. She looked at Oscar as if he'd just told her he was giving her the Star of India.

"Cause of death?" she asked excitedly.

"Advanced tertiary syphilis."

"Neuro?"

"Gummatous."

"Oscar, I can't thank you enough," Sarah said. "We've *never* had a cadaver with gumma tumors. Are they suppurating?"

"A bit. You've got a good deal of necrosis. Granulation. Some hyalinization, too. Next time I get an extrapulmonary tuberculosis death, I'll send it your way. Those ulcers can be deceptively similar to syphilitic gummas. It's good to see both so you can learn to tell the difference."

"This is a tremendous opportunity," Sarah gushed. "Thank you again. I can't wait to tell the others!" She smiled at Eddie and Jo. "Oscar's so thoughtful. We don't get many cadavers at the women's college. They mostly go to the men's schools. But he always comes up with something for us. Just like magic."

"Abracadavra," Oscar said, waving his soupspoon like a wand.

Sarah burst into laughter. She sounded like a goose honking. Her glasses slipped down her nose. She pushed them up again, said goodbye, and headed for the counter.

Oscar watched her go. "Isn't she wonderful?" he said dreamily.

"Go sit with her, Osk," Eddie said.

He shook his head glumly. "I can't. Both stools next to her are taken. And anyway, what would I say? I already told her about the cadaver."

"You could always talk about pus," Eddie suggested.

Oscar brightened. "You're right. I could."

"Oh, look!" Jo said. "The man sitting next to her just stood up. He knocked her gloves off the counter. Go return them to her, Oscar!"

"He's crazy about her," Eddie said as he watched his friend go.

Jo smiled. "I never would have guessed. Is she really a medical student?"

Eddie nodded. "Her father disowned her when she declared she was going to be a doctor. Her grandmother gives her a bit of money, though. Enough to pay her school fees. She works nights at Belle-vue Hospital to pay her rent. That's where Oscar met her."

Jo and Eddie both watched as Oscar picked up Sarah's gloves. Sarah patted the seat next to her, and Oscar, glowing like a light-bulb, sat down. Watching them made Jo feel happy, and sad, too. She looked away and turned the conversation back to Kinch.

"Eddie, the man who attacked me . . . he was left-handed, too," she said. "Oscar's demonstration brought the whole thing back to me. Since Kinch is right-handed, he can't be the attacker, which means Scarface probably is. After all, he attacked you, didn't he? If he's unhappy that you're snooping, he'd be unhappy with me for the same reason." She paused, then said, "Beekman's killer is also left-handed. What if it's Scarface? What if he's behind Scully's murder and my father's, too?"

Eddie sighed. "You don't give up, do you?"

"No, I don't."

He looked at her as if he were deciding something, then said, "I went to Darkbriar early this morning."

Jo banged her hand on the table. "Ha! I knew it! *Who* doesn't give up? You want to know the truth as much as I do."

Eddie ignored her exultant tone. "I was hoping I could talk to

Kinch, but I couldn't get near him," he said. "No one can. The warden held a press conference. He said Kinch is a danger to himself and everyone else. I tried to find Francis Mallon, but he wasn't around. I even tried to bribe an orderly—but no luck."

Jo frowned, thwarted. "If only we could find Della McEvoy," she said. "Maybe *she* knows something."

"Just for the record, Jo, there is no *we*. There's *you* and there's *me*. And even if one of us found Della, and she knew something, you think she'd share the information? Especially with a reporter? The last thing she wants right now is attention."

Jo digested this, then said, "What about Esther?"

"Esther who?"

"Madam Esther. She's in the same line of work, isn't she?"

"What's your point?"

Jo thought of all the catty girls she knew. "Della is Esther's competition, right? Her rival. Esther might have heard something. If she has, she might tell us. Just to make things hot for Della."

Eddie's eyebrows shot up. "You could be right about that."

"Let's go pay Esther a visit. I still have some time before I'm expected home."

"No, Jo. Like I said before, you're done. I can't stop *you* taking chances with your life, but *I* refuse to do it."

"If you won't go with me, then I'll go alone."

"Are you nuts?" Eddie scoffed. "You can't go to a place like that by yourself."

Jo's determined gray eyes locked with Eddie's. "I'm going. I started this and I'm going to finish it."

Eddie shook his head angrily. He stared out of the window at the traffic on Park Row.

"Tell me something, Eddie," Jo said softly. "Are you sorry?"

He didn't answer.

"Because *I'm* not sorry," she said. "I'm not sorry I overheard you at the *Standard*. I'm not sorry I opened my father's diary. I'm not sorry I kissed you. I'm not sorry I fell in—"

"*Don't*," Eddie said brusquely. "You made your choice. You left whatever it was we had behind you the night you accepted Bram. Let me leave it, too."

Jo nodded. "All right. But know this: I'll never be sorry for what we had, but I will be sorry if I don't see this story through to the end. I'll be sorry for the rest of my life." She rose, scooping the bill and Oscar's paper off the table. "Are you coming?"

Eddie looked at her for a long moment before he said yes.

➤ CHAPTER SEVENTY-ONE ◄

"Sit *down*, Jo!" Eddie said through gritted teeth.

Jo, peeking through a pair of red velvet curtains trimmed with gold fringe, didn't even hear him.

They were in a small parlor inside the residence of Esther Arinovsky, on East Twenty-Fifth Street in the Tenderloin. She and Eddie had told the burly man at the door, Benny, that they were from a newspaper and wanted to speak with Esther. He'd nearly tossed them off the stoop, but assurances that they were only after information about Della McEvoy, and a dollar placed into his hand, had softened him. He'd led them through a garish foyer to the parlor and told them to wait there while he spoke with Esther.

"Why is it called the Tenderloin?" Jo had asked as they walked uptown, past the area's flashy restaurants, hotels, and bars.

"The cops gave it that name because it's rich and tasty, and they want a piece of it. Esther, like every other madam in the city, only keeps her houses open because she pays the cops," Eddie replied.

"There's more than one disorderly house here?" Jo had asked, astonished.

"In the Tenderloin? Are you kidding? There are scores of them. And thousands of girls."

Jo, saucer-eyed, was watching some of those very girls now. They were clad only in skimpy silk combinations—one-piece under-garments that served as both chemise and knickers. Some wore stockings. Others were bare-legged. They had powdered cheeks and painted lips. Most were drinking.

Jo found their bareness shocking, but it was their eyes that truly unnerved her. They were empty and dead. The girls sat slumped on chairs and settees, retying a ribbon, twirling a tendril of hair, or smoking—until a customer walked in. Then, like windup dolls, they came to life. They sat up and blew kisses, displayed a pretty leg, or undid a few buttons to better show their wares.

"Most of them look like they're my age," Jo said, still staring out from the curtains.

"They probably are. Will you *please* sit down?" Eddie asked, ex-asperated.

Jo watched as a scrawny man in a cheap suit and scuffed shoes came in. He puffed his chest out like a rooster and strolled among the girls, eyeing them each in turn. "You," he finally said, pointing to a petite brunette. She dutifully stood and followed him up the dark stairwell. Jo couldn't bear to imagine what happened next.

"He didn't even ask her name," she murmured, sitting down.

"I told you not to come here," Eddie said.

"He eyed her the way Mrs. Nelson eyes a rib roast."

"This is yet another bad idea. We should leave."

Jo went silent. She thought about Oscar and his cadaver. He said the body was a female's and that she'd died from syphilis. Had she been a prostitute, too? Jo had heard the disease whispered about. She'd seen beggars with their faces eaten away by it and Katie had told her hair-raising tales of people going insane from it.

"Who writes about *them*, Eddie?" she asked.

"Who?" Eddie asked, his wary eyes on the doorway.

"Esther's girls."

Eddie's gaze shifted from the doorway to Jo. "You could have," he said, his blue eyes wistful.

Jo flinched. His words cut deeply. Not because they were thoughtless or cruel, but because they were true. She could have written about these girls, if she hadn't accepted Bram's proposal. Now she never would.

"Esther'll see you two now," a voice said.

It was Benny. Jo and Eddie stood.

"Let me do the talking," Eddie whispered as they followed Benny out of the parlor.

He led them to what Jo assumed was a study, though it was nothing like her father's study, or her uncle's. Gilded furniture—its finish chipped, its cushions worn and dusty—had been placed haphazardly. Three toy poodles roamed the room. As Jo watched, one lifted its leg and soaked the wallpaper. At the far end of the room, a large woman sat at a desk, writing in a ledger.

"Sit," she said without looking up.

Eddie took one of the chairs in front of her desk; Jo took the other. Jo tried not to stare but couldn't help it.

Esther Arinovsky looked to be about fifty. Her hair, dyed black and thinning, was worn in a high roll. Powder had settled into the creases of her cheeks; lip rouge had bled into the lines around her mouth. She wore ropes of fake pearls. Her enormous breasts strained at the front of her dress, which was covered with a dusting of confectioner's sugar. A plateful of pastries rested on the desk.

After another minute or so, Esther closed her ledger and looked at them.

"Good afternoon, Mrs. Arinovsky," Eddie said. "I'm—"

"I know who you are, *pisher*," Esther said with a Russian accent. "You think I let just anyone come in here?"

She looked at Jo next, cocking her head like a bird of prey. "But you? What brings you here, my darling? I cannot imagine such a pretty girl would need to go looking for work, but if you *are*—"

Jo blushed. Eddie cut Esther off. "This is Miss Jones. She's a reporter, too. We're looking for information," he said.

"What kind of information?"

"Information that will help secure justice for the murder of Alvah Beekman," Jo said.

Esther laughed. "You are looking for justice in New York? Good luck." She leaned back in her chair and picked a piece of food from her teeth with a fingernail. "I give you what information you want. The police, as always, have it wrong. Alvah Beekman was not killed by the *meshuggener* with the tattoos."

"Could one of Della's girls have done it?" Jo asked. "Or Della herself?"

Esther gave her a contemptuous look. "You ever cut a man's throat?"

Jo shook her head.

"It takes strength, let me tell you. Della's as thin as a piece of old rope. Her girls, they're not so strong, either. Della doesn't feed them well. Too afraid to spend a little money. She doesn't have my standards," Esther sniffed as a poodle squatted in a corner behind her desk. "There was a fourth man on the sidewalk that night. Montfort, Beekman, Kinch, plus one more," she continued. "This I know for a fact. I was told it by one of the girls at the *farshtinkener* Della's house. Lucy's her name."

I was right, Jo thought smugly. *Esther Arinovsky can't resist the chance to bury a rival.*

"How do you know?" Eddie asked skeptically.

"Because I paid her to tell me."

"Beekman would meet with this girl Lucy?" Eddie asked.

"No, *chochem*, he would meet with a chimpanzee!" Esther said, shaking her head. "Of *course* he meets with the girl! Beekman, he goes to her three times a week. She's seventeen years old. Print *that* in your paper! He was late coming to her that night. She looked out of the window for him and saw him standing on the sidewalk, one house over from Della's. He was talking with his friend the *macher,* Montfort. As they stood there, two other men came up to them."

"Two?" Jo echoed.

"Yes. One had tattoos all over him. The other was big. According to Lucy, the big one cut Beekman and hit Montfort, and then Montfort struggled with the tattoed one."

"Did she tell the police?" Jo asked. "Is she helping them track the men down?"

"Help the cops? *Us?*" Esther spat on the floor. "We hate them. That is the one thing, the only thing, we have in common, Della and I. They take half what we make—half!—and use the girls for free."

"Did Lucy see the big man's face?" Eddie asked.

"Well enough to see that he had dark hair and a scar on his cheek," Esther replied.

Jo and Eddie traded excited glances.

"The other one, the one with the marks on him, Lucy said he looked sick," Esther added. "He was staggering. Shouting. Like he wasn't right in the head."

Jo wondered at that. Kinch hadn't been staggering or out of his mind when he was with Scully. He'd been perfectly lucid.

Esther smiled at them then with a mouthful of coffee-stained teeth. The smile did not touch her eyes. "I give you good information about what goes on at Della McEvoy's house. For free," she said. "You use it and I am happy, but you write one word about *my* house, children, and I send Benny to cut off your hands. Then you never write nothing no more. We have an understanding?"

"We do," Eddie said.

Jo quickly nodded. She'd seen Benny and didn't doubt for a minute that he'd do it.

Esther returned her attention to her ledger. Jo and Eddie were dismissed. They thanked her. She acknowledged their thanks with a flap of her hand.

"That's strange," Jo whispered to Eddie as they left Esther's study. "Lucy said *two* men attacked my uncle and Mr. Beekman—Kinch and the scar-faced man—but when my uncle recounted the attack, he only spoke of Kinch."

"Your uncle was dazed. Maybe all he remembers is the last part of the attack, when he struggled with Kinch," Eddie said.

"If Lucy's right, then they were there *together*," Jo said. "Kinch and the scar-faced man are working together!"

"It certainly looks that way," Eddie agreed. "But only one of them's behind bars. You've *got* to be careful. Promise me you won't go out alone at night anymore. Promise me right now, or I'll . . . I'll go tell your mother."

Jo laughed. "Really, Eddie? You'd *tattle* on me?"

"It's not funny, Jo, and I swear to God I will. I don't want to wake up one morning and hear the newsboys shouting that *you've* been found dead in an alley," he said solemnly.

"I can't promise that," Jo said. "I'm too close to finding out why my father was killed to stop now." She was as scared of the man who'd attacked her as she'd ever been, but she would no longer let that fear stop her. Scarface was scared, too—scared that she and Eddie were getting close to him, and to the truth. That was why he'd attacked them.

As they made their way to the front door, Jo saw that business had picked up while they'd been with Esther. At least half a dozen men were surveying the merchandise now. One was kissing a red-headed girl. Another was fondling a brunette's bottom.

Eddie grabbed Jo's hand and hurried her along. They passed a man sitting in a chair with a blond girl in his lap. She was trying to engage him.

"C'mon, handsome," she cooed. "Come upstairs. You won't be sorry."

She leaned in to kiss the man, but he pushed her off his lap. She hit the floor hard, banging her head against a table.

"I wan' a blon', dammit!" the man yelled drunkenly. "A *real* blon' who can *prove* it!"

The girl, dazed, struggled to sit up. Jo stopped dead, furious. She yanked her hand free.

"What are you doing?" Eddie hissed.

But it was too late. She marched over to the girl and helped her up. Then she turned to the man, eyes blazing, and said, "You owe this girl an apology."

Eddie's eyes widened in alarm. "Jo! Come *on!*" he said.

The drunken man looked up at Jo, astonished. *"What?"* he said.

"You heard me," Jo said. "Would you like someone to treat your mother, or sister, or daughter the way you just treated this young lady?"

The man guffawed. "She ain't no lady, you silly bitch. She's a whore!"

"And *you*, sir," Jo said loudly—so loudly that everyone in the room stopped to listen to her—"are a vile, drunken pig!"

The man growled a nasty reply, but Jo didn't hear it. She'd turned on her heel and was marching back to Esther's office. Esther was still buried in her accounts as Jo walked up to her desk.

"Please don't buy Fay from the Tailor," she said.

Esther looked up. "How do you know about that?" she asked, a note of menace in her voice.

Eddie, who'd caught up with Jo, took hold of her arm and tried to pull her away, but she shook him off.

"This is no place for her. She's had a hard life. If she comes here, it'll only get harder," Jo said, pleading for her friend.

"We've all had hard lives, my darling. This is business. Between myself and the Tailor. I've already bought her. I was the highest bidder. The deed's done and it's none of your affair."

"I have nine hundred dollars," Jo said. "I'll buy her from you."

Esther snorted. "It would take a lot more than that for me to sell her. She's young and pretty. She can work for a good ten years if she doesn't get sick. She'll bring me thousands."

"But she's a human being," Jo protested, heartsick at the thought of Fay's fate. "You can't just buy and sell her. That's slavery. Have you no sense of morality?"

"Morality is a luxury, my darling. A very expensive one," Esther said.

"But—"

Esther cut her off. Her eyes, cold and calculating, locked on Jo's. "I know who you are Miss *Jones*," she said. "I read the papers. I look at the pictures. And I know you've just gone to the highest bidder yourself."

Jo felt as if she'd been slapped. "I *beg* your pardon!" she said, outraged.

"You're engaged to Abraham Aldrich, are you not? No doubt your dear mama—if she's worth a damn—tallied the fortunes and prospects of every young man of means in the city, weighing their dollars against your assets: beauty and breeding." She paused to let her words sink in, then said, "One day soon, my darling, you'll be doing the very same thing the girls here do, only *you* won't get paid for it."

Jo, cheeks burning, was too mortified to reply. Eddie grabbed her arm again, and this time she let him pull her away.

"Esther shouldn't have said that. Just forget about it," he told her, once they were on the sidewalk. "It was harsh and cruel and it's not true."

But Jo barely heard him. Instead, she heard her mother's voice. *It doesn't do to be absent from the market too long,* she'd said, the night of the Young Patrons' Ball.

And Grandmama's, at Herondale: *We make matches with our heads, not our hearts, in order to preserve our families and fortunes.*

And suddenly Jo saw her engagement to Bram for what it was: a business deal, and she was the commodity that had been traded. She didn't love Bram. And he didn't love her. He cared for her in his way, as she did for him. But it wasn't love. It wasn't what she felt for Eddie.

"She was only trying to embarrass you and get you to leave. She was wrong to say it, and—"

Jo, her hands balled into fists, turned to him and yelled, "Oh, Eddie, shut up!"

Eddie looked dumbfounded. "Gee, thanks. I was only trying to—"

"Well, *stop* trying! Don't you see? Madam Esther's not harsh and she's not cruel. Madam Esther's *right.*"

She didn't wait for Benny to get the door for her; she pushed it open herself. Outside on the street, Eddie spotted an empty cab and hailed it. As the driver pulled to the curb, Eddie gave him Jo's address. She tried to hide her face from him as she climbed in, so he wouldn't see the tears welling in her eyes, but failed. He made a motion for her to lower the window and handed her his handkerchief.

"Did you know Fay saved me once?" Jo asked him, dabbing at her eyes. "When I was in Brooklyn, paying a call on Mr. Markham. I was nearly robbed and dumped in the river. She got me out of it. We walked over the Brooklyn Bridge afterward. We were talking about . . ." She hesitated, not wanting him to know they had talked about him. "About *choices,*" she finally said. "I asked her what the best thing was and she said freedom. Freedom, Eddie."

"Oh, Jo." Eddie covered one of her hands with his own.

"I want her to be free. Why does no one ever get to break free? Not Fay. Not Eleanor Owens. Not the girls at Esther's. Or—"

"Or you," Eddie said.

The cabbie cracked his whip and the carriage slowly rolled away.

❯❯ CHAPTER SEVENTY-TWO ❮❮

"An exaggerated sleeve on one so young is aging," said Madame Gavard. "I suggest a small pouf, a pointed bodice, and a gathered skirt with a sensible train. Three feet in length, no more."

"I agree," Anna said. "The trains are becoming ridiculous. Why, the elder Adams girl, the one who married last year, was practically at the altar, and her train was still in the carriage!"

Jo eyed herself in Madame Gavard's enormous gilt mirror. She was in the dressmaker's atelier, trying on sample wedding dresses.

Anna glanced at the pretty painted clock on the atelier's wall and frowned. "Can you bring a veil, please, Madame Gavard? Oh, I *do* wish Madeleine were here to give us an opinion. I wonder why she's so late?" She turned to Jo almost as if she were an afterthought. "What do *you* think of the dress, Josephine?" she asked.

"It's very pretty," Jo said dutifully.

"It's more than pretty. You look like an absolute dream in it."

"Sorry, Mama. My mind was elsewhere. It's beautiful."

A worried frown creased Anna's face. "Are you all right? What *is* it?"

Ever since yesterday, when Esther had spoken the ugly truth to her, Jo had been restless, tense, and unable to think of anything but the woman's words. Esther had opened her eyes. Her engagement *was* a business transaction. She loved Eddie and he loved her. Yet here she was, deciding on the dress she'd wear to wed Bram.

Marriage wasn't a dance, or a party, or a summer flirtation. It was forever. Once she said her vows to Bram, all she would ever have of Eddie was memories. Only weeks ago, at school, she'd lamented the idea of Trudy marrying a man she didn't love, and now she was doing the very same thing.

Mornings whiled away with a breakfast tray in bed. Luncheon with friends. Afternoons spent strolling in the park, or embroidering. That would be her life. Supper with Bram. And then, when the dull day was finally over, back to bed to make all those babies Grandmama wanted. Lovemaking, they called it. But shouldn't one be in love to make love?

She couldn't do it. She *wouldn't* do it. She would tell her mother. *Right now.* She would tell her she was going to break it off with Bram because she loved someone else. Surely her mother would understand.

"Is the dress not to your liking? Is that it?" her mother asked. "You could be right. The cut suits you, and yet something's not quite correct."

"The veil, Mrs. Montfort," Madame Gavard said, returning to the room with a length of lace.

"Wait on that for a moment, please. Take the gown off her," Anna instructed. "It's not falling correctly. You need to pull her corset tighter."

"Mama, there's something I have to *say*," Jo whispered, her voice heavy with emotion. She felt Madame Gavard's brisk fingers at her back, undoing the gown's buttons.

Jo needed to tell her mother the truth. About the stories she wanted to write. The boy she wanted to love. The life she wanted to lead. Her feelings raged inside her like a hurricane, gathering force, trying to push their way out.

"What is it, Josephine?" her mother asked.

"I—I can't go through with this."

Her mother smiled understandingly and for the briefest of seconds, Jo thought everything would be all right.

"Don't be silly. Of course you can. You're just having a case of nerves. Every bride-to-be suffers from them," Anna said, shattering Jo's hopes.

"No, it's more than nerves," Jo insisted. "I can't go through with this wedding. I don't love—"

"Stop it. Right now," Anna ordered, gently but firmly. "I forbid another word on this topic. It's one thing to have nerves, another to give in to them. Dwelling on your worries will only upset you and you shouldn't have more upsets. Not with everything we've endured these past few weeks. Not with a wedding coming."

"Mama, listen to me. Please," Jo cried. "I don't *want* this wedding!"

"Josephine, that is *enough*!"

Her mother's sharp words rang out in the quiet room. Jo stopped speaking, shocked. Her mother never raised her voice. *Never.* Jo saw anger sparking in her eyes. But there was something else there, too: *fear.*

Why? Jo wondered, mystified. *What is she afraid of?* Whatever it was, Jo decided, it would not stop her. She was going to win this battle.

Before she could open her mouth to argue, however, her aunt bustled into the room.

"Oh, Anna, my dear! There you are!" she said. She was breathless and red-cheeked.

"Of course I'm here," Anna said, turning to her. "Why are you so late? And so flushed?"

Jo's aunt sat down across from her mother in a whirl of silk and fur. One of Madame Gavard's assistants immediately brought her a cup of tea.

"Thank you," Madeleine said, handing the girl her stole. "I'll keep my coat for now. I'm chilled through. Simply can't stop shivering. I've had quite a shock."

"What's the matter, Aunt Maddie?" Jo asked, putting her own upset aside.

"Oh, Jo! I didn't see you there," Maddie said, pressing a hand to her heaving chest. "You look like an angel, my darling." She turned to Madame Gavard. "Might we have a moment alone, please?" It was phrased as a question but was unmistakably a command.

The dressmaker dipped her head. She motioned for her assistant and they left the room, closing a pair of double doors behind them. Jo joined her mother and aunt on some slipper chairs near a low table.

"Madeleine, *what* is going on? You're making me anxious," Anna said.

"Oh, Anna! That disturbed man, Kinch, the one who killed Alvah, killed *himself*!" Madeleine said breathlessly. "They found him this morning. He hanged himself with his belt in his cell sometime during the night, they think."

"How dreadful!" Jo's mother said.

Jo sat as still as a statue, unable to believe her aunt's words. Kinch was dead. He was gone. There were answers she needed that only he could supply. Now she would never get them.

"Did he talk to the police, Aunt Maddie?" she asked, hoping against hope. "Did he tell them anything?"

"Yes. The police say last night he confessed to Alvah's murder and the attack on Phillip. He told the orderly caring for him what he'd done. He was anguished by guilt, apparently, and terrified of facing a trial."

That can't be right, Jo thought. *Oscar said Kinch couldn't have done it because Beekman's killer is left-handed and Kinch is right-handed. Why would he confess to a crime he didn't commit? And then kill himself over it?* She would go to Eddie as soon as she could, to see if he knew anything more.

"According to the orderly, Kinch was a morphine addict and he may have been in some sort of drug-induced rage during the attack," Madeline explained. She reached for Anna's hand and then Jo's. "I'm afraid there's more," she said gravely. "Kinch also confessed to killing Richard Scully—"

"Oh, no, Maddie. Please. Please don't," Anna said, squeezing her eyes shut.

"—and our beloved Charles."

Anna nodded, struggling to keep her emotion in check. "I suppose the papers have gotten hold of this?" she asked, opening her eyes.

"You have no idea, Anna. It's as if the entire city has turned into some mad choir of shrieking newsboys," Madeleine said. "They're shouting the headlines from every sidewalk."

Anna's mask of calmness suddenly cracked. She balled her hands into fists. "So we can hear it over and over again," she said bitterly. "It was hard enough losing him . . . but now *this* . . . a murder . . . This man Kinch *killed* him. . . . He killed my husband. . . . I don't—"

A sob escaped her. She pressed her free hand to her mouth, as if to stop any others from getting out, but she couldn't contain her sorrow. With a low moan of pain, she doubled over. Jo rushed to her and put an arm around her, her questions about Kinch's confession forgotten in the face of her mother's grief.

She'd never seen her stoic, self-contained mother weep, and it both devastated and frightened her. She remembered her own grief when she found out the truth of her father's death and wished she could do something—anything—to take her mother's pain away, to make it better.

"I'm sorry, Anna. I'm so, so sorry," Madeleine whispered.

After a few moments, her mother straightened. Her face was ravaged. Her eyes were filled with anguish. She looked completely helpless.

"What does one do?" she asked. "How does one go on after something like this?"

Her voice, so small and bewildered, broke Jo's heart.

Madeleine took her hand again. "By looking ahead of ourselves, Anna, not back," she said resolutely. "By watching what Charles left behind—our beautiful Jo—take her first steps into the future with a wonderful companion by her side. By dandling their children on our knees, and seeing Charles in their sweet faces, and knowing that all he was, all he stood for, his goodness and kindness, lives on."

Anna nodded brokenly.

"We *must* be strong, Anna. This awfulness will pass. Come summer, we'll have a beautiful wedding at Herondale. With a lovely couple to toast and a new beginning to celebrate. And it *will* be beautiful, won't it, Jo?"

Jo gazed at her aunt's hopeful face. She looked at her mother—always so straight-backed, always so strong—struggle like a wounded animal. As she did, Jo's resolve drained away. How could she break her mother's heart? Her entire family's?

"Yes, Aunt Maddie," she said, utterly defeated. "It will."

❧ CHAPTER SEVENTY-THREE ❧

A fine rain pattered over Jo's black umbrella and dampened the hem of her black coat.

"Another funeral. Another member of our circle buried. It seems we will never get out of black," her uncle said.

They were walking arm in arm out of Grace Church's graveyard, together with dozens of other mourners. Moments ago, they'd all stood by Alvah Beekman's grave as his casket was lowered into the ground.

Cries pierced the air now. Outside the cemetery gates, newsboys yelled the day's headlines.

"'Thanksgiving Tragedy! Beekman Buried Today'!"

"'Third Victim of Tattoo Terror Laid to Rest'!"

"'Murder and Mayhem in Manhattan'!"

"No peace for the departed, even here," Phillip observed dryly. "None for the living, either."

The story of Kinch's confession and suicide had broken two days ago, and the newsboys had barely taken a break since. Most of New York had celebrated Thanksgiving yesterday, though the Beekmans, Montforts, and other mourners had not, and the topic of conversation over every dining table had been the lunatic Kinch and how he had murdered three of Van Houten Shipping's partners. But why? That was what all of New York wanted to know, and what the papers—all except the *Standard*—were only too happy to tell them.

A spokesman for Darkbriar, a Dr. Ellsworth, told the press that from the moment Kinch had been brought to the asylum to the night of his death twenty-four hours later, several doctors had tried to get sense out of him but had found it impossible. He would rave one moment and become almost catatonic the next.

They'd tried to examine him, but when an orderly went to remove Kinch's clothing, Kinch became so incensed, he tried to kill the man. That same orderly, Francis Mallon, expressed the opinion that Kinch was under the influence of drugs. It was decided to wait a day or two for whatever substance Kinch had injected to clear from his system; then the doctors would try again to question him.

Unfortunately, before that could happen, he'd hanged himself with his belt from one of the bars of his cell window.

The papers reported that Kinch had finally become clearheaded the night of his death and had begged Mallon to sit with him so that he could unburden himself. He did, and Kinch told him his story. He said he was an ex-employee of Van Houten and had crewed on several of the firm's ships. Phillip Montfort was asked by the police to confirm this. He said he could recall neither Kinch's name nor his face, but that it was certainly possible that Kinch had worked for the firm. He was not familiar with the faces and names of every man who sailed on their ships.

Kinch claimed that Van Houten had done him out of a vast fortune and said he would have his revenge. When Mallon asked him what the fortune was, he told him it was a chest full of treasure. Mallon expressed disbelief and Kinch grew enraged. He told him he'd learned the address of Charles Montfort and went to his house late one night with the aim of getting his treasure back.

Charles recognized him and let him in. They went to Charles's study, where he'd been cleaning a revolver. Kinch demanded his treasure, and when Charles could not produce it, he grabbed his revolver, which Charles had placed on his desk, and shot him. Frightened, he placed the revolver in Charles's hand to make it look like an accident, or a suicide, anything but a murder. Then he escaped by climbing out a study window. It had been difficult but not impossible for an ex-sailor used to climbing ships' rigging. He'd had to open the window, balance on the shallow ledge outside it, close it again, then drop twenty feet to the ground. He hadn't broken anything, but he'd bruised himself badly.

Kinch also told Mallon that he'd accosted Richard Scully on Van Houten's Wharf, hit him over the head, and thrown him, unconscious, into the water. He'd cut Alvah Beekman's throat and tried to do the same to Phillip Montfort.

It was concluded that he was hopelessly insane. No one at Darkbriar had been able to find out who he really was, where he'd come from, or what had led to his mental breakdown. His orderly prepared his body, and he was buried, in the clothes in which he'd been apprehended, in Darkbriar's lonely cemetery. No one attended the burial.

"I do hope this is the last visit I make to a graveyard for quite some time," Phillip said now.

"How are you feeling?" Jo asked. There was an ugly bruise on his cheek where he'd been hit and the knife wound on his chest hadn't healed yet.

"I'm perfectly well. And so very glad this is over. The papers will grow tired of the story in a few days, things will calm down, and we can resume our lives."

"So we won't have to rent a place in the country after all?" Jo asked, gently teasing him. She remembered his threat to move them all out of the city if reporters hounded them.

"Hopefully not," he said, smiling. He covered her hand with his, and as he did, his smile faded. "Josephine, I've been remiss. I want to thank you."

"For what, Uncle Phillip?" Jo asked, struck by his sudden seriousness.

"For warning me," he said. "I should have listened to you more carefully when you told me about seeing a strange man outside your house. I was so convinced that Charles had committed suicide, there was no room in my mind for any other explanation. I was wrong, Jo. Dangerously so. But we've arrived at the truth at last, and Charles, Richard, and Alvah have justice of a sort. We must leave it at that."

Yes, Jo thought. *We must.*

It was easier to stop digging, stop probing, stop asking questions that never seemed to get answered. If only she could.

She would have to cut away a part of herself—the restless, questing part. She'd have to cut away many parts of herself in the weeks and months to come. She'd decided, in Madame Gavard's, to do her duty by her mother, and her family, and marry Bram. And now, and for the rest of her days, she would have to make good on that decision.

Yet questions remained. And they gnawed at her.

"I would like to leave it, Uncle Phillip," she said. "But there are still so many answers I wish I had. I know now how Papa's murderer escaped when the door to his office had been locked from the inside—that's something, though I'm amazed he didn't break his legs. But Kinch's confession doesn't explain the bullet I found under the draperies."

"Your father might've dropped it ages ago, Jo. And accidentally kicked it under the curtains himself."

"I suppose so," Jo said. "But Oscar Edwards believes that Beekman's killer was left-handed and Kinch was right-handed? And that Kinch had an accomplice—a man with a scar on his face?"

Jo continued to use her fictional private eye to pose the more objectionable questions. There were places she'd never told her uncle she'd visited. The morgue and Madam Esther's were among them.

"I don't know what to say about that. All I can tell you is what I remember—Kinch punching me and then coming at both Alvah and me with a knife," Phillip explained.

Jo recalled Oscar's assertion that her uncle had taken a blow to the head and therefore was not a reliable witness. It was certainly possible that all her uncle remembered of the attack was Kinch, not the scar-faced man.

Jo also recalled how confident Oscar was that Kinch could not be Beekman's killer. She had taken Oscar at his word, but Eddie said most people dismissed his theories. Had she been rash to put so much faith in them? What if he was wrong? Kinch's right-handedness certainly wouldn't have stopped him from shooting her father or hitting Richard Scully over the head. She told herself now that Oscar *was* wrong. And tried her best to believe it.

But a myriad of other questions lingered, too. "What of Eleanor Owens and the manifests?" she asked her uncle. "What was the *Bonaventure* carrying?"

"I'm not sure we'll ever know," Phillip replied.

Absorbed by her questions presented, Jo did not catch the note of weariness in her uncle's voice.

"The thing that haunts me most of all," she continued, "is Papa's sadness. You yourself said he was feeling distraught right before he died. I can't shake that, or the feeling that his despair had something to do with his death. I go around and around in circles, and always end up back there, at Papa's sadness."

Phillip abruptly stopped walking. "Josephine, why do you *insist* on seeking out darkness?" he asked, dismayed. "Have we not had enough of it?"

Because I want answers, Uncle Phillip. I want the truth! Jo wanted to shout. *Because that's the way I'm made!*

Instead she said, "I've upset you, Uncle Phillip. I'm sorry."

"You've become obsessed," her uncle said, his faced creased with concern. "Your father's sadness was just a coincidence. We all go through times when we're not ourselves. But now we *must* put this ugly chapter behind us. You most of all. You cannot embrace the future if you refuse to let go of the past. A good marriage, a comfortable home, children—that's where your mind should be now. That's what your father would have wanted for you."

"*There* you are, Jo," a voice said from behind them.

Jo turned. It was Bram. The party of mourners had reached the cemetery gates. Jo and her mother had ridden with the Aldriches to the church and then the graveyard, and would now continue on with them to the Beekmans' home.

"May I steal her from you, Mr. Montfort?" Bram asked.

"I'm afraid you already have, Bram. Heart and soul," Phillip replied, a smile replacing his anxious frown.

"Blast it, Lolly! You come out of there this instant!" a voice bellowed from behind them.

Bram grimaced. He recognized his grandmother's voice. They all did.

Addie suddenly appeared, flushed and breathless. "Bram, can you help Grandmama? She's lost one of her dogs in the bushes. Why did she bring them here? To a *cemetery*!" She nodded at Phillip. "Hello, Mr. Montfort. Please pardon me for intruding. I am, of course, mortified. Bram, *do* come!"

"I'm sorry about this," Bram said.

"Go ahead," Jo said. "I'll meet you at your carriage."

As Bram loped off to corral the errant spaniel, Jo released her uncle's arm. "And I'll meet you at the Beekmans', Uncle Phillip," she said.

"Jo," her uncle said, catching her sleeve.

"Yes?" She turned back to him. His face had taken on a fearful look. "What is it, Uncle Phillip?" she asked alarmed. "Are you unwell?"

His hand tightened on her arm. "I'm fine. It's *you* I'm worried about. Terribly so," he said. "Don't let the darkness that's been visited upon this family pull you in so deeply, you cannot get out. Turn back from it, darling Jo. *Now.* While you still can."

➼ CHAPTER SEVENTY-FOUR ↢

Jo entered her room and flopped onto her bed. She was exhausted. The funeral reception at the Beekmans' was over. It had tired her, and so had her uncle's lecture.

He wanted the best for her and for his own children—good marriages, happy lives. He wanted them to be surrounded by people like himself—decent, kind, and upstanding. She understood that and loved him for it, but she wondered if perhaps money and privilege had made him blind to the realities of the world.

Don't let the darkness that's been visited upon this family pull you in so deeply, you cannot get out. Turn back from it, darling Jo . . . , he'd warned her. He didn't seem to understand that turning your back on the darkness didn't mean the darkness would turn its back on you.

Jo stared up at the ceiling. It was late afternoon and already the light was fading. The Aldriches had dropped Jo and her mother at their home. Anna had asked Mrs. Nelson to send a supper tray up to her room. She was worn out, too, and wished to dine alone and retire early. Katie had drawn Jo a hot bath and made her a fire, and Jo was grateful for both. In a few minutes, Katie would return to help her undress.

Jo sat up, wanting to get into the tub before the water cooled. Two dozen cream roses in a vase atop her vanity table caught her eye. She hadn't noticed them before but knew without looking at the card tucked between the blooms that they were from Bram. He sent roses to her every week now. Propped against the vase were several buff-colored envelopes. *Invitations*, she thought, *to parties for us, the newly engaged couple.* There would be dresses to order for them. The thought did not excite her.

Sighing heavily, Jo took her boots off and carried them to her wardrobe. As she bent to put them away, she noticed the newspaper that she had folded up and hidden against the side of her wardrobe had flopped over. It was a copy of the *World*—the one Oscar had given her at Child's Restaurant. As she pulled it out now, it seemed to her like a souvenir from a faraway place.

"No need for this anymore," she said, carrying it to her fireplace.

Printed on the front was the article about Kinch's arrest. In the photo, he was frozen in time with the police officer Dennis Hart on one side and the orderly Francis Mallon on the other.

Jo pulled the fire screen away from the hearth, but just as she was about to toss the paper onto the flames, she stopped. She knelt down on her carpet, smoothed the paper flat, and scrutinized the photo.

It wasn't Kinch she was staring at now, but Mallon. Even though his face was blurred, there was something familiar about it. Her eyes followed the thin shadow that crossed one cheek. She traced it with her finger.

And suddenly she knew.

"Oh dear God," Jo said aloud.

She scrambled to her feet. She knew where she had to go. Her mother had retired for the evening and wouldn't be asking for her. She could get out of the house unnoticed if she was quiet.

She wrote a note to Katie explaining her absence, folded a dollar inside it to buy her silence, and left the note on the vanity. She tip-toed downstairs, got her coat and hat, and let herself out the front door. As soon as she turned off Gramercy Square, she ran as fast as she could to Irving Place and hailed a cab.

She wasn't worried about the scar-faced man attacking her if she left her house. Not anymore. He was done with her. Eddie, too. He'd thrown them off the scent.

"Park Row, please," she said as she climbed inside the cab. "The *Standard*."

➤ CHAPTER SEVENTY-FIVE ✦

"Nope. Not happening. It's over. Really and truly this time. Kinch is dead."

"Forget it's me who's asking."

"That's kind of impossible."

"Please. You *have* to," Jo said. "Because if I'm right, then the theory we came up with at Madam Esther's was wrong: Kinch and Scarface *weren't* working together. So why were they together when Beekman was killed?"

Eddie relented. "All right, let's see the page," he said.

Jo was sitting by Eddie's desk in the *Standard*'s newsroom. It was a Friday evening. Most of his coworkers had left. She'd been lucky to catch him.

She pulled the newspaper out of her purse now. "It's him," she said, smoothing it on Eddie's desk.

"How can you tell? The image is totally blurry."

"See that?" she said, pointing to the discoloration across the man's face. "I thought it was a shadow. It's not. It's a scar. Were any other photos taken? That's what I need to know. If so, he might be in them. And we might be able to see his face more clearly."

"All right, we'll take a look. Come on."

They walked out of the *Standard*'s offices and down the block to the *World*'s. Eddie talked to a fellow reporter, a friend of his, and told him what they were after. He led them to the paper's photography department. The editor was just tidying up for the night.

Eddie showed him the photograph in question and asked if they could see any other shots in the series. A few minutes later, they were staring at three more photographs. Kinch was blurry in all of them, but the man on his right was not.

Jo's blood turned to ice in her veins as she saw the jagged scar, the cruel face. In two of the photos, he had Kinch by the arm. In one, however, he was shielding his eyes from the camera's flash.

"I'll be damned," Eddie said. "They're one and the same. And look . . . he's using his left hand to protect himself—his dominant hand. The same hand he used to pull a knife on you. And to cut Alvah Beekman's throat."

"I *knew* it," Jo said. "It's him. Francis Mallon is the scar-faced man."

CHAPTER SEVENTY-SIX

Eddie was walking down Park Row. Away from Jo.

"You know I'm right!" she called after him, heedless of who heard her.

"Don't care!" he called back, not bothering to turn around.

"It's not a coincidence that Mallon was Kinch's orderly!"

"Still don't care!"

Mallon had followed them to Walsh's. He'd attacked Eddie and Jo as well. According to one of Della McEvoy's girls, a scar-faced man was the one who'd killed Beekman. And then Mallon turned out to be Kinch's orderly. That was an almost impossible set of co-incidences. There was a reason for them, a connection. Jo was certain of it. But what *was* it?

She had to come up with an answer and had only seconds to do it before Eddie turned the corner and disappeared. From her view. From her life. Forever.

"This is finished now, Jo. I mean it. I won't go any further with it," he'd said, when they were still at the *World*—right after she'd told him she wanted to go to Darkbriar to talk to Mallon.

"If you think we're going to confront Francis Mallon, think again.

He attacked us. He may well be a killer, too. Do you really think I'm going to let you put yourself in that kind of danger? And for what? What's he going to do? Confess to three murders just because you ask him to? It's over, Jo. Accept it."

But she *couldn't* accept it. She felt like she had when she was little and playing Blind Man's Buff and knew her playmates were right there in front of her, only inches from her outstretched hands.

She and Eddie had never been as close to the truth as they were now. They couldn't see it yet, but it was there. Francis Mallon was a part of it, but it was bigger than him. Jo felt it in her bones. If only she could convince Eddie.

Think, Jo, think! she told herself as she stood on the sidewalk, watching him walk away.

She tried to recall the meeting between Kinch and Scully. Snatches of their conversation came back to her. Could the answer be in those bits and pieces? Where? She'd already sifted through them a thousand times.

She heard Scully's voice in her head: *I would not have known you....* And then Kinch's *Seventeen years without the company of another Christian soul.... Look upon me and see the monster you have wrought....* She remembered Kinch explaining how his fellow crewmen had put the tattoos upon him. And then she knew.

"Oh my goodness. That's *it!*" she exclaimed.

But Eddie was nearly at the end of the block and didn't hear her.

"Stop, Eddie, *please!*" Jo called out.

Eddie kept right on going.

"Eddie Gallagher, you stop right *now!*" Jo bellowed.

Eddie stopped, then turned around. "What?" he shouted, annoyed.

Jo ran to him. "Kinch touched his chest!" she said breathlessly. "He touched his chest when he said it!"

"Said *what?*"

"'It's written on my heart, and that's where it will stay.'"

"So?"

"So he *meant* it! It *is* written on his heart. Don't you see? The man was positively covered in tattoos! 'They use tattoos to tell their stories. They told mine,'" she said, quoting Kinch again.

"But, Jo, it doesn't make any difference. Even if the story *was* written on his heart. Kinch is dead. He and his tattoos are six feet under."

Jo licked her lips nervously, then said, "How long does it take for a body to rot? Oscar would know."

Eddie gave her a puzzled look. Then her meaning dawned on him. "No. Absolutely not. You cannot be serious," he said.

"Two days? Three? Maybe a bit longer at this time of year? We could ask him. We could bring him with us," Jo ventured.

"*We* are doing nothing. You want to do this, you do it alone."

"But I won't be," Jo said, her eyes locked on his. "You'll be there. You want your story, Eddie. I know you do. That's who you are."

"This is not a trip to the goddamned morgue, Jo!" Eddie said angrily. "It's not a trip to Esther's or the Tailor's. This is a *crime*. Do you have any idea what will happen to us if we get caught?"

"Please, Eddie. One last time."

Jo had told herself *one last time* before, when she found him at Child's and convinced him to go to Madam Esther's with her. This trip would truly be their last together. She could see in his gaze that it would.

Eddie looked up at the sky for quite some time. When he finally met Jo's eyes again, she saw a fire burning there that matched the one inside her. "Tomorrow night," he said. "Corner of Irving and Fifteenth. Ten o'clock. I'll be waiting."

✥ CHAPTER SEVENTY-SEVEN ✥

"The thing is, you can't ever really know just how rotten someone will turn out to be," Oscar Rubin said philosophically. "It's always a surprise."

"And who doesn't love a surprise?" Eddie muttered darkly.

Jo, Eddie, and Oscar were shoveling dirt off a newly mounded grave in Darkbriar's cemetery.

They'd met Flynn, the gravedigger, an hour ago at the asylum's tall black gates, timing their arrival to coincide with the watchman's nightly trip to the main kitchens for a cup of hot coffee. Flynn had them through the gates and into the wooded grounds by the time the watchman returned to his hut.

Oscar had made the arrangements. Eddie had filled him in about the photograph and told him that Francis Mallon and the scar-faced man were one and the same. Oscar knew Flynn and offered him twenty dollars of Jo's money to let them dig up Kinch. Flynn had provided them with a small lantern, shovels, and a crowbar. He'd walked them to the grave and then he'd left them on their own.

Darkbriar mainly catered to rich clients. The bodies of patients who died there were almost always whisked away for burial in a family plot. The few that went unclaimed were buried in a lonely patch of land at the farthest reaches of the asylum's extensive grounds.

From the graveyard, Jo could see the asylum buildings silhouetted against the moonlit sky. A mournful wind moved through the trees, rattling their bare branches and sweeping dead leaves across the cold ground. A moment ago, her courage had failed her. She'd wanted to run from this place, and from what she was about to do. She couldn't shake the feeling that she was crossing a final and terrible border, and that once she opened Kinch's coffin, there would be no going back. And yet she hadn't run. Her fear was strong, but her need for the truth was stronger.

As she, Eddie, and Oscar all continued to dig, Oscar continued to talk.

"There are so many variables. Age. Weight. Manner of death. Time of year," he said. "Say you pull a ten-day-old corpse out of a warehouse in January . . . you'll get discoloration, some odor—mainly from the bowels evacuating. The eyes will be gone. The nose, too. Rats *love* noses. But pull the same corpse out in July? You've got liquid putrescence then. Maggots. Bloating. Slippage—that's when the skin comes off when you try to move the guy. And the stench? Indescribable." Oscar chuckled heartily. "You'll lose your lunch. I guarantee it."

"I'm about to lose my dinner, so can you stop?" Eddie asked.

"I'm only trying to point out the fact that Mr. Kinch might be well preserved," Oscar said. "He died only four days ago, and the weather's been cold. We're lucky the ground isn't frozen or we wouldn't be able to do this."

"*Lucky* isn't the first word that comes to mind," Eddie grumbled. "I can't believe I'm doing this. I'm a grave robber now. And so are you two."

"Technically, we're not. Not unless we take Kinch with us. We're *disturbing* a grave, certainly, but not robbing it."

"Really? That's so great, Oscar. I feel much better. You know something? You're as crazy as she is," Eddie said, nodding at Jo.

"I'm not crazy; I'm curious. That's why I came. What if Jo's right? What if the answers *are* written on Kinch's body? Imagine that—a dead man who *does* tell tales. I'm certainly adding this to my casebook."

"Let's pick up the pace, shall we?" Eddie said. "The faster we dig him up, the faster we can get out of here."

Jo tried her best to keep up with the two men, but it was impossible. She'd never held a shovel in her life except for the little tin one she'd played with as a child on the beaches of Newport. The one she'd been given was heavy, and digging out a hole with two other people was awkward. As soon as they'd shoveled down a foot, it became too hard for all three of them to maneuver around the grave. Eddie asked her to stop digging and hold the lantern instead.

The two men took turns then, working mostly in silence for the next hour, huffing and grunting in the light of the lantern, their breath visible in the chilly air. And then, when they were about four feet down, Oscar's shovel struck wood. A sickly-sweet smell wafted up. Jo did her best to ignore it.

"A shallow grave," Oscar said. "Flynn's not only crooked, he's lazy, too."

Eddie and Jo watched as Oscar cleaned the rest of the dirt off the top of Kinch's coffin and dug out little hollows on either side of it so he'd have somewhere to stand when the lid came off.

"Crowbar," he said.

Eddie handed it to him. Oscar placed his feet firmly in the hollows. He hooked the crowbar under the coffin's lid, took a deep breath, then yanked as hard as he could. There was a screech as the nails pulled free. The lid flipped up on its side. Oscar nimbly lifted his left leg over the lid, then braced himself against it. He handed the crowbar back to Eddie. The smell of death, punishingly strong, rose like a specter.

Jo gagged. She covered her nose and mouth with her hands.

Eddie swore.

Oscar rubbed his hands together. "Hand me the lantern, kids!" he crowed.

In the glare of the kerosene flame, Jo saw an image she knew would haunt her for as long as she lived.

Kinch's face was purple and grotesquely swollen. His tongue protruded through his lips. His eyes were half closed. Jo wanted to scream. She wanted to run. She stayed where she was by sheer force of will, watching as Oscar went to work.

"You have a pad and pencil on you?" he asked Eddie.

Eddie, looking green, nodded.

"Good. Write down what I say." Oscar turned back to the body. "Talk to me, Kinch," he murmured, carefully inspecting the corpse's clothing. "Jacket, shirt, trousers, belt, socks, and boots . . . According to the papers, Kinch refused to remove his clothing when he was brought to the asylum. Not much blood on them, is there? For a man who allegedly cut someone's throat."

He parted Kinch's swollen eyelids with this thumb and forefinger. Jo swallowed her revulsion and leaned in, the better to see what he was doing.

"Petechial hemorrhages in both the sclera and inner lids," he said, pointing to red dots in Kinch's eyes.

He looked at Kinch's fingers and palms next. He pushed his sleeves up and peered at his skin. "No lividity to hands or forearms. Extensive bruising and puncture marks inside the elbows."

"There's no bruising on his arms besides the inner elbow?" Jo asked. "What about his legs?"

Oscar pulled up one trouser leg, then the other. "Nothing major. Why?" he asked.

"Because he jumped from a window twenty feet off the ground," replied Jo. "At least, according to his confession to Mallon."

"You're right," Oscar said, frowning. "I remember reading that in the papers."

"What about the puncture marks? Was he injecting himself with morphine?" Eddie asked. "That was the word in the newsroom."

"Looks like he was injecting *something*. It also looks like he wasn't very good at it. The bruising is extensive. Seems like he'd try for a vein, miss, and try again," Oscar said. He parted Kinch's jacket and stared at his waist. "Why'd they leave your belt on you, Mr. Kinch? Loonies aren't supposed to have belts or shoelaces."

He undid Kinch's collar, revealing a deep black groove around his neck. "Horizontal ligature furrow approximately one-half inch deep. Bruises and abrasions above and below furrow." He gently felt the front of Kinch's neck, probing his Adam's apple. "Suspected fracture to thyroid cartilage." Next, he examined Kinch's belt. "Belt approximately one and one-half inches wide. Noncorroborative with furrow dimensions."

Eddie stopped writing. "Hold on a minute, Oscar. . . . *Non-corroborative?*"

Oscar nodded grimly.

"What does that mean?" Jo asked, looking from Eddie to Oscar.

"It means that our friend Mr. Kinch *didn't* hang himself," Oscar replied.

"With his belt, you mean. He used something else as a noose," Eddie ventured.

"No. I mean he didn't hang himself," Oscar said.

"But there's a mark on his neck," Jo countered.

"Yes, but it wasn't made by a noose," Oscar said. "Kinch was strangled."

⇒ CHAPTER SEVENTY-EIGHT ⇐

Jo took a step back from the grave, stunned. When her aunt had first broken the news about Kinch's suicide, Jo had found it hard to believe. Guilt over Beekman's death had driven him to it, her aunt said, but why would Kinch feel guilty if—as Oscar claimed—he hadn't killed Beekman?

She'd tried to talk herself out of her doubts. She'd tried to stop asking questions. Because that was what everyone around her wanted. But now the questions came flooding back.

"How can that be, Oscar? The papers all reported that he hanged himself. Dr. Ellsworth, the asylum's spokesman, said Kinch was overcome by remorse."

"He was overcome, all right. By a large and strong man," said Oscar, standing up straight. "Had he hanged himself, the furrow left by his belt would be wider, not as deep, and higher on his neck. The petechial hemorrhages and congestion of the face would likely be absent. His hands and arms would show at least some livor. I doubt I'd see a fracture in the thyroid cartilage. Someone wrapped a cord around his neck and pulled it. Hard."

"Francis Mallon," Eddie said. "I'd bet a thousand dollars. He had both access and opportunity. He was one of the very few—besides the doctors, and a handful of cops—who did. He probably strangled him, then strung him up with his belt."

"But *why?*" Jo asked.

"To frame somebody else for Beekman's murder," Eddie said. "One of Della's girls saw Mallon kill Alvah Beekman and attack Phillip Montfort, right? Since Kinch was also there at the murder scene, we thought he and Mallon might be accomplices, but we were wrong."

"You're saying Kinch just happened to be in the wrong place at the wrong time?" Jo asked skeptically.

"Yes. He saw what was happening and tried to stop Mallon, but he couldn't because he was under the influence of morphine," Eddie said. "He managed to raise the alarm, though, and the cops came. Your uncle, who's dazed from the blow he took, is confused and blames Kinch for the murder. Kinch can't argue, because he's out of his mind. He's taken to Darkbriar, where Mallon works. Mallon kills Kinch and says Kinch confessed."

"It's possible," Oscar allowed. "Barely."

"Why would Mallon say that Kinch had confessed to *all three* Van Houten murders?" Jo asked.

"Because *he* committed them. And he was worried he'd be found out. That's why he came after us, Jo. He must've seen us following up our leads and felt we were getting too close," Eddie said.

Jo shook her head. "It still doesn't make sense," she said, trying to put it all together. "What reason would Francis Mallon—an orderly at Darkbriar—have to kill three members of Van Houten? *Kinch* was the one who believed the firm was guilty of wrongdoing. *He* was the one who claimed to have proof of it. *He* was blackmailing the firm, not Mallon."

"She's got you there, pal," Oscar said.

"Just because we don't know what the reason is doesn't mean there isn't one," Eddie said stubbornly.

"True," Jo conceded, irked that no matter how many layers of the mystery they peeled back, the answers still eluded them.

Oscar handed Eddie the lantern, then reached into the corpse's trouser pockets, one after the other, but found nothing. He took off Kinch's shoes and felt around inside them. Again nothing. He fished through the corpse's jacket pockets, then ran his hands over the jacket for good measure.

"Aha!" he said, stopping near the hem. "You have a pocketknife?" he asked Eddie.

Eddie handed him one and Oscar sliced the jacket's lining open. He reached inside and pulled out a pendant on a gold chain. Jo's breath caught as he handed it to her.

It was gold and shaped like half a heart, and it glinted warmly in the lantern's light. A name was inscribed upon it.

"Eleanor," Jo said in a hushed voice. "Oh, Eddie . . . Oscar . . . it's *him*. There were two halves of this heart. Eleanor wore one half with the name *Stephen* engraved on it and Stephen wore the other with *Eleanor* on it." She paused, overcome by emotion, then said, "He came back for her, just as he promised he would—seventeen years too late."

"Kinch *is* Stephen Smith," Eddie said, amazement in his voice. "Just as you suspected, Jo."

"He *didn't* die at sea. He somehow survived the storm that took his ship and came home," said Jo, astonished by the enormity of their discovery.

"Kinch—pardon me, Mr. *Smith*—has been very talkative so far," Oscar said, unbuttoning the corpse's shirt. "He told us how he died. Now maybe he'll tell us why."

➤ *CHAPTER SEVENTY-NINE* ⤛

Jo, Eddie, and Oscar all fell silent as they gazed upon Stephen Smith's bare chest. It was like a page of a book, covered with words. Some were legible; others were blotted out by decay.

Jo was the first to speak. "It's his story. Written on his heart. Just like he said." She was so hopeful that the words might finally tell her what she needed to know.

"He told Scully that the ones who tattooed him were Lascars and Africans, but the words are all in English," said Eddie.

"He probably wrote it out for them. They didn't have to understand the symbols, just re-create them," Oscar said. "Give me your pad. And shine the lantern down here."

Eddie, kneeling on the edge of the grave, leaned down over the coffin and held the lantern just above Kinch's chest. Oscar wrote down everything, leaving spaces to indicate letters that had become indecipherable. When he finished, he showed the pad to the others.

```
I   M   EPH   SM   H. TH   ONAV          CARRI
     I TRI          TOP IT B      AS    ANDON    IN
          BY                            E DEVI    E HIS
SOUL F      OD WILL NOT.
```

They puzzled it out together.

"'I am Stephen Smith . . . ,'" Oscar started.

"'The *Bonaventure* carried . . . ,'" Eddie added.

"Carried *what*?" Jo said, beside herself. "Oscar, can you make out those letters?"

"No, there's too much discoloration."

Jo continued to stare at the notepad. "'I tried to stop it but was abandoned in . . . ,'" she said, deciphering more of the words. She looked at Oscar. "In *what*?"

"Can't make *those* letters out, either," Oscar said. "Or the ones after *by*."

"He was *abandoned*," Jo said in a hushed voice. "He didn't perish in a storm; he was left somewhere to die."

"I bet the letters we can't make out spell the name of the person who abandoned him. And where he was left," Eddie said. "And I bet the person who did it was also behind the wrongdoing he discovered."

"'The devil take his soul, for God will not,'" Jo said, deciphering the final few words.

Eddie gave her a long look. "You still think nothing bad happened at Van Houten?" he asked.

Jo raised her eyes from the notepad and met his gaze. "All along it's been so hard to believe that the firm was involved in anything illicit, but now it's hard not to," she said. "Was one of the partners who died behind it—Scully or Beekman? Or one who's still alive? Asa Tuller? John Brevoort?"

"This person, whoever he is, could be the one directing Mallon," Oscar offered. "That could be the connection you're looking for between Mallon and Van Houten."

Jo nodded. "You're right, Oscar," she said. "It makes sense."

Eddie was oddly quiet. Then he said, "There are two more partners you neglected to mention, Jo. Two besides Stephen Smith. And they were both in Zanzibar *with* Smith."

Jo took his meaning. *"No,"* she said vehemently. "It's simply not possible, Eddie. You're saying my uncle or my father was behind the wrongdoing? That one of them is the man who left Smith to die? I can't believe that."

"Can't? Or won't?" he demanded.

Jo, angry now, didn't answer right away. Eddie didn't know what he was talking about. He didn't know her uncle, and hadn't known her father. They were no more capable of hurting another human being than she was.

"You're spending too much time at the *World* and the *Herald*. You must be," she finally said. "That sort of sensationalist nonsense is worthy of them, not you."

The comment came out louder, and meaner, than she'd intended. The corpse, the pendant, learning that Kinch was indeed Stephen Smith—these things had brought her emotions to the surface.

"Sensationalist? Why? Because I can see the truth and you can't?" Eddie said hotly.

"But it's *not* the truth!" Jo retorted.

"Why, Jo? Because no one in your pretty, perfect little world can do any wrong? Only those of us outside it?"

He was talking about more than her uncle, more than their investigation. He was talking about the mistake she'd made in accepting Bram's proposal.

"That's unfair, Eddie!" she shot back. "I *said* I was sorry. I tried to explain the night we went to Pitt Street, but you wouldn't let me. It's not only about the two of us. You'd know that if you'd bothered to listen to me. But you walked away, and—"

"Um, Eddie? Jo? Sorry to interrupt another tiff," Oscar said. "But are we still talking about the dead man? This one whose coffin I'm standing in? Because if we are, *I* have a question. . . ."

"Sorry, Osk. What is it?" Eddie said as Jo took a deep breath to calm herself.

"Why did Smith do this? I can see why he'd tattoo his face—to avoid being recognized. But putting all these words on himself doesn't make sense. Ship tattoos are done with dirty needles. They hurt. They get infected. People die from them. So why not just write the story down on paper? Why have it written on your body?"

"So it couldn't be taken from him. Because everything else had been," Jo said softly, embarrassed to suddenly find herself in tears. "We were looking for the wrong man for so long. Stephen Smith threatened the partners of Van Houten, but he didn't kill them. Mallon did. I'm certain of that now."

"Why?" Eddie asked, his voice gentler.

"The pendant," Jo said. She was still holding it. She looked at it again and was deeply moved by what it stood for—constancy, faith, love. "God only knows what Stephen Smith went through, and how he survived it, but he never stopped trying to get home to Eleanor. How can a man like that be a cold-blooded killer? He was only trying to claim what was his—the woman he loved and their child."

A gust of wind swirled through the cemetery. Jo shivered. Eddie was standing close to her and must've felt her tremble. "Do you want my jacket?" he asked.

"No, thank you," Jo replied. The chill she felt had nothing to do with the wind. "The killer's still out there. Everyone thinks it's over now that Kinch is dead, but if we're right, then Mallon killed three men and he's still walking the streets. What if it's not over? What if my uncle's still at risk?"

"Are you going to tell him about Mallon?" Eddie asked.

"I have to," Jo replied.

But how? she wondered. He didn't want her even to *think* about the events of the past few weeks anymore. How would he react when she told him what she'd learned tonight, and how she'd learned it? Would he believe her? She'd take the pendant with her. Hopefully, it would convince him.

Somewhere in the city, a clock struck the hour.

"Midnight," Eddie said.

"As much fun as this has been, we'd better finish up and go," Oscar said. He pulled the corpse into a sitting position, hastily slid its shirt off, and inspected its back. There were no tattoos on it. Oscar reclothed the body, then folded Smith's hands neatly across his chest. He was about to ease the coffin lid back down when Jo stopped him.

"Shouldn't we say something?" she asked. She doubted that Flynn had taken the time to bestow any final words on Stephen Smith.

"Like what?"

Jo thought for a few seconds, then said, "I'm sorry we disturbed you, Mr. Smith, but thank you for telling us the truth. I wish Eleanor had survived. I'd find her for you. I'd tell her you loved her and did your best to get back to her. I'd tell her the story that was written on your heart."

➤ CHAPTER EIGHTY ◄

"We made it," Eddie said, stepping out of the cab at Lexington and Twenty-Second Street.

"Thank you," Jo said to the driver as she paid him.

Her body was aching. They'd walked part of the way from the asylum to get the smell of death out of their noses, and their clothing, though Oscar still reeked. It had been hard work to shovel the dirt back over Stephen Smith's coffin, and tricky business to sneak through the gates. Luckily, the watchman had fallen asleep, despite his big mug of coffee.

Jo's heart was aching, too. This was the end of the line. She could do no more. The manifests Stephen Smith had sent to Eleanor Owens would remain hidden, for both she and Eddie had tried—and failed—to find them. Mallon would remain unquestioned, at least by them.

Eddie was right—Mallon was too dangerous to approach. She would tell her uncle what she'd learned, and then he would go to the authorities. They would be the ones to approach Mallon. Jo's time as a sleuth was over. With all her heart she wished it weren't. She wished things could be different. She wished *she* were different—the sort of girl who could forget her duties to her family and follow her own heart's desires. But she wasn't.

"Anyone hungry?" Oscar asked. "The Portman's not far. I bet they'd scare up a sandwich for us."

"How can you even *think* about food after where we've just been?" Jo asked.

"Dead people always make me hungry," Oscar said. "Once you're in the ground, there's no more noodle kugel for you. No more roast chicken or potato latkes. So eat, drink, and be merry, I say. But especially eat."

"I would love to go with you, Oscar, but it's almost one o'clock in the morning and I have to sneak back into my house," Jo said. Then, impulsively, she hugged him.

"What's that for?" Oscar asked, as she released him.

"I don't know when I'll see you again. Or *if* I'll see you again. And I just wanted to say thank you. For everything. I've never met anyone quite like you. I know you'll make the most wonderful doctor, and here's something else I know: Sarah Stein wishes you'd take her to dinner."

Oscar blushed. He kissed Jo's cheek.

Then Jo turned to Eddie. The look that passed between them was one of love and loss. It was naked and sad, and Oscar saw it. "I . . . uh . . . I think I'll just walk down the street now. For no good reason," he said.

"Can't imagine you'll be seeing much of me again, either," Eddie said. He was looking at Jo, not Oscar.

Jo lowered her head so he wouldn't see the tears brimming in her eyes. "I'll miss you every day of my life. Because you changed my life, Eddie. I'll never, ever forget you."

"No more, Jo," Eddie said, his voice husky. "Please."

Jo nodded. She raised her head and tried for a smile. "Goodbye," she said, hugging him.

He hugged her back, holding her tightly, his cheek against hers, his eyes closed. And then he let her go.

"You need me to walk you home?" he asked.

"It's only a block away," Jo said. "I'll be fine."

"All right, then. There's a cab coming," he said, looking up the street. "I'm going to take it and pick up Oscar."

The hansom cab Eddie had seen was occupied. It rolled by them and then abruptly stopped. The door opened. A young man, slender and tall, stepped out.

"Jo? Jo Montfort?" he called. "Is that you?"

Jo turned around slowly, her heart in her throat.

It was Bram.

➤ CHAPTER EIGHTY-ONE ➤

Bram looked at Jo as if he didn't trust his own eyes.

"Josephine, what in God's name are you doing out on the streets at this hour?" he demanded.

"W-well, I . . . I was j-just . . . ," Jo stammered. She couldn't tell him the truth, but she had to say *something*.

"Who is this man? Has he hurt you?" he asked, eyeing Eddie suspiciously.

"*Hurt me?* No!" she said. "He's my *friend*, Bram. Abraham Aldrich, I would like you to meet Edward Gallagher. Edward Gallagher, Bram Aldrich."

Eddie offered his hand. Bram did not take it.

"And Oscar Rubin, too. Well, Oscar's not here at the moment. He's over there." She pointed down the street. Bouncing on the balls of her feet nervously, she smiled and racked her brain for something to say. Finally she asked, "What brings *you* out at this hour?"

"Teddy Farnham's going-away party."

Jo remembered that Teddy was leaving for a tour of the Continent soon. "Did you have fun?" she asked, as if it were perfectly normal to be having this conversation out on the street in the middle of the night.

Worry filled Bram's face. "Jo, are you all right? Please come inside the cab. I'll take you to your door."

"You good with that, Jo?" Eddie asked.

"*What?*" Bram said, turning to look at Eddie.

"You heard me. Even though I wasn't talking to you," Eddie replied, standing his ground.

"What perfect timing!" Jo quickly said, moving toward the cab. "I won't have to walk through the square. Good night, Mr. Gallagher."

"Miss Montfort," Eddie said, tipping his cap.

Bram put a protective arm around Jo's shoulders and led her to his cab. "Gramercy Square. Number Twenty-Six," he said to the driver as Jo climbed in.

The cab moved off and Jo settled herself on the seat. As she did, Bram's gaze traveled over her, from her dirt-streaked hands to her muddy shoes. She could see the confusion in his eyes and realized how she must look to him. She was wearing an ancient coat. Her dress was filthy. Her hair had straggled out of its knot.

"Jo, where have you been? What have you been doing?"

"Bram, you have to trust me," she said earnestly, taking his hand.

"Jo, I *must* know what you were doing with those men," he insisted.

"I'll tell you, but I doubt you'll believe me," she said, fervently hoping that he *would* believe her. That she could confide in him. That he would help her. If he could do those things, it might be the beginning of something between them, something real.

She took a deep breath and plunged ahead. "I've been at the Darkbriar Asylum digging up a corpse."

Bram sank back against his seat, ashen-faced.

"The corpse belongs to the man I suspected of murdering not only Alvah Beekman, but also Richard Scully and my father," she continued, talking quickly. "However, a story tattooed on the corpse's chest has convinced me otherwise."

"Oh my God," Bram said, his voice barely a whisper.

"I know this must be a terrible shock for you, and I'm sorry," Jo said, unhappy to have upset him.

"If I'd only known," Bram said. "I didn't see it. Phillip—"

"Knows nothing," said Jo. "Not about this. I plan to tell him to-morrow. He'll know what to do."

"First your father, then Richard, then Alvah. . . . It's all been too much for you. My poor girl. We've been so worried. . . . Your uncle, your mother, your friends, even Katie."

Jo, looking out the window, barely heard him. The cab was now moving along the east side of the square. She didn't want to go any farther. "Stop here, please," she said, agitated.

"But we're not at your house," Bram objected.

"I don't want the cab to stop in front of it in case the noise wakes Theakston."

"But we *must* wake the servants. They'll be needed to help you. Your mother, too."

"*No!*" Jo said. "Bram, I *must* get to my room unseen. My mother mustn't find out about tonight. Not yet. Not before I tell my uncle. She won't understand."

"All right, Jo, all right," Bram said, in a soothing voice. "But you must allow me to see you to your door. I refuse to leave until I know you're safely inside your house."

Bram stopped the carriage. He helped Jo down and walked her to the servants' door.

"Promise me you'll get some rest," he said.

"I will. Thank you for listening to me, Bram. Thank you for believing me."

"It's all right, Jo. Go in the house now."

Jo nodded. She carefully opened the door, slipped inside, and pulled it closed, locking it behind her. Then she tiptoed up the back stairs, hoping not to wake anyone. When she reached her room, she looked out the window.

Bram was still standing on the sidewalk, motionless. He raised his hand to his eyes and brushed at something. Then he turned and slowly walked back to his cab.

❧ CHAPTER EIGHTY-TWO ❧

Jo barely slept a wink all night.

She'd taken off her filthy clothing and muddy shoes, rolled them up in a ball, and shoved them into an old carpetbag at the back of her wardrobe. She took a hot bath, scrubbing every inch of herself, then climbed into bed, where she tossed and turned for the rest of the night, haunted by images of Stephen Smith in his coffin.

At dawn, she was out of bed. After dressing and doing her own hair, she slipped out of the house. Her mother was usually a late riser, but today was a Sunday and there was church to attend. Jo had to get to her uncle's house and back before breakfast.

Her aunt and cousin usually slept late, too. Her uncle, however, did not. He always said that dawn was his favorite time of day, and he usually worked for a few hours in his study before breakfasting with his family. Jo hoped that was the case today.

She hurried up the steps to her uncle's front door now and knocked lightly. Seconds later, it was opened.

"Miss Montfort, good morning. Is Mrs. Montfort expecting you?" Harney asked, ushering her inside.

"It's my uncle I've come to see, Harney," Jo explained. "Can you please let him know I'm here?"

As Jo waited in the foyer, Admiral Montfort gazed at her with his hard eyes. *"Fac quod faciendum est,"* she whispered, drawing strength once again from the Montfort family motto.

Harney returned. "Right this way, Miss Montfort," he said, leading Jo to her uncle's study.

Phillip was standing in the doorway as she reached it. "Jo? This is a most unusual hour for a visit. Is everything all right?" he asked.

Jo waited until she was inside the study and Harney had closed the door before she spoke.

"No, Uncle Phillip, it's not. I have some very difficult news to share with you, and you are going to be angry with me when you hear it. Very angry. But please hear me out."

Jo sat down. She looked at her uncle's kindly face, now etched with concern, and wished that she didn't have to tell him what she knew, but she had no choice. She needed his help. He was kind, yes, but he was also strong and shrewd and would do what needed to be done.

Jo squared her shoulders, took a deep breath, then began. She started with her trip to Child's Restaurant and ended with her visit to Darkbriar and her carriage ride home with Bram. She came clean about Oscar Edwards, too. She had to. Bram had seen Eddie and Oscar and might mention them to her uncle.

Phillip turned white as she spoke. He sat as still as death, listening to her every word. When she finished, he silently rose, poured himself a glass of brandy, and downed it in one gulp. Though his back was to her, Jo could tell by his clenched hand and the tremor in his shoulders that he was doing his best to compose himself. He turned, finally, and looked at her.

"Can this *possibly* be true?" he asked.

"I'm sorry, Uncle Phillip. I'm so sorry," Jo said, distressed by all the fresh pain she was causing him.

Phillip sat down again, heavily. "Kinch was Stephen Smith. . . . *How?*" he asked. "Smith was lost at sea. His ship went down in a storm."

"I don't know how, but somehow he survived and returned to New York to look for Eleanor Owens and the manifests he'd sent her."

"And he didn't kill himself at Darkbriar, you say? He was murdered?"

"Yes. I believe his orderly at Darkbriar did it . . . Francis Mallon. I think Mallon killed Mr. Beekman, Mr. Scully, and my father, as well."

Phillip covered his face with his hands. He shook his head violently, as if trying to clear it. "Have you any proof of the things you've just told me?"

"I'm afraid I have very little proof of anything," Jo admitted. "Only this." She dug in her purse and placed Stephen Smith's pendant on the tea table.

Phillip stared at it. He picked it up and read the inscription. "Dear God, Jo. Tell me you did not really do what you said you did to get this thing."

"I *had* to, Uncle Phillip," Jo said. "I want my father's murderer—his real murderer—brought to justice. I want the truth. And though I may not have hard proof, I've heard enough, and seen enough, to think that your life might still be in danger." She crossed the room, knelt down by his chair and took his hands. "Uncle Phillip, *listen* to me. You must act. *Please.* You must go to the police. I've lost my father to a murderer. I couldn't bear it if something happened to you."

Phillip said nothing for nearly a minute. He just stared straight ahead helplessly. Finally, he nodded. "Yes, Jo. You're right," he said decisively.

Jo felt a rush of relief. He was rallying. His color had improved. He sat up straight, in command of himself once again.

"I'll go to the authorities immediately," he said. "I'd like to show them the pendant, if I may."

"Of course," said Jo. "Shall I come with you?"

"No, not yet. I'm sure the police will wish to speak with you at some point, but you are to do nothing more. *Nothing.* Do you understand me? You've put yourself in enough danger. You said this man Mallon attacked you once—what if he tries to do so again? My God, Jo, I still can't believe I'm having this conversation with you. The things you've seen . . . No young woman should *ever* see such horrors."

Jo nodded, looking at her hands.

"Look at me, Josephine," Phillip said sternly.

Jo raised her eyes to his. *Here it comes*, she thought, wincing.

"I cannot begin to tell you how angry I am with you. For doing the things you've done. For the risks you've taken. For deceiving us all—your mother, me, Bram. I only hope he has not told Grandmama. If he has, your engagement may well be in jeopardy."

"I would sacrifice my future with Bram to save your life," Jo said, tears springing to her eyes.

Phillip, who was about to continue his tirade, faltered. "You are a very foolish girl, Josephine. Very foolish," he said, his voice breaking. "And very brave."

"What about Mama? What do I tell her?"

Phillip cleared his throat. "Nothing. Not yet. Let me do it. I don't want your mother, aunt, and cousin scared witless. I won't go to church this morning. I'll say I'm unwell. I think you should do the same. You've had too great a shock to be out and about this morning."

Jo nodded.

"After Madeleine and Caroline leave, I'll go to the police and tell them about Mallon," Phillip continued. "Then I'll inform Tuller and Brevoort. They should know, too. I'll tell your aunt everything as soon as we both return home again. She'll be less upset if I can tell her that the police and the other partners have been alerted. When that's done, I'll have a word with Bram. He's bound to be worried about you. And then I'll come to your house and talk to your mother. She'll be quite distraught when she hears about your activities, but I think she'll take it better coming from me than from you."

Jo agreed, grateful to her uncle for dealing with her mother.

"There's one more thing, Uncle Phillip," she said. "No matter how angry you are at me, you are not to be angry with Eddie Gallagher or Oscar Rubin. This was all my idea, not theirs." She paused, then said, "If I am to go on with my life and become Bram's wife, I must know that they'll be allowed to go on with theirs, without suffering any consequences for helping me." Her meaning was veiled, but she was sure her uncle would understand it.

And he did. "You have my assurances that Mr. Gallagher and Mr. Rubin are safe from my wrath," he said. "But I must have your promise that you won't see either of them again. This is out of your hands now, Jo. It's a matter for the authorities."

"I give you my word," Jo said.

Phillip rose. "I think you should go home now. You look very tired and I have much to do."

Jo stood, too. "I feel like I could sleep for ten years," she said.

Phillip embraced her. She hugged him back tightly.

"I was so afraid to tell you, but I'm glad I did," she said.

"I'm glad, too," he said, releasing her. "You're not to worry about it anymore, my dear Jo. I'll take care of it. I'll take care of everything."

CHAPTER EIGHTY-THREE

There was no sneaking into the house unobserved by the time Jo returned from her uncle's.

It was nearly eight-thirty. The household staff were up, and preparations for breakfast were under way.

"I felt a headache coming on and went out for some air, but it hasn't helped," she fibbed to Mrs. Nelson. "Would you send some tea and toast to my room and let my mother know I'm under the weather and won't be attending church?"

Jo went up to her room and changed into her nightgown. Her mother, having gotten Jo's message, came in about fifteen minutes later to check on her, followed by Katie, who had Jo's tea tray. When Anna had satisfied herself that Jo was not feverish, she left her to rest. Jo ate a bit of breakfast, then closed her eyes. She only meant to nap for an hour or so, but it was four-thirty in the afternoon by the time she woke. She immediately rang for her maid.

"Katie, has my uncle been here?" she asked.

"No, Miss Jo, but he sent word that he intends to pay a call at seven this evening."

Jo was relieved she hadn't missed him. She thanked Katie, then asked her to draw a bath and lay out her clothing. She'd only had a quick wash very early that morning and wanted a long hot soak.

By six-thirty, she was scrubbed, dressed, and neatly coiffed. At precisely seven, the doorbell rang. She walked downstairs when she heard it, summoning the strength she knew she would need to get through the next hour.

"Good evening, Uncle," she said as she entered the foyer.

Theakston was already reaching for Phillip's coat, but he said he wished to keep it on. Jo thought that odd but made no comment, as Theakston was still hovering

Phillip gave Jo a quick kiss on her cheek. "I'll go in to your mother now," he told her in a low voice. "After I've said what I've come to say, I'll call you in. I assume she's in the drawing room?"

"She is," Jo said.

Theakston ushered Phillip into the drawing room, and Jo decided to wait for her uncle's summons in her father's study. She left the study door open, and distracted herself from her anxiousness by looking out the bay windows. In the glow of a gas lamp, she saw a figure, slight and hunched, near the servants' entrance to the Cavendishes' house, which was kitty-corner to her own. It was Mad Mary. The door opened and Mrs. Perkins, the Cavendishes' cook, handed her a small bundle. Mary dipped her head, then hurried to their stoop. She sat down, opened the bundle, and greedily started to eat.

"Jo? Are you there?" Her uncle's voice carried up the stairs.

Jo hurried to the drawing room. Phillip held the door open, then closed it behind her. Her mother was sitting on a divan clutching a handkerchief. Her eyes were red and swollen. She was trembling.

"Oh, Mama," Jo said, her voice breaking. She sat down next to her.

Her mother took her hand. She looked at her searchingly, then at Phillip. "I don't believe it," she said. "I *can't* believe it. It's not true!"

"Jo, your mother is having a bit of difficulty with what I've told her. Would you repeat the story for her? Start at the very beginning."

"Yes, Uncle," Jo said. She sat down next to her mother and told her everything, starting with her trip to the *Standard* to give Mr. Stoatman her father's bequest.

Anna listened, shaking her head at times, pressing her handkerchief to her eyes, murmuring the word *no*. It was dead silent in the room when Jo finished. The only sound was the ticking of the grandfather clock.

Phillip was the first to speak. He turned to Anna and said, "Do you see now? It's just as I told you."

Jo was so glad he was here. She was grateful for his calmness and his strength. She could not have done this alone.

"It's dreadful," he continued, looking at Jo's mother. "A shattering thing to face, especially after all you've been through. But I told you, Anna. All along, I told you. You wouldn't believe me. Do you now? Do you finally see? Our poor, dear Jo has lost her mind."

❧ CHAPTER EIGHTY-FOUR ❧

"*What?*" Jo said, laughing in disbelief. "For goodness' sake, Uncle Phillip, what are you saying? I haven't lost my mind!"

"Josephine, please," said Anna tearfully. "Think about the horrible things you just told us you've done . . . walking the streets at night with strange men, going to morgues and houses of ill repute, digging up a *corpse*—" Her voice broke. She struggled to regain her composure. "It's obscene!"

Jo felt the first pricklings of fear run up her spine. "But, Mama, it was all to find out the truth about Papa's death," she said.

"And when, exactly, did you do these things? When?" her mother asked.

"At night, mostly. Sometimes during the day."

"At night? That is a *lie*, Josephine," her mother said. "I check on you at night. I have since you were a tiny girl. And every night since you came home from school for your father's funeral, you have been in bed. Sound asleep."

"You saw Katie. I traded places with her. Several times," Jo said, becoming more nervous. "Mama, these things are *true!*" She turned to her uncle. "Tell her, Uncle Phillip! Tell her the truth!"

"My darling Jo," Phillip said, his faced creased with pity, "I told her what I know—that this morning you came to me very upset with a wild and sordid story. And that it was not the first time you'd done so. I foolishly took no action before today, hoping this mania was born of grief and would pass. I was wrong. You've grown worse, not better. Last night, instead of imagining you'd left your house, you actually *did* leave it."

"But you . . . you believed me!" Jo said.

"I played along hoping to keep you calm."

"You lied to me. You said you were going to the authorities," Jo said, her voice rising.

Phillip shook his head sorrowfully. "Please don't say that, Jo. I didn't mean to. I needed time."

"Time? For what?"

"To find you the care you need."

"But I don't need any care!" Jo shouted, her fear growing. Anna and Phillip traded glances, and Jo realized she was only confirming their suspicions by becoming hysterical.

In a quieter, calmer voice, she said, "I assure you that I am perfectly fine."

"You are a sensitive girl, Josephine, and you have sadly fallen prey to all manner of delusions," said Phillip. "I, your aunt, your mother, we all tried. We asked you to stop dwelling on dark thoughts. We allowed you to bend the rules of mourning. Encouraged you to see friends. We desperately hoped your engagement would pull you out of your moroseness, but even that has failed to turn you around."

"You've been acting so strange," her mother said. "In the carriage on the way to the Scullys'. At the dressmaker's, too. Like your uncle, I didn't want to face what I was seeing. Now I have no choice."

Jo remembered being at the dressmaker's. She remembered the fearful look on her mother's face when she'd tried to tell her she didn't want to go through with the wedding. And the look that had passed between her mother and her aunt on the way to the Scullys'. It seemed *everything* she'd said or done fed her uncle's assertion that she'd gone mad.

"This is all a terrible misunderstanding," she insisted, trying to keep her voice level, "but I know how to clear it up. Send for Eddie Gallagher and Oscar Rubin. They'll confirm everything I've told you."

"I spoke with them both this afternoon, Jo," Phillip said. "They both said they'd never met you until last night when you approached them on the street, covered in dirt. They also told me they were relieved when Bram appeared and took you home."

Jo felt as if she'd been struck. "*What?* That's preposterous! It's not true! I've been to Eddie's room several times. Of *course* he knows me!" she said without thinking.

Anna's eyes widened with alarm. "If this gets out, Phillip . . . if people hear that she's saying such things . . ."

"I also looked up your private detective—Oscar Edwards," Phillip said. "There's no investigator by that name in the city."

"I told you, I—I made him up. I had to. To protect Eddie," she stammered.

"You made it *all* up, didn't you, Jo?" Phillip gently prompted.

"Fetch Katie! She'll tell you that what I said is true," Jo said, relieved to have hit on the idea. Katie's account of Jo's recent activities would certainly corroborate Jo's.

"I've given Katie and the other maids the night off. Mrs. Nelson, too," her mother said. "Only Theakston's still here, and I'm hoping he's gone downstairs to polish the silver."

"Why have the servants been sent away?" Jo asked warily.

"Because they listen at doors and then they tell tales. I do not want this all over the city. It's bad enough that Bram knows," said Anna.

Emotion choked her words off. When she could speak again, she said, "God only knows what he makes of all this. He found you on the *street* at one in the morning with two strange *men*! It's a testimony to his kind nature and good character that he didn't immediately break off your engagement. He may yet. If Grandmama finds out, he'll have no choice."

"We hope to prevent this, Jo," Phillip said "We plan to say that all the excitement of the past few months has led to nervous exhaustion and that we've sent you on a trip to regain your strength."

Jo felt as if a net was closing around her. "A trip? To where?" she asked.

"Consider it a brief respite," Anna said. "We'll say you've gone to visit my sister in Winnetka. And when you recover, which I hope will be very soon, you'll come home."

"But where am I going?" Jo asked, genuinely afraid now.

"Don't worry, Josephine," Phillip said. "Your mother had Katie pack a few things. Enough to see you through the first few days. We'll send the rest on later." He stood then, and pulled a small traveling case from behind a chair. Her coat had been folded over it. "Come along now. Put your coat on."

Jo turned to her mother. "Mama, *please*," she cried. "Stop this!"

"My poor, darling girl, it's for the best," Anna said. She turned away and wept into her handkerchief.

Phillip handed Jo her coat. "Please, Jo. Don't make this any harder than it already is."

Jo's head was spinning. Everything felt completely unreal. *How can this be happening?* she wondered.

When she'd buttoned her coat, Phillip took her by the arm and led her to the front door. As he opened it, she saw his shiny black carriage waiting on the street. Panic overwhelmed her. She tried to break free, but her uncle's grip only tightened.

"Please, Uncle Phillip, please don't do this," she begged.

But Phillip was adamant. He led her across the sidewalk to the carriage. Mad Mary was walking by as Jo was pleading with her uncle. The woman stopped to stare.

"Move on," Phillip barked at her.

Mary flinched. She backed away, onto Jo's stoop. Phillip handed Jo's suitcase to his driver, then bundled her into the cab. Jo looked out the open window as her uncle settled himself across from her, hoping to see her mother appear on the stoop, hoping she'd changed her mind. But her mother wasn't there, only Mary. Jo caught the beggar woman's eyes and saw her fear reflected in them.

"Where to, Mr. Montfort?" Phillip's driver asked.

"East, please, Thomas," Phillip replied. "To the Darkbriar Insane Asylum."

➤ CHAPTER EIGHTY-FIVE ◄

I'm not here, Jo thought, squeezing her eyes closed. *This isn't happening.*

But it was. She opened her eyes and saw that nothing had changed. She was seated next to her uncle. They were in his carriage, heading to Darkbriar. She was going to be committed. The feeling of unreality became so strong, so dizzying, she thought she might be sick.

Maybe my mother and uncle are right, she thought. *Maybe I am insane. Isn't that how it is with crazy people? They think everyone else is crazy.* She covered her face with her hands, moaning softly.

Phillip, noticing her agitation, said, "It will be all right, Josephine. I promise you."

"Will it?" Jo asked.

"Yes, it's only for a short while. Take the time at Darkbriar to heal your nerves and restore your mind. I know you're angry with me, but what else could I do after what you yourself told me? That you'd been in morgues and brothels. That you'd dug up a dead man. That Stephen Smith came back from the Amirantes. . . ."

Jo froze.

But I didn't tell you that, Uncle Phillip, she thought. *Because I didn't know.*

Until now.

The part of Smith's tattoo that named the place where he'd been abandoned had been blotted out by decay. As had the name of the one who'd abandoned him.

Jo knew that the Amirantes, a small cluster of islands in the Indian Ocean, were part of the larger Seychelles chain. She'd heard Stephen Smith's death referred to occasionally when she was a child, but no one had ever mentioned the Amirantes in connection with it.

How could her uncle know where Smith had been abandoned?

Unless *he* was the one who'd abandoned him?

Jo's heart was slamming. Terror, pure and blinding, coursed through her. She understood now. She saw it all.

Eddie was right. His words, spoken at the waterfront, came back to her. *You better get used to the idea that maybe someone at Van Houten isn't so upstanding. . . .* He'd tried again to get her to open her eyes, just last night at Stephen Smith's grave. If only she'd listened to him!

Her uncle, her own beloved uncle, was the one behind the wrongdoing Smith had uncovered. Smith must've threatened him with exposure, so he arranged for him to disappear. Maybe her uncle suggested the scouting trip and paid the ship's captain to somehow get rid of Smith. But Smith had come back. And this time, it was Mallon who'd gotten rid of him—undoubtedly at her uncle's behest.

Jo realized something else, too—her uncle didn't really think she was crazy. He was only pretending to, so he could have her committed. Because she'd become a threat to him.

She glanced at him now. He was looking out the window, which was closed now, still talking. Fear, anger, and revulsion filled her heart. Instinctively, she shrank away from him.

". . . Why, the story grows more outlandish with each telling," he was saying. "You must see that. And you must also see the necessity of our getting you help, Jo. Jo?"

He turned to her. His gaze sharpened as he saw that she'd moved away from him, and suddenly there was another expression under his mask of concern—one that was much darker.

Play along, a voice inside Jo warned. *You can't let him know you know.*

She quickly forced a smile. "I do see, Uncle Phillip. It's just that I'm . . . I'm so frightened," she said.

"You don't need to be," he assured her. "The sooner you admit your illness and cooperate with the doctors, the sooner they can cure you."

"Yes. Of course," Jo docilely agreed.

Only they won't cure me, she thought. *They won't get the chance. You'll hand me over to Darkbriar tonight and then he'll come—Mallon. Maybe tomorrow night. Maybe next week. But he'll come. He'll strangle me and make it look like I hanged myself. Just like he did with Stephen Smith.*

The voice inside Jo went silent for a moment, and then it said one last thing.

If you want to live, Jo, you've got to run.

➤+ CHAPTER EIGHTY-SIX +◄

Jo saw the high stone wall first, then the black gates. DARKBRIAR ASYLUM FOR THE INSANE, the sign on them read.

Jo knew the carriage door to her right was locked. She'd seen her uncle lock it after his driver closed it. Had he, by some miracle, forgotten to lock the one to her left? She glanced at it. Phillip saw her.

"Do not be difficult, Josephine. Both doors are locked. And even if you could get out of the carriage, Thomas and I would come after you," he said. His soothing smile and sympathetic tone were gone. Jo had never seen this side of him before.

A moment later, they were passing through the gates. Jo had been here just last night and she knew that once the watchman locked the gates behind the carriage, she wouldn't be able to get out. There was no other exit from Darkbriar except the river, and its cold temperature and fast currents would guarantee a quick death. Witless with fear, Jo made a desperate lunge at the door on her left, but her uncle pushed her back.

"I'm not going to tell you again," he said coldly.

Thomas drove on. The gates closed. Jo had lost her chance. As the carriage stopped in front of the main building—a gothic mon-

strosity with towers and turrets and bars on the upper windows—
a wave of despair engulfed her.

Thomas opened the door. Phillip stepped out, then helped Jo
down, keeping a firm grip on her arm. A flight of stone steps led
from the drive to the main building's front doors. A matron in uniform was waiting at the bottom of them.

"Welcome, Miss Montfort. We've been expecting you," she said
briskly. "I'm Nurse Williams, and I'll be looking after you."

Jo glanced around wildly, still hoping to find a way out. Phillip's
grip was like a vise now. "Miss Montfort is very agitated," he told
the matron.

"That sometimes happens," the matron said. She gave Jo a fake
smile. "There's no need to fret, dear. We'll take good care of you."
She turned and beckoned to someone behind her. "Would you help
Mr. Montfort settle his niece, please, Mr. Mallon?"

Jo gasped. Her head snapped up. Standing at the top of the stairs
was the scar-faced man. He was here. *Now.* Her uncle wasn't going
to wait; he was going to have her killed tonight.

"No! Let me go!" she shouted, struggling to break free. "He's a
murderer!"

"Mr. Mallon, if you would?" the matron said sternly.

Jo realized that arguing was futile. She remembered *Ten Days in
a Mad-House,* and how none of the staff listened to patients who
insisted they were sane. She knew the matron wouldn't listen to
her, either.

Mallon trotted down the stairs. "I'll take her, sir," he said as his
hand closed around Jo's wrist.

Phillip released her and started up the steps, side by side with
the matron.

Jo fought to break free, but Mallon twisted her arm behind her
back. "Stop," he hissed in her ear. "Or I'll break it."

Jo had no choice but to walk up the steps.

"See? He calmed her already. He's wonderful with the patients. So soothing. He has a great deal of experience, you know. He's one of our longest-serving orderlies," the matron said. "Your niece will be seen to by female staff, of course, but we have male orderlies escort new patients to their rooms. They're better able to restrain anyone who becomes violent."

"I'm sure she'll be in excellent hands," Phillip said. "I would like her to have a sedative tonight to ease her mind and help her sleep. I do not want restraints used on her."

"Of course, Mr. Montfort."

Jo saw how the scenario would play out: Mallon would drug her. Later, he'd come back and strangle her. Then he'd tie something—maybe her own bedsheet—to a bar on her window. The other end would be looped around her neck.

The next day, the matron will recall how upset I was, she thought. *She'll say that the sedative wore off and I hanged myself and that it would not have happened if only my too-kind uncle had let them use restraints.*

Terror shrieked in Jo's head now. She was halfway up the steps. If she didn't run this very instant, she never would. But she couldn't; Mallon had her in a death grip. *I'm going to die here,* she thought. The door loomed ahead of her. Mallon forced her on and she stumbled, nearly losing her shoe.

Which gave her one last, desperate idea.

As she took the next step, she wiggled her foot all the way out of her shoe and kicked it behind her.

"My shoe!" she cried out. "It fell off!"

Nurse Williams turned around. Phillip did, too, an expression of annoyance on his face. "Fetch it for her," he barked at Mallon.

Mallon, not wanting the matron to see how he was twisting Jo's arm, released it, but he still had her by the wrist as he bent down to retrieve her shoe.

Jo was no match for him physically, but she had the element of surprise on her side and she used it. As Mallon reached down, she grabbed the back of his head with her free hand and brought her right knee up—directly into his face.

It was a move she'd seen used at Mick Walsh's, and one that Fay had taught her how to execute, and by some miracle it worked.

There was a sickening crack as her knee smashed Mallon's nose. He reared up, roaring in pain. His hands went to his face. The instant Jo felt him let go of her wrist, she ran.

Down the steps she fled and into the dark grounds of the asylum. She heard Mallon bellowing behind her. She risked a glance over her shoulder as she made for a grove of trees. He wasn't chasing her. He was doubled over by the steps, his hands cupping his nose, blood dripping between his fingers.

It was Phillip who was coming after her. And from the look in his eyes, Jo could see that he wouldn't settle for catching her and dragging her back up the asylum stairs.

He would kill her where she stood.

⇥ CHAPTER EIGHTY-SEVEN ⇤

Jo ran for her life.

Through the grove of trees, through a meadow, through the darkness.

Her breath sounded like a howling wind in her ears, her heart like thunder. Surely they would give her away.

She heard her uncle and Mallon in the distance, shouting. And then they were closer. She couldn't keep running. She would have to hide and hope they ran past. The asylum gates were behind her. They were the only way out. She would have to double back through the grounds to get to them.

A thicket of boxwood loomed ahead, green even in December. She pulled her remaining shoe off, placed it on the path to the left of the bushes, and crawled inside the thicket, grateful to be wearing a black coat. It would help her blend in. She looked through the branches so she could see the path she'd run down.

Jo held herself perfectly still, trying to quiet her breathing and slow her thumping heart. As she did, she saw her uncle appear on the path, panting and swearing. The shoe immediately caught his eye.

"Mallon! Over here!" he shouted, continuing down the path. Just as she'd hoped.

As soon as he was gone, Jo broke from the bushes and ran in the opposite direction, heading for the shelter of some birch trees. She assumed that Mallon was behind her uncle and would run down the same path he had.

It was a mistake. As she neared the birches, Mallon burst from them and lumbered toward her, blood still streaming down his face. Screaming, Jo wheeled around, saw a building in the distance, and raced toward it.

"I've got her!" Mallon yelled.

Jo's stockinged feet flew over the ground. She was lighter and faster than Mallon and quickly put distance between them. When she reached the building, she launched herself at the door, but it was locked. She shot around to the side, hoping to find another way in, and spotted a basement window that was slightly ajar. It was a casement window, hinged at the top. She wriggled through it backward, held on to the sill with her fingers, and let go. The drop wasn't far, only two feet. She stepped back out of the moonlight that was shining in through the glass—praying that Mallon hadn't seen her. Seconds passed, and then a minute, and then she saw a pair of legs stop by the window. They were joined by another pair.

"Out here? How? They'll know we did it!" a voice said. It was Mallon's. The window was still ajar and Jo could hear him. "We'll say she fell and hit her head on a rock." That was her uncle.

"We've got to find her first," said Mallon.

"You head that way. I'll double back," her uncle said.

They left and Jo sat down heavily on the dirt floor, exhausted. Her uncle was trying to kill her—a man she'd loved and trusted her entire life. A sob burst out of her. She bit her fist to stifle the rest, knowing that if she started, she wouldn't be able to stop. Crying wouldn't get her out of this; thinking would. She calmed herself and tried to figure out her next step.

There would be no help from anyone here. Her uncle had told them all she was insane and had likely signed papers attesting to that. Her only hope was to get to Eddie. He and Oscar would back up her story.

To do that, though, you have to get up, get out of this basement, and get through the gates, she silently told herself.

But how? her mind countered. *They're locked, and the watchman has the key. Flynn had to sneak you in last—*

"Flynn! That's it!" she whispered.

The gravedigger lived on the grounds. He might agree to smuggle her out if she offered him enough money. All she had to do was find his cottage.

If he could get her through the gates, she could work her way south to Reade Street and Eddie's boardinghouse. She stood, heartened by her plan, and fumbled her way across the basement until she found some stairs. She had no idea what lay above her.

"*Fac quod faciendum est,*" she said to the darkness.

And started to climb.

➤ CHAPTER EIGHTY-EIGHT ◄

Jo stood at the top of the basement stairs, her hand on the knob, for nearly a minute before she worked up the courage to turn it.

She opened the door slowly, trying to be as quiet as possible. The hinges whined, but only a little. Stepping through the doorway, she saw that she was in a large kitchen. A range loomed to her right. Pots hung overhead. Two sinks. A wooden icebox.

And a guard.

He was sitting with his back to her. His head, cushioned by his arms, was resting on the large wooden table in front of him. His jacket was draped over the back of his chair. A brass key ring hung from his belt. He was snoring loudly.

Looking all around, Jo saw that the kitchen had a row of windows on the right and an open doorway on the left. She tiptoed through the doorway and found herself in a long, narrow hallway that ran from the back of the building to the front. Directly across that hallway was another, shorter one that terminated in a dead end. It had a single door on its right side.

She walked to that door now, hoping it might be an exit, and saw a sign bolted to it. DANGER: AUTHORIZED ACCESS ONLY, it read.

And below that, MALE WARD FOR THE CRIMINALLY INSANE. A warning followed advising staff to enter in pairs, tuck in loose clothing, and refrain from confrontational behavior.

Thwarted, Jo turned back. She started down the long hallway, walking quietly past the kitchen, where the guard was still snoring peacefully. There were no doors on the left wall of the hallway. On the right, she saw one with a sign that said DAY ROOM and another with a sign that said SUPPLIES, both of which were locked. At the top of the hallway was the front door. To its left was another short hallway, mirroring the one across from the kitchen. It was a second door to the men's ward.

Jo tried the knob to the front door. It was locked. She needed the key to get out. And she knew who had it.

Flattery, Flirtation, Finesse, Fay had said. Those were what was needed to pick a pocket, or lift a ring of keys.

I can do without the first two, Jo thought, hurrying back to the kitchen, *but I'll need plenty of finesse.* Slowly, she tiptoed up behind the guard. Halfway there, a board creaked under her foot and she froze. The guard snorted but didn't wake. She waited for two whole minutes, timing herself by a clock on the wall, then continued. Crouching by his side, she examined his key ring. Five long brass skeleton keys hung from it. Using a light, deft touch—as Fay had taught her—she threaded the fingers of her left hand through the keys to make sure they didn't clink.

Next, she unbuckled the thin leather strap that connected the ring to the guard's belt. Carefully, one hand grasping the brass loop, the other still cushioning the keys, she pulled the key ring free. Now all she had to do was get back down the hallway to the front door. She made her way out of the kitchen and had just stepped into the long hallway when she heard it—a pounding, loud and insistent.

"Open up! Open up in there!" Mallon shouted. His face appeared in the window of the front door. Jo gasped and flattened herself against the wall. There was a light on by the door, but it was dark at this end of the hall. Hopefully, Mallon hadn't seen her.

"What the hell?" said the guard groggily. Jo heard his chair scrape across the kitchen floor. "Who is it?" he bellowed, stumbling across the room.

In two seconds, they'd be face to face. Jo shot into the short hallway that led to the men's ward. She ran past the door to the end of the hallway and squeezed herself into a dark corner. An instant later, the guard rushed out of the kitchen and down the main hallway, buttoning his jacket.

"Let me in! It's an emergency!" Mallon shouted.

"Keep your hair on, will ya? I'm coming!" the guard yelled back. And then, in a panicked voice, he said, "Where are my keys? I haven't got my keys! Wait there, I'll get the master! Wait right there!"

He raced back to the kitchen. Jo heard him swearing and fumbling and then he was running back to the front door. Mallon would soon be in the building. Was her uncle with him?

I'm trapped, she thought frantically. *They'll search this place and find me cowering here. There's nowhere to run.*

And then her eyes fell on the door to the men's ward. There was that second door, covered in warnings like this one, at the front end of the building. The ward ran parallel to the hallway. If she could walk through it while Mallon was coming down the hallway, she might be able to get to the front door. While he was searching the building, she'd be on her way to Flynn's cottage.

Jo jammed one of the skeleton keys into the lock of the men's ward and turned it. Nothing happened. She tried another. And another. And then, just as she heard Mallon enter the building, the fourth key worked. She wrenched the ward door open, stepped inside, and locked it behind her, hoping that her pursuers' footsteps and voices had covered up her noise.

She took a deep breath to steel herself—and immediately

regretted it. The stench of urine and dirty bodies hit her hard. Sighs and moans filled her ears.

Clutching the key ring tightly, she took a step forward. The door to the men's ward had a small window of thick glass. It let in a little light, enough that she could make out a walkway about five feet wide with barred cells at either side of it. Ahead of her, she could see dim light coming in the window of the opposite door.

All she had to do was get to it.

❧ CHAPTER EIGHTY-NINE ❧

"I want to touch you."

"I want to kiss you."

"I want to kill you."

Do you? Well, you'll just have to get in line, sir, Jo thought.

She moved slowly down the walkway, doing her best not to veer from the center. Hands were thrust toward her; fingers clawed at the air. She kept her eyes on the square of light ahead of her and tried not to look at any of the faces pressed to the bars—some furious, some anguished, others hateful. She tried not to see the bodies clothed in nightshirts, straitjackets, or nothing at all. Or hear the voices whispering, wheedling, and hissing.

Heel to toe she walked, one foot in front of the other. The square of light came closer with every step. She was almost at the door when it happened.

One of the patients hurled something at her—something warm and sticky. It hit her arm. Recoiling, she lost her balance, stumbled, and fell. Suddenly there were hands all over her, tugging at her skirt, clutching at her feet and legs. The whispers and growls became shouts.

Jo forced herself not to scream. Someone got hold of her coat and started to pull her toward the bars of his cell.

The keys! Her mind shrieked. *Don't let them get the keys!*

She tossed the ring away, aiming for the center of the path, but it landed well past it. More hands shot from between the bars, straining toward the splayed keys.

Jo's arms were still free. She grabbed the front of her coat and ripped it open. The man tugging on it pulled it off her. She kicked her feet hard, connecting with someone's head. He fell back, howling. She was able to rip her skirt out of someone else's hands, crawl back to the middle of the walkway, and snatch the keys.

Shaking with fear, she scrambled to the door and started jamming keys into the lock. The second one worked. As she pulled the door open, the one at the other end of the ward opened, too.

"Quiet down in there!" the guard bellowed. "What are you— *Hey!*" His eyes widened as he spotted Jo. "Hey, you! Stop!"

Jo shot out of the ward. She ran for the front door and yanked on the knob. It opened and she nearly cried with relief. The guard must've forgotten to lock it after he'd let Mallon in. Slamming it shut, she fumbled a key into its lock, and luckily, her first try worked. Just as the tumblers turned, she felt a hard thump against the door. She looked up and saw Mallon's blood-streaked face in its window. He threw himself against the door again, then shouted for the guard.

Jo yanked the key out of the door, stumbled down the stairs, and ran for Flynn's cottage. She was getting out of this place. She wasn't going to die. Not here. Not tonight.

She didn't see her uncle step out from behind the huge old oak tree in front of her until it was too late.

✶ CHAPTER NINETY ✶

The blow knocked Jo to the ground.

She tried to get up but couldn't. Phillip hauled her to feet and began to drag her through a carpet of wet, rotting leaves to the main building. She fought as hard as she could, kicking, clawing, and slapping her uncle. She screamed the word *murderer* over and over until he backhanded her across the face so hard that she sank to the ground once again, blood dripping from her lip.

He stood over her, breathing heavily. "You stupid little fool!" he spat, his eyes dark with fury. "Why did you have to meddle? You had *everything*! You had Bram Aldrich and a life of ease ahead of you. I saw to it myself. But that wasn't good enough for you, was it? You threw it away!"

Jo, her head bent, started to weep. She would never get to the gates. Would never see her home or her mother again. She would never see Eddie.

"Mallon!" Phillip bellowed. "Over here!"

Footsteps crashed through the brush.

"Get her up," Phillip ordered.

"Why? I say we kill her right here, right now. Bitch broke my nose!" Mallon hissed. He was carrying a good-sized rock in his hand.

"No, too many people are hunting for her. They might see us. We have to go back to the original plan."

"To hell with the plan," Mallon growled.

Jo heard a sickening sound then—a small, metallic click. She recognized it, having shot guns with her father. She closed her eyes, sobbing with fear. She prayed that Mallon had good aim, grateful that at least it would be a bullet—quick and clean, not a rock.

The shot, when it came, was deafening. Jo smelled gunpowder. She felt blood on her cheek, warm and wet. She waited for the pain and the darkness, for the voices around her to fade.

But they didn't.

Instead, a new voice spoke up, loud and clear. "Move an inch, Montfort, and I'll blow your head off as well as your kneecap."

⤚ CHAPTER NINETY-ONE ⤙

"Fay?" Jo whispered, unable to believe her eyes.

"Get her!" Phillip roared, holding his gushing kneecap.

Mallon advanced.

"Sit down, you ugly bastard," Fay said.

When he didn't, she raised her little silver revolver and shot him in the knee, too. He dropped to the ground, screaming in pain. He looked at the ugly hole in his leg, and the dark blood pulsing out of it, and passed out.

"Get up, Jo," Fay said.

Jo rose and staggered to her friend, wiping Phillip's blood off her face as she did. "How did you get here?" she asked, her voice shaking as badly as the rest of her.

"Mad Mary," Fay replied, her eyes on the two men. "Tumbler saw her running up Fourteenth Street like someone had set her on fire. She was crying and carrying on and yelling my name. I was working Union Square, like I do at night. He brought her to me. I got her to calm down and she told me a man had taken you away. She heard him say Darkbriar, told me it was a wicked place and begged me to help you. She knew we were friends; she'd seen us together at the

Brooklyn Bridge. I found a cab and got over here. Mary's still in the cab. She won't come out. What the hell is going on?"

"My uncle's trying to kill me," Jo said. "He's the murderer, not Kinch. Eddie, Oscar, and I . . . we found out that Kinch was Stephen Smith. My uncle tried to have him killed in the Seychelles, but Smith survived, so my uncle had Mallon kill him here at Darkbriar. I never saw the connection. I stupidly told him everything I'd found out and he used it to convince my mother that I'm insane."

"I'll be damned. Your *uncle?*" Fay said. "Why?"

"I don't know," Jo said.

Fay's face hardened. Without any warning, she shot at Montfort again. The bullet buried itself in the ground an inch away from his good knee.

"Talk, Montfort, you son of a bitch," Fay demanded. "Or next time I won't miss."

Phillip Montfort glared at her hatefully. "I've nothing to say to you. Go ahead. Kill me. They'll hang you within a week."

"Oh, I'll kill you, all right," said Fay. "But they won't hang me. I'll be long gone by the time the cops get here. I'll leave this place and melt back into the shadows like I always do. But one night, I'll come out of the shadows and I'll burn your house down. With your family in it. My friend Tumbler will get me in. Ashcan will set the fire. In fact, he'll set two. One at the bottom of your front stairs, one at your back stairs. No one will be able to get out. I'll take them all—your wife, your son, and your daughter—unless you talk. *Now.*"

Jo thought Fay was bluffing, but her uncle must've thought she meant every word she said.

For he closed his eyes as if gathering his strength, then opened them again and began to talk.

✤ CHAPTER NINETY-TWO ✤

"It started in 1871," Phillip said, taking off his belt. He looped it above his knee and pulled it tight. "Van Houten was in trouble. We took on a new partner, Stephen Smith. The money he paid to buy in propped us up for a bit, but it wasn't enough. So we made a plan and bought a ship to carry it out."

"The *Nausett*," Jo said.

"Yes," said Phillip, grimacing in pain.

"But it sank off the Cape of Good Hope."

"No, it didn't. We paid the captain and crew to say it did so we could collect insurance money on it. We changed the ship's name to the *Bonaventure*. We had papers forged identifying her as a Portuguese vessel."

"We?"

"The Van Houten partners."

Jo was afraid to ask her next question. She dreaded the answer. "All of the partners?"

Phillip smiled baitingly. "Are you asking if your father was involved? He was. Everyone was except Stephen Smith. He was too new. We didn't know if we could trust him. We kept the whole thing—the ship, its cargo—a secret from him."

"What cargo?" Jo asked.

Phillip didn't answer her.

"Speed it up, Montfort. We don't have all night," Fay growled, her eyes, and her revolver, trained on him.

"Smith meddled. He discovered what we were doing and tried to make us stop. He found some documents and threatened to make them public if we didn't."

"The manifests. The ones he sent to Eleanor Owens," Jo said.

"Yes," Phillip said. "They contained accounts of the ship's cargo. There were also contracts made with its captain, signed by me. Records of payments made to its crew. And a passbook for a bank in Dar es Salaam into which we funneled the profits. Van Houten would have been ruined if these documents came to light. I couldn't let that happen, so I did what needed to be done. As Montforts always have."

"You abandoned Stephen Smith in the Amirantes," said Jo. "Or had someone else do it. That story about a ship going down in a storm—that was a lie, too, wasn't it?"

Phillip nodded. "I told Stephen we would stop sailing the *Bonaventure* and find new avenues of income. I persuaded him to scout out the Amirantes to see if we could start our own spice plantations there. He went in a small ship, the *Gull*. Smith didn't know it, but the *Bonaventure* preceded him. It waited off the coast of one of the islands, and when it spotted the *Gull*, it approached her. The crew of the *Gull* scuppered their vessel and left Smith on board."

"To *drown?*" Jo said, shocked.

"Yes. The *Bonaventure* carried the *Gull*'s crew to the port of Cochin, in India. There were only four of them, and they were paid well to disappear."

"You tried to take an innocent man's life!" Jo said, her hands clenched. "How could you *do* it?"

"Because no one else had the nerve to. *Fac quod faciendum est*," he said bitterly.

"Did my father know the truth about Smith?"

"I think he suspected. He never challenged me, though. It was easier that way. If he *had* asked me, he would've had to live with the knowledge that his own brother was a murderer. The *Bonaventure* sailed for two more years, until a fire took her." Phillip paused; he smiled darkly. "I have to hand it to Stephen, he kept his word."

"What do you mean?" Jo asked.

"The *Bonaventure*'s captain told me that Smith stood on the deck of the *Gull* as it sank and watched them sail away. There was a moment when the wind died down and they heard him screaming. He said he would come for us one day. For all of us. And he did."

"But why?" Jo asked brokenly. "Why did you kill him?"

"I've just told you," Phillip said coldly.

"No, you haven't. You haven't told me what it was that was worth a man's life."

Phillip was silent.

"Uncle Phillip, what was the *Bonaventure*'s cargo?" Jo demanded.

Phillip looked at her, clear-eyed and unremorseful.

"Slaves," he said.

CHAPTER NINETY-THREE

Jo was reeling. Her entire life, she'd loved her uncle. Over the last few hours, she had come to fear him. Now, she hated him.

"Van Houten sold slaves," she said, trying to fathom the unfathomable. "I don't believe you. You're lying. My father would never do such a thing. *Never.*"

"We sold Africans to buyers in Arabia, Egypt, and Brazil—all of us, your father included. I told you, the firm was on the brink of ruin. How do you think the beautiful life you've always lived was funded? The Gramercy Square mansion, the Adirondack estate, the summers in Newport?" Phillip asked tauntingly.

"That's why you were all afraid," Jo said. "No upstanding companies would do business with slave traders. Especially after the war. No decent people would receive you. Stephen Smith knew that. And when he finally got back to New York, he used it against you."

"Smith made it to one of the islands. That was in '73. He was there for nine years, until a pirate ship picked him up. He was with them for another eight years. He served the captain well, and they let him go eventually. They gave him a bit of money. He used it to get home. He arrived in New York in September, determined to find Eleanor and their child. He didn't know they were both dead."

Jo remembered Smith sitting with Scully. She could hear his voice echoing in her mind.

Seventeen years without the company of another Christian soul. Without kin. Without comfort. Seventeen years of hunger, scurvy, and fever. My aspect is as you have made it. Look upon me and see the monster you have wrought.

Her heart ached for Stephen Smith. For Eleanor. For everything they'd lost.

"How do you know about the island? The pirates?" she asked.

"Charles told me. After the luncheon at his house. After the others had left. He'd seen Smith the night before and wanted to do what Smith demanded. He wanted to hand over Van Houten. He saw no other way."

"But you did," Jo said, bitterness rising in her like bile. She knew what was coming next. She knew what he'd done. And it made her sick to her very soul.

"I wanted to get rid of Smith. Just *him*. But your father wouldn't listen to me. He actually wanted to *help* him. To make reparations. Charles turned on me. After all I'd done for him. The things he had—wealth, respect, influence—he owed them all to me. Because I had the courage to do what had to be done."

"Did you kill Scully and Beekman yourself? Or did Mallon do it?" Jo asked.

Phillip went silent again. Fay, who'd picked up a sturdy stick, whacked his bloodied knee with it as hard as she could. He groaned with the pain, his teeth clenched. Then he leaned over and threw up. Jo watched dispassionately.

"*Talk*. I'm not telling you again," Fay growled.

"I hoped Mallon would find Smith before Smith could get to any of the other partners," Phillip said, wiping his mouth with his sleeve, "but Smith was slippery. He got to Scully and Beekman. They turned on me, too, but Mallon took care of them. And then he found Smith. And when I finally had him, I had my solution—a way to make it all go away."

"By killing him, but not before you pinned all three deaths on him," Jo said.

Phillip hesitated. Fay tapped her stick on the ground and he continued. "There are cells under Darkbriar. Disused. Forgotten. Mallon kept Smith there. He gave him large doses of morphine for several days, and then, when I was ready, he withdrew the drug. I had a plan. I invited Beekman to dine with me so we could discuss Smith. It was a fruitless conversation. When we finished, Beekman headed to Della McEvoy's, as he often did. I walked with him. Mallon was waiting for us in an abandoned building next to Della's with Smith. I'd helped him get Smith there under cover of darkness the night before. We left him in the basement, bound and gagged. Mallon returned the next night, hauled Smith up to the ground floor, and kept watch. When he saw us outside of Della's, he cut Smith's restraints and dragged him out of the building. By that time, Smith was suffering from morphine withdrawal. Badly. He was staggering and raving."

"You made sure you were with Beekman so that you could be attacked, too. To make yourself look like a victim," Jo said.

Phillip nodded. "Mallon killed Beekman immediately. I had him cut me and hit me in the face. Then he put the knife in Smith's hand. I held it there and shouted for help. When the police arrived, they saw me struggling with Smith. I told them Smith had killed Beekman and attacked me. They saw Smith holding a knife, and ranting like a madman, and they believed me."

"Where was Mallon?" asked Jo.

"He'd run back to Darkbriar to change his bloody clothing, start his shift, and wait. Smith was bundled off to Darkbriar at my suggestion. Mallon took over and you know the rest—Kinch the crazed ex-employee confessed his crimes and committed suicide."

"You nearly got away with it," Jo said.

"I still can, if you'll let me."

Jo looked at him uncomprehendingly. "Who *are* you?" she asked.

Her uncle locked eyes with her. "Do you understand what you're setting in motion?" he asked. "The end of everything. Of Van Houten. Our family. Your future. It's not too late. I can make this go away. Just like I made Stephen go away. You can have Bram, Herondale, a life of ease. What more could you want?"

"My father," Jo said, her voice breaking.

For a second, something flickered in Phillip's eyes. Something familiar. Something human. Jo tried to appeal to that as she asked the question that terrified her the most.

"You killed him yourself, didn't you? You, not Mallon."

Before Phillip could answer her, shouts rang out in the darkness.

"Orderlies," Fay said. "They're getting closer. We have to go."

But Jo barely heard her. In her mind, she was no longer on the grounds of Darkbriar; she was inside her father's study. She saw the wrong turns she and Eddie had taken in pursuit of the truth, and the right ones. She saw how it had happened.

"You stayed after the luncheon that day," she said. "You and my father argued. Theakston heard you. You left, and as you did, you took Mrs. Nelson's key, didn't you? The police report said you went to the kitchen to compliment her. It also said she was distraught after my father's body was discovered because she'd *lost* her key and thought the killer might've used it to get inside the house. But it *wasn't* lost. Theakston found it right where it was supposed to be—hanging on its hook in the kitchen. You took it before you left and used it to let yourself into the house later that night so that none of the servants would see you. My father didn't shout for help when you walked into his study. Why would he? He probably welcomed you. You closed the door. The two of you talked. It turned into another argument. He wouldn't go along with your plan to get rid of Smith, so you got rid of him instead. You shot him with your own revolver. He was never suicidal. You made that up to throw the police off the scent. And me as well."

"It was an accident," Philip said pleadingly. "I only meant to scare him. The gun went off in my hand."

Jo shook her head. "You don't know how much I want to believe that," she said.

"It's the truth, Jo. I swear it," Phillip said, pressing a bloody hand to his chest.

"The noise from the gunshot woke the household," Jo continued, ignoring his attempt to sway her. "But you were ready for that. You locked the study door to give yourself a few minutes, then you took my father's revolver out of his cabinet, took a single bullet out of the chamber, put your spent casing in it, and put the gun in his hand. You couldn't leave the bullet to be found, so you slipped it in your coat pocket and hid behind the draperies, but the bullet fell out because there's a hole in your pocket. I know there is. I remember coins falling out of your coat and onto the sidewalk the day of Mr. Scully's funeral."

Phillip nodded, defeated.

"You stayed behind the draperies, perfectly still, until Mrs. Nelson took my mother to her room, and the maids went upstairs to dress, and Dolan went for the coroner, and Theakston and Officer Buckley went to check the back door. Then you hurried down the stairs and out of the front door to your own home. And that's where you were when Pauline arrived to fetch you. After you saw my father's body, you insisted on going to the kitchen for a glass of water. Dr. Koehler and the police captain went with you. You bribed them then to call the death a suicide. They returned to the study to finish their work, and you put Mrs. Nelson's key back on its hook. Just in time for Officer Buckley to do his inventory of the house keys."

Phillip closed his eyes.

"He was your brother," Jo said, anguished. *"Your brother."*

Voices called back and forth. They were much closer this time. Lantern beams shone in the darkness.

"We've *got* to go," Fay said tersely.

But Jo still had questions. "Do you know where the manifests are?"

Phillip said nothing.

"Does Mallon know?" Jo asked. "He was Eleanor's orderly. Did she tell him? Do you have them? Answer me!"

"There they are!" someone shouted. Jo looked up; she saw a man in a white uniform running down the path toward them.

"Story time's over," Fay said. "We're leaving. *Now.*"

➤ CHAPTER NINETY-FOUR ◄

Fay stuffed her revolver into her skirt pocket and grabbed Jo's hand. They ran through the woods until they hit the asylum's stone wall.

"We've got to get to the gravedigger's cottage," Jo said, gasping for breath. "The gates are locked."

"Not anymore. The watchman opened them to let my cab through. I persuaded him to give me the gate key."

"You did? How?" Jo asked.

Fay rolled her eyes.

"Right. The revolver," Jo said.

They set off again, following the wall until they reached the front of the asylum. Fay stopped short of the gates, keeping herself and Jo hidden behind some shrubs. Jo was relieved to see that the gates were wide open, but alarmed by the scene unfolding directly in front of the asylum.

"What's happening? Is that Mary?" she asked.

"Yes, it is, damn it!" Fay hissed. "She's gone *totally* nuts! Look at her!"

Mad Mary was singlehandedly attacking the asylum. The watchman was lying on the ground, unconscious, a rock near his head.

The matron was inside the building, shrieking from a first-floor window. The glass in the front door was smashed. Lights were going on in windows on all the floors. The cab Fay and Mary had arrived in was nowhere to be seen.

"What the *hell* is going on? Why are all the lunatics *outside* the asylum tonight?" Fay asked.

Mary picked up a rock and smashed another window.

"This is not what we need," Fay said. She started toward Mary with Jo on her heels. "Mary! Hey, Mary! Knock it off!" she shouted.

Mary turned around and Jo saw that her face was wet with tears. "Let me go!" she shouted, stamping her foot. "I can't stay here!"

"Who said you had to, you loon!" Fay shouted back. "Come on! Let's *go*!"

In the distance, a siren wailed. Fay grabbed Mary's arm and yanked her away.

"I just shot a man, Mary," she said. "Two, actually. So I need to be gone when the cops show up or I'm going to jail. And you"—she jabbed a finger at Jo—"need to be gone, too. Unless you want to give your uncle another crack at having you committed."

As the siren grew louder, Fay, Jo, and Mary started running for the gates. They'd just reached them when a police wagon turned into the driveway.

Everything happened at once. Jo had no time to react. Five officers jumped out of the police wagon. They surrounded her, Fay, and Mary. The matron dashed out of the asylum, shouting for the officers to put Mary in jail. Orderlies came out of the woods carrying Phillip Montfort and a still-unconscious Francis Mallon on stretchers.

"I'm Sergeant Terence Cronin," the officer in charge yelled. "What's going on here?"

"I'm Phillip Montfort. And that girl there shot me! She also shot an orderly," Phillip said, pointing at Fay. "I want her arrested. That's my niece next to her, Josephine Montfort. She belongs inside the asylum."

"He's lying!" Jo shouted. "He's a murderer. As is that man there." She nodded at Mallon. "He killed my father, Charles Montfort. He's responsible for the deaths of Richard Scully, Alvah Beekman, and Stephen Smith, too. Tonight he tried to kill me. He confessed it all. My friend heard him."

"Who? Fairy Fay?" Cronin said, snorting. "She's a pickpocket! I don't trust anything *she* says."

Jo saw how it would go; the officers would believe her uncle, a powerful man, over herself and Fay.

"Sergeant Cronin, Fay saved my life," Jo said frantically. "I don't belong in Darkbriar and she doesn't belong in jail. You've got to believe me. *Please.* If you put me in that asylum, I won't survive."

"Now, now, miss. We're being a bit dramatic, aren't we?" He walked up to Jo and peered at her face, frowning. "Who put those bruises on you?" he asked.

"My uncle."

"Don't listen to her, you fool! She's a lunatic!" Phillip shouted.

The sergeant's eyebrow shot up at Phillip's arrogant tone. He turned to him. "Now then, sir, who might you be calling a fool?" he asked.

"Do as I say, or I'll have your badge!" Phillip ordered.

"Will you, now?" Cronin turned to his men. "Robinson! Gates!" he barked. "There's an infirmary in the main building. Find some doctors and get these men medical attention. Ryan! Bauer! Take the women downtown. Ladies, you're all under arrest. A judge can sort this mess out in the morning. I'll be damned if I'm doing it."

An officer manhandled Fay over to the police wagon. It took two more to get a howling, struggling Mary over to it.

"I can manage, thank you," Jo said curtly to the officer who approached her.

As she walked to the wagon, the orderlies carrying Phillip's stretcher passed her. Phillip's hand shot out. He grabbed Jo's wrist, his fingers curled painfully into her flesh. The orderlies stopped short. Her uncle's eyes were hard and cold as Jo looked into them. Whatever humanity she'd glimpsed earlier was gone.

He pulled her to him, and in a low, menacing voice said, "Make your next move carefully, Josephine. I've buried quite a few . . . and I can bury you, too."

➤ CHAPTER NINETY-FIVE ➤

Sergeant Cronin and his men searched the three women thoroughly before they put them into the wagon.

Mary didn't like it. She tried to pull away, but Cronin was adamant.

"Can't have one of you knifing another one on the way downtown," he said.

He reached into pockets, inspected collars and cuffs, and searched shoes and boots. He turned up nothing on Jo. Mary had a few coins in her pocket, and an apple, which he gave back to her. She was wearing a necklace. He pulled it out of her blouse, examined it, then let it fall against her chest.

"Have yourself a beau, do you, Mary?" he asked teasingly.

Mary scowled at him and tucked the necklace back inside her shirt. Cronin found Fay's revolver and confiscated it. He knew she had a razor in her mouth and made her spit it out. He also took a man's pocket watch and billfold that he found in her jacket.

"Assault, theft . . . murder, too, if that big lug doesn't wake up. You'll go down this time for certain, Fairy Fay. Hold on, what's this?" he said, pulling Fay's rag doll out of her skirt pocket.

"My good-luck charm," Fay said sarcastically.

Mary grabbed for the little doll. "I want that! Give it to me!" she shouted, over and over. She wouldn't stop.

"Would you give it to her, please, so she shuts up?" Fay asked the sergeant. "We're the ones who have to ride with her."

Cronin handed Mary the doll. She stopped yelling and stared at it intently. "In you go now, Mary," he said.

Mary obediently climbed into the police wagon; then Fay did. Jo was about to follow her when someone shouted her name.

Jo knew who it was before she even turned around. "Eddie!" she cried, overjoyed to see him.

"Inside please, miss," said an officer. He put a firm hand on her back and pushed her into the wagon. Then he slammed the door and locked it. The wagon was enclosed, but it had barred windows on its sides.

Eddie looked through one now. "Jo, my God, it *is* you! Fay? Mad Mary?"

"How'd you find us, Newsie?" Fay asked.

"Tumbler. After you took off with Mary, he came to get me." He snaked a hand through the bars. Jo took it. "What happened?" he asked her. "Are you hurt? Where's your uncle?"

"I'm all right, Eddie, I—"

"Get lost," an officer said, pushing Eddie away from the wagon.

"Where are you taking them?" Eddie demanded.

"To the Tombs."

"What did they do?"

"Escaped from the loony bin, assaulted a watchman, and shot two people."

"You're joking, right?" Eddie said to him.

"There are two men in the asylum's infirmary who'll never walk right again. That sound like a joke to you?" the officer asked. He rapped on the side of the wagon. "All clear!" he shouted. The wagon rolled off.

"Jo!" Eddie shouted, running after it. "I'll get down to the Tombs as soon as I can. Is there anyone—"

The driver snapped his reins. The wagon picked up speed.

"Get Bram, Eddie! Tell him I need a lawyer!"

"I will!" Eddie yelled.

Jo knew that Bram was her only hope. But would he come? He might not. He thought she was crazy. If he didn't, she was lost.

The wagon rolled out of the asylum's gates and Eddie disappeared from Jo's view. It was dark inside the wagon, but one of the officers had left his lantern in the back with them, so they had a bit of light to see by. Narrow wooden benches lined both walls. Jo sat down on one.

Fay sat down across from her and stretched her legs out, a disgusted expression on her face. "How the hell am I going to get out of *this*?" she fumed.

Mary sat down next to Fay. She was still staring at the little rag doll in her hands, and she'd gone dead quiet. Her eyes were brimming with tears.

"What's wrong, Mary?" Jo asked. "Why are you crying?"

Mary didn't say a word. Instead, she pulled the doll's head off.

"Hey! Easy there!" Fay said angrily. "What do you think you're doing?"

But Mary, intent upon her work, continued to rip the doll apart.

"Thanks a lot. I had that doll my whole life," Fay said as she watched pieces of her good-luck charm fall to the wagon's dirty floor. She shook her head. "In case neither of you has noticed, we're in a lot of trouble. Especially me. Can you, Jo, be quiet and can you, Mary, stop ripping things up and let me think?"

As Fay finished speaking, they all heard a metallic clink. A small object had dropped out of the doll's torn body and hit the floor. It glinted in the lantern's light. Jo leaned down to pick it up. It was a ring. Set with sapphires and diamonds.

"Fay," she said quietly. "Give me the lantern."

Fay passed it to Jo, squinting at the ring. "*That* was inside the doll?" she said, sounding surprised. "Wish I'd known."

Jo held the ring close to the light, turning it so she could look inside its band. There was an inscription: *Stephen & Eleanor, March 12, 1873.*

Jo's heart skipped a beat. Her eyes sought Mary's. "It's her, isn't it?" she said. "But how is that possible?"

Mary nodded. She was looking at Fay now. Tears were streaming down her face. She reached for Fay's hand.

Fay took it and patted it distractedly. She wasn't paying any attention to her, or to Jo. "There you are, Mary. Be still now, won't you?" she said.

She didn't *die,* Jo thought. *Mallon took her out of the asylum and sold her. He sold a* child, *damn him.*

"Mary," Jo said, "your necklace . . . the one the policeman was looking at. May I see it?"

"It's mine!" Mary shouted.

"For God's sake, Jo, don't get her going again," Fay said, exasperated.

"Please, Mary, I just want to look at it," Jo said, trying to keep her voice calm, even though her mind was racing. "You've kept it safe for so long. I know you have. I won't take it from you, I promise."

Mary warily pulled the necklace out of her blouse. Without taking it off, she held it up for Jo to see. It was a gold pendant in the shape of half a heart. There was a word inscribed on it. *Stephen.*

Jo leaned back against the wagon's wall, speechless. Charles Montfort, Richard Scully, Alvah Beekman, Stephen Smith . . . they were all victims of her uncle, but there were two more.

"Mary," she finally said. "A woman's body was pulled out of the East River back in 1874. Her face was gone, but she was wearing a jacket and watch that belonged to you. Who was she? Who did your parents bury if they didn't bury you?"

Mary's eyes narrowed. "Lizzie the Cat," she said angrily. "She robbed people, and bit and scratched if they resisted. She took my watch and my jacket. Took my money. Left me to die on the street. But I couldn't die. I had to live. I had to find her. Lizzie got drunk on my money. She fell into the river and drowned. But *I* lived."

"Can you tell me about Stephen?"

Mary shook her head; she started to rock back and forth on the bench.

"Please, Mary," Jo said.

"He gave me a ring. I put it inside the doll I made for her. And I put the doll in a little basket with the clothes I made. I didn't trust them. I thought they would take her from me. I hoped that if they did, they would take the things I made, too, so she wouldn't be cold. I hoped she would keep the doll with her, and that one day she'd feel the ring inside it and take it out and know who she was—mine and Stephen's. Lizzie didn't get Stephen's heart, either, I kept it safe all these years. Stephen died at sea. I heard the newsboys say so. Years and years ago. But his ghost came back. A fearsome ghost with devil's marks on its face. I was afraid when I saw it. Afraid it was angry with me because I lost our baby and couldn't find her again no matter how hard I tried. But now, if I see the ghost again, I can tell it I *did* find her. I can tell it our heart is mended."

Jo handed the ring to Mary. She was in tears now, too, but she was smiling.

Fay, still preoccupied with their dire situation, glanced at Jo. "What's wrong with you? How come you're crying and smiling at the same time? Maybe Montfort's right. Maybe you *have* lost your mind," she said.

Jo reached across the wagon's narrow aisle and took her friend's hand. "Fay, listen to me. . . . You don't know who she is," she said. Her voice, like her heart, was full of emotion.

"Jesus, Jo!" Fay snapped. "I *am* listening! I'm listening to the sound of this wagon on its way to the Tombs. Half an hour from now, I'll be listening to the sound of a cell door slamming shut. A few days from now, I'll be listening as a judge gives me ten years for kneecapping Phillip Montfort. And yes, damn it, I do know who she is. She's Mad Mary!"

"No, Fay, she's not," Jo said. "She's Eleanor Owens. Your mother."

✥ CHAPTER NINETY-SIX ✥

Jo paced back and forth in her cell like a caged tiger.

The Tombs had been built decades ago over a polluted pond, and the stone cells within them were cold, damp, and foul-smelling. Jo had to keep moving just to keep warm.

She stopped suddenly and stared down the dimly lit aisle. *He'll come*, she told herself. *He said he would, and he will.*

She resumed her pacing, exhausted but too anxious to sit down. Behind her on a metal bench, Fay was stretched out asleep, her head in Mary's lap. Mary, smiling, was stroking her hair.

Jo smiled, too. She'd never seen Fay cry, but Fay had cried in the police wagon. The hard, cynical girl had cried buckets. Mad Mary had, too.

Eleanor, Jo told herself. Not Mad Mary. Not anymore.

She looked down the aisle again, wrapping her hands around the bars of her cell, and this time she was rewarded. The security door way down at the end of it opened and a man walked through it.

When she saw him hurrying toward her, a knight in a rumpled tweed jacket, she thought, *No matter what happens to me in the coming days, no matter how bad this all gets, I have been so lucky to know him.*

"Where's your coat?" Eddie Gallagher asked, rushing up to the bars.

"I loaned it to a madman," Jo replied, remembering with a shudder how it had been snatched off her at the asylum.

Eddie immediately took his jacket off and pushed it through to her.

"Did you speak with Bram?" she asked urgently.

"I did. He's on his way," Eddie replied.

As if on cue, the security door opened again and Bram, accompanied by a balding and bespectacled man who looked to be in his early thirties, walked briskly down the aisle.

Relief washed over her. "Thank you, Bram," she said as he reached her cell. She knew he hated the Tombs and all that the place represented, but he'd still come. Because she'd asked him to. Because that was the kind of man he was.

Bram's eyes traveled over her swollen lip, bruised face, and her torn, bloodstained clothing. He swallowed hard. For a second or two, it looked to Jo as if his emotion would get the best of him, but he squared his shoulders and bested it. He was, after all, an Aldrich.

"Jo, this is Winthrop Choate, a friend of mine and a very fine lawyer," he said. "He'll help you."

Choate shook Jo's hand through the bars, then asked her to tell him her entire story—start to finish. She'd just begun when the security door opened a third time. A short man, well-dressed and well-fed, came bustling down the hall, accompanied by an officer.

Jo recognized him; he was John Newcomb, a lawyer retained by her father. And her uncle.

"I want Miss Montfort released into my custody immediately!" he bellowed at the officer. "A jail cell is no place for a frail and unstable young woman. She is supposed to be under a doctor's care!"

"Can't do that, sir. You can talk to her, but that's all. Miss Montfort was arrested, along with the other two women. She'll be arraigned in the morning," the officer explained.

"Arrested? Why? She didn't do anything! She didn't shoot Mr. Montfort, the other girl did!"

"Who did what is for the judge to decide," the officer said.

Newcomb came to a halt at Jo's cell. "Miss Montfort!" he exclaimed, pressing a hand to his chest. "My poor dear girl. I'm so sorry to see you in such a terrible place. I've been sent to fetch you away from here, but I find I am unable to do so. I will, however, secure your freedom tomorrow morning."

Jo should've been relieved to see Newcomb, but she wasn't. Instead, something inside her told her to be wary of him. "Where will you be taking me after I'm released?" she asked him.

"Why, home, of course," Newcomb replied with a smile.

"Who sent you?" she pressed.

"Your family."

"You mean my uncle," Jo said flatly. "My mother doesn't even know I'm here, does she?"

Newcomb hesitated. Only for an instant, but that was long enough for Jo to realize her instincts were correct.

"You're not here to take me home," she said, furious. "You're here to take me back to Darkbriar." For the first time, she was grateful she'd been arrested. While she was in this cell, she was beyond her uncle's reach. "You're Phillip Montfort's lawyer, not mine. I've taken my own counsel. Mr. Winthrop Choate will be representing me, as well as Miss Eleanor Owens and Miss Fay *Smith*. Good evening, Mr. Newcomb."

Newcomb, flushing with anger, said, "Your uncle and mother have signed the papers necessary to have you committed. I'd advise you to come peacefully after I've posted your bail. If you do not, I'll have you forcibly removed from the courtroom and brought to the asylum."

"Try it, fat boy," Eddie said.

"Where are the papers you cite, counselor?" Winthrop Choate asked, stepping forward. "I'd like to see them."

"Who the devil are you?" Newcomb spat, looking him up and down.

"Winthrop Choate. Miss Montfort's attorney. The papers?"

"At the asylum, of course!"

Choate frowned regretfully. "I'm afraid you'll have to present them to a judge for verification before I can allow you to take custody of my client."

Newcomb turned crimson. He leaned in close to the bars. "You're playing a dangerous game, Miss Montfort. One you can't hope to win," he warned. Then he stalked off, slamming the security door on his way out.

Jo flinched at the sound. Choate had brought a briefcase with him. He was digging through it now.

"We need to work fast, Miss Montfort," he said, pulling out a pad and pen. "If the papers Newcomb spoke of actually exist, he could make trouble for us. Tell me everything that led up to tonight. Leave nothing out."

Jo looked at Eddie, the man she'd lost. Her eyes traveled to Bram and knew—by the expression on his ashen face—that she'd lost him, too. She thought of her mother, their home, Miss Sparkwell's School, her friends . . . and realized that she would lose more, much more, before the night was over.

She took a deep breath, and began.

➤ CHAPTER NINETY-SEVEN ⤙

Two hours later, just past midnight, Winthrop Choate stopped writing. He looked at Jo and said, "Is that everything?"

"Yes," Jo replied tiredly.

She sat down on the cell's bench. Fay was still asleep, her head still resting in Eleanor's lap. Eleanor, wary and watchful, was awake. Eddie, who hadn't been present for most of what occurred at Darkbriar, was busy writing down everything that had transpired there. Bram was leaning against the bars of the cell opposite Jo's, looking as if he'd been hollowed out.

Choate's glasses had slid down his nose. He pushed them back up.

"Phillip Montfort will be a lethal opponent, but I expect you already know that," he said. "Any hope we have of besting him rests on finding the letters Stephen Smith sent to Miss Owens. Without them, we have no proof of Van Houten's crimes. What Phillip Montfort confessed to you on the grounds of the asylum, he can—and will—deny. He'll say he feared for his life and made the whole thing up to keep Miss Smith from killing him."

Jo nodded. A heavy sense of dread had settled over her. Choate had questioned her closely as she'd told her story. Again and again he'd asked her if she had any proof of her claims. It was with a sinking feeling that she told him she had very little—only her father's agenda. Jo recalled showing it to her uncle in his study, weeks ago. He'd asked if he could have it, but she'd kept it. She *had* unwittingly given him the only other piece of evidence, though—the pendant with *Eleanor* on it. He'd probably gotten rid of it the moment she'd left his house, just as he would've gotten rid of her father's agenda.

"Mr. Choate," she said.

"It's Win."

"Win, can you have the police enter the Owenses' home and search for the manifests?"

"With a warrant, yes," Choate said, looking at her over the top of his glasses. "The question is: can I convince the judge who would issue the warrant that the manifests still exist?"

Jo realized that there was one person who could answer that question. She turned to the woman sitting next to her.

"Eleanor," she said. "Mr. Choate and I are going to try very hard to make sure that we all gain our liberty, but you have to help us. Can you do that?"

Eleanor bit her lip. She stroked Fay's hair. And said nothing.

"I need you to think back a long time ago, to when Stephen was still alive."

Eleanor clenched one hand into a fist and banged it repeatedly on the bench.

"Did Stephen send you letters from Zanzibar?"

Eleanor stopped banging her fist. She nodded. "He said he would come for me," she whispered, looking at the floor. "He said he would, but he died before he could, and then the ghost came instead." She pounded the heel of her hand against her forehead.

Jo gently took her hand and held it. Eleanor Owens was a broken human being, a woman who'd had everything taken from her. She'd survived the loss of the man she loved and their baby. She'd survived incarceration in an asylum and life on the streets of New York. But despite it all, she'd never given up hope that one day she'd find her daughter.

It was to that survivor, to that fighter, that Jo now appealed.

"Can you remember where those letters are, Eleanor? Please, for Fay's sake, for your daughter's sake, tell me where they are."

Eleanor leaned close to Jo. "Safe under the heavens," she whispered. "The gods watch over them. And us."

Jo tried to mask her frustration. She'd heard this nonsense from Sally Gibson, who'd heard it from the Owenses' former cook.

"Please, Eleanor," she said. "*Tell me where the letters are.* If we can't find them, then I'm going to the madhouse, Fay's going to prison, and you're back on the streets."

"Safe under the heavens," Eleanor repeated. "Guarded by the sun and the moon."

Eddie, listening to Eleanor's replies, said, "Jo, maybe she's referring to something. You searched her room. I searched the basement. No one searched the rest of the house. Is there something—a painting, maybe—that has a sun and moon in it? Did you see anything on your way to her room?"

Jo closed her eyes and tried to picture the Owenses' house. She saw the servants' quarters in her mind's eye. The kitchen. The back stairs. The hallway. Eleanor's room. And the back garden. She saw Stephen Smith standing in it. Looking up at her with his fierce eyes from the bower. Under the marble statues of Helios and Selene.

Jo's eyes flew open. "I know where they are!" she cried.

"Where?" Eddie said.

"In the bower. There are two statues there. One's Helios, the sun god. The other's Selene, goddess of the moon."

"Guarded by the sun and moon," Bram echoed.

"Good job, Jo!" Eddie said excitedly.

Win said, "I'll draw up the papers right away and take them

to the judge myself. We'll serve the warrant first thing. With any amount of luck, we'll have the manifests in hand before Newcomb gets back from the asylum. But, Jo, I must ask you something. . . ."

"Yes?"

"Are you sure about this? Not just about the manifests, about all of it? Because none of it will stay private. In a day, two at the most, all of New York will know about your uncle and your father and what they did. There's no putting the genie back in the bottle."

Jo looked at Win, trying to voice her answer. She thought about the photograph hanging in the foyer of Van Houten's Wharf—the one of her father and uncle in Zanzibar, so many years ago. Her heart clenched. She'd loved her father, and she missed him, but she knew that she would spend the rest of her life trying to reconcile the good man she remembered with the terrible thing he'd done.

How many lives had he and her uncle already stolen when that picture was taken? How many people had they enslaved? Wives and husbands torn apart. Children ripped from their parents' arms. She thought about another stolen child—Fay. She remembered the expression on her face, and on Eleanor's, when they realized they were mother and daughter. Sixteen long years it had taken Eleanor Owens to find her daughter. Poor Stephen Smith never did.

"Yes, Win," Jo finally said. "I'm sure."

Bram stepped forward. "My God, Jo, don't do this," he said. "There must be another way."

"There's only one right way, though," Jo said. She gave him a smile, one made up of courage, fear, and loss all mixed together. She was finally stepping off that cliff.

"You'll destroy your entire family," he said.

"My uncle destroyed my family. My father, too. Years ago in Zanzibar."

She turned to Eddie then. He'd finished writing. He'd closed his notebook. She knew that what he had on those pages would ruin her life, and launch his. It was a huge scoop and would surely land him the job he wanted.

"I don't have to, Jo," he said, reading her mind. "Somebody else can report this one."

Jo shook her head. "I thanked you when I first met you. Thank you again, Eddie."

"For what? Landing you in a nuthouse? And then in jail?" he joked, walking up to the bars of her cell.

"For helping me find the truth."

Eddie grasped one of the cold iron bars. "The truth costs, Jo. Dearly," he said. "I hope you know that."

She nodded, and covered his hand with her own. For an instant, their fingers entwined. For an instant, she'd never doubted him. She'd never faltered. She'd never said yes to Bram. For an instant, he was hers again.

"Lies cost more," she said regretfully.

She stepped back from the bars and with a sad smile said, "Go, Eddie. Hurry. Before the rest of Park Row gets wind of it. You finally have your story."

➤ CHAPTER NINETY-EIGHT ◄

Gramercy Square
March 3, 1891

Jo moved through the empty rooms of her house one by one, feeling every bit as hollow as they were.

She ran a hand over the marble mantel in her dining room and traced a shadow on the wallpaper where a picture had hung. Her boot heels echoed on the bare wood floors.

She'd had so many happy times in this house—Christmases, birthday parties, fancy dinners. She could almost hear her father's voice welcoming family and friends.

Those times were gone now, as he was, never to return.

The furniture had been auctioned off. The house had been sold. A family from Philadelphia had bought it. The father was a new sort of man, one who owned a typewriter factory. He would make an unusual addition to Gramercy Square.

The *Standard* had been sold, too. Eddie now worked at the *Tribune*. He'd been hired for his scoop on the sensational Van Houten story. Almost overnight, he'd become the most widely read reporter in New York. Jo was happy for him. She'd written to tell him so. She hadn't seen him since the trial. He was very busy now. At least, that's what he said.

Jo was waiting to say goodbye to her mother. Anna was leaving for Winnetka this afternoon, to live near her sister.

"It's far away from New York," she'd said after she'd announced her plan to Jo, "but not far enough, I fear. Nowhere is far enough. Not after all that has happened."

The Montforts were no more. They no longer existed. Not to anyone, as Grandmama would say, who mattered. They existed for the *rest* of New York, though. Their story had been on the front page of every city paper for the last three months—ever since the day Jo had walked out of the Tombs.

Early that morning, Win Choate had traveled to Gramercy Square to inform Anna Montfort what had happened at Darkbriar. As soon as Anna had recovered from the shock, she'd rescinded the papers she'd signed to have Jo committed. At the arraignment for Jo, Fay, and Eleanor, the judge had charged Fay with shooting Phillip Montfort and Francis Mallon. Eleanor had been charged with assault, for knocking out Darkbriar's watchman, as well as vandalizing the asylum. No charges were leveled against Jo. Her assault on Francis Mallon was seen as self-defense. Win had persuaded a judge to set bail for Fay and Eleanor, and Anna paid it.

"We're jumping bail, me and Eleanor," Fay had whispered to Jo as they'd left the courtroom. She was terrified that the charges against her would stick and she'd be sent to prison. She didn't trust the cops or the courts to give her a fair shake. "I'll pay you back the bail money someday. I swear it," she'd said.

"You'll do no such thing," Jo had told her. "Van Houten owes you and Eleanor that money. That, and a great deal more. Go now. Hurry. And for God's sake, Fay, be careful."

As Fay and Eleanor had dropped out of sight, Jo found herself thrust directly into the spotlight.

With Win Choate at her side, she'd leveled her own charges. She accused her uncle and Francis Mallon of a host of crimes, including slave trading, insurance fraud, battery, kidnapping, attempted murder, and murder.

A grand jury had been convened, and its members had listened to testimony from Jo, Eddie, and several others involved in the case. Win Choate thought Eddie might try to invoke his First Amendment rights as a member of the press, and refuse to testify, but he didn't. He'd told the jury everything he'd seen, heard, and done in connection with the case. His account had corroborated Jo's and had been instrumental in obtaining indictments against both Phillip Montfort and Francis Mallon.

Newsrooms had erupted when the charges were made public. Reporters had camped out at the courthouse and on the steps to the Montfort home. Jo's picture, descriptions of her gestures, her clothing, even details of how she wore her hair, were all anyone talked about.

New Yorkers had devoured every detail of the story. Every man in the street knew how the Owenses had refused to believe their daughter was alive, and had tried to bar the police from entering their home. Win had had a search warrant issued, and the mysterious manifests had been found—right where Jo thought they'd be. They'd been wrapped up well and protected from weather, and they clearly detailed Van Houten's slave trading.

Because of them, Phillip Montfort had been doomed in the court of public opinion even before his actual trial had even begun. Throughout the trial, Phillip's lawyer, John Newcomb, maintained that his client was innocent of all charges. Mallon, however, folded on the second day.

On that morning, the prosecution called two eyewitnesses—a

sailor and a barkeep—who'd come forth after reading Eddie's reports. Both men swore under oath that they'd seen Mallon at Van Houten's Wharf with Scully the night of Scully's death. Scared, Mallon turned on Montfort and made a full confession. He told the court that Montfort had paid him to kill Richard Scully, Alvah Beekman, and Stephen Smith, and to assault Edward Gallagher and Josephine Montfort. Mallon insisted he hadn't killed Charles Montfort, however—Phillip Montfort had done that himself.

While on the stand, Mallon explained how his and Montfort's relationship had begun—and how Eleanor Owens's child had ended up with Jacob Beckett, a denizen of Mulberry Bend who was also known as the Tailor.

Montfort, Mallon said, had first approached him in 1874, during a trip home from Zanzibar. He'd returned to New York, ostensibly to visit his wife, young son, and baby daughter, but the trip's real purpose was to deal with Eleanor Owens. He knew she was Smith's fiancée and that Smith had sent her proof of the firm's slave trading.

Mallon explained that a private detective had done some sleuthing for Phillip and had found out that Eleanor was in Darkbriar and why. The detective put Mallon, who admitted that he was always looking for a way to make a few extra dollars, in touch with Phillip Montfort.

Phillip, convinced that Eleanor and her child posed a threat, asked Mallon to take care of them. Mallon told Phillip the child was supposed to go to an orphanage, but that wasn't good enough for Phillip. He worried that she might one day try to find out who her real parents were and what had happened to them, and he didn't want that.

Mallon found that he could not kill a child, but he still wanted Phillip's money. So with the help of a crooked undertaker, he procured a dead infant and switched it with Eleanor's baby. The asylum's overworked doctor merely glanced at the baby, signed the death certificate, and continued on his rounds. The switched baby was buried at Darkbriar, but Eleanor was never told her child had died. The doctor thought her too fragile to bear such hard news, so he instructed Mallon to tell her that the baby had been taken to an orphanage, where it would find a loving home.

Mallon, meanwhile had spirited the child, along with the basket of things Eleanor had made for it, out of Darkbriar and sold her to the Tailor—with a warning that she must never learn the truth of her parentage. Neither Mallon nor the Tailor had any idea that the little rag doll tucked into the baby's basket contained her mother's engagement ring.

A subpoena had been issued to the Tailor to answer Mallon's accusation. He'd objected but had been hauled into court anyway. There, he'd denied buying Fay and claimed that he'd found her abandoned in a tenement stairwell clutching the rag doll. He'd insisted he'd raised her with great care, loved her as if she were his own, and wanted her found and returned home to him.

Oscar Rubin had also been called to testify. He stated that the injuries on all four dead men were inconsistent with the official reports of their deaths and then explained why to the jurors. Newcomb had objected to almost everything Oscar said, but to everyone's surprise, the judge had overruled him. Both judge and jury were fascinated by Oscar's compelling arguments and by the science behind them.

Eddie had followed Oscar to the stand and had repeated for the jury everything he'd told the grand jury. The late Charles Montfort's household staff had been called, as well as Van Houten partners Asa Tuller and John Brevoort; Jackie Shaw; Samuel and Lavinia Owens; Sally Gibson; Simeon Flynn, Darkbriar's gravedigger; Ada Williams, one of its matrons; Alfred Black, its watchman; Lucy Taggart, a young woman in the employ of Della McEvoy; and various police officers who'd either arrested Jo, Fay, Eleanor, and Kinch or who'd been involved in the investigations of the death of Charles Montfort, Richard Scully, and Alvah Beekman. The *Bonaventure*'s manifests had been shown to the jury, as well as Charles Montfort's agenda and the bullet Jo had found on the floor of her father's study.

When Jo herself had finally taken the stand, a hush had fallen over the courtroom. The reporters present had strained to hear her every word. After all, what she said could well send her own uncle to death row. Newcomb had done his best to trip Jo up during his cross-examination, but he'd failed. Jo had recounted the events that followed her father's death clearly and with conviction, and it had been obvious to everyone in the courtroom that the jury believed her.

Though the case against Phillip Montfort and Francis Mallon had been built entirely on circumstantial evidence, by the time closing arguments had begun, all of New York had been certain both defendants would be convicted. And they almost were, but at the last moment, John Newcomb pulled off a shocking surprise.

The very morning that the prosecution was scheduled to begin its closing arguments, Newcomb had stunned the jury by declaring that Phillip Montfort had confessed to killing his brother.

The courtroom had erupted into such chaos that the judge had broken a gavel trying to restore order. When everyone had finally settled down, Newcomb had stated that the night before, a highly agitated Phillip Montfort had summoned him to the Tombs and had told him that he had to confess. He'd shot his brother, yes, but it had been a terrible accident.

Phillip Montfort, Newcomb had said, had been driven insane by remorse over Van Houten's slave trading. He'd started having visions of hell, and believed he would go there because of his crimes. He'd begun to carry his gun with him everywhere he went. One night, he'd gone to visit Charles, desperate to unburden himself. While he was there, he'd become certain that Charles himself was the devil. In a fit of terror, he'd pulled out his gun, and somehow it had gone off. Scared that another demon would come after him for killing his own brother, Phillip made the death look like a suicide, hid behind the study's curtains, and later escaped.

Newcomb had then informed the court that upon hearing Montfort's confession, he'd sent for a doctor. The doctor had examined Montfort and had declared him to be delusional and completely unfit to stand trial.

Newcomb had then produced the doctor, who'd repeated his diagnosis for the court. Court had been adjourned and a second doctor had been summoned. He'd confirmed the first doctor's findings, and the next day, Phillip Montfort was on his way to the Asylum for Insane Criminals in Auburn. The newspapers had all opined that the doctors had been paid off by Newcomb, but nothing could be proved.

Jo hadn't accepted her uncle's claim that the shooting was an accident. He'd tried to get her to believe the very same thing at Darkbriar. Nor had she believed he was mentally unsound. Newcomb had made a bold last-ditch effort to save her uncle's neck, and it had worked. Jo would have felt no happiness had her uncle received the death penalty, and she felt no anger at the turn of events—just a deep, abiding grief. Her father was dead. Now her uncle was, too. Dead to her, at least. He had been ever since their carriage ride to Darkbriar.

The papers were disappointed that Montfort had escaped the electric chair—the state's recently adopted means of dispatching death row inmates—but most agreed that there was poetic justice in his ending up in an asylum after he'd tried to force his niece into one.

A day after Phillip Montfort was packed off to Auburn, Francis Mallon was convicted of two counts of battery, three counts of murder in the first degree, and one count of kidnapping. Jacob

Beckett steadfastly maintained that he had never seen Mallon in his life, and that he'd found Fay, not bought her. No charges were brought against him.

Mallon was sentenced to death, but the judge commuted the sentence to life in prison in consideration of his testimony against Montfort.

And then the whole ugly thing was over, and Jo was left to cope with the aftermath. As Bram predicted, she destroyed not only Phillip, but her entire family. The old guard no longer received the Montforts. Madeleine, Caroline, and Robert had moved to Oregon. Asa Tuller and John Brevoort were shunned for their participation in the slave trade and, together with their families, also left New York.

Anna had taken it all very hard, but she weathered her losses with courage and grace. Phillip Montfort, a man she'd loved and trusted, had killed her husband. That same husband had been a party to slave trading. And she'd nearly committed her own child to a madhouse—an act she deeply regretted and one for which she had apologized to Jo.

All that Charles had procured for the family was sold and the monies donated to various charities. The things Jo's mother had brought to the marriage—the Gramercy Square town house, jewels, and many fine heirlooms—were also sold. Anna planned to live on the proceeds.

Anna had also set up an investment fund for Jo, one that would give her about five hundred dollars a month. It was nowhere near the money Jo would have had at her disposal if she'd said nothing, done nothing, and married Bram, but it would keep her.

Throughout the ordeal, Jo had gained a new appreciation for her mother. She admired her toughness, her resilience, and her insistence on doing not just what was required, but what was right. *Breeding*, Grandmama Aldrich would have called it. Jo liked the word *character* better.

"Josephine!" Anna called out now.

She'd just come downstairs and was full of last-minute instructions. The plan was for her to go to Winnetka ahead of Jo and ready their new home. It was a modest house, but it was in the best neighborhood. Jo would stay behind for a week to make sure their last few pieces of furniture were taken to the auction house and that any remaining bills were paid.

There was no question of her returning to Miss Sparkwell's. She'd received a letter from the headmistress saying that in light of the tragic death of her father, and other subsequent events, it might be better for Jo, who must be in a very fragile state, to not return to school this year. *Or ever,* Jo thought, reading between Miss Sparkwell's lines.

"You'll need to take the papers to the lawyer's office, and don't forget to bring the keys to the new owners. They're staying at—"

"The Fifth Avenue Hotel! You told me five times, Mama!" Jo protested.

Anna buttoned her fur coat up around her neck. "Do you have your own train tickets? Yours and Katie's?" she asked.

"Yes, Mama." Katie was to accompany Jo to Winnetka as her chaperone.

"Make sure you lock the doors at night and leave no lamps burning. Mr. Theakston is no longer here to check."

They'd let him go last week.

"I will. Your cab is here," Jo said. "If you don't leave now, you'll miss your train."

Anna kissed Jo, bade her goodbye, and headed for the door. She stopped as she reached it, however, and turned around one last time.

"I am very sorry, Josephine," she said with a voice full of feeling.

"For what?" Jo asked, unused to such a tone from her mother.

"For all the things you've lost," Anna replied. And then, in a rare display of emotion, she walked back to Jo, took her face in her hands, and kissed her again. "But you are a different sort of girl. Not at all what I expected you to be. And this is a different sort of time. And so I am hopeful for all the things you may yet find."

And then she was gone, out the door and down the steps, and it felt to Jo as if they'd said *adieu*, not *au revoir*. She had the urge to run to her mother and embrace her, but she told herself she was being childish. And she knew full well how her mother would react to dramatic scenes enacted upon the sidewalk. So she simply watched her carriage until it turned off Gramercy Square and disappeared.

How odd it feels to be standing in my own doorway, she thought. It had always been Theakston's job to see people off. For a few seconds, she almost missed him.

She shivered in the cold winter air and turned to go inside. As she did, a voice called her name.

Jo turned and smiled at the handsome young man at the bottom of the stoop.

It was Bram Aldrich, Elizabeth Adams's fiancé.

➤ CHAPTER NINETY-NINE ◀

"January's come and gone already. We're well into the new year. Time moves so fast," Bram said wistfully, staring at the bare trees, their branches dusted with snow. He turned to Jo. "I hear you're heading to Winnetka. What will you do there?"

"I haven't the faintest idea," Jo said. "Something, I hope."

"You liked to write. Couldn't you do that? During the trial, you said you posed as a reporter."

Jo laughed. "I did, yes. But posing as one and being one are two different things. Winnetka is not New York. Not every town is eager to have its very own Nellie Bly."

She and Bram were sitting on a bench in Gramercy Park. He'd brushed the snow off it. He'd been walking past her house on his way to the Rhinelanders' for tea when he'd spotted her on her stoop and asked her to take a walk with him.

Jo had immediately agreed and fetched her coat, hat, and gloves. She felt her mother's absence keenly and wasn't looking forward to being in her sad, empty house with only Katie for company.

Bram had broken off their engagement weeks ago. Grandmama had had such severe heart palpitations when she'd been told about

Jo's arrest that the doctor had been called. She'd insisted she was on her deathbed and that the only thing that would bring her out of it would be for Bram not to marry into a family with such a strong streak of insanity running through it.

Jo had expected this and was not saddened by it, only relieved. She returned his ring, telling him that the one thing she would like to keep was his friendship. He'd smiled at that and said, "Always, Jo."

"I—I've wanted to tell you something," he said now. He'd removed his hat and was fidgeting with the brim. "With everything that happened, I never got the chance."

"What is it?" Jo asked.

"I wanted to say that I'm sorry. For thinking you were insane."

"It's all right, Bram. I can hardly blame you. Anyone would have thought I was mad if they'd seen me as you did—on a city street in the dead of night, filthy as a pig, saying I'd just dug up a body. Everyone else in this city *still* thinks I'm crazy."

"I'm so glad you sent for me. I'm glad I brought Win. I'm glad your uncle and Francis Mallon are behind bars. When I think of what could have happened to you . . ." He trailed off.

"I played right into Phillip's hands from the very beginning. He couldn't have plotted it more perfectly. He almost got away with it."

"But you're free now," Bram said.

"Thank goodness."

"From Phillip. From everything and everyone and all their expectations."

"I suppose I am."

"I wonder what that's like," Bram said, so quietly that Jo almost didn't hear it. He looked at his watch. "Four o'clock already." He sighed. "I'd best not be too terribly late to the Rhinelanders' tea." He turned to her. "I'm glad we had the chance to talk. I'll miss you, Jo. You've made the last few months very exciting."

"You'll have plenty of excitement with a wedding to plan," Jo said. "I hear Elizabeth went to Paris to be fitted for her gown by Monsieur Worth himself. If I know her, it will be the event of the year."

"Yes, it will. I'll be a married man in June, I'm afraid. I won't be able to get out of *this* engagement unless Elizabeth, too, ends up in jail," Bram joked.

Jo laughed. "There are worse things than marrying a beautiful and charming girl," she said. "Elizabeth will make a good wife. She cares for you. Why, I've heard she's even succeeded in winning Grandmama over. If that's not love, what is?"

Bram laughed, too. "She likes Herondale very much, it's true. And spaniels."

"You are of one mind, then. That's important."

"On most things, yes," Bram allowed. And then with a sudden, fierce honesty he said, "You're very brave, Jo. I wish I were half as brave."

Jo heard the emotion in his voice and realized that they'd talked more honestly in the last half hour than in all the years they'd known each other.

"I don't feel brave, Bram. I feel scared," she said. "I always thought I knew what life held in store. Miss Sparkwell's. Dances and parties. You, one day. I thought, right up to the end, that I would find my way back to my world. To *our* world. But I didn't. I got lost. I *am* lost." She shook her head. "*Winnetka?* My God. What on earth will I do there? Wither and die."

"No, Jo. Not you. Withering's not in your nature."

He had said so much to her, and yet—looking into his eyes—Jo had the feeling there was much he had not said. She wondered if she'd misjudged him. Maybe there were secret dreams hidden in his heart, too. Things besides land deals and railway routes that he wished he could pursue. If there were, she would never know them. Such secrets were for Elizabeth to unlock now, not her.

They both stood. Jo offered him her hand, but instead of taking it, he folded her into his arms and held her tightly. "Goodbye, my darling Jo," he said. "I'd wish you good luck, but you won't need it. You get to write your own story now. Nothing's luckier than that."

He walked away from her then, down the well-trodden path through the park. With each step, he got smaller. More indistinct. Until he was only one figure among many.

As she watched him go, Jo felt like she was looking at a man in a photograph.

An image of the past.

Blurry and faded.

And gone.

✦ CHAPTER ONE HUNDRED ✦

"Come on, Katie!" Jo shouted. "Run! We're going to miss the train!"

"We wouldn't if you hadn't dallied!" Katie shouted back.

Jo and Katie were hurrying into the Grand Central Depot. Their train was due to leave in five minutes. It would take them to Chicago where they would change to one bound for Winnetka. Jo hadn't intended to leave Gramercy Square quite so late, but things had come up.

Jo had been busy in the week since her mother had left and today was no exception. Her mother's lawyer had stopped by that morning with a sheaf of papers for Jo to take to her. And then she'd remembered she hadn't been to the post office to have their mail forwarded. The clerk had given her a form to fill out and handed her a stack of letters that had just arrived. She'd thanked him and had run back home to get Katie.

At least they didn't have many bags to slow them down—only one valise each. Katie would be paid well for making the trip out and back, but she wasn't happy about it. She had a new beau and wanted to be with him.

"*You* need a chaperone?" she'd scoffed, when Jo asked her to accompany her. "For what? In case a man looks at you the wrong way?

Just pull out a gun, like your good friend the pickpocket, and blow his kneecaps off."

Jo searched the departures board for their train's track number and learned that it was delayed by twenty minutes. "Oh, thank goodness!" she said. "Let's take a seat and catch our breath."

She and Katie settled themselves on a wooden bench near the ticket window. As Katie opened a newspaper she had with her, Jo looked around at the people nearby. She saw a family with five boisterous children. Two elderly women—sisters, from the looks of them. A traveling salesman with a sample case. A handful of businessmen. Two women wearing hats with heavy veils over them passed in front of her. A newsie bellowed the day's headlines. A boy shouted his shoe-shining services. A girl walked by selling pretzels.

And Jo realized, with a heavy heart, that these passing minutes were the last ones she'd spend in New York, the city where she'd been born and raised. Her heart felt as if it were breaking. *How can I leave?* she wondered. But how could she stay? The house was sold. Her train tickets were bought.

She decided to distract herself from her sadness by going through the mail she'd picked up earlier. There was a letter to her mother from the bank. Another from the auction house. There were various bills from tradesmen.

And there was a letter for her. From Eddie. Her heart leapt when she saw it. She tore it open eagerly and read it.

March 9, 1891

Dear Jo,
I owe you something—an answer.
You asked me some time ago at Child's if I was sorry.
I didn't give you a reply then. I couldn't.
I can now, so here it is: I'm not sorry.

I'm angry and sad, but I'm not sorry and I never will be.
Good luck to you in Winnetka. I'll miss you.
New York won't be the same without you.

Yours,

Eddie

Jo put the letter back in its envelope with shaking hands. *Bram said I'm brave,* she thought. *But I'm not. I'm a coward. I'm more scared right now than I was when my uncle tried to kill me.*

Because I love Eddie Gallagher.

I love him and I'm scared to death he doesn't love me anymore. That it's too late. That he can't forgive me and he'll always be angry at me for foolishly choosing Bram.

Jo heard a man's voice shout that the Chicago train was boarding.

"That's us," Katie said. She unbuckled her valise to tuck her newspaper inside it.

But Jo remained where she was, unable to move.

The two women wearing veils whom she'd seen earlier walked by her again. They were only about two yards away, and she could hear them talking. The taller one was urging the shorter one along. They went to the ticket window and the taller one told the agent that she needed two tickets to Chicago. Her voice sounded confident, but Jo saw that her gloved hand was knotted into a fist.

Jo knew that voice.

"I'm sorry, miss," the window agent said. "Today's train is sold out. I can sell you tickets for tomorrow's."

"There's no other train we can take today?" the tall woman asked, her voice fraught with worry.

And no wonder, Jo thought. *She's a fugitive. The police are after her. She jumped bail and was declared in contempt of court for failing to testify at my uncle's trial. I wonder if she knows that. I wonder if she knows the Tailor's after her, too, because Madam Esther wants the goods she paid for.*

Jo stood up. She walked up to the women. "Here," she said, handing the tall one her tickets. "Use our names until you get to Chicago so the police don't catch wind. Or the Tailor. Then make up new ones. Be careful."

She turned to go, but the tall woman grabbed her wrist. "Do you remember the walk we took? Over the Brooklyn Bridge?"

Jo nodded.

"We talked about freedom," the woman said. "It's all I ever wanted and now I have it, thanks to you. My mother, too. Without you, she'd still be on the streets and I'd be at Madam Esther's, and neither of us would ever have found the other. Freedom *is* the best thing. Thank you for mine, Jo Montfort. I'll never be able to repay you."

Jo pulled her into a fierce embrace. "You already have."

The two women held each other tightly. And then a conductor hollered a final boarding call for the train to Chicago.

"Go," Jo said. "Hurry."

Fay Smith and Eleanor Owens rushed to the train. As Jo watched them go, Katie walked up to her.

"Are we getting on or not?" she asked, buckling her valise.

"We are not," Jo said. "I've changed my mind. I'm not going to Winnetka. Or anywhere else. I just gave our tickets away."

"You did *what?*" Katie squawked. "Who'd you give them to?"

"To a friend," Jo said. "The best one I ever had."

She kept watching until Fay and Eleanor stepped onto the train; then she walked out of the gloom of Grand Central with Katie on her heels, and into her city's gray winter light.

➤ *EPILOGUE* ◄

Chelsea
March 23, 1891

"Goodbye, Jo! Knock 'em dead!" Sarah Stein called out.

"I will, and then I'll bring the bodies to you!" Jo called over her shoulder.

Sarah laughed her noisy honking laugh and waved goodbye with a bloody scalpel. She was busy dissecting a cow's eyeball at their kitchen table. Jo closed the door to their apartment and trotted down the stairs of their building.

They were roommates, Jo and Sarah. Jo had bumped into Sarah in the office of a rental agency. Sarah had come to post an ad for a roommate, as hers had just left to get married, and Jo had come to post an ad for a room. Now they lived together in the Jeanne d'Arc, a redbrick building on Fourteenth and Seventh, in what was called a French flat—a small, self-contained suite of rooms complete with a tiny kitchen and private bathroom. For the first time in her life, Jo could come and go from her home as she pleased without reasons and excuses and chaperones.

Freedom, she thought as she pushed the building's door open and walked outside. *It is the best thing.*

Today was Jo's first day at her new job. She was excited and nervous as she walked downtown. She'd had to work up the courage to apply for it, but her new employer had hired her on the spot, telling her that she was a natural. He'd shown her where she would sit.

Her weekly paycheck would not be huge. She had the income from her investment account, but she was being careful with its proceeds. Already she'd had to contend with some unforeseen expenses, like galoshes to protect her shoes from slush. She'd never walked the streets in winter before. There had always been Dolan.

After she'd given her tickets to Fay and left Grand Central, she'd gone directly to a jeweler's and sold her watch, a pair of earrings, and a bracelet. She'd paid Katie what was owed to her, said goodbye, and then checked herself into a modest hotel. From it, she'd written to her mother to tell her she wasn't coming to Winnetka because her heart was here in New York.

Our old world is closed to me now, Mama, she'd written, *but that's all right. I don't miss it. It's a darker place than I'd ever realized. And there's a new world that I'm just discovering, with so many people in it. Wonderful people. And terrible ones. More people than I ever knew existed, with more stories than I can possibly imagine.*

Anna had responded that she was not entirely surprised, and that Winnetka, she now saw, could never hold her daughter.

Please be careful, Josephine, she'd written. *And always remember that you are a Montfort. It was a good name once. Perhaps you can make it so again.*

After half an hour's walk, Jo was well downtown. She suffered a bout of nerves now as she stood on the corner of Broadway and Murray Street, waiting for the traffic to slow so she could cross. She reached into her coat pocket, feeling for the postcard inside it. It had been forwarded to her new address. There was a picture of Lake Michigan on the front. On the back was written: *Wish you were here.* There was no signature, no return address. Jo knew who'd sent it, though, and she hoped that the good citizens of Chicago were guarding their wallets. She felt glad to know that Fay and Eleanor had made it. She hoped they were safe and warm and had plenty to eat. She knew they had each other.

She put the card back in her pocket. She kept it there for when she needed courage. And she needed courage now.

A wagon loaded with beer kegs stopped dead in front of Jo and nearly caused a collision with a lumber wagon behind it. As the two drivers exchanged words and traffic snarled around them, Jo saw her chance. She dashed across the street, past city hall to Park Row, and then on to Nassau Street, where she arrived at her destination. She paused at the door of an imposing nine-story building. *The New York Tribune* was emblazoned above it.

"*Fac quod faciendum est,*" she whispered, and pushed the door open.

Jo told the harried-looking woman at the front desk who she was and the woman pointed at the stairwell.

Jo made her way upstairs to the noisy, smoke-filled newsroom. As she walked down one side of it, she saw the city editor chewing out some hapless reporter, and the editor in chief, Mr. Johnson, looking at a group of photographs spread across his desk. He noticed her walk by and gave her a brisk nod. She nodded back. He was the one who'd called her a natural.

There was one more office, down at the very end. It belonged not to an editor but to a senior reporter—the one who covered the crime beat. He'd been out of his office the day she'd come for her interview. She wondered if he even knew she'd been hired. The door was open now. She stopped in front of it, waiting until the man inside, furiously typing away with a pencil clamped between his teeth, looked up and saw her.

"Jo?" Eddie Gallagher said after he'd taken the pencil out of his mouth. "What are you doing here?"

Smiling, she pulled a notepad out of her bag—it was the same brand he used—and held it up.

Eddie stared at it, confused for a moment. Then he smiled. "Welcome to the newsroom, Miss Montfort," he said. "Nellie Bly better watch her back." He put the pencil back in his mouth and went back to his story.

A smile, Jo thought. *It's something. It's a start.*

She kept walking. When she reached the very back of the room, where the cubs started out, she sat down at a battered wooden desk that had nothing but a typewriter and a stack of paper on top of it.

For an instant, she saw herself as she had been the day she'd gone to the *Standard*'s newsroom to give Arnold Stoatman her father's bequest.

That girl was gone. And so were the illusions she had carried.

Jo had come full circle and found herself back where she'd started, back where she wanted to be.

Working on stories.

And writing her own.

AUTHOR'S NOTE

This story started with a dead guy.

A man with weird markings on his face showed up in my head. He had long, dark hair and was wearing clothing from another time.

Who are you? I asked him. *What do you want?*

But he wouldn't answer. Not right away. He just lay in his coffin with his hands folded over his chest, decay beginning to creep. He wouldn't leave, either. And since he wasn't going to explain himself, I needed someone who could.

That's when other people started showing up: a teenaged reporter named Eddie, a thief lord called the Tailor; Oscar, a coroner's assistant. And a girl. Her name was Josephine Montfort.

Jo immediately intrigued me. I could tell she was wealthy and educated from the way she dressed and spoke. And yet, something wasn't quite right. I sensed that her porcelain coolness was only a veneer, and that underneath it, a fierce intelligence burned. In her gray eyes, I glimpsed a restless longing.

As my characters do, Jo made me work to get to know her. As she labored to uncover the dead man's story, I labored to uncover hers.

I learned that she'd been born into an old and distinguished New York family and that she led a life of privilege. Jo was fortunate in many ways, but she didn't have the one thing she wanted the most: freedom.

So few young women of the 1890s did. Poor girls were expected to work, as early as possible. Wealthy ones were expected to marry, as well as possible. As I researched *These Shallow Graves*, I met many of these young women.

I met Edith Jones, brilliant and misunderstood, and watched her marry the wrong man and live the wrong life—until she found the right life and became Edith Wharton.

I met eighteen-year-old Lizzie Schauer, who was arrested, imprisoned, and subjected to medical examinations to determine whether she was of good character—all for the "crime" of being an unaccompanied female walking alone in the city at night.

I met Consuelo Vanderbilt, a teenage heiress, forced to marry the Duke of Marlborough, a man she didn't love, to satisfy her domineering mother's social ambitions.

I met scores of teenage girls for whom an education was only a dream—and the factory floor or scullery or sweatshop, a reality.

Edith eventually broke free. Consuelo, too. I doubt poor Lizzie or the scullery girls ever did.

I so badly wanted Jo to. And thanks to the dead man, she finally did. He gave Jo her life, and by the end of the book, he gave me my answers, and my peace. He stopped haunting me and went on his way.

Jo's on her way now, too. And I can't wait to see where life takes her.

ACKNOWLEDGMENTS

Once again, I owe a huge thank you to my wonderful editor, Krista Marino, for her insight, encouragement, humor, and wise counsel; to publisher Beverly Horowitz for her enthusiasm for this New York story; to designer Alison Impey for her beautiful cover; to copy editors Colleen Fellingham, Jenica Nasworthy, and Alison Kolani for saving me from myself; and to the whole Penguin Random House team for all the hard work you do on behalf of your authors and their books.

Thank you to the Museum of the City of New York and the New-York Historical Society for making your digital collections free and easily accessible, and to the Lower East Side Tenement Museum for being the most awesome time machine ever.

Thank you to Steve Malk for being the best agent an author could ask for.

Thank you to Doug and Daisy for always, always being there for me, and for making room in our home for all my imaginary friends, be they reporters, morgue attendants, or pickpockets.

And lastly, thank you to New York City, for making a writer of Jo Montfort. And of me.

> *The only credential the city asked was the boldness to dream.*
> *For those who did, it unlocked its gates and its treasures,*
> *not caring who they were or where they came from.*
> *—Moss Hart*

BIBLIOGRAPHY

The following works provided information and inspiration and I would like to acknowledge my debt to their authors:

Anbinder, Tyler. *Five Points: The 19th-Century New York City Neighborhood That Invented Tap Dance, Stole Elections, and Became the World's Most Notorious Slum.* New York: Simon & Schuster, 2001.

Asbury, Herbert. *The Gangs of New York: An Informal History of the Underworld.* Dorset Press, 1989.

Bly, Nellie. *Ten Days in a Mad-House.* Lexington: University of Kentucky Press, 2014.

Collins, Paul. *The Murder of the Century.* New York: Crown Publishers, 2011.

Gilfoyle, Timothy J. *A Pickpocket's Tale: The Underworld of Nineteenth-Century New York.* New York: W. W. Norton & Co., 2006.

Gillotti, Susan. *Women of Privilege: 100 Years of Love and Loss in a Family of the Hudson River Valley.* Chicago: Academy Chicago Publishers, 2013.

Husband, H. Aubrey. *The Student's Handbook of Forensic Medicine and Medical Police,* Edinburgh, Scotland: Edinburgh, E. & S. Livingstone, 1883.

Koehler, Dr. Steven A., and Dr. Cyril H. Wecht. *Postmortem: Establishing the Cause of Death*. Buffalo, NY: Firefly Books, 2006.

Lee, Hermione. *Edith Wharton*. New York: Knopf, 2007.

Riis, Jacob. *How the Other Half Lives: Studies Among the Tenements of New York*. New York: Dover Publications, 1971.

Stuart, Amanda Mackenzie. *Consuelo and Alva Vanderbilt: The Story of a Daughter and Mother in the Gilded Age*. New York: Harper Perennial, 2007.

Wharton, Edith. *A Backward Glance: An Autobiography*. New York: Simon & Schuster, 1998.

Zacks, Richard. *Island of Vice: Theodore Roosevelt's Quest to Clean Up Sin-Loving New York*. New York: Anchor Books, 2012.

Ziegelman, Jane. *97 Orchard: An Edible History of Five Immigrant Families in One New York Tenement*. New York: Harper, 2011.

The Reporters Committee for the Freedom of the Press (www
.rcfp.org) provided valuable information on the reporter's privilege, as did "The Reporter's Privilege: Then and Now," accessed at http://shorensteincenter.org/wp-content/uploads/2012/03/r23_bates.pdf. The website emedicine.medscape.com provided information on forensic medicine.

ABOUT THE AUTHOR

Jennifer Donnelly is the author of three adult novels, *The Tea Rose, The Winter Rose,* and *The Wild Rose;* the young adult novels *These Shallow Graves, Revolution,* and *A Gathering Light,* winner of Britain's prestigious Carnegie Medal, the *Los Angeles Times* Book Prize for Young Adult Literature, and a Michael L. Printz Honor Award; and the Waterfire Saga, a series for middle-grade readers. She lives and writes full-time in New York's Hudson Valley. You can visit her at jenniferdonnelly.com and follow her on Twitter at @jenwritesbooks and on Facebook at jenwritesbooks.